Turning under a blood-red sun, Darkover was a crossroads planet. Yet the Terran Empire knew little of its incredibly high mountains, its deadly winds, or its hostile and distant inhabitants. Dan Barron, spaceport dispatcher, had never cared to know this cold world—until a nightmare vision robbed him of his job and thrust him among its alien races.

Disoriented, self-doubting and plagued by deepening visions, Barron found himself irresistibly drawn into a struggle which called forth powers wielded by what the Terrans called witchcraft. He was an unlikely candidate to shape the destiny of worlds—but the tension between Terran technology and the ancient rites of Darkover snapped within him.

Turn this book over for
second complete novel

CHRONOLOGICAL ORDER OF THE DARKOVAN NOVELS:

STAR OF DANGER. Dealing with the first contact between Terran and the secret caste of the Darkovan Com'yn.

THE BLOODY SUN. Kennard, sub-hero of *STAR OF DANGER*, has grown to middle age; Jeff Kerwin, half-caste of Terra and Darkover, renounces Terra for Darkover, yet discovers that Terra has a hold he cannot quite detach.

THE DOOR THROUGH SPACE. A tale of revenge and blood-feud in the Dry Towns far to the north of Darkover.

FALCONS OF NARABEDLA. A Terran of the pre-space era stumbles upon an alien world of the far future, where Terran and Darkovan have meshed and become decadent.

THE SWORD OF ALDONES. The son of Kennard Alton by a daughter of Montray and Aldaran, returning to Darkover, tries desperately to hold the decadent and degenerating Com'yn together—and fails, for Terra and Darkover are shown as irresistible force and immovable object.

THE PLANET SAVERS. Regis Hastur, who alone of the Com'yn has chosen to remain and guide his world in the days of the Terran's apparent triumph, brings about true understanding and amity and peace between the alien worlds of Terran Empire and Darkover.

THE WINDS OF DARKOVER

MARION ZIMMER BRADLEY

AN ACE BOOK

Ace Publishing Corporation
1120 Avenue of the Americas
New York, N.Y. 10036

THE WINDS OF DARKOVER

Copyright ©, 1970, by Marion Zimmer Bradley

All Rights Reserved

Cover art by Kelly Freas.

THE ANYTHING TREE
Copyright ©, 1970, by John Rackham

Printed in U.S.A.

BARRON dumped the last of his gear into a duffel bag, pulled the straps tight, and said to nobody in particular "Well, that's that and the hell with all of them."

He straightened, taking a last look around the neat, tight little world of spaceport living-quarters. Built to conserve materials (it had been the first Terran building on Darkover, in the zone later to become Trade City), it had something in common with a spaceship's cabin; it was narrow, bright, clean and cramped, the furniture functional and almost all built-in. It would have suited a professional spaceman perfectly. Ground crews were another matter; they tended to get claustrophobia.

Barron had complained as much as anyone else, saying the place might be a decent fit for two mice, if one of them were on a stiff diet. But now that he was leaving it, he felt a curious pang, almost homesickness. He had lived here five years.

Five years! I never meant to stick to one planet that long!

He hoisted the duffel bag to his shoulder and closed the door of his quarters for the last time.

The corridor was as functional as the living quarters; reference charts and maps papered the walls up to the height of a tall man's eye level. Barron strode along, not seeing the familiar charts, but he did cast a brief bitter glance at the dispatch board, seeing his name there in red on the dreaded rep-sheet. He had five reps—official reprimands—when seven would put one out of the Space Service for good.

And no wonder, he thought. *I didn't get any dirty deal; in fact, they went easy on me. Pure luck, and no credit to me, that cruiser and the mapping ship didn't crash and blow the damned spaceport right off Darkover, and half Trade City with them!*

He set his mouth tight. Here he was, worrying about demerits like a kid in school—and yet it wasn't merely that.

Many people in Terran Space Service went through their whole twenty years without a single rep—and he'd piled up five in one disastrous night.

Even though it wasn't his fault.

Yes it was, damn it. Who else could I blame it on? I should have reported sick.

But I wasn't sick!

The rep-sheet read: gross neglect of duty, grave danger of causing accident to a landing spacecraft. They had found him literally napping on duty. *But damn it, I wasn't asleep either!*

Daydreaming?

Try telling them that. Try telling them that when your every nerve and muscle should have been alert over the all-important dispatch board, you were—somewhere else. You were caught up in a deep dream, bewildered with colors, sights, sounds, smells, blazes of brilliance. You were leaning into an icy wind, under a deep purple sky, a blaze of red sunlight overhead—the Darkovan sun—the sun that the Terrans called The Bloody Sun. But you'd never seen it like that, reflected in rainbow prisms through a great wall of crystalline glass. You heard your own boots ringing on ice-hard stone—and your pulse was pounding with hate, and you felt the surge of adrenalin in your blood. You broke into a run, feeling the hatred and blood-lust rise to a crest inside you; before you something reared up—man, woman, beast—you hardly knew or cared—and you heard your own snarl as a whip came crashing down and something screamed——

The dream had dissolved in the thundering nightmare noise of klaxons, the all-quarters alarm of sirens and whoopers and bells, the WRECK *lights blazing everywhere, and your reflexes took over. You'd never moved so fast. But it was too late. You had slammed the wrong button and the dispatch tower was fouled up by that all-important eight-second margin, and only a minor miracle of seat-of-the-pants navigation by the young captain of the mapping ship —he was getting three medals for it—had saved the space-port authority from the kind of disaster that waked people up—what people were left—in screeching nightmares for twenty years afterward.*

Nobody had wasted words on Barron since. His name on

the rep-sheet had made him a pariah. He had been told to vacate his quarters by 2700 that night and report for a new assignment, but nobody bothered telling him where. It was as simple as that—five years in Darkover Spaceport and seventeen in the service had been wiped out. He didn't feel especially mistreated. There wasn't room in the Terran Spaceforce for that kind of mistake.

The corridor ended in an archway; a plaque, which Barron ignored after seeing it every day for years, told him he was now in Central Coordinating. Unlike the building where quarters were located, this one was constructed of native Darkovan stone, translucent and white as alabaster, with enormous glass windows. Through them he could see flaring, blue spaceport lights, the shapes of groundcraft and resting ships, and, far beyond the lights, pale greenish moonlight. It was half an hour before dawn. He wished he'd stopped for some breakfast; then he was glad he hadn't. Barron wasn't thin-skinned, but the way the men ignored him in the cafeteria would put anyone off his food. He hadn't bothered eating much in the last couple of days.

There was always the Old Town, the Darkovan part of Trade City where he sometimes slipped away for exotic food when he was tired of the standard fare of the quarters; there were not a few restaurants which catered to spacemen and tourists who came for "exotic delicacies." But he hadn't felt like trying to pass the guards; he might have been stopped. They might have thought he was trying to escape an official process. He wasn't officially under arrest, but his name was mud.

He left the duffel bag outside the narrow bank of elevators, stepped in and pressed the topmost button. The elevator soared up, depositing him outside the dispatch room. He lowered his head, passing it without a glance inside and headed for the coordinator's office in the penthouse.

And then, without warning—he was standing on a high parapet, winds flowing icily around his body, ripping at him with enough force to tear his clothes off, ridging his skin with gooseflesh and pain. Below him, men screamed and moaned and died over the sounds of clashing steel; and somewhere he heard stone falling with a great crunching rumble like the end of the world. He could not see. He clung hard to the stone, feeling frost bite with fiery teeth at his stiff fingers, and fought the sickness rising in his throat. *So many men. So many dead, all of them my people and my friends . . .*

He let go of the stone. His fingers were so cramped that he had to pry them off with his other hand. He caught his blowing garments around him, feeling an instant of incongruous physical comfort in the thick fur against his cold hands, and went swiftly, on groping feet, through the blind dark. He moved as in a dream, knowing where he was going without knowing why; his feet knew the familiar path. He felt them move from flagstone to wood parquet to thick carpeting, then down a long flight of stairs and up another flight—farther and farther, until the distant sounds of battle and falling walls were muffled and finally silenced. His throat was thick and he sobbed as he went. He passed through a low archway, automatically ducking his head against the stone arch he had never seen and would never see. A current of chill air blew on him. He fumbled in the darkness for something like a loose hood of feathery textures; he drew it downward swiftly and he thrust his head through the feathers, pulling it down.

He felt himself falling back and in the same instant he seemed to rise, to soar upward and swoop outward on the wings of the feathery substance. The darkness suddenly thinned and was gone, and light broke around him—not through his darkened eyes, but through the very skin of his body—and he felt cold reddish light and frosty clouds. Weightless, borne on the feather dress, he soared outward, guiding himself through the sudden brilliance of dawn.

Quickly he grew accustomed to the bird dress, and balancing on one wing (*It's a long time since I dared to do this.*) he turned to look below.

The colors were strange, flat, shapes distorted and concave; he was not seeing them with ordinary mortal eyes. Far below a swarm of men in rough, dark clothing clustered around a rude tower covered in skins, next to an outwork. Arrows flew, men screamed; on the wall a man toppled with a long despairing shriek, and fell out of his sight. He beat harsh pinions, trying to swoop down, and . . .

8

He was standing on firm flooring, wiping the sweat of terror from his face.

He was here. He was Dan Barron. He was not flying bodiless except for a few feathers over a weird tipping landscape, fighting a biting current of wind. He stared at his fingers and put one into his mouth. It felt numb, frostbitten. *The stone was cold.*

It had happened again.

It was so real, *so damnably real.* His skin was still gooseflesh and he mopped eyes still streaming from the bitter wind. *Good God,* he thought, and shuddered. Had someone been slipping him hallucinogenic drugs? Why would anyone do that? He had no enemies, as far as he knew. He had no real friends—he wasn't the type to make them at a strange outpost—but no enemies either. He did his work and minded his own business, and he knew no one who envied him either his few possessions or the tough and somewhat underpaid job he had been doing. The only explanation was that he was mad, psychotic, freaked-out, off his landing base. He realized that in that weird dream, obsession or hallucination, he had been speaking and thinking in Darkovan—the strong accented mountain Darkovan which he understood, but could not speak except for the few words necessary to order a meal or buy some knickknack in Trade City. He shivered again and mopped his face. His feet had carried him within a few feet of the coordinator's office, but he stopped, trying to get his breath and his bearings.

This made five times.

The first three times had struck him as abnormally vivid daydreams, born of boredom and hangover and based on his infrequent but colorful excursions into the Old Town. He had dismissed them without much thought, even though he woke shuddering with the reality of the surges of fear or hatred which possessed him in these dreams. The fourth —the fourth had been the near-catastrophe of the spaceport. Barron wasn't an imaginative man. His possible explanations went as far as a nervous breakdown, or someone with a grudge slipping him a hallucinatory drug as a grim joke, and not a step further. He wasn't paranoid enough to think that someone had done it for the purpose it achieved, his disgrace and a spaceport catastrophe. He was confused, a little scared and a little angry, but not sure if the anger was his own or part of the strange dream.

He couldn't continue to delay. He waited a minute more, then straightened his shoulders and knocked at the co-ordinator's door. A light flashed a green COME IN, and he stepped in.

Mallinson, Coordinator of Spaceport Activities for the Terran zone of Darkover, was a hefty man who looked, at any hour of day or night, as if he'd slept in his uniform. He appeared unimaginative and serious. Any notion Barron might have had about revealing his experiences to his superior, died unspoken. Nevertheless, Mallinson looked straight at Barron, and he was the first person who'd done so for five days.

Without preamble he said, "All right, what the hell happened? I pulled your file; you're listed as a damned good man. In my experience, men don't pile up a perfect record and then rack it up like *that;* the man who's heading for a big mistake starts out by making dozens of little mistakes first, and we have time to pull him off the spot before he really piles something up. Were you sick? Not that it's an excuse—if you were you should have reported and requested a relief man. We expected to find you dead of a heart attack—we didn't think anything else would slow you down like that."

Barron thought about the dispatcher's room and its enormous board which patterned all traffic in and out of this spaceport. Mallinson said, not giving him time to answer, "You don't drink or drug. You know, most men last about eight months on the dispatch board; then the responsibility starts giving them nightmares, they start making little fumbles, and we pull them off and transfer them. When you never made even a little fumble, we should have realized that you just didn't have sense enough—the little fumbles are the mind's way of yelling for help, yelling 'This is too much for me, get me out of here.' When you didn't, we should have pulled you off anyway. That's why you weren't cashiered, kicked out with seven reps, and slapped with a millicred fine. We left you on the board five years, and we should have known we were asking for trouble."

Barron realized that Mallinson hadn't expected any answer. People who made mistakes of that caliber never could explain why. If they'd known why they could have guarded against it.

"With your record, Barron, we could transfer you out to the Rim, but we have an opening here; I understand you speak Darkovan?"

"Trade City language. I understand the other, but I fumble in it."

"Even so. Know anything about mapping and exploring?" Barron jumped. It had been a ship from M & E which had nearly crashed five days ago, and that sector was in his mind, but a second glance at Mallinson convinced him that the man was simply asking for information, not needling. He said, "I've read a book or two on xenocartography —no more."

"Lens grinding?"

"The principles. Most kids make a small telescope some time or other; I did."

"That's plenty. I didn't want an expert," Mallinson said with a grim smile. "We've got plenty of them, but it would put Darkovan backs up. Now, how much do you know about general Darkovan culture?"

Wondering where all this was leading, Barron said, "Orientation Lectures Two, Three and Four, five years ago. Not that I've needed it much, working in the port."

"Well then, you know the Darkovans never bothered a great deal with small technology—telescopes, microscopes and the like? Their supposed sciences go in other directions, and I don't know much about them either; nobody does except a few anthropologists and sociological experts. The facts remain; we, meaning the Board of Terran Affairs, sometimes get requests for minor technological help from individuals. Not from the government—if there is any government on Darkover, which I personally am inclined to doubt—but that's beside the point. Somebody or other out there, I'm not sure about the details, decided that for forest-fire control and fire watching, telescopes would be handy little gadgets to have around. Somehow the idea crawled up whatever channels it had to come through, and came to the Council of Elders in Trade City. We offered to sell them telescopes. Oh, no, they said politely, they'd rather have someone teach their men how to grind them, and to supervise their construction, installation and use. It's not the sort of thing we can send up a slip to Personnel for and find, just like that. But here you are, out of a job, and lens grinding listed in your comprehensive file as a hobby. Start today."

Barron scowled. This was a job for an anthropologist, a liaison officer, a specialist in Darkovan language, or—*fire watching! Hell, that's a kid's job!* He said stiffly, "Sir, let me remind you that this is out of my sector and out of my specialty. I have no experience in it. I'm a scheduling expert and dispatch man—"

"Not as of five days ago, you aren't," Mallison said brutally. "Look, Barron, you're through in your own line; you know that. We don't want to ship you out in disgrace—not without some idea of what happened to you. And your contract isn't up for two years. We want to fit you in somewhere."

There was nothing Barron could say to that. Resigning before a contract was up meant losing your holdback pay and your free passage back to your home planet—which could strand you on a strange world and wipe out a year's pay. Technically he had a right to complain about being assigned outside his specialty field. But technically they had a right to fire him with seven reps, blacklist him, fine him, and press charges for gross negligence. He was getting a chance to come out of this—not clean, but not wrecked for good in the service.

"When do I start?" he asked. It was the only question he had left.

But he did not hear the answer. As he scanned Mallison's face, suddenly it blurred.

He was standing on a stretch of soft grass; it was night, but it was not dark. All around him the night flamed and roared with a great fire, reaching in tendrils of ravening flame far above his head. And in the midst of the flame there was a woman.

Woman?

She was almost inhumanly tall and slender, but girlish; she stood bathed in the flame as if standing carelessly under a waterfall. She was not burning, not agonized. She looked merry and smiling. Her hands were clasped on her naked breasts, the flames licking around her face and her flame-colored hair. And then the girlish, merry face wavered and became supernally beautiful with the beauty of a great goddess burning endlessly in the fire, a kneeling woman bound in golden chains. . . .

. . . "and you can arrange all that downstairs in Personnel and Transportation," Mallinson finished firmly, shoving back his chair. "Are you all right, Barron? You look a bit fagged. I'll bet you haven't been eating or sleeping. Shouldn't you see a medic before you go? Your card is still good in Section 7. It's going to be all right, but the sooner you leave, the better. Good luck." But he didn't offer to shake hands, and Barron knew it wasn't all right at all.

He stumbled over his own feet leaving the office, and the face of the burning woman, in its inhuman ecstasy, went with him in terror and amazement.

He thought, *what in the world—any world—has happened to me?*

And, in the name of all the gods of Earth, space and Darkover—why?

II

THE BREACH in the outwork was being repaired.

Brynat Scarface had gone out to watch, and was standing on the inner parapet supervising the work. It was a cold morning and mists flowed up the mountainside; in the chill the men moved sluggishly. Little dark men from the mountains, most of them ragged and still battle-stained, fought the rough ground and the cold stone; they were moved by shouts and the occasional flick of a whip in the hands of one of Brynat's men.

Brynat was a tall man, dressed in ragged and slashed finery, over which he had drawn a fur cloak from the spoils of the castle. A great seamed scar ridged his face from eye to chin, giving to a face which had never been handsome the wolfish look of some feral beast which had somehow put on the dress of a man. At his heels his sword bearer, a little bat-eared man, scurried, bowing under the weight of the outlaw's sword. He cringed when Brynat turned to him, expecting a blow or a curse, but Brynat was in high good humor this morning.

"Fools we are, man—we spend days tearing down this wall," he complained, "and what is the first thing we do? We build it up again!"

The bat-eared man gave a nervous sycophant's laugh, but Brynat had forgotten his existence again. Drawing the fur around himself, he walked to the edge of the parapet and looked down at the ruined wall and the castle.

Storn Castle stood on a height defended by chasms and crags. Brynat knew he could congratulate himself for the feats of tactics and engineering which had broken the walls and poured men through them to storm the inner fortress. Storn had been built in the old days to be impregnable, and impregnable it was and had remained through seven generations of Aldarans, Aillards, Darriels and Storns.

When it had housed proud lords of the Comyn—the old, powerful, psi-gifted lords of the Seven Domains of Darkover —it had been known to the world's end. Then the line had dwindled, outsiders had married into the remains of the families, and finally the Storns of Storn had come there. They had been peaceful lords without any pretense to be more than they were—wilderness nobility, gentle and honorable, living in peace with their tenants and neighbors, content to trade in the fine hunting hawks of the mountains and sell fine wrought metals from the forges of their mountain tribe, which dug ore from the dark cliffs and worked it at their fires. They had been rich and also powerful in their own way, if by power one meant that when word went forth from the Storn of Storn, men obeyed; but they smiled instead of trembling when they obeyed. They had little contact with the other mountain peoples and less with the lords of the farther mountains; they lived at peace and were content.

And now they had fallen.

Brynat laughed smugly. In their prideful isolation, the Storns could no longer even send for help to their distant lordly neighbors. With care, Brynat would be established here as lord of Storn Castle long before the word went out through the Hellers and the Hyades that Storn Castle had a new lord. And would they care that it was ruled no longer by Storn of Storn, but by Brynat of the Heights? He thought not.

A cold wind had come up, and the red sun was covered in scudding clouds. The men toiling at the lugged stones were moving faster now to keep warm in the biting wind, and a few flakes of snow were beginning to fall. Brynat jerked a careless shoulder at Bat-ears, and without looking to see if the little man followed—but woe to him if he hadn't —strode inside the castle.

Inside, far from watchers, he let his proud grin of triumph slide off. It had not been all victory, though his followers revelling in the rich spoil of the castle thought it had been. He sat in Storn's high seat, but victory eluded him.

He walked swiftly downward, until he came to a door padded with velvet and hung with curtains. Two of his mercenaries lolled here, drowsing on the comfort of cushions; an empty wineskin showed how they whiled away their guard. But they sprang up at the sound of his heavy tread, and one sniggered with the freedom of an old servitor.

"Ha, ha! Two wenches are better than one—hey, Lord?"

Seeing Brynat scowl the other said swiftly, "No more weeping and wailing from the maid this morning, Lord. She is still, and we have not entered."

Brynat scorned answer. He moved his hand imperiously and they flung open the door.

As the door hasp creaked, a small blue-clad form sprang up and whirled, long red braided hair flying about her shoulders. The face had once been piquantly lovely; now it was swollen and dark with bruises; one eye was half shut with a blow, but the other blazed in quenchless fury.

"You whelp of a bitch-wolf," she said low, "take one step further—I dare you!"

Brynat rocked back loosely on his heels, his mouth drawn to a wolfish smile. He set hands on hips and didn't speak, surveying the girl in blue. He saw the white, shaking hands, but noted that the swollen mouth did not tremble nor the eyes drop. He approved with inward laughter. Here he could feel genuine triumph.

"What, still unreconciled to my hospitality, Lady? Have I offered you word or deed of insult, or do you blame me for the roughness of my men in offering it?"

Her mouth was firm. "Where is my brother? My sister?"

15

"Why," he drawled, "your sister attends my feasts nightly; I came to invite you to attend upon my lady wife this morning; I believe she pines for a familiar face. But, my Lady Melitta, you are pale; you have not touched the fine food I sent to you!" He made a low, burlesque bow and turned to pick up a tray laden with wine and rich food. He proffered it to her, smiling. "See, I come in person, at your service—"

She took one step, snatched the tray, picked up a roast bird by one leg, and hurled it into his face.

Brynat swore, stepping backward and wiping the grease from his chin—with a great burst of laughter. "Zandru's hells! *Damisela*, I should have taken you, not the whimpering, whining creature I chose!"

Breathing hard she surveyed him defiantly. "I'd have killed you first."

"I make no doubt you'd have tried! Had you been a man, the castle might never have fallen—but you wear skirts in place of hose and the castle lies in ruins and my men and I are here and all the smiths in Zandru's forges can't mend a broken egg. So I advise you in good sadness, little mistress: wash your face, put on your fine robes, and attend on your sister, who is still Lady of Storn. If you have good sense, you'll advise her to have patience with her lot, and you shall both have robes and jewels and all things that women prize."

"From you?"

"Who else?" he said with a laughing shrug, and flung the door open to the guards.

"The Lady Melitta is to come and go as she wills within the castle. But attend me, Mistress—the outworks, the parapets and the dungeons are forbidden, and I give my men leave—hear me well—to stop you by force if you attempt to go near them."

She started to hurl a curse at him and then stopped herself, visibly toying with the thought of what even limited freedom could mean. At last she turned away without a word, and he shut the door and moved away.

Perhaps this would be the first step in his second victory. He knew, though his men did not, that Storn Castle conquered was only the first victory—and hollow without the second conquest. He bit off another curse, turned his back on the room prisoning the girl and strode on. Upward and upward he went, high into the old tower. Here there were no windows. There were only narrow slits which admitted, not the red daylight but a strange, eerie, flickering blue light like chained lightning. Brynat felt a strange, cold shiver pass over him.

Of ordinary dangers he was fearless. But this was the ancient Darkovan sorcery, the bare legends of which protected such places as Storn Castle long after their other defenses had fallen. Brynat clutched the amulet round his neck with suddenly nerveless fingers. He had guessed that the old magic was merely a show, had hardened his mercenaries to storm the castle and had won. He had caroused in Storn Castle and had laughed at the old tales. Their magic hadn't saved the castle, had it? He had thought it a show to frighten children, no more harmful than the northern lights.

He strode through the ghostly flickers, through a pale arch of translucent stone. Two of his hardened and brutal men, the most nerveless he could bribe to the task, lounged there on an old carven settee. He noted that they were neither gaming nor drinking, and that their eyes were averted from the arch beyond, where a flickering curtain of blue light played like a fountain between the stones. There was naked relief in their faces at sight of their chieftain.

"Any change?"

"None, Lord. The man's dead—dead as Durraman's donkey."

"If I could believe that," Brynat said between his teeth and strode boldly through the curtain of blue flame.

He had been through it before and it had been his bravest act—bold enough to dwarf the single-handed taking of the last barbican. He knew his men held him in awe for it, but this alone he did not fear. He had seen such things beyond the mountains; they were fearsome, indeed, but harmless. He felt and endured with distaste the electric tingle, the hairs bristling on head and forearms. He stiffened his backbone against the surge of animal fear and strode through.

The blue light died. He stood in a dark chamber, lit with a few pale tapers in fixed cressets; soft hangings of woven fur circled a single low couch, on which a man lay motionless.

The still form seemed to glow softly in the darkness; he was a slender, frail man, with pale hair streaming from a high forehead and deep-sunken eyes. Though he was still young, the face was drawn and stern. He wore a tunic and plain hose of woven silk, no furs and no jewels but a single star-shaped stone like an amulet around his neck. His hands looked white, soft, and useless—the hands of scribe or priest, hands which had never held a sword. The feet were bare and soft; the chest did not stir with breathing. Brynat felt the old frustrated fury as he looked down on the pale, soft-looking man. Storn of Storn lay there, helpless—yet beyond Brynat's reach.

His mind whirled him back to the hour of the castle's fall. The servants and soldiers had been seized and subdued; trusted men had been sent to bind, but not to harm, the ladies. The younger Storn, no more than a boy and bleeding from many wounds, Brynat had spared with grudging admiration—a boy to defend this castle alone? The lad was dungeoned, but Brynat's own surgeon had dressed his wounds. Storn of Storn was Brynat's real prey.

His men did not know; they had seen only the spoil of a rich house, the power of holding an ancient fortress where they could be secure. But Brynat sought choicer game: the talismans and powers of the old Storns. With Storn of Storn in his hands, a Storn of the true blood, he could wield them—and Storn, he had heard, was a fragile, sickly, unwarlike man—born blind. Hence had he lived in retirement, leaving the management of his castle to his young sisters and his brother. Brynat had maidens and boy, *now for the feeble Lord!*

He had found his way through weird lights and magical fire curtains to the private apartments of the Lord of Storn —and found him escaped; lying unrousable in trance.

And so he had lain for days. Now Brynat, sick with rage, bent over his couch, but no stir of muscle or breath revealed that the man lived.

"Storn!" he bellowed. It was a shout that he felt must rouse even the dead.

No hair stirred. He might as well have howled into the winds around the parapet. Brynat, gritting his teeth, drew the skean from his belt. If he could not use the man, he held one power, at least: to send him from enchanted sleep to death. He raised the knife and brought it slashing down.

The knife turned in mid-air; it writhed, glowed blue, and exploded into white-hot flame from hilt to tip. Brynat howled in anguish, dancing about and shaking his burnt hand, to which the glowing skean clung with devilish force. The two mercenaries, trembling and bristling in the blue lights, faltered through the electrical curtain.

"You—you called us, *vai dom?*"

Savagely Brynat hurled the knife at them; it came un-stuck and flew; one of them fumbled to catch it, yelled and shook it off to the floor, where it lay still hissing and sizzling. Brynat, with a low, savage stream of curses, strode from the chamber. The mercenaries followed, their eyes wide with terror and their faces like animal masks.

In marmoreal peace, far beyond their reach in unknowable realms, Storn slept on.

Far below, Melitta Storn finished bathing her bruised face. Seated before her toilet table, she concealed the worst of the marks with cosmetics, combed and braided her hair, and brought a clean gown from the press and donned it. Then, conquering a sudden spasm of sickness, she drank deeply of the wine on the tray. She hesitated a moment, then retrieved the roast bird from the floor, wiped it, and, deftly tearing it with her fingers, ate most of it. She did not wish Brynat's hospitality, but sick and faint with hunger she was useless to herself or her people. Now, with wine and food, she felt a measure of physical strength, at least, returning. Her mirror told her that except for swollen lip and darkened eye, she looked much as before.

And yet—nothing could ever be the same.

She remembered, shuddering, the walls crashing with a sound like the world's end; men surging from the gap; her youngest brother, Edric, bleeding from face and leg and white as a ghost after they tore him away from the last defenses; her sister Allira, screaming insanely as she fled from Brynat; the mad screams suddenly silenced in a cry of pain—then nothing. Melitta had run after them, fighting with bare hands and screaming, screaming until three men had seized and borne her, struggling like a trussed hen, to her own chamber. They had thrust her roughly within and barred the door.

She forced away the crowding memories. She had some freedom, now she must make use of it. She found a warm cape and went out of the room. The mercenaries at the door rose and followed her at a respectful, careful ten paces.

Apprehension throbbed in her, she walked through the deserted halls like a ghost through a haunted house, dogged by the steps of the strange brutes. Everywhere were the marks of siege, sack and ruin. Hangings were torn away, furniture hacked and stained. There were marks of fire and smoke in the great hall, and, hearing voices, she tiptoed past; Brynat's men caroused there and even if he had given orders to leave her alone, would drunken men heed?

Now, where is Allira?

Brynat, in hateful jesting—had he been jesting?—had referred to Allira as his lady wife. Melitta had been brought up in the mountains; even in these peaceful days she knew stories of such bandit invasions: castle sacked, men killed, lady forcibly married—if rape could be called marriage because some priest presided—announcement made that the bandit had married into the family and all was peaceful— on the surface. It was a fine subject for sagas and tales, but Melitta's blood ran cold at the thought of her delicate sister in that man's hands.

Where had Brynat taken her? Doubtless, to the old royal suite, furnished by her forefathers for entertaining the Hastur-Lords should they ever honor Storn Castle with their presence. That would be the sort of mixed blasphemy and conquest that would appeal to Brynat. Her heart racing, Melitta ran up the stairs, knowing suddenly what she would find there.

The royal suite was a scant four hundred years old; the carpeting felt new underfoot. The insignia of the Hasturs had been inlaid in sapphires and emeralds over the door, but hammer and pick had ripped the jewels from the wall and only broken stone remained.

Melitta burst into the room like a whirlwind, inner conviction—the old, seldom-used, half-remembered *knowing* inside her mind, the scrap of telepathic power from some almost-forgotten forefather—forcing her to look here for her sister. She sped through the rooms, hardly seeing the ravages of conquest there.

She found Allira in the farthest room. The girl was huddled in a window seat with her head in her arms, so quenched and trembling that she did not lift her head as Melitta ran into the room, but only cowered into a smaller and smaller bundle of torn silks. She started with a scream of weak terror as Melitta put a hand on her arm.

"Stop that, Allira. It's only me."

Allira Storn's face was so bleared with crying that it was almost unrecognizable. She flung herself on the other girl, wrapped her arms round her, and burst into a hurricane of sobs and cries.

Melitta's heart quailed with sickening pity, but she grasped Allira firmly in both hands, held her off and shook her hard, until her head flapped loosely up and down. "Lira, in Aldones' name, stop that squalling! That won't help you —or me, or Edric, or Storn, or our people! While I'm here, let's think. Use what brains you have left!"

But Allira could only gasp, "He—he—huh—Buh—Brynat—" She stared at her sister with such dazed, glassy eyes that Melitta wondered in a spasm of terror if harsh usage had left Allira witless or worse. If so, she was frighteningly alone, and might as well give up at once.

She freed herself, searched, and found on a sideboard a half-empty bottle of *firi*. She would rather have had water, or even wine, but in these straits anything would do. She dashed half the contents full into Allira's face. Eyes stung by the fiery spirits, Allira gasped and looked up; but now she saw her sister with eyes at least briefly sane. Melitta grasped her chin, tilted the bottle and forced a half-cup of the raw liquor down her sister's throat. Allira gulped, swallowed, coughed, choked, dribbled, then, anger replacing hysteria, struck down Melitta's arm and the cup.

"Have you lost your wits, Meli?"

"I was going to ask you that, but I didn't think you were in any shape to answer," Melitta said vigorously. Then her voice became more tender. "I didn't mean to frighten or hurt you, love; you've had more than enough of that, I know. But I had to make you listen to me."

"I'm all right now—as much as I can ever be," she amended, bitterly.

"You don't have to tell me," Melitta said quickly, flinching from what she could read in her sister's mind; they were both wide open to each other. "But—he came and mocked me, calling you his lady wife—"

"There was even some mummery with one of his red-robed priests, and he sat me in the high seat at his side," Allira confirmed, "with knife near enough my ribs that I didn't dare speak—"

"But he didn't harm you, apart from that?"

"He used neither knife or whip, if that's what you mean," Allira said, and dropped her eyes. Before the accusing silence of the younger girl, she burst out, "What could I have done? Edric dead, for all I knew—you, Zandru knew where—he would have killed me," she cried out on another gust of sobs. "You would have done the same!"

"Had you no dagger?" Melitta raged.

"He—he took it away from me," Allira wept.

Melitta thought, *I would have used it on myself before he could make me his doxy-puppet in his high hall*. But she did not speak the words aloud. Allira had always been a fragile, gentle girl, frightened by the cry of a hawk, too timid to ride any horse but the gentlest of palfreys, so shy and home-loving that she sought neither lover nor husband. Melitta subdued her anger and her voice to gentleness. "Well, love, no one's blaming you; our people know better and it's no one's business else; and all the smiths of Zandru can't mend a broken egg or a girl's maidenhead, so let's think what's to be done now."

"Did they hurt you, Meli?"

"If you mean did they rape me, no; that scarface, a curse to his manhood, had no time for me, and I suppose he thought me too fine a prize for any of his men offhand—though he'll probably fling me to one of them when the time comes, if we can't stop it." In a renewed spasm of horror, she thought of Brynat's rabble of renegades, bandits, and half-human things from far back in the Hellers. She caught Allira's thought, even the brutal protection of the bandit chief was better than that rabble's hands. Well, she couldn't blame Lira—had she had the same choice what might she have done? Not all porridge cooked is eaten, and not all brave words can be put into acts. Nevertheless, a revulsion she could not quite conceal made her loose her sister from her arms and say dispassionately, "Edric, I think, is in the dungeons; Brynat forbade me to go there. But I think I would feel it if he were dead. You are more psychic than I; when you pull yourself together, try to reach his mind."

"And Storn!" Allira broke out again in frenzy. "What has he done to protect us—lying like a log, safe and guarded by his own magic, and leaving us all to *their* tender mercies!"

"What could he have done otherwise?" Melitta asked reasonably. "He cannot hold a sword or see to use it; at least he has made sure that no one can use him for a puppet —as they are using you." Her eyes, fierce and angry, bored into her sister; "Has he gotten you with child yet?"

"I don't know—it could be."

"Curse you for a whittling," Melitta raged. "Don't you, even now, see what it is he wants? If it were only a willing girl, why not one—or a dozen—of the maids? Listen. I have a plan, but you must use what little sense the gods gave you for a few days at least. Wash your face, robe yourself decently, try to look like the Lady of Storn, not some camp follower torn from the kennel! Brynat thinks he has you tamed and well-married, but he is a ruffian and you are a lady; you have the blood of the Seven Domains; you can outwit him if you try. Play for time, Allira! Have the vapors, play at mourning, put him off with promises— at worst, tell him that the day you know you are pregnant you will throw yourself from the battlements—and *make him believe it!* He daren't kill you, Allira; he needs you robed and jewelled in the high seat beside him, at least until he can be sure no follower or enemy will try to topple him from this height. Put him off for a few days, no more, and then—"

"Can you waken Storn to help us?" Allira gasped.

"By all the gods, what an idiot you are! Storn in trance is all that keeps us safe, Lira, and gives us time. Storn roused and in his hands—that devil's whelp would stick a knife in Edric's guts, toss me to his soldiers for a few hours' sport while I lived, and who knows if he'd even want a child from you? No, Lira, pray Storn keeps safe in trance till I can think of a plan! You do your part, keep up your courage, and I'll do mine."

In her heart a small desperate plan was maturing. She dared not tell Allira. They might be overheard, or, if she formulated it in words, there might be among Brynat's rabble, some half-human telepath who would win favor from his outlaw lord by bearing tales of the plot. But a seed of hope had been born in her.

"Come, Allira, let us dress you as befits the Lady of Storn, and bedazzle that ruffian into respect," she said, and prepared, again, to face Brynat without revealing anything.

III

BARRON had been in the service of the Terran Empire since he was a lad in his late teens and he had served on three planets before coming to Darkover. He discovered that afternoon that he had never left Terra. He found it out by leaving it for the first time.

At the designated gate 'from the Terran Zone, a bored young clerk looked him over as he examined the slip from Transportation and Personnel, which stated that Barron, Class Two, was being released on liaison assignment beyond the Zone. He remarked, "So you're the fellow who's going back into the mountains? You'd better get rid of those clothes and pick up some sort of suitable outfit for travelling here. Those togs you're wearing might do for the Zone, but back in the hills you'll get frozen—or maybe lynched. Didn't they tell you?"

They hadn't told him anything. Barron felt nonplussed; was he expected to go native? He was a Terran Empire liaison man, not a secret agent. But the clerk was the first person since the accident who had treated him like a human being, and he was grateful. "I thought I was going as an official representative. No safe-conducts, then?"

The clerk shrugged. "Who'd give it? You ought to be planet-wise after five years here. Terrans, or any Empire men, aren't popular outside Trade City. Or didn't you bother reading Official Directive Number Two?"

"Not the fine print." He knew that it made it illegal, on penalty of instant deportation, for Empire men to enter, without permits, any portion of the planet outside the designated trade zones. Barron had never wanted to, and so it never entered his head to wonder why. An alien planet was an alien planet—there were thousands of them—and his work had always been inside the Zone.

But it was no longer.

The clerk was feeling talkative. "Almost all the Terrans in Mapping and Exploring or the other liaison jobs wear Darkovan clothes. Warmer, and you don't collect a crowd that way. Didn't anybody tell you?"

Barron shook his head stubbornly. He didn't remind the clerk that nobody had been telling him anything for some days. In any case, he was feeling stubborn. He was doing his proper work for the Empire—he was officially appointed to it—and the Darkovans were not to tell him how to dress or act. If the Darkovans didn't like the clothes he was wearing, they could start learning the tolerance for alien customs which was the first thing required of every man who accepted work for the Terran Empire. He was satisfied with his light, warm synthetic tunic and breeches, his soft, low-cut sandals, and his short lined overcoat, which kept out the wind. Many Darkovans had adopted them in Trade City; the clothing was comfortable and indestructible. Why change it? He said a little stiffly, "It isn't as if I were wearing Spaceforce uniform. I can see where that might be a breach of good taste. But these?"

The clerk shrugged enigmatically. "It's your funeral," he said. "Here, I imagine this is your transport coming now."

Barron looked down the roughly cobbled street, but saw no sign of any vehicle approaching. There were the usual crew of loungers, women in heavy shawls going about their business, and three men leading horses. He started to say "where" and then realized that the three men, who were coming straight toward the gate, were leading *four* horses.

He swallowed hard. He had known in a general way that the Darkovans had small technology and used no motor transit. They used various pack and draft animals, indigenous relatives of the buffalo and the larger deer, and horses —probably descended from a strain imported from Nova Terra about a hundred years ago—for riding. It made sense. The Darkovan terrain was unsuited to roadbuilding on a large scale, the population didn't care about it and in any case there were none of the massive mining and manufacturing operations which are necessary for surface transit. Barron, safely inside the Zone, had noticed all this and his reaction had been "So what?" He hadn't really cared how the Darkovans lived; it had nothing to do with them. His world was spaceport dispatch: spaceships, cargo, passenger transit —Darkover was a major pivot on long-distance hyper-travel because it was situated conveniently between the High Arm and Low Arm of the Galaxy—mapping ships, and the various tractors and surface machinery for servicing all of those. He was not prepared for the change from spaceship to pack animals.

The three men paused, letting go the reins of the horses, which were well-trained and stood quietly. The foremost of the three men, a sturdy young man in his twenties, said, "You are the Terran representative Daniel Firth Barron?" He had some trouble with the name.

"*Z'par servu.*" The polite Darkovan phrase, *at your service,* brought a faint agreeable smile from the young man as he replied in some formula Barron couldn't understand and then shifted back to Trade City language, saying, "I am Colryn. This is Lerrys, and this, Gwynn. Are you ready? Can you leave at once? Where are your baggages?"

"I'm ready when you are." Barron indicated the duffel bag, which held his few possessions, and the large but light case which held the equipment he must use. "The bag can be knocked around as much as you like; it's only clothes. But be careful not to drop the crate; it's breakable."

"Gwynn, you see to that," Colryn said. "We have pack animals waiting outside the city, but for the moment we can carry them with us. It isn't easy to manage pack animals on the streets here, as narrow as they are."

Barron realized that they were waiting for him to mount. He reminded himself firmly that this assignment was all that stood between him and ruin, but that didn't seem very important at the moment. He wanted, for the first time in his adult life, to run. He set his mouth hard and said very stiffly, "I should warn you, I've never been on a horse in my life."

"I am sorry," Colryn said. His politeness was almost excessive. "There is no other way to go where we are going."

The one introduced as Lerrys swung Barron's duffel bag

up to his saddle. He said, "I'll take this, you'll have enough trouble with your reins, then." His Terran was substantially better than Colryn's, being virtually accentless. "You'll soon pick up riding; I did. Colryn, why don't you show him how to mount? And ride beside him until he gets over being nervous."

Nervous! Barron felt like snarling at the youngster that he had been facing strange worlds when this boy was playing with his toys, then he relaxed. *What the hell, I am nervous, the kid would have to be blind not to see it.*

Before he realized how it had happened, he was in the saddle, his feet slipped through the high ornate stirrups, moving slowly down the street and away from the Terran Zone. He was too confused and too busy keeping his balance to give it a single backward look.

He had never been at close quarters with Darkovans before. At the restaurants and shops in Trade City, they had been dark impassive faces serving him and strangers at a safe distance to be ignored. Now he was among them for an indefinite period of time, with only the most casual of warnings, the dimmest of preparations.

This never happened in the Terran Empire! Damn it, you were never supposed to be assigned work outside your specialty; then if they actually sent you into the field on a strange planet, you were supposed to get all sorts of briefing and training! At the moment it was taking all the concentration he could muster to stay on his horse.

It was the better part of an hour before he began to relax, to feel that a fall was less imminent, and to spare a few minutes to look at his three companions.

All three were younger than Barron, as well as he could judge. Colryn was tall, lanky yet delicately built, and his face was narrow and fine, with a shadow of brown curly beard. His voice was soft, but he seemed unusually self-possessed for so young a man, and he talked and laughed with animation as they rode. Lerrys was sturdy, with hair almost red enough for a Terran, and seemed hardly into his twenties. Gwynn, the third, was swart and tall, the oldest of the three; except for a nod and brief greeting, he had paid no attention to Barron and seemed a little aloof from the younger men.

All three wore loose heavy breeches, falling in flaps over

high, carefully-fitted boots, and laced tunic-like shirts in rich, dark colors. Gwynn and Colryn had thick, fur-lined riding cloaks, and Lerrys a short loose fur jacket with a hood. All three wore short gauntlets, knives in their belts and smaller knives in pockets at the top of their boots; Gwynn had a sword as well, although for riding it was swung across the crupper of his horse. They all had hair cut smoothly below their ears and a variety of amulets and jewelry. They looked fierce, bright and barbaric. Barron, aware of his own thoroughly civilized clothing, hair, grooming and manner, felt queerly frightened. *Damn it, I'm not ready for this sort of thing!*

They rode at first through cobbled streets, between the crowded houses and markets of the Old Town; then along wider stone roads where the going was smoother, between high houses set back behind gardens and unfamiliar high towers. Finally the stone road ended to become trampled grass and the riders turned aside toward a long, low enclosure and through wooden and stone fences and gateways into a sort of compound of reddish, trampled earth, where several dozen unfamiliarly dressed men were doing various things: loading and unloading animals, saddling and grooming them, cooking over open fires or on braziers, washing and splashing in a wooden trough, and carrying buckets of feed and water to the beasts. It was very cold and very confusing, and Barron was glad, at last, to reach the lee of a rough stone wall, where he was permitted to slide from his horse and turn it over, at Colryn's nod, to a roughly dressed man who came to lead it away.

He walked between Gwynn and Lerrys, Colryn remaining behind to see to the animals, under a shelter roofed and walled against the wind. Lerrys said, "You're not used to riding; why don't you rest while we get food ready? And haven't you any riding clothes? I can bring your bag— it would be better to change into them now."

Although Barron knew that the youngster was trying to be kind, he felt irritated at the continued harping on this point. "The clothes I have with me are just like this; I'm sorry."

"In that case you'd better come with me," Lerrys said, and led him out of the shelter again, through the opposite end of the long enclosure. Heads turned to follow them as they passed; someone shouted something and people laughed loudly. He heard repeated murmurs of *Terranan*, which didn't need any interpreting. Lerrys turned and said firmly, *"Chaireth."* That caused a momentary silence and then a brief flurry of quiet words and mutters. They all moved away with some deference as the young redhead motioned to them. Finally the two came out into a market or shop—mostly clay jars and coarse glassware, a multitude of loose garments lying over baskets and barrels. Lerrys said firmly, "You can't possibly travel into the mountains in the outfit you're wearing. I don't mean to sound offensive, but it's impossible."

"I wasn't given any orders—"

"Listen, my friend"—Lerrys used the Darkovan word *com'ii*—"You have no idea how cold it gets, travelling in the open, especially back in the hills. Your clothes may be warm"—he touched a fold of the light synthetic—"but only for conditions between walls. The Hellers are the very bones of the earth. Your feet will be sore, riding in those things, not to mention—"

Barron, now fiercely embarrassed, had to say flatly, "I can't afford it."

Lerrys drew a deep breath. "My foster father has ordered me to provide everything that is necessary for your well-being, Mr. Barron." Barron was surprised at the manner of address—the Darkovans did not use honorifics or surnames —but then, Lerrys apparently spoke excellent Terran. He wondered if the young man were a professional interpreter. "Who is your foster father?"

"Valdier Alton of the Comyn Council," Lerrys said briefly. Even Barron had heard of the Comyn—the hereditary caste of Darkovan rulers—and it silenced him. If the Comyn had anything to do with this and wanted him to wear Darkovan clothes, there was no use arguing.

After a brief period of spirited bargaining of which Barron—who knew considerable of the Darkovan language, more because he was quick and fluent at languages than because he had been interested—could follow very little, Lerrys said, "I hope these will meet with your approval. I knew you would not care to wear bright colors; I do not myself." He handed Barron a pile of clothing, mostly in dark fabrics that looked like linen, with a heavy fur jacket like the one he himself was wearing. "It's hard to manage a cloak, riding, unless you grew up wearing one." There was also a pair of high boots.

"Better try the boots for fit," he suggested.

Barron bent and slipped off his sandals. The clothing seller chuckled and said something Barron couldn't follow about sandals and Lerrys said fiercely, "The *chaireth* is Lord Alton's guest!" The merchant gulped, muttered some phrases of apology and fell silent. The boots fitted as if they had been made for him, and though they felt strange along his ankles and calves, Barron had to admit they were comfortable. Lerrys picked up the sandals and stuck them in Barron's pocket. "You could wear them indoors, I suppose."

Barron would have answered, but before the words reached his lips a curious dizziness swept over him.

He was standing in a great, vaulted hall, lighted only by a few flickering torches. Below him he could hear the shouts of drunken men; and he could smell torches, roasting meat, and an odd acrid odor that confused him and made him feel sick. He grasped at a ring in the wall, found that it was not there; the wall was not there. He was back in the blowing wind and cloudy sunlight of the fenced compound, his pile of clothing fallen to the grass at his feet, and young Lerrys staring up at him, shaken and puzzled.

"Are you all right, Barron? You looked—a bit odd."

Barron nodded, glad to conceal his face by stooping to gather up his clothing. He was relieved when Lerrys left him in the shelter and he could sink down on the rough floor and lean against the wall, shuddering.

That again! Was he going mad? If it had been due to the stress of his job, now that he had been removed from the dispatch board it should have stopped. Yet, although brief, this time had been more vivid than the others. Shivering, he shut his eyes and tried not to think until Colryn, coming to the edge of the open wall of the shelter, called to him.

Two or three men in rough, dark clothing were moving around the fire; Colryn did not introduce them. Barron, in response to gestures, joined Gwynn and Lerrys at the trough where men were washing. It was growing dusky and the icy evening wind was coming up, but they all washed long and thoroughly. Barron was shivering uncontrollably and thinking with some longing of the Darkovan fur jacket, but he took his turn and washed face and hands more than he'd normally have done; he didn't want them to think Terrans were dirty—and in any case riding had left him dirtier than pushing buttons and watching circuit relays. The water was bitterly cold, and he shook with the chill, his face bitten by the bitter wind.

They sat around the fire out of the wind, and after murmuring a brief formula, Gwynn began handing food around. Barron accepted the plate he was given, which held some sweet boiled grain covered with a splash of acrid sauce, a large lump of meat and a small bowl of thick bittersweet stuff vaguely like chocolate. It was all good, although it was hard to manage the tough meat which the others sliced into paper-thin slices with the knives in their belts; it had been salted and dried in some manner and was almost like leather. Barron pulled a pack of cigarettes from his pockets and lighted one, drawing the smoke gratefully into his mouth; it tasted ambrosial.

Gwynn scowled at him and said in an undertone to Colryn, "First the sandals and now this—" looking with direct rudeness at Barron, he asked a question of which Barron could make out only the unfamiliar word *embredin*. Lerrys raised his head from his plate, saw Barron's cigarette and shook his head slightly, then said *"Chaireth"* again, rather deprecatingly, to Gwynn and got up to drop down beside Barron.

"I wouldn't smoke here if I were you," he said. "I know it is your custom, but it is offensive among the men of the Domains."

"What was he saying?"

Lerrys flushed. "He was asking, to put it in the simplest possible terms, if you were an—an effeminate. It was partly those damned sandals of yours, and partly—well, as I say, men do not smoke here. It is reserved for women."

With an irritable gesture Barron ground out his cigarette. This was going to be worse than he thought. "What's that word you used—*chaireth?*"

"Stranger," Lerrys said. Barron picked up a lump of meat again, and Lerrys said, almost apologizing, "I should have provided you with a knife."

"No matter," Barron said, "I wouldn't know how to use it anyway."

"Nevertheless—" Lerrys began again, but Barron did not hear him. The fire before them slid away—or rather, flared up, and in the midst of the flames, tall, bluish, and glowing, he saw——

A woman.

A woman again, standing in the midst of flames. He thought he cried out in the moment before the figure changed, grew and was, again, the great chained Being, regal, burning, searing her beauty into his heart and brain. Barron gripped his hands until the nails bit into the palms.

The apparition was gone.

Lerrys was staring at him, white and shaken. "Sharra," he breathed, "Sharra, the golden-chained—"

Barron reached out and grabbed him. He said, hoarsely, disregarding the men at the fire, which was once again the tiny, cooking fire, "You saw it? *You* saw it?"

Lerrys nodded without speaking. His face was so white that small freckles stood out. He said at last with a gasp, "Yes, I saw. What I can't understand is—how *you* saw! What in the Devil's name are you?"

Barron, almost too shaken to speak, said, "I don't know. That keeps happening. I have no idea why. I'd like to know why you can see it, too."

Struggling for composure, Lerrys said, "What you saw—it is a Darkovan archetype, a Goddess form. I don't completely understand. I know that many Terrans have some telepathic power. Someone must be broadcasting these images and somehow you have the power to pick them up. I—" He hesitated. "I must speak to my foster father before I tell you more." He fell silent, then said with sudden resolution; "Tell me, what would you rather be called?"

"Dan will do," Barron said.

"Dan then. You are going to have trouble in the mountains; I thought you would be an ordinary Terran, and not aware—" He stopped, biting his lip. "I am under a pledge," he said at last, "and I cannot break it even for this. But you are going to have trouble and you will need a friend. Do you know why no one would lend you a knife?"

Barron shook his head. "Never occurred to me to ask. Like I said, I can't use one anyway."

"You are a Terran," Lerrys said. "By custom and law here—a knife or any other weapon must never be lent or given, except between sworn friends or kinfolk. To say 'my knife is yours' is a pledge. It means that you will defend the other—therefore, a knife or any weapon, must be bought, or captured in battle, or made for you: Yet," he said, with a sudden laugh, "I will give you this—and I have my reasons." He stooped down and drew a small sharp knife from the pocket in his boot. "It is yours," he said, suddenly very serious. "I mean what I say, Barron. Take it from me, and say 'yours and mine.' "

Barron, feeling embarrassed and strange, fumbled at the hilt of the small blade. "Mine, then, and yours. Thank you, Lerrys." The intensity of the moment caught him briefly up into it, and he found himself staring into the younger man's eyes almost as if words passed between them.

The other men around the fire were staring at them, Gwynn frowning in surprised disapproval, Colryn looking puzzled, and vaguely—Barron wondered how he knew—jealous.

Barron fell to his food, both puzzled and relieved. It was easier to eat with the knife in his hand; later he found it fitted easily into the little pocket at the top of his boot. Lerrys did not speak to him again, but he grinned briefly at Barron now and then, and Barron knew that, for some reason, the young man had adopted him as a friend. It was a strange feeling. He was not a man to make friends easily—he had no close ones—and now a young man from a strange world, guessing at his confusion, had thrust unexpected friendship on him. He wondered why and what would happen next.

He shrugged, finished his meal, and followed Colryn's gestured directions—to rinse his plate and bowl and pack them with the others and to help with the spreading of blankets inside the shelter. It was very dark now; cold rain began to spray across the compound; and he was glad to be inside. There was, he realized, a subtle difference in the way they treated him now; he wondered why, and though he told himself it made no difference, he was glad of it.

Once in the night, wrapped in fur blankets, surrounded by sleeping men, he woke to stare at nothingness and feel his body gripped with weightlessness and cold winds again.

Lerrys, sleeping a few feet away, stirred and murmured, and the sound brought Barron back to the moment.

It was going to be one hell of a trip if this keeps on happening every few hours.

And there wasn't a thing he could do about it.

IV

A VOICE called in Melitta's dreams.

"Melitta! Melitta, sister, *breda,* wake! Listen to me!"

She sat up in the dark, desperately grasping at the voice. "Storn," she gasped, half aloud, "is it you?"

"I can speak to you only a little while like this, *breda,* so listen. You are the only one who can help me. Allira cannot hear, and in any case she is too frail and timid, she would die in the hills. Edric is wounded and prisoned. It must be you, little one. Dare you help me?"

"Anything," she whispered, her heart pounding. Her eyes groped at the dark. "Are you here? Can we escape? Shall I make a light?"

"Hush. I am not here; I speak to your mind only. I have tried to waken hearing in you for these last four days and at last you hear me. Listen, sister—you must go alone. You are only lightly guarded; you can shake them off. But you must go now, before snow closes the passes. I have found someone to help you. I will send him to you at Carthon."

"Where . . ."

"At Carthon," the fading voice whispered and was silent. Melitta whispered aloud, "Storn, Storn, don't go," but the voice had failed and faded into exhaustion. She was alone in the darkness, her brother's voice still ringing like an echo in her ears.

Carthon—but where was Carthon? Melitta had never been more than a few miles from her home; she had never been beyond the mountains and her ideas of geography were hazy. Carthon might be over the next ridge, or it might be at the world's end.

She flung agonized queries into the darkness. *How can I, where shall I go?* But there was no answer, only darkness and silence. Had it been a dream born of her frenzy to escape, or had her brother in his magical trance, somehow managed to reach her mind in truth? If it were so, then she could do nothing but obey.

Melitta of Storn was a mountain girl with all that implied. The prime root of her being was the clan loyalty to Storn, not only as her elder brother, but as the head of his house. That he was blind and incapacitated, that he could not have defended her and her sister and younger brother—not to mention their people—in this crisis, made no difference. She did not censure him even in her thoughts and believed, when Allira did so, that the girl's sufferings at Brynat's hands had turned her brain. Now he had laid the task on her to escape and find help, and it never occurred to her not to obey.

She rose from her bed, pulled a fur robe around her shoulders—for the night was bitterly cold and the stone floors had never known fire—and thrust her feet into furry socks, then, moving surely in the dark, found flints and tinder and struck a small lamp—so small that the light was not much bigger than the head of a pin. She sat down before the light, cheered a little by the tiny flame, and began to plan what she could do.

She knew already what she must do—escape from the castle before snow closed the passes, and somehow make her way to Carthon, where her brother would send someone to help her. But how this could be accomplished, she found it hard to imagine.

Guards still followed her at a respectful distance, everywhere she went through the halls. Dark and late though it was, she was sure that even if she left her room they would rouse from where they slept and follow. They feared Brynat more than they longed for sleep. Their fear of him was made clear to her when she realized that not one of them had ventured to lay a hand on her. She wondered if she should be grateful for this, and thrust the thought aside. That was to fall into his trap.

Like all mountain girls, Melitta was enough of a realist to think the next logical step: could she seduce one of the guards into letting her escape? She thought it unlikely. They feared Brynat, and he had ordered them to let her alone. More likely the guard would accept her advances, take what she offered, then go directly to Brynat with the story and win approval of his chief as well. After which, Brynat might well punish her by turning her over to the outlaws for a plaything. That was a blind alley—she could have made herself do it, but it would probably be no use.

She went to the window, pulling her furs closer about her, and leaned out. *You must be gone before the snow closes the passes.* She was a mountain girl, with weather and storms in her blood. It seemed to Melitta that she could almost smell from afar, borne on the chill night wind, the smell of far-off clouds pregnant with snow.

The night was not far advanced. Idriel and Liriel swung in the sky; Mormalor, faint and pearly, hung half-shadowed on the shoulder of the mountain. If she could manage somehow to leave the castle before dawn . . .

She could not go now. Brynat's men were still at their nightly drinking party in the great hall; Allira might send for her still, and she dared not be found absent. But in the hours between deep night and dawn, when even the air was sluggish, she might devise a plan, and be far away before mid-morning discovered that she was not in her room. She closed the window, cuddling herself in the furs, and went back to make plans.

Once out of the castle she wondered where she could go. It would be to Carthon, wherever that was, eventually. But she could not make Carthon in a single night; she would need shelter and food, for it might be a journey halfway to the world's end. Once clear of Castle Storn, perhaps some of her brother's vassals would shelter her. Although they were without power to protect against Brynat's attack, she knew that they loved Storn and many of them knew and loved her. They would at least let her hide among them for a day or two until the hue and cry died down; they might help provide her with food for the journey, and it might be that one of them could set her on the road to Carthon.

The nearest of the great lords were the Aldarans, of Castle Aldaran near High Kimbi; they had, as far as she knew, no blood feud with Storns and no commitment to Brynat, but it seemed unlikely that they would, or could, come to the aid of Storn at this time. Her grandmother's kinfolk had been Leyniers, related to the great Comyn Domain of Alton, but even the Comyn Council's writ did not run here in the mountains.

It did not occur to Melitta to censure her brother, but it did occur to her that, knowing himself weak, he might well have attempted to place himself under the protection of one of the powerful mountain lords. But always before, the chasms and crags surrounding Storn had made them impregnable; and—a Storn swear fealty to another house? Never!

He could have married Allira—or me—to some son of a great house. Then we would have had blood kin to protect us—bare is the back with no brother to guard it!

Well, he had not, and the time for fretting was long past —*chickens can't be put back into eggs!* The evil bird that had hatched from this oversight was out and flying, and only Melitta had the freedom and the strength to save something from the wreck.

Carrying the tiny lamp, she went to her chests. She could not go in long skirts and mantles. At the bottom of her chest was an old riding cloak, woven of thick heavy fabric from the valley and lined with fur; it was not rich enough to rouse greed in anyone she passed, but it was warm and durable. There was an old and shabby pair of her brother's riding breeches, patched with leather, which she had worn for riding about the estate; it was a wiser choice than her own long, loose riding mantle. She added a knitted blouse, a long, thick, lined tunic, socks knitted from the spun fur of the forge folk, and her fur boots. She made a small parcel of a change of linen and some small trinkets, which she might sell or barter for help on the way. Finally she braided her hair and tied it into a woolen cap. This done, she put out the lamp and went to the balcony again. Until this moment, the actual preparation for the journey had obscured the really basic fact: exactly *how* was she to get out of the castle?

There were secret passages. She knew some of them. There was one, for instance, leading from the wine cellars near the old dungeon. The only thing necessary was to get into the wine cellar so that she could get into the secret passage. Perfectly simple. And what would her guards be doing while she descended the stairs and went into the wine cellar, conveniently managing to leave them outside? Drinking wine? That might be fine, if she could get them drunk enough, but they would certainly be suspicious at anything she offered them, on guard for a trick.

Another exit from the castle—calling it secret was a mere technicality, a way of saying that it had been unused for years and nobody bothered guarding it any more—was the passageway that led down into the cliffs and the abandoned forges where, in an earlier day of Darkover, the dark, stunted mountain people had worshipped the fires that lit their forges. There they had made the ancient swords and the strangely propertied artifacts which those who had never seen them used, called magical. The fires and forges had been silent for centuries; the little people withdrawn into the deeper hills; the Storns had come long after they were gone. As a child Melitta, with her brothers and sister, had explored the caves and abandoned dwellings of the forge folk. But they and all their magic, were gone. Their poor and scattered remnants now dwelt in villages near Storn, and they had been captured and driven along with the farm folk; they were more helpless than Melitta herself.

She looked over the balcony again, her mouth curving in what might have been a smile in better days. *I need wings*, she thought. *My guards are too much afraid of Brynat to molest me here; while I stay in this room, they will stay outside in that hallway, and swear to him that I am inside here. I should have managed these things better; I should have spent my childhood in a room with one of the secret passages. I can think of a dozen ways to get out of the castle—but I have to get out of this room first, and I can't think of a way to do that.*

A faint glimmer of light wavering beneath her showed her that, on a lower floor and some rooms away, Allira moved in the Royal Suite. She thought, despairingly, *Storn should have wakened Allira. There is the old hidden way from the Royal Suite, down into the cliff people's village. Allira could simply wait till Brynat was sleeping, and slip away. . . .*

Mad schemes spun in her mind. She had access to her sister; the guards would follow her to the doors of the Royal Suite but not follow her inside, could she manage to get in there and find the old entrance to the passage. At what hour could they be safe from Brynat's intrusion? Could she count on Allira to trick him, drug him, even hold him in talk or in sensual play while she, Melitta, slipped past?

I dare not depend on Allira, she thought with something like despair. *She would not betray me, but she would not have courage to help me, or risk angering Brynat, either.*

If I went down to her rooms, with the guards following me—how long could I count on being alone with her before they summoned Brynat, or grew suspicious when I did not return? And if I vanished from her rooms—they would tear her to pieces, to find out what way I had gone, and I would be pursued before the sun was well up. That's no help.

But the thought persisted. It might very well be her only chance. It was, of course, to risk everything on one throw; if Brynat returned while she was with Allira, something might rouse his suspicions and she would be consigned to securer custody. For all she knew, her guards had orders to report to Brynat if she and her sister spoke together for more than a few minutes.

But if no one knew I was with Allira?

How could she get to Allira's room unseen?

The old Darkovans had mastered the secrets of such things. The magic electrical net which protected Storn's trance was only one of the powers with which Melitta was familiar—but none of them were of use to her now. There were magical cloaks which threw a veil of illusion around the wearer and let them walk unseen, by bending the light, but if Storn had ever owned one, Melitta did not know where it was, or how to use it. She could slip up to the Sunrise Tower, if she could get there, and pull the magical bird plumage over her head, and fly out and away from the castle—but only in illusion. What she saw would be real enough—Storn, she knew, had watched the battle that way—but her body would lie in trance in the Tower, and sooner or later, she would be drawn back to it. That was not the kind of escape which would do any good. *I need wings,* she thought again. *If I could fly right off this balcony and down into that same Royal Suite where Brynat has taken Allira . . .*

She stopped in mid-thought, grimly. She had no wings. Thinking about them was no good. But she had two sturdy arms, two sturdy legs, ten strong fingers and she had been trained since childhood in rock climbing.

She went to the edge of the balcony, fantasies and plans vanishing in a cold, realistic assessment of the problem. She could not fly down to the Royal Suite. But, with strength, caution, and good luck, it was remotely possible that she could *climb* down to it.

She leaned over, fighting a sudden surge of dizziness. A hundred feet of rough, sheared stone fell away into a chasm below. But the castle wall was not sheer, not smooth. Centuries ago, it had been built of rough stone, the very bones of the mountain, hewn in great lumps and cemented into place with ancient tools which would have blunted too swiftly if the stone had had to be smoothed. A wealth of window ledges, archer's slits, balconies, outside stairways and projections lumped and ridged the gray sides of the old castle.

When I was a child, she thought, *Storn and I used to climb everywhere. I was whipped once for frightening our nurse out of her senses by climbing to a third-level balcony and making faces at her from the arbor. I taught Edric to climb on the balconies down lower. I've never climbed this high—I was afraid of falling. But this part of the castle should be as climbable as the lower part.*

She knew that if she fell she would be broken on the crags far below. *But why should I fall from two hundred feet in the air, if I could manage not to fall from fifteen feet?*

You never thought about that because it wouldn't have mattered if you did fall from fifteen feet, her common sense told her, but she hushed the voice, packed up the thought into a tiny box, shoved it into the back of her mind and left it there. *And suppose I do get killed,* she told herself defiantly. *Edric didn't mind risking being killed in the siege, or if he did mind, he risked it anyway. I took bow and arrow myself, and I could have been shot or knifed down on the ramparts. If I was willing to die then, in the hope of defending Storn Heights, then why should I hesitate to take the same sort of risk now? If I get killed, I get killed, and at least I won't have to worry about Brynat's rabble lining up to take turns raping me.*

It wasn't exactly a comforting thought, but she decided

that she could make it do for the moment. She hesitated only a moment, her hands on the railing. Off went the fur-lined gloves; she thrust them deep into the pockets of Edric's breeches. She buttoned the cloak back and tied it into the smallest possible compass at her waist, hoping it would not catch on a projection of stone. Finally she slipped off her boots, standing shivering on the stone balcony, and tied them together by their laces round her neck. If the thongs caught on a stone she might strangle, but without boots she would be helpless in the snow, and her trained weather sense told her that the snow could not be very long delayed. Then, without giving herself time to think she swung herself up and over the edge of the balcony, sat there for a moment taking the exact bearings of the room and balcony she wanted—forty feet below her and almost a hundred feet away to the left—and slipped down, lodging her stockinged feet in a crevice of the stone, finding a handhold to spread-eagle herself against the rough wall.

The crevices between the stone seemed smaller than when she had climbed about on them as a child, and she had to move by feel on the cold stone. Her feet ached with the cold before she had moved five yards, and she felt first one, then another of her nails split back and break as she clutched the dark, rough stone. The moonlight was pale and fitful, and twice a white streak that she took for a crevice in the paleness turned out to be a crumbling, evil-smelling bird-dropping. But Melitta clung like a limpet to each crevice, never moving more than one hand or one foot until she was securely anchored in some new hold.

Evanda be praised, she thought grimly, *that I'm strong and tough from riding! If I were a girl to sit over my sewing, I'd drop off in two yards!* Even strong as she was, she felt every muscle trembling with cold and tension. She felt, also, that in the pale moonlight, she must be clearly visible against the side of the castle, a target for an arrow from any sentry who happened to look up on his rounds. Once she froze, whimpering as a small light and a fragment of voice, blown on the wind, came round the corner, and she knew one of Brynat's soldiers on some business below passed beneath her. Melitta shut her eyes and prayed he would not look up. He did not; he went on singing drunkenly and, almost exactly beneath her, a hundred feet below, and on the narrow path between the castle and the cliffs, opened the fly of his breeches and urinated into the abyss. She held herself taut, trembling against hysterical laughter. After what seemed an hour he stooped, picked up his lantern, shrugged his clothes into place and stumbled on his way again. Melitta thought she had forgotten how to breathe, but she managed it again, and forced her taut fingers, gripping at a stone, to move again toward the lighted balcony below.

Inch by slow inch—a finger, a toe, a cold yard at a time —the girl crept like an ant down the wall. Once, her heart flipped over and stopped as a pebble encrusted in cement broke away under her fingers, and she heard it slide away and ricochet off a projection beneath her, rebound with what sounded like gunfire off the rocks below, and finally clatter into the darkness. Every muscle tight, she held her breath for minutes, sure that the sound would bring soldiers running, but when she opened her eyes again, the castle still lay bathed in the empty light of the setting moons and she still clung to the wall in her comforting solitude.

The moonlight had dimmed considerably past the shoulder of the mountains, and thick mists were beginning to rise below, when at last her feet touched the stone of the balcony and she let go and slid, dropped down on the stone railing, and crouched there, just breathing in deep gasps of relief. When she could move again, she slipped her hands into her gloves, her feet into the fur-lined boots, and wrapped herself tightly in the cloak, grabbing it tight to lessen her shivering.

The first hurdle was passed. But now she must get inside and attract Allira's attention without running the risk that Brynat would see. She had come too far to be stopped now!

She crept like a small shaking ghost across the stone balcony and pressed her face against the veined colored glass, joined with strips of metal, which closed the double doors of the balcony. The doors were bolted inside and lined with heavy thick curtains of tapestry, and Melitta had a sudden hysterical picture of herself perched out there like a bird for days, uselessly rapping like a bird at the glass, unheard, until somebody looked up and saw her there.

She also feared that it might be Brynat who drew aside those curtains and looked straight out into her eyes.

She tried to force herself to approach the window, but the picture of Brynat's fierce face was so compelling that she literally could not make herself raise her hand. She *knew* he was behind that tapestry. She sank down, nerveless and shaking, and waited, her mind spinning.

Storn, Storn, you came to me before, help me now! Brother, brother! Gods of the mountains, what shall I do? She begged and commanded her weak limbs to move, but she kept on crouching there, frozen and motionless, for what seemed like hours. Finally, slowly, her frozen body and brain began to work again, and she began to think.

When we were children, Allira and I could reach one another's minds like this. Not always and not often, but if one of us was in danger the other would know; when the wild bird pack had her cut off on the island, I knew and I brought help. She was fourteen then, and I was only eight. I cannot have lost that power, or Storn could not have reached me tonight. But if all my mind is giving off is fear, Allira wouldn't know if she did hear me; she'd think it was just part of her own panic.

She had had almost no training. Storn, being blind and thus debarred from the usual pursuits of men of his caste, had explored the old telepathic ways. But to his brother and sisters, these had been dreams, fantasies, games and tricks—pleasant perhaps for pastime, but not worthy of serious study. There was too much else that was real and present and necessary to the moment. Melitta spent a moment berating herself for not spending more time with Storn learning about the old speech of mind to mind, but common sense came to her rescue. She reminded herself of the old proverb, *Foresight could make wise men of Durraman's donkeys!* She might as well blame herself for Allira's not having been married to a strong husband with eighty fighting men to defend them.

She put her hand out to rap on the glass sharply, and again the clear picture of Brynat looking out into the storm came to her; it was so instant and compelling that she physically shrank back and pressed herself against the railing, folding herself up into her cloak. It was just in time; a browned hand drew the tapestry aside, and Brynat's scarred visage turned from side to side, trying to penetrate the darkness.

Melitta shrank against the railing and tried to make herself invisible. After a minute that seemed endless, Brynat turned away and the lamp went out. The tapestry dropped back into place. Melitta dropped, gasping, to the stones, and lay there trying not to breathe.

Time dragged. The moon set, and the shivering girl grew colder and colder. After hours, so long that she began to wonder if the sun would come up and find her there, a thin fine rain began to fall, and this spurred her; she realized that whatever she risked, she must be gone by sunrise; she must be somewhere that she could lie hidden by day. Even if she must chip the glass of the doors and cut Brynat's throat while he slept, she must make some move!

As she poised her muscles for action, a faint light glimmered again between the tapestries. Melitta gathered herself to spring against the bolts; then a fine hand moved through the gap, the bolt shuddered in the wood and her sister Allira, wrapped in a long woolen shift, her hair disheveled, thrust the door outward and, her eyes great and staring, looked straight into Melitta's face.

Melitta raised a hand to her mouth, frightened of Allira's nerves and a sudden outcry, but Allira only clasped her hands to her heart with a gasp of relief. She whispered "I *knew* you were there, and I couldn't believe—Melitta, how did you come here?"

Melitta replied only with a jerk of her head toward the rocks and a whispered "No time now! Brynat—"

"Asleep," Allira said laconically, "He sleeps with one eye, like a cat, but just now—never mind that. Melitta—are you armed?"

"Not with a weapon I could kill him with, without outcry," Melitta said flatly. "And you'd still have his men to deal with, and they would be worse." Watching Allira flinch, she knew that her sister had already considered and rejected that escape.

"The secret passage through the old cliff-town; have any of Brynat's men discovered it?"

"No—Melitta, you cannot go that way; you'll be lost in the caves, you'd die in the mountains if you ever found your way out—and where would you go?"

"Carthon," Melitta said briefly, "wherever that is. I don't suppose you know?"

44

"I know only that it's a city beyond the passes, which was great in the days of the Seven Domains. Melitta, are you really going to dare this?"

"It's this or die here," Melitta said bluntly. "You seem able to stand it here, though—"

"I don't want to die."

Allira was almost sobbing and Melitta hushed her roughly. It was not Allira's fault that she was so timid. Perhaps even such protection as Brynat could give seemed better than a desperate trek through strange crags, passes and mountains. *Maybe I ought to be like that too,* Melitta thought, *maybe that's a woman's proper attitude, but I suppose there's something wrong with me—and I'm glad. I'd rather die taking the chance of doing something to help Storn.*

But the brief moment of censure for her sister passed. After all, Allira had already faced, or so it seemed to Allira herself, the worst that could happen to her; what more had she to fear? By escaping now, she would only lose the life she had saved at such cost.

"You must go, then, before sunrise," Allira said with quick resolution. "Quick, while Brynat sleeps and before the guards come in"—a brief flicker of something like her old smile— "as they do each night, to make sure I have not killed him while he sleeps."

The wind blew briefly into the room and was barred out again as the two girls slipped inside. Brynat lay sprawled and ugly in the great bed, breathing stertorously. After one blazing look of hate, Melitta averted her eyes, creeping past him silently, holding her breath and trying not to think, as if her very hate might wake their enemy. She breathed more freely when they were in the ornate reception room of the suite, but her hands were still clenched with tension and terror.

There were the carven chests, the hangings and the strange beasts around the elaborate false fireplace. She pressed the hilt of the marble sword there and the stone slid away, revealing the old stair. She clutched Allira's hands, wanting to say something but falling silent in desperation. She went forward. Whatever somehow happened, she was safe or dead.

Allira might somehow summon up the courage to come— but the escaping, Melitta knew with a practical grimness, was only the beginning. She had a long way to go, and she could not encumber herself with anyone who did not share her own desperate resolve; at this point, even if Allira had begged to come with her, she would have refused.

She said briefly, "The guards outside my room think I'm still in there. Try anything you can to keep them from finding out how I'm gone. You saw nothing; you heard nothing."

Allira clutched at her, a frightened hug and kiss. "Shall I—shall I get you Brynat's knife? He would search me for it, but when he didn't find it, he'd only think he lost it."

Melitta nodded, a tardy spasm of admiration for her frightened sister touching her. She stood frozen, not daring to move, as Allira crept back into the bedroom, and then returned with a long, unsheathed knife in her hand. Allira thrust it into the top of Melitta's boot. Allira had something else in her hand, wadded together in a torn linen coif. Melitta glanced hastily at the soggy mess; it was a torn half-loaf of bread, some cut slices of roast meat, and a large double handful of sticky sweets. Uncritically, she wrapped it up again and put it into her deepest pocket.

"Thank you, Lira. It will keep me going for a day or two, and if I don't find any help by then, it's no use anyhow. I must go; it will be light in three hours." She dared not frame a goodbye in words; it would have loosened the floodgates of her fear. "Give me your gold chain, unless you think Brynat will miss it; I can hide it in a pocket and the links will pass current, though it's not as good as a copper one would have been."

Allira smiled a wavering smile. "The amulet didn't protect me, did it? Maybe it will do better for you. *Lucky charms protect you only if you have your own luck.*" She pulled off the long chain, looping it twice and put it over Melitta's head. Melitta clutched at the small amulet, suddenly touched—Allira had worn it since she was three years old; it had been their mother's and grandmother's.

She said quietly, "I'll bring it back," gave Allira a quick kiss, and without another word, plunged into the long deep stairwell. She heard Allira sob softly, as above her the passage darkened and the light went out.

She was alone in the depths of the castle.

V

"WE SHOULD reach Armida by nightfall." Colryn drew his horse to a walk in the neck of the narrow pass, waiting for the others to draw abreast of them, and looked across at Barron with a brief smile. "Tired of travelling?"

Barron shook his head without answering. "Good thing, because, although the Comyn Lord may want us to break our journey there for a day or two, after that we start into the hills."

Barron chuckled to himself. If, according to Colryn, they started into the *hills* tomorrow, he wondered what they had been travelling for these past four days. Every day since they had left the plains where the Terran Trade City lay, they had been winding down the side of one mountain and up along the side of another, till he had lost count of the peaks and slopes.

And yet he was not tired. He was hardened now to riding, and sat his horse easily; and, although he would not have known how to say so, every inch of the road had held him in a sort of spell he did not understand and could not explain.

He had expected to travel this road filled with bitterness, resentment and grim resignation—he had left behind him everything he knew: his work, such friends as he had, the whole familiar world made by the men who had spanned great giant steps across the Galaxy. He had been going into exile and strangeness.

Yet—how could he explain it even to himself?—the long road had held him almost in a dream. It had been like learning a language once known but long forgotten. He had felt the strange world reach out and grip him fast and say "Stranger, come; you are coming home." It gave him a sensation, of riding through a dream, or under water, with everything that happened insulated by a curtain of un-reality.

Now and then, as if surfacing from a very long dive, the old self he had been, during those years when he sat at the

47

dispatcher's board in the Terran Trade City would come to the surface and sit there blinking. He tried, once, to make it clear to himself.

Are you falling in love with this world, or something? He would breathe the cold, strangely scented air, and listen to the slow fall of his horse's hooves on the hard-frozen road, and think, *What's wrong? You've never been here before, why does it all seem so familiar?* But familiar was the wrong word, it was as if, in another life, he had ridden through hills like these, breathed the cold air and smelled the incense that his companions burned in their campfires in the chilly fog of evening before they slept. For it was new to his eyes, and yet—*it's as if I were a blind man, newly seeing, and everything strange and beautiful and yet just the way I knew it would be. . . .*

During these brief interludes when the old Barron came to life in his mind, he realized that this sense of *deja vu,* of living in a dream, must be some new form of the same hallucinated madness that had cost him his job and his reputation. But these interludes were brief. The rest of the time he rode in the strange dream and enjoyed the sense of suspension between his two worlds and the two selves which he knew he was becoming.

Now the journey would break, and he wondered briefly if the spell would break with it. "What is Armida?"

Colryn said "The estate of the lord Valdir Alton, the Comyn lord who sent for you. He will be pleased that you speak our language fluently, and he will explain to you just what he wishes." He looked down into the valley, shading his eyes with his hand against the dimming sunlight, and pointed. "Down there."

The thick trees, heavy, gray-blue conifers that cast dark spice-smelling small cones on the ground, thinned as they rode downward, and here and there in the underbrush some small bird called with perpetual plaintiveness. Thin curls of mist were beginning to take shape in the lowlands, and Barron realized that he was glad they would be indoors before the nightly rain began. He was tired of sleeping on the ground under tarpaulins, though he knew that the climate was mild at this season and that they were lucky it was only rain and not snow. He was tired, too, of food cooked over open fires. He would be glad to sleep under a roof again.

He guided his horse with careless expertness down the slope, letting his eyes fall shut, and drifted off into a brief daydream. *I do not know the Alton lords, and I must keep my real purpose secret from them, until I am certain they would help and not hinder. Here, too, I can find some information about roads and the best way to travel—snow will close the passes soon, and before then I must somehow find the best road to Carthon. The way to the world's end . . .*

He jerked himself out of his dream. He wondered what rubbish was he daydreaming. Where was Carthon, for that matter, *what* was Carthon? As far as he knew, it might be the name of one of the moons! *Oh, hell, maybe I've seen it on a survey map somewhere.* He did look at such things now and then when he had nothing better to do. Perhaps his unconscious—they said the unconscious mind never forgets anything—was weaving dreams with these half-forgotten fragments.

If this went on, he'd be ready for Bedlam. *Ready? Hell, I'm going Tom-o-Bedlam one better!* His brain juggled with scraps of a song learned years ago on another world; it was about the world's end.

"I summoned am to journey/
   Three leagues beyond the wild world's end,/
   Methinks it is no journey . . ."

No, that's wrong. He frowned, trying to recapture the words; it fixed his mind on something other than the strangeness around him.

Lerrys drew his horse even. "Did you say something, Barron?"

"Not really. It would be hard to translate unless—do you understand the Terran language?"

"Well enough," Lerrys said with a grin.

Barron whistled a scrap of the melody, then sang in a somewhat hoarse but melodious voice:

"With a host of furious fancies
   whereof I am commander,
   With a burning spur and a horse of air,

Through the wilderness I wander;
By a queen of air and darkness
I summoned am to tourney
Three leagues beyond the wild world's end;
Methinks it is no journey."

Lerrys nodded. "It does seem a little like that sometimes," he said. "I like that; so would Valdir. But Armida isn't *quite* at the wild world's end—not yet."

As he spoke, they rounded a bend; a faint smell of wood smoke and damp earth came up to them from the valley, and through the thin mist they saw the great house lying below them.

"Armida," said Lerrys, "my foster father's house."

Barron did not know just why he had expected it to be a castle, set high among impassable mountain crags, with eagles screaming around the heights. On the downslope, the horses neighed and picked up speed, and Lerrys patted his beast's neck.

"They smell their home and their stable-mates. It was a good trip; I could have come alone. This is one of the safest roads; but my foster father was afraid of dangers by the way."

"What dangers?" Barron asked. *I must know what I may face on the long road to Carthon.*

Lerrys shrugged. "The usual things in these hills: catmen, wandering nonhuman bands, occasional bandits—though they usually prefer wilder country than this, and in any case we aren't enough to tempt the more dangerous ones. And if the Ghost Wind should blow—but I'll be frightening you away." He laughed. "This part of the world is peaceful."

"Have you travelled much?"

"Not more than most," Lerrys said. "I crossed the Kilghard Hills leading out of the Hellers with my foster brother, when I was fifteen; but it wasn't any pleasure trip, believe me. And once, I went with a caravan into the Dry Towns, crossing the passes at High Kimbi, beyond Carthon—"

Carthon! The word rang like a bell, kicking something awake in Barron and sending a jolt of adrenalin into his system; he physically twitched, missing the next sentence or two. He said, cutting almost rudely through the younger man's reminiscences, "Where and what is Carthon?"

Lerrys looked at him strangely. "A city, or it used to be; it lies well to the east of here. It's almost a ghost town now; no one goes there, but caravans go through the passes; there's an old road, and a ford of the river. Why?"

"I—seem to have heard the name somewhere," said Barron lamely, and lowered his eyes to his saddle, using as his excuse the horse's increasing pace as the road levelled and led toward the low ramparts of Armida.

Why had he expected it to be a castle? Now that he was at the gates, it seemed reasonable that it should be a wide-flung house, sheltered by walls against the fierce winds from the heights. It was built of blue-gray stone with wide spaces of translucence in the stone walls, behind which lights moved in undefined patches of color and brilliance. They rode through a low arch and into a warm, sheltered courtyard; Barron gave up his horse to a small, swart man clad in fur and leather, who took the reins with a murmured formula of welcome. The Terran slid stiffly to the ground.

Shortly afterward he was beside a high blazing fire in a spacious, stone-flagged hall; lights warred with the dark behind the translucent stone walls and the wind safely shut outside. Valdir Alton, a tall, spare, sharp-eyed man, welcomed Barron with a bow and a few brief formal words; then paused a minute, his eyes resting on the Terran with a sudden, sharp frown.

He said, "How long have you been on Darkover?"

"Five years." Barron asked, "Why?"

"No particular reason, except that—perhaps it is that you speak our language well for such a newcomer. But no man is so young he cannot teach, or so old he cannot learn; we shall be glad to know what you can teach us about the making of lenses. Be welcome to my hearth and my home." He bowed again and withdrew. Several times during that long evening, the warm and plentiful meal, and the long, lazy period by the fire—which came between the end of supper and the time they were shown to their beds—the Terran felt that the Darkovan lord's eyes were resting on him with a curious intentness.

Some Darkovans are mind-readers, I've heard. If he's read my mind, he must have seen some damn funny things in it. I wonder if there are loose hallucinations running around the planet and I've simply caught a few somehow.

Nevertheless, his sense of confusion did not keep him from eating hugely of the warm, good meal served for the travellers, and enjoying the strange green, resinous wine they drank afterward. The fuzziness from the strong wine seemed to make him less confused about the fuzziness which blurred his surprise at all things Darkovan, and after a while it was pleasant to feel simply drunk instead of feeling that he was watching the scene through two sets of eyes. He sat and sipped the wine from the beautifully carved, green crystal of the goblet, listening to Valdir's young foster daughter Cleindori playing a small harp which she held on her lap, and singing in a soft pentatonic scale some endless ballad about a lake of cloud where stars fell on the shore and a woman walked, showered in stars.

It was good to sleep in the high room hung with translucent curtains and filled with shifting lights; Barron, accustomed to sleeping in a dark room, looked for twenty minutes for a switch to shut them off, then gave up, got into bed and lay watching them drowsily. The shifting colors shifted his mind into neutral gear, and produced colored patterns even behind his closed eyelids, until he slept.

He slept heavily, dreaming strange swooping dreams of flight, watching landscapes tipping and shifting below, and hearing a voice calling in his dreams, again and again, "Find the road to Carthon! Melitta will await you at Carthon! To Carthon ... Carthon ... Carthon. ..."

He woke once, half-dazed, the words still ringing in his ears when he thought sleep had gone. Carthon. Why should he want to go there; and who could make him go? Banishing the thought, he lay down and slept again, only to dream again of the voice that called—murmuring, beseeching, commanding—*"Find the road to Carthon ..."*

After a long time the dream changed. He was toiling down endless stairs, breaking sharp webs with his outstretched hands, blinded except for a greenish, phosphorescent glow from damp walls that pressed all around him. It was icy cold, and his steps came slow, and his heart beat hard, and the same question pounded in his head: *"Carthon. Where is Carthon?"*

With the sunrise and the thousand small amenities and strangenesses of life in a Darkovan home, he tried to drive the dream away. He wondered again, dispassionately, if he was going mad. *In God's name, what spell has this damned planet woven around me?*

In an attempt to break the bondage of these compelling dreams or sorceries, half through the day, he sought out Lerrys and said to him, "Your foster father, or whatever he is, was supposed to explain my work to me, and I'm anxious to get started. We Terrans don't like idling around when there is work to be done. Will you ask your father if he can see me now?"

Lerrys nodded. Barron had noticed before that he seemed to be more practical and forthright than the average Darkovan and less concerned with formalities. "There is, of course, no pressure on you to begin your work at once, but if you prefer it, my guardian and I are at your service whenever you wish. Shall I have your equipment brought up?"

"Please." Something he had said touched Barron with incongruity. "I thought Valdir was your father."

"Foster father." Again Lerrys appeared to be on the point of saying something, but he withheld it. "Come, I'll take you to his study."

It was a smallish room, as Darkovans counted space. Barron thought that at home it would have been a good-sized banquet hall. It looked down on the enclosed court, with alternating layers of glass and translucent stone. It was bitterly cold, although neither Valdir nor Lerrys appeared to suffer from it; the two wore only the linen shirts Darkovan men wore beneath their fur tunics. Outside below them, men were coming and going in the courtyard; Valdir stood and watched them for some minutes, while seeming courteously not to notice how Barron hung over the one small brazier to warm his hands; then he turned back, smiling in welcome.

"Last night in the hall I could give you only formal greetings; I am very glad to see you here, Mr. Barron. It was Lerrys and I who arranged that someone from the Terran city should come to teach us something of lens grinding."

Barron grinned a little sourly. "It's not my regular work, but I know enough about it to show beginners. So you arranged for me to come here? I thought you people didn't think much of Terran science."

Valdir gave him a sharp look. He said, "We have nothing against Terran science. It is Terran *technology* we fear—that Darkover will become just another link in a chain of worlds, all as much alike as sands scattered on the shore, or weeds along the path of the Terrans. But these are matters of politics—or, perhaps, of philosophy, and to be discussed over good wine at night, not offhand while we work together. I think you will find us ready to learn."

For the last several moments, while he spoke, Barron had been conscious of some low-keyed irritation, like a sound just at the edge of consciousness, which he couldn't quite hear. It made his head ache, and made it hard to hear Valdir's words. He looked around to identify, if he could, what was making the—noise? He couldn't quite hear it. He tried to concentrate on what Valdir was saying; he had missed a sentence or two.

"—and so, you can see, in the foothills, the sight of a sharp-eyed man may be enough, but in the high Sierras, where it's absolutely imperative that any trace of fire must be discovered before it gets out of hand, a lens—what do you call it, a telescope?—would be an invaluable help. It could save acres and acres of timber. Fire in the dry season is such a constant hazard—" He broke off; Barron was moving his head restlessly from side to side, his hand to his forehead. The sound or vibration or whatever it was seemed to fill every crevice of his skull. Valdir said in surprise, "The telepathic damper disturbs you?"

"Telepathic which? But *something* seems to be making one hell of a racket in here. Sorry, sir—"

"Not at all," Valdir said. He went to what looked like an ornamental carving and twisted a knob on it; the invisible noise slackened, and Barron's head quieted to normal. Valdir looked surprised.

"I am sorry; not one Terran in five hundred will know such a device exists, and I had simply forgotten to disconnect it. My deepest apologies, Mr. Barron; are you well? Can I offer you anything?"

"No, I'm all right," Barron said, realizing that he was back to normal again, and wondering what the gadget was. He had the usual Terran notion that Darkover, being a planet without a great deal of manufacturing or technology, was a barbarian one, and the idea of some sort of electronic device functioning out here well beyond the Terran Zone seemed as incongruous as a tree growing in the middle of a spaceport.

"Is this your first trip into the mountains?" Valdir asked.

"No, but the first time I had crossed the plains." Barron caught himself. What was the matter with him? That gadget and its weird noises seemed to have unsettled his brain. "Yes, I've never been outside the Terran Zone before this."

"Of course you haven't seen any real mountains yet," Lerrys said. "These are just foothills, really, compared to the Hellers or the Hyades or the Lorillard Ranges."

"There's quite enough mountain for me," Barron said. "If these are foothills, I'm not in any hurry to see anything higher."

As if to refute what he had said, a picture sprang to swift life in his brain: *I had expected Armida to be like this, a great gray peaked castle lying beneath the chasmed tooth of the mountain, beneath the snow-laden crag with its high plume of snow.*

Barron let his breath out as the picture faded, but before he could think of anything to say, the door opened and Gwynn, now wearing what looked like a green and black uniform, came in, accompanied by two men carrying between them Barron's crate of lens materials and grinding tools. They set it down, under his instructions, and removed the heavy straps, buckles and padding which had protected it on the trip. Valdir thanked the men in an unfamiliar dialect, Gwynn lingered to ask a couple of routine questions, and when the men went away, Barron was once more composed and in possession of himself. *Okay, maybe I've had something like a nervous breakdown in the Terran Zone, and it's still showing in intermittent brainstorms. It doesn't necessarily mean I'm going insane, and it certainly needn't inhibit the work I'm going to be doing.* He was glad to have the chance to collect himself by talking about familiar things.

He had to admit that for men without a standard scientific education, Valdir and Lerrys showed a good deal of comprehension and asked intelligent questions about what he had told them. He gave them a very brief history of lenses—from microscope to telescope to refracting lens for myopia, to binocular lens.

"You realize this is all very elementary," he added apologetically. "We've had simple lenses from our prehistory; it's a pre-atomic development on most planets. Now we have the various forms of radar, coherent light devices, and the like. But when men on Terra first started experimenting with light, the lens was our first step in that direction."

"Oh, it's quite understandable," said Valdir, "you needn't apologize. On a planet like Terra, where the random incidence of clairvoyance is so low, it's perfectly natural that men would turn to such experiments." Barron stared; he hadn't been apologizing.

Lerrys caught his eye and gave Barron a brief, humorous wink, then frowned slightly at his guardian, and Valdir caught himself and continued. "And of course, it's our good fortune that you have developed this technique. You see, Mr. Barron, here on Darkover, throughout *our* prehistory, we were a world where the so-called ESP powers were used, in place of gadgets and machinery, to augment and supplement man's five senses. But so many of these old powers have been lost, or forgotten, during what we call the Years of Chaos, just before the Compact, that now we are forced to supplement our unaided senses with various devices. It's necessary, of course, to be very careful which devices we allow into our society; as the history of all too many planets will show, technology is a two-edged weapon, which can be abused more often than it is used. But we have studied the probable impact on our society quite carefully, and decided that with elementary caution the introduction of lenses will do no palpable harm in the foreseeable future."

"That's good of you," said Barron ironically. If Valdir was conscious of the sarcasm he let it pass without comment. He said "Larry, of course, has a fairly good technical education, and can make things clear to me if I can't understand. Now, about power sources for your machinery and equipment, Mr. Barron. I trust you were warned that very little electricity is available, and only in the lowest of voltages?"

"That's all right. I have mostly hand equipment, and a

small generator which can be adapted to work by wind power."

"Wind is something we have plenty of back here in the mountains," said Lerrys with a friendly grin. "I was the one who suggested wind power instead of storage batteries."

Barron began putting the various bits of equipment back into their case. Valdir rose and went to the window, pausing beside the carved ornament which hid the strange electronic gadget. He asked abruptly, "Mr. Barron, where did you learn to speak Darkovan?"

Barron shrugged. "I've always been fairly quick at languages." Then he frowned; he had a good working knowledge of the language spoken in the city near the Trade Zone, but he had given what amounted to a long and fairly technical lecture, without once hesitating, or calling on the young man—Larry or Lerrys or whatever Valdir called him—to interpret. He felt strangely confused and troubled. *Had* he been speaking Darkovan all that time? He hadn't stopped to think what language he was speaking. *Damn it, what is wrong with me?*

"Nothing is wrong," said Lerrys quickly. "I told you, Valdir. No, I don't understand, either. But—I gave him my knife."

"It was yours to give, fosterling, but I don't disapprove."

"Look out," Lerrys said quickly, "he can hear us."

Valdir's sharp eyes swept in the direction of Barron, who suddenly realized that the two Darkovans had been speaking in yet another language. Barron's confusion made him angry. He said, with dry asperity, "I don't know Darkovan courtesy, but among my people it is considered fairly rude to talk over someone's head, *about* them."

"I'm sorry," Lerrys said. "I had no idea you could hear us, Dan."

"My foster son, of all people, should know about latent telepaths," Valdir said. "I am sorry, Mr. Barron; we intended no rudeness. Telepaths, among you Terrans, are not common, though they are not unknown, either."

"You mean I'm reading your minds?"

"In a sense. It's far too complex a subject to explain in a few minutes. For the moment I suggest you think of it as a very good sort of talent to have for the work you're going to be doing, since it will make it easy for you to talk to people, when you know only a little of their language."

Barron started to say, *But I'm no telepath, I've never shown any talent for that sort of thing, and when the Rhines gave me the standard psi test for the Space Service, I tested out damn near flat negative.* Then he withheld it. He had been learning a lot about himself lately, and it was certain that he wasn't the same man he had been before. If he developed a few talents to go with his hallucinations, that was perhaps the law of compensation in action. It had certainly made it easier to talk to Valdir, so why complain?

He finished carefully putting the equipment in the crate, and listened to Valdir's assurances that it would be securely wrapped and crated for the trip up to the mountain station where he would be working. But when, a few minutes later, he took his leave and went down the hall, he was shocked and yet unsurprised to realize that Valdir's voices and Lerrys' continued, like distant whispers inside his head.

"*Do you suppose the Terrans chose a telepath purposely?*"

"*I don't think so, Foster Father; I don't believe they knew enough about choosing or training them. And he seems too surprised by the whole thing. I told you that from somewhere he had picked up an image of Sharra.*"

"*Sharra, of all conceivable!*"—Valdir's mental voice blurred out in astonishment and what seemed like dismay. "*So you gave him your knife, Larry! Well, you know what that will mean. I'll release you from your pledge, if you like; tell him who you are when it seems necessary.*"

"*It's not because he's a Terran. But if he's going to be running around Darkover in that state, someone's got to do something about it—and I can probably understand him better than most people. It isn't all that easy, to change worlds.*"

"*Don't jump to conclusions, Larry. You don't know that he's changing worlds.*"

Larry's tone in answer sounded positive, and yet somehow sad. "*Oh, yes, he will. Where would he go among the Terrans, after this?*"

VI

MELITTA crept down the long, tunneled stairway, groping through the darkness. After the faint light from the cracks behind her had died, she was in total darkness and had to feel each step with her feet before setting her weight on it. She wished she had thought to bring a light. But on the other hand, she would need both hands to find her way and to brace herself. She went carefully, never putting her full weight on a step without testing it. She had never been down here before, but her childhood had been soaked in stories of her Storn forefathers and the builders of the castle before them, and she knew that secret exits and tunnels could be honeycombed with nasty surprises for people who blundered through them without appropriate precautions.

Her care was not superfluous. Before she had gone more than a few thousand feet down into the darkness, the wall at her left hand fell away and left her feeling a breath of dank air which seemed to rise out of an immense depth. The air was moving, and she had no fear of suffocation, but the echoes stirred at such distance that she quailed at the thought of that drop to her left; and when she dislodged a small pebble with her foot and it slipped over the edge it seemed to fall forever before landing at last, a distant whisper, far below.

Abruptly her hands struck cold stone and she found that she had run into a blank wall. Taken aback for a moment, she began to feel about and discovered that she was inching, foot by foot, along a narrow shelf at the foot of the stairs. She felt her hands strike and break thick webs, and cringed at the thought of the unseen creatures in the darkness that had spun them; she had no fear of ordinary spiders, but who could tell what horrors might spawn here, out of sunlight since the beginning of the world, and what they would crawl over in the darkness and what ghastly things they would find to eat. She braced herself, setting her small chin, thinking, *They won't get to eat me, anyhow.* She gripped the hilt of her knife and held it before her.

To her left, a small chink of pale greenish light wavered. Could she have come to the end of the tunnel already? It was no normal daylight or moonlight. Wherever the light came from, it was not outside. The ledge suddenly widened and she could step back and walk at ease instead of inching along.

The greenish light grew slowly, and now she saw that it came through an arched doorway at the end of the stone passageway along which she walked. Melitta was far from timid, but there was something about that green light which she disliked before she saw more than a glimmer of it, something which seemed to go beneath the roots of consciousness and stir old half-memories which lay at the very depths of her being. Darkover was an old world and the mountains were the most ancient bones of the world, and no man knew what might have crawled beneath the mountains when the sun first began to cool, ages ago, there to lie and grow in unseen horror.

She had been walking silently in her fur-lined boots; now she ghosted along hardly disturbing the air she walked through, holding her breath for fear it would disturb some hidden *something*. The green light grew stronger, and, although it was still no brighter than moonlight, somehow it hurt her eyes so that she slitted them to narrowness against it and tried not to let it inside her eyelids. There was something very awful down here.

Well, she thought, *even if it's a dragon, it can't be much worse than Brynat's men. At worst a dragon would only want to eat me. Anyhow, there haven't been any dragons on Darkover for a thousand years. They were all killed off before the Ages of Chaos.*

The doorway from which the green light emanated was very near. She felt the poisonous brightness as a positive assault on her eyes. She stepped to the doorway and peered through, holding her breath against screaming at the ghastly glare which lay ahead.

She could see that the green light came from some thick, poisonous fungus that grew in the slow currents of air. The room ahead was high and arched, and she could see carvings covered with fungus, and at the far end, blurred and overgrown shapes which had once been a dais and something like chairs.

Melitta took a firm hold of her nerves. *Why should it be evil just because it's green and slimy-looking,* she demanded of herself. *So is a frog, and frogs are harmless. So was the moss on a rock. Why should plants growing in their own way give me this overwhelming feeling of something wicked and sinister?* Nevertheless, she could not make her feet move to take the first step into that arched room. The green light made her eyes ache, and there was a faint smell, as if of carrion.

Slowly, as her eyes grew accustomed to the green, she saw the things that crawled among the fungus.

They were white and sluggish. Their eyes, great and curiously iridescent, moved slowly in her direction, and the girl felt her stomach heave at that blind regard. She stood there paralyzed, thinking frantically, *This must be new, they can't have been here all along, this passage was in good shape forty years ago; I remember my father speaking of it, though he hadn't been down here since years before I was born.*

She stood back, studying the green stalactites of fungus and the crawling things. They looked dreadful, but were they dangerous as well? Even though they made her skin crawl, they might be as harmless as most spiders. Perhaps, if she could simply summon up the nerve to run through them, that was all that was needed.

A small restless rustle behind her made her look down. Near her skirts, sitting up on his hind legs and surveying her with curiosity, a small red-furred, rodentlike animal hung back from entering the cave. He gave a small, nervous chitter which seemed to Melitta to mirror her own apprehension. He was a dirty-looking little creature, but by contrast with the things in the green cave he looked normal and friendly. Melitta almost smiled at him.

He squeaked again and, with a sudden burst of speed, set off running through the fungus.

The green branches whipped down on the little creature. It screamed thinly and was still, smothered in the green, which seemed to pulse with ghastly light. Through the phosphorescence the small golden-eyed horrors moved, swarmed, and moved away. Not even the bones were left; there was only an infinitesimal scrap of pinkish fur.

Melitta crammed her fist in her mouth to keep from

screaming. She took a convulsive step backward, watching
the slow subsiding of the fungus. It took some minutes to
subside.

After a long time her heartbeat slowed to normal and she
found herself frantically searching for solutions. *I wish I
could get through here somehow and lure Brynat's men
down after me,* she thought grimly, but that line seemed to
go nowhere.

*Fire. All living things fear fire, except man. If I could
carry fire . . .*

She had no light; but she did have steel and tinder in
her pocket; on Darkover to be outdoors without the means
of making fire in the snow season, was to die. Before she
was eight years old she had known all the tricks of firemaking anywhere and everywhere.

Trying not to breathe hard, she pulled out her firemaking
materials. She had nothing she could use for a torch, but
she tore off her scarf, wound it round a small slab of rock,
and set it alight. Then, carrying it carefully in front of her,
she stepped into the fungus cave.

The green branches whipped back as the firelight and
heat struck them. The sluggish crawling at her feet made
her gasp with horror, but they made no effort to attack,
and she began to breathe again as she began to walk,
steadily, across the cave. She must go quickly but not too
fast to see where she was going. The scarf would not burn
more than a minute at most. Fortunately the patch of green
seemed to be less than a hundred yards; beyond the further
arch was darkness again.

One of the crawling things struck her foot. It felt
squishy, like a frog, and she gasped, staggered a little for
balance, and dropped the blazing scarf. She swooped to re-
trieve it . . .

A high shrill yeeping came from the crawling thing. The
green fungus near her feet moved, and Melitta held her
breath and waited for it to strike.

The blazing scarf touched the green branch and it caught
fire. A blaze of ghastly green-red light licked up to the
ceiling; Melitta felt the blast of heat as the fire blazed up,
catching branch after branch. In half a minute the walls of
the cave were ablaze; the small crawling things screamed,
writhed and died at her feet as the green branches, agi-

tating violently, struggled to get out of range, were caught by the blaze and burned.

It seemed an eternity that she stood there in terror, trying to draw her clothing back from the flames, her ears hurting with the screams and her eyes burning from the greenish tint of the fire. Rationally she knew that it must have been only a few minutes before the flames, finding nothing more to feed on, sank and died, leaving her alone in unrelieved, blessed darkness.

She began to move slowly across the cave, in the remembered direction of the other door, holding her breath and trying not to breathe the scorched, poisonous dust of the burnt fungus. Under her feet it crumpled unpleasantly and she hated setting her feet on the ground, but there was no help for it. She kept moving, numbly, in the direction of that remembered patch of darkness beyond the fungus cave.

She knew when she had passed through it, for almost at once the air was cleaner, and under her feet there was nothing but hard rock. There was also faint light from somewhere—a glimmer of moonlight, perhaps, from a hidden airshaft. The air felt cool and sweet; the builders of these tunnels had gone to some pains to make them pleasant to walk in. Far off she heard a trickle of water, and, her throat still full of the dust of the burnt fungus, it was like a promise.

She went down, moving toward the sound of distant water. Twice she shrank, seeing on the walls a trace, hardly more than a smear, of the greenish stuff, and made a mental note: *If I ever get back I'll come down and burn it out. If not, I hope it grows fast—and Brynat comes down here some day!*

After what seemed like hours of slow descent she found the water—a trickling stream coming out of the rock and dripping slowly down along the stairs beside her path. She cupped her hands and drank. The water was good, and she drank well, cleansed her grimy face, and ate a few bites of food. She could tell, by the feel of the air on her face, that the night was far advanced. She must be safely hidden by morning.

Must I? I could lie hidden in the tunnel for a day or two, till pursuit quiets.

Then she knew she could not. She simply could not trust Allira that much. Her sister would not intentionally betray her; but if Brynat suspected Allira knew, he would try anything to extract the information from her. She had no faith in Allira's ability to resist questioning for any length of time.

As she went downward, she realized that the slope of the tunnel was lessening, until she walked on a grade that was just downhill. She must be coming near the end of the long stair. She was a fair judge of distances, and she knew that she had walked a considerable distance in the night; the tunnel must have led far beneath the castle and down into the caves and cliffs beneath. Then she came upon a great pair of bronze doors, thrust them outward, and stood in the open air, free.

It was still dark, although the smell of the air told her that dawn was less than two hours away. The moons had set, and the rain had stopped, though mist still lay along the ground. She looked back at the closed doors behind her.

She knew where she was now. She had seen these doors from the outside when as a child she played in the forge village. She stood now in an open square of stone, surrounded on every side by the doors cut in the cliffs that rose around her. The sky was only a narrow cut above. She looked at the dark house doors, some of them still agape, and thought with all the longing in her weary body of how good it would be to crawl into one of the abandoned houses to lie down and sleep for hours.

She forced herself upright again and went down the path that led between the cliffs. Like the tunnel, the empty forge village would be the first place searched if Brynat managed to force the secret of the passage from Allira. She passed the open-air hearths where countless years ago, smiths had worked, making their beautiful and curious ironwork, copper jewelry and the iron gates of their own castle now crumpled and thrown down in the siege. She cast a look upward. From here she could see a portion of the outworks. Brynat had spared no time in repairing the fortifications of Storn. Evidently he thought he might have to hold them against invaders.

He will. I swear it by Avarra and Zandru, I swear it by

Sharra, Goddess of Forges and Fires! He shall struggle tenfold ...

There was no time for that. If she wanted to make Brynat suffer, there was only one way to achieve it, she must get away herself. Her own safety must be the first thought. She passed the old circle of fireplaces, cold and rusted. Even the carven image of Sharra above the central forge was dulled and the gold of her chains, set against the duller metal of the statue, covered with spiderwebs and bird-droppings. She flinched at the sacrilege. She was no worshipper of the Flamehair, but like every child of the mountains, she had a deep respect and awe for the secret arts of the smith.

If I come back—when I come back Sharra's image shall be purified and served again ... There was no time for that now, either.

The horizon was reddening perceptibly when footsore, Melitta, her steps dragging, clung to the doorway of a small house in a village far below the castle, and beat weakly on it. She felt at her last strength. If no one heard her or helped her, she would fall down here and lie there until Brynat's men found her, or she died.

But it was not more than a few moments until the door opened a cautious crack, and then motherly arms grasped her and drew her inside and to a fire.

"Quick—bar the door, draw the curtain—*damisela*, where did you come from? We thought you dead in the siege, or worse! How did you get free? Evanda guard us! Your poor hands, your face—Reuel, you oaf, bring some wine, quickly, for our little lady."

A few minutes later, drinking hot soup, her boots drawn off and her feet to the fire, wrapped in blankets, Melitta was telling a little of her escape to a wide-eyed audience.

"Lady, you must hide here until the search is quiet—" but their faces were apprehensive, and Melitta said a swift "No. Brynat would surely kill you all," and saw shamed relief in their eyes. "I can lie hidden in the caves up the mountain until darkness tonight; then I can get away to Nevarsin or beyond. But you can find me food to carry, and perhaps a horse that can face the passes."

It was quickly arranged and by the time the day broke, Melitta rested, wrapped in furs and rugs in the labyrinthine caves which had for centuries been a last hiding place of the Storns. For one day she was safe there, since Brynat would surely search nearer places first; and by tonight she would be gone. It was a long road to Carthon.

Exhausted, the girl slept, but the name tolled in her dreams—*Carthon*.

VII

BARRON had believed, on the journey from the Terran Zone to Armida, that he had seen mountains. True, his Darkovan escort had repeatedly called them foothills, but he had put that down to exaggeration, to the desire to see the stranger's surprise. Now, half a day's ride from Armida, he began to see that they had not exaggerated. As they came out of a miles-long, sloping pathway along a forested hill, he saw, lying before him, the real ranges. Cool purple, deep violet, pale grayed blue, they lay there fold on fold and height behind height, each successive fold rising higher and farther away, until they vanished in cloudy distances that might have been thunderheads—or further ranges.

"Good God," he exploded, "we're not going over the top of *those*, are we?"

"Not quite," Colryn, riding at his side, reassured him. "Only to the peak of the second range, there." He pointed. "The fire tower is on the crest of that range." He told Barron its name in Darkovan. "But if you look far enough, you can see all the way back into the mountains, as far as the range they call the Wall Around the World. Nobody lives beyond there, except the trailmen."

Barron remembered vague stories of various groups of Darkovan nonhumans. The next time they paused to eat cold food from their saddlebags and rest the horses, he looked for Lerrys, who was still the friendliest of the three, and asked him about them. "Are they only beyond the far ranges? Or are there nonhumans in these mountains too?"

"Oh, yes. You've been on Darkover how long, five of our years, and you still haven't seen any of our nonhumans?"

"One or two *kyrii* in the Terran Trade Zone—from a distance," Barron told him, "and the little furred people at Armida—I don't know what you call them. Are there others? And are they all—well, if they're nonhumans, I can't ask, 'are they human,' but do they meet Empire standards for so-called intelligent beings—time-binding culture, viable language capable of transfer to other I.B.'s?"

"Oh, they're all I.B.'s by Terran Empire standards," Lerrys assured him. "The reason the Empire doesn't deal with them is fairly simple. Humans here don't have much interest in the Empire *per se*, but they are interested in other humans as individuals. The nonhuman races—I'm no expert on them, but I suspect they have never tried to get in touch with the Empire for the same reason they don't have much contact with humans on Darkover. Their goals and wishes and so forth are so completely different that there's no point of contact; they don't want any and they don't have any."

"You mean even Darkovans have no contact with nonhumans?"

"I wouldn't say *no* contact. There's some small amount of trade with the trailmen—they're what you might call half-human or subhuman, and they live in the trees in the forests. They trade with the mountain people for drugs, small tools, metal and the like. They're harmless enough unless you frighten them. The catmen—they're a race something like the *cralmacs*, the furred servants at Armida. *Cralmacs* aren't very intelligent; feline rather than simian, but they do have culture of a sort, and some of them are telepathic. Their level is about that of a moron, or a chimpanzee who suddenly acquired a tribal culture. A genius among the *cralmacs* might learn a dozen words of a human language but I never heard of one learning to read; I suspect the Empire people gave them pretty wide benefit of the doubt in classifying them as I.B.'s."

"We tend to do that. We don't want later squawks that we treated a potential intelligent race as higher animals."

"I know. *Cralmacs* are listed as real or potential I.B.'s and let alone. The catmen, I suspect, are a hell of a lot more intelligent; I know they use metal tools. Fortunately I've never been close to them; they hate men and they'll attack when they feel safe in doing it. I've heard that they have a very elaborate feudal culture with the most incredible tangle of codes governing face-saving behavior. The Dry-towners believe that some of the elements of their own culture came from cultural interchange with the catmen millennia ago, but an I.B. xenthropologist could tell you more about that."

"Just how many races of I.B.'s are there on Darkover anyway?" Barron asked.

"God only knows, and I'm not being funny. Certainly no Terran knows. Maybe a few of the Comyn know, but they're not telling. Or the *chieri;* they're another of the nearly human races, but they're as far above humans, most people think, as the *cralmacs* are below 'em. It's for sure no Terran knows, though; and I've had more opportunity than most."

Barron hardly heard the last sentence for a minute, in his interest in the nonhumans, then suddenly it penetrated. "*You're* a Terran?"

"At your service. My name is Larry Montray; they call me Lerrys because it's easier for a Darkovan to pronounce, that's all."

Barron felt suddenly angry and irked. "And you let me make a fool of myself trying to speak Darkovan to you?"

"I offered to interpret," Larry said. "At the time I was under a pledge to Valdir, never to mention that I was a Terran—not to anyone."

"And you're his ward? His foster son? How'd that happen?"

"It's a long story," Larry said. "Some other time, maybe.* In brief, his son, Kennard, is being schooled on Terra with *my* family, and I'm living here with *his* people." He scrambled to his feet. "Look, Gwynn's looking for us; I think we ought to get on. We want to reach the fire tower before nightfall tomorrow, if we can—the rangers there are due to be relieved—and it's still a long way into those hills."

It gave Barron plenty to think about, as they rode on, but his thoughts kept coming back, with an insistence he could

*cf. *Star of Danger*: Ace 1965.

not understand—it was as if some secret watcher, far back in his mind, kept dwelling on that point almost with frenzy.

A Terran could pass as a Darkovan. A Terran could pass as a Darkovan. A Darkovan could pass himself off as a Terran. A Terran could pass as a Darkovan. In these mountains, where Terrans are never seen, a Terran willing to pass as a Darkovan would be safe from anything human, and attract no unusual attention from nonhumans . . .

Barron shook his head. *That's enough of that.* He wasn't interested in the Darkovan mountains except from the viewpoint of doing his job well enough to redeem himself with the Empire, and get his own job, or something like it, back, and start over again on another planet, in a spaceport job. *If Larry, or Lerrys, or whatever he calls himself, wants to amuse himself living with a family of weird, Darkovan telepaths and learning more than anyone else cared to know about nonhumans and such, that's his business; everybody gets their kicks in his own way and I've known some dillies.* But he wasn't having any.

He clung to that with an uneasy concentration all that day, doggedly ignoring the beauty of the flowers that lined the mountain road, snubbing Larry's friendly attempts to pick up the conversation. Toward evening, as the ride steepened, Colryn whiled away the time by singing Darkovan legends in a tuneful bass voice, but Barron shut his ears and would not listen, closing his eyes and letting his horse take the road along the mountain trail; the horse knew more about it than he did.

The sound of hoofs, the slow jogging in the saddle, the darkness behind his closed eyes, was first hypnotic, then strangely familiar; it seemed normal to sit unseeing in his saddle, trusting himself to the horse beneath him and his other senses alert—the smell of flowers, or conifers, of the dust of the road, the sharp scent of some civet-smelling animal in the brush. When Lerrys drew abreast of him, Barron kept his eyes closed and after a time Lerrys spurred his horse and overtook Colryn. Colryn went on singing in an undertone. Without knowing how he knew, Barron recognized that the singer had shifted to the opening bars of the long *Ballad of Cassilda.*

How strange it sounded without the water-harp accom-

*paniment. Allira played and sang it well, though it was
really a song for a man's voice:*

> The stars were mirrored on the shore,
> Dark was the dark enchanted moor,
> Silent as cloud or wave or stone,
> Robardin's daughter walked alone.
> A web of gold between her hands
> On shining spindle burning bright,
> Deserted lay the mortal lands
> When Hastur left the realms of light.
> Then, singing like a hidden bird . . .

He lost track of the words, hearing a far-off hawk-cry
and the small wounded scream of some animal in the
bush. *He was here, he was free, and behind him, ruin
and death.*

The song went on, soft and incessant;

> . . . A hand to each, he faltering came
> Within the hidden mountain hall
> Where Alar tends the darkened flame
> That brightened at Cassilda's call. . . .
> And as his brilliance paled away
> Into the dimmer mortal day,
> Cassilda left the shining loom,
> A starflower in his hand she laid;
> Then on him fell a mortal doom:
> He rose and kissed Robardin's maid.
> The golden webs unwoven lay . . .

His mind spun in a strange dream as he listened to the
song of the love of Cassilda, the sorrows of Camilla, the
love of Hastur and the treachery of Alar. *It must be strange
to be Comyn and Hastur, and know oneself sib to the
God. . . .*

I could use a god or two for kinsmen now!

*What are these old gods really? The forge people used to
say that Sharra came to their fires—and they didn't mean
the spirit of fire, either! The old telepaths could raise powers
as far beyond my bird forms, or the fire shields, as these
are beyond a trailman's knife!*

"Barron! Don't fall asleep here, man; the trail gets dangerous!" The voice of Gwynn, the big Darkovan, broke into his dream, and Barron shook himself awake. Was it another hallucination?— No, only a dream. "I must have been asleep," he said, rubbing his eyes. Gwynn chuckled. "And to think that five days ago you'd never been in the saddle. You learn fast, stranger. Congratulations! But you'd better keep your eyes open from here; the path gets rough and narrow, and you probably have better judgment than your horse—even though there *is* an old proverb that says, 'on an uphill road give your horse his head.' But if you fell here—" He gestured at the thousand-foot drop on either side of the pass. "We ought to try and get through and down into the valleys, before nightfall. There are Ya-men around these heights, and perhaps banshees; and although there's no sign of the Ghost Wind, I'm not any too eager to meet them just the same."

Barron started to ask what they were and stopped himself. *Damn it, I don't care; I'm already too entangled in this business, and Gwynn and the others are here to guard me.* There was no reason he should think about these supposed dangers or even know what they were.

Nevertheless, the unease of the others penetrated to him, and he found himself pulling close to them in the narrow neck of the pass. It was almost an anticlimax when they topped the pass without incident and began to ride downward.

They camped that night in the valley under a shelter of the gray-blue boughs, which smelled of spice and rain; there was less talk and singing than usual. Barron, lying awake in his blankets and listening to the nightly rain sliding off the thick boughs, felt an apprehension he could not check. *What a hell of a world, and why did I have to get stuck in it?*

Already he had half forgotten the delight and fascination he had felt during the first journey through the foothills. It was part of that strangeness within which he wanted to forget.

They arrived at the ranger station late the next day; Barron, unpacking his crates by lamplight in the large, airy room allotted to him; he realized grudgingly that at least Valdir had spared no pains to make a guest comfortable.

There were ample shelves and cupboards for his working tools, benches and space with good light—the pressure lamps produced unusual amounts of light from the relatively crude fuels extracted from resins and oils of the local trees. A broad window of clear glass—not common on Darkover, not much desired, and evidently provided for the comfort of the Terran guest—provided an unbelievable panoramic view of mountains, and ridge after ridge of forested and rocky slopes and heights. As Barron stood at the window, watching the huge red sun of Darkover setting behind the peak—the mountains here were so high that the sun was hidden even before the night's mist formed—he was touched again with that uncanny sense which made his heart race; but by sheer force of will he kept himself from succumbing to it, and went out to explore the station.

From where it sat at the top of one of the tallest peaks, it commanded a view—even without climbing to the tower behind—of what seemed like hundreds of square miles of forested country; Barron counted fifteen small villages, each lying sheltered in a fold of the hills, each only a cluster of dim roofs. At this distance he could see why telescopes would be needed; the view stretched so far that it vanished in haze through which no unaided eye could penetrate and which could easily hide a thin coil of smoke. He could even see the faraway roofs of Armida, and, high in the hills, a dim pale spire which looked like a castle.

"With your lenses," Larry told him, joining him at the doorway of the station, "we will see forest fires while they are still only small blazes, and save our timber. Look." He pointed to the side of a faraway ridge which was a black scar in the green. "That burned five years ago; it was out of control only for a day or two, but even though every man from seven villages turned out, we lost I forget how many square miles of good timber and resin trees. Also, from here, we could see and give the warning, if bandits or something attacked."

"How do you give warning? There seem to be no sirens or any such things here."

"Bells, fire beacons—" He pointed to a high pile of dry weed carefully isolated behind a ditch filled with water, "And also, signaling devices—I don't think I ever knew the Terran name for them." He showed Barron the shiny metal plates. "Of course they can only be used on sunny days."

"Heliograph," Barron said.

"That's it."

Barron had expected to feel like a fish out of water, but the first few days went smoothly enough. There were six men at the ranger station, serving tours of duty of fifteen days each and then being replaced by others, in a staggered rotation system which sent three new men every seven days. Currently Gwynn was in command of the station. Larry seemed a sort of supernumerary, and Barron wondered if he was there only to interpret, or to keep an eye on the stranger. From something Gwynn said, he eventually decided that Larry was there to learn the management of the station, so that he could take his place in a series of responsible duties held in sequence by all younger men of Darkovan families. Colryn was there as Barron's assistant, specifically to learn the work of lens-grinding and to teach the making and use of the telescopes and lenses to any of the rangers who were willing to learn.

Barron knew, from his orientation lectures years ago, that Darkover was a world without complex technology or industry, and he had expected that the Darkovans would not be very adept at learning what he had come to teach. He was surprised to see the swiftness with which Colryn and the others picked up the rudiments of optics, his instructions on the properties of reflected and refracted light, and, later, the technical work of grinding. Colryn in particular was apt at picking up the technical language, the meticulous scientific techniques; so was Larry, who hung around when he was not out on patrol, but then Barron had expected it of Larry, who was a Terran and seemed to have at least the rudiments of a Terran education. But Colryn was a surprise.

He said as much one afternoon, when they were working in the upstairs workroom; he had been showing the younger man how to set and adjust one of the complex grinding tools and how to check it with the measuring instruments for proper set. "You know, you really don't need me," he said. "You could have picked this up on your own with a couple of textbooks. It was hardly worth Valdir's trouble to bring me all the way out here; he could simply have gotten books and equipment from the Terran Zone and turned them over to you."

Colryn shrugged; "He'd have to have me taught to read 'em first."

"You can speak some Terran Standard; you wouldn't have that much trouble learning. As nearly as I can tell, the Darkovan script isn't so complicated that you'd have any difficulty with Empire letters."

Colryn laughed this time. "I couldn't say. Maybe if I could read at all, I could read Terran Standard. It's nothing I've ever stopped to think about."

Barron stared in frank shock; Colryn *seemed* intelligent enough! He looked at Larry, expecting to exchange a look of consternation at this barbarous planet; but Larry frowned slightly and said, almost in reproof, "We don't make a fetish of literacy on Darkover, Barron."

Suddenly he felt condemnatory and like a stranger again. He almost snarled, "How in the hell does anyone learn anything, then?"

He could see Colryn visibly summoning up patience and courtesy toward the boorish stranger, and felt ashamed. Colryn said, "Well, I'm learning, am I not? Even though I'm no sandal-wearer, to sit and wear my eyes out over printed pages!"

"You're certainly learning. But you mean you have no system of education?"

"Probably not the way you mean it," said Colryn. "We don't bother with writing unless we're in the class that has to spend their time reading and writing. We've found that too much reading spoils the eyes—weren't you telling me, a few days ago, that about eighty per cent of your Terrans have imperfect vision and have to wear false lenses to their eyes? It would seem to make more sense to set those people to doing work which doesn't need so much reading—anyway, too much writing things down spoils the memory; you don't remember a thing properly if you can go and look it up. And when I want to learn something, why should I not learn it the sensible way, from someone who can show me if I am doing it properly, without the intermediary of printed symbols between us? With only a book to learn from, I might misunderstand and get into the way of doing things wrong, whereas here, if I make a mistake you can set me right at once, and the skill gets into my hands, so that my hands will remember how the work is done."

Not really convinced, Barron let the discussion drop. He had to admit that the arguments were singularly coherent for someone he now had to reclassify as an illiterate. His systems of thinking were shaken up; communications devices had always been his field. Colryn said, evidently trying to bend over backward and see his point of view, "Oh, I didn't say there was anything *wrong* with reading, in itself. If I were deaf or crippled, I'm sure I would find it useful—" But understandably, this did not calm Barron's ruffled feelings.

Not for worlds would he have admitted what was really bothering him most at the moment. His hands went on, with almost automatic skill, adjusting the delicate micrometric measurements on the grinding tool, and connecting it to the small wind-powered generator. While Colryn was talking, the argument somehow seemed *familiar*. It was as if he had heard it all before, in some other life! He thought, with black humor, that if this went on, he would come to believe in reincarnation!

His eyes blurred before him, colors running into one another and blearing into unfamiliar patches, shapes and groups without reference. He looked at the equipment in his hands as if he had never seen it before. He turned the pronged plug curiously in his hands; what was he supposed to do with this thing? As it focused and came clear, he found that he was staring wildly at Colryn, and Colryn looked strange to him.

All the strange colors flooded together again and sight went out; he found himself standing on a great height, looking down at a scene of ruin and carnage, hearing men shrieking, and swords clashing. As it blotted out sight, he found himself once again looking up at rushing flames, and in the midst of the fire was a smiling woman, flame-haired, lapped in fire as another woman might stand beneath a waterfall. Then the woman faded and was only a great female shape, fire-crowned and golden-chained. . . .

"Barron!" The cry cut through his consciousness and he came briefly back, rubbing his eyes, to see Colryn and Larry staring at him in consternation. Larry caught the lens machine from his hands as he swayed and crashed to the floor.

When he came to himself again, water trickling down his throat, they were both staring down at him with troubled concern in their faces. Colryn was apologetic. "I think you've been working too hard. I shouldn't have gotten into that argument with you; you have your ways and we have ours. Have you had seizures like this often?"

Barron simply shook his head. The argument hadn't bothered him that much, and if Colryn wanted to explain it away as an epileptic fit or something of that sort, that was all right with him and probably a saner explanation than whatever it really was. Perhaps he was suffering some sort of brain damage! *Oh, well, at least when it happens out here in the Darkovan mountains, I'm not likely to be responsible for crashing a couple of spaceships!*

Colryn might have accepted this explanation but it was quickly obvious that Larry hadn't. He sent Colryn away, saying that he was sure Barron wouldn't feel like working for the rest of the day; then he began slowly to put the lens-grinding equipment away. Barron started to get up and help him, and Larry gestured to him to stay put.

"I can manage; I know where this stuff goes. Barron, what do you know of Sharra?"

"Nothing—less than nothing." *It's damned unhandy having a telepath around.* "You tell me."

"I don't know that much. She was an ancient goddess of the forge people. But gods and goddesses, here on Darkover, are more than just something you say your prayers to, or burn incense to, or ask for favors. They seem to be real—tangible, I mean."

"That sounds like rubbish, gobbledygook."

"I mean, what they call gods, we'd call forces—real, solid forces you can touch. For instance—I don't know much about Sharra. The Darkovans, especially in the Comyn, don't like to talk about Sharra worship. It was outlawed years ago; it was thought to be too dangerous. Also, it seemed to involve human sacrifice, or something like it. What I mean is, the forge people called on Sharra, using the proper talisman or whatever—these things concentrate forces, I don't know how—and Sharra would bring the metallic ore up out of the mountains for them."

"And you a Terran? And you believe all that stuff? Larry, there are legends like that on every planet in the Empire."

"Legend be damned," said Larry. "I told you I don't think they're gods as we use the term. They may be some form of—well, entity or being—maybe from some other dimension. For all I know, they could be an invsiible race of nonhumans. Valdir told me a little about the outlawing of Sharra worship—it happened here in the mountains. His people, the Altons and the Hasturs, had a lot to do with it; they had to go into the hills and confiscate all the talismans of Sharra so that the forge people couldn't call up these forces any more. Among other things, I gather, the fires sometimes got out of control and started forest fires."

"Talismans?"

"Stones—they call them matrix stones—blue crystals. I've learned to use them a little; believe me, they're weird. If you have even rudimentary telepathic force, you concentrate your thoughts on them and they—well, they do things. They can lift objects—psychokinesis—create magnetic fields, create force-field locks that no one can open except with the same matrix, and so forth. My foster sister could tell you more about them." Larry looked distressed. "Valdir should know, if Sharra images can even get to you, a Terran. I should send to him, Barron."

Barron shook his head urgently. "No! Don't trouble Valdir; this is my problem."

"No trouble. Valdir will want to know. Valdir is of the Comyn. He *must* know if these things are coming into the mountains again. They could be dangerous for us all, and especially for you." He smiled a troubled smile. "I shared a knife with you, and it is a pledge," he said. "I have to stand your friend whether you want me to or not. I'll send for Valdir tonight."

He finished closing the box with the lens blanks, and turned to go. "You'd better rest; nothing is urgent, and I have to go out on patrol," he said. "And don't worry; it is probably nothing to do with you. You have evidently picked up something that is loose in these mountains, and Valdir will know how to deal with it." He paused at the door, said urgently, "Please believe that we are your friends, Barron." He left.

Alone, Barron lay on the wide bed, that smelled of the resin-needles used to stuff the mattress. He wondered why it seemed so urgent to him that Valdir should not be sent for. He heard Larry ride away with the patrol; he heard Colryn singing downstairs; and he heard the wind rise and begin blowing from the heights. He got up and went to the wide window. Down in these valleys and hills lay villages of unsuspecting men, little knots and nests of nonhumans in the thickest and most impenetrable forests, and birds and wildlife; they would be safer for protection against forest fire and raiding bandits—catmen and nonhumans and the terrible Ya-men. He would help with that, he was doing good work, why then was he gripped by this sense of fearful urgency and despair, as if he sat idling while around him a world fell into ruins? Disoriented, he covered his eyes.

It was quiet at the station. He knew that in the tower a ranger in the usual green and black uniform scanned the surrounding countryside for any signs of smoke; the resin trees, in spite of the nightly rain, were so volatile, that an unexpected thunderstorm could strike one and send it ablaze. The only sound was the wind that never changed and never died; Barron hardly heard it now. And yet there was something—something in the wind. . . .

He tensed, throwing the window open and leaning out, closing his eyes the better to focus attention.

It was almost imperceptible except to senses sharpened like his—almost lost in the overpowering smell of the resins —a faint, sweet, yellow-dusty smell, almost lost, borne on the wind. . . .

The Ghost Wind! Pollen of a plant which flowered erratically only once in several seasons—was released in enormous quantities, scattering its scent and queer hallucinogenic qualities from the valleys to the heights; blessedly rare, it produced euphoria and a queer drunkenness and, occasionally, if one breathed too much of it, brain damage in men. It released the animal instincts of rage and fear and anger, sending men cowering in corners or raving on the hills. But into the nonhumans it went deeper, penetrating into their strange brains and releasing very old things, very terrible things. . . . The catmen would howl and strike and kill wantonly, and the Ya-men—when it reached the Ya-men—

He moved fast. He was not Barron now; he was not

conscious of himself or who or what he was, he knew only that he must act to warn the others at the station, to warn the men in the valleys to take shelter. It would not be strong enough for any ordinary nose to smell for two or three more hours, and by that time the rangers would be too far from the station to take shelter, and the nonhumans would already be out and ravening. By the time the Ghost Wind was strong enough to affect humans it might even be too late to take shelter.

His vision was blurring. He closed his eyes, the better to let his feet find their way around, and ran down the stairs. He heard someone call to him in an unfamiliar language, pushed past and ran on.

The beacon. He might light the beacon! He did not know the alarm systems here but the beacon would certainly alert everyone to danger. There was a fire burning in the lower hall, he could feel its heat on his face. He bent over, carefully reaching, picked out a long stick blazing at one end and cool and charred at the other. He ran with it in his hand out the door and across the graveled horse path and the lawn; almost falling into the ditch around the beacon, he thrust the blazing torch into the tinder-dry wood and leaped back as it flamed up and a tall column of fire reared to the sky. Then someone yelled at him, hands were gripping him, and Colryn was demanding, as he held him in a steel-strong grip, "Barron, damn you, have you gone mad? That's going to rouse the countryside! If you were a Darkovan, you'd be hanged on the spot for raising a false fear!"

"False fear be———" he swore atrociously. "The Ghost Wind! I smelled it! By night it will be everywhere!"

His face slowly blanching, Colryn stared at him. "The Ghost Wind? How do you know?"

"I smelled it, I tell you! What do you do here to rouse the countryside for taking shelter?"

Colryn looked at him, only half believing but gripped by his obvious sincerity. "The beacon will alert them," he said, "and I can signal with the mirror, after which they will ring bells in the villages. We have a good alarm system here. I still think you're insane, I don't smell it at all, but then for all I know you could have a better nose than mine. And I won't take a chance on letting the Ghost Wind—or the Ya-men—get anyone." He shoved Barron out of his way. "Look where you're going! Damn it, what's the matter, are you *blind?* You'll be in the ditch in a minute!" He forgot Barron again, and ran toward the station for the signaling device. Eyes closed, Barron stood listening to the beacon crackle. He was aware of the pungency of the burning beacon and through it, the growing, sick scent of the pollen-laden Ghost Wind blowing from the heights.

After a while, still disoriented, he turned and made his way, on faltering feet, inside the station. Colryn was on the tower, signaling. Paradoxically, the thing which surprised Barron most was that he was not surprised at himself; he had a vague sense of split selfhood, in the same sort of divided, underwater consciousness that he had felt once or twice before.

The next hour was insane confusion: shouts and voices, bells beginning to ring in the villages below, and the rangers at the station running about on errands they didn't bother explaining. He kept his eyes closed against further disorientation and kept out of the way. It seemed natural to sit by while others acted; he had done his part. Presently men came riding up the slope in crazy haste and he became aware that Larry had come in and was standing with Colryn in front of him.

"What happened?"

"He smelled the Ghost Wind," Colryn said tersely.

"And in good time," Larry said. "Thank the gods we have warning. I had just barely begun to wonder if I smelled it myself when I heard the bells and ordered everyone back—but it's still so faint I can hardly make it out! How did you know?" he demanded. Barron did not answer, but only shook his head. After a little while Larry went away.

He thought, *I have done a foolish thing; before, he only suspected something strange, but now he will know, and if he does not, Valdir will. Valdir is Comyn and he will know exactly what has happened.*

I don't care what they do to the Earthman, but I must get away. I should have kept quiet and escaped in the confusion of the Ghost Wind.

But I couldn't let them all go through that danger; and Lerrys would have been caught on the hills. I owe him something. There is a blade between us.

Nothing human will dare to move in these mountains

tonight. I must lie low and keep from attracting any more attention to Barron until then.

And then—then I must be gone, long gone, before Valdir comes!

VIII

It seemed eternities that he watchfully waited, that curious doubled consciousness keeping him nerve-strained, but holding himself back from being noticed. He kept out of the way while the men at the station hurried around, making all secure as the wind rose higher, screaming around the corners of the station and the fire tower. The sickish smell grew stronger by the moment and he fancied he could feel it penetrating to the rest of his nose, into the brain, subtly eating away at his humanity and his resolution.

Nor were the others unaffected; at one point Colryn stopped in his work of nailing heavy shutters tight and bent over, crouching, his arms wrapped round his head as if in terrible pain. He began a low, crazy moaning. Gwynn, hurrying through the room on some errand or other, saw him there, went to him, knelt beside him, put an arm around his shoulders and talked to him in a low, reassuring voice, until Colryn shook his head violently as if to clear it of something. Then he stood up and swung his arms, swore, thanked Gwynn and went on with his work.

The man who was not sure at the moment whether he was Dan Barron or someone else, stayed where he was, fighting for self-control; but he was not unaffected. As the wind rose and the smell of the Ghost Wind grew stronger, strange images spun in his mind—primordial memories laden with fear and terror—frightening hungers. Once he jerked upright from a waking nightmare of kneeling over a prone man, tearing at his throat with his teeth. He shuddered, rose and began to walk feverishly around the room.

When all was secure they sat down to food, but no one ate much. They were all silent, all tormented by the rising scream of the wind, which tore at their ears and their nerves, and by the spinning of vague hallucinatory images in their eyes and their minds. Barron kept his eyes closed. It seemed easier to eat that way, without the unfamiliar distraction of sight.

Halfway through the meal, the faraway shrieking began; a high, keening, space-filling howl and yelp that rose higher and higher, through the audible frequencies, and seemed to go on even after it could be heard no more.

"Ya-men," said Gwynn tersely, and let his knife drop to the table with a clatter.

"They can't get into the station," Colryn said, but he didn't sound sure. No one after that made much more than a pretense at eating, and before long they left the food and dishes uncleared on the table and went into the shuttered and barricaded main room of the station. The yelping and howling went on—at first distant and intermittent, then constant and close. Eyes closed, Barron saw in his mind's eye a ring of towering plumed forms, raging and shrieking and hurling themselves, in a maddened dance, around the peak of the hill.

Once Colryn tried to drown out the sound by beginning a song; but his voice died away, halfway through the first verse.

The night wore on. Toward the deepest part of the darkness, the pounding and banging began; it sounded as if a heavy form hurled itself, again and again, against the barred doors, and fell back, howling with bruised, insensate rage. Once begun, it went on and on, until their nerves were screaming.

Once Larry said low in the darkness, "I wonder what they're really like? It seems hell that the only time they come out of the deep woods, they're maddened—and we can't communicate with them."

Gwynn said, with bleak humor, "I'll unbar the door, if you want to try a little nonhuman diplomacy."

Larry shuddered and was still. Colryn said, "Upstairs in the lens-grinding room there's a glass window. We could get a look at them from there."

Gwynn refused, with a shudder, and so did the other rangers; but Colryn, Larry and Barron went up the stairs together. It was something to do. At this height, the window had not been covered or barricaded. They did not light the lamp, knowing the light would attract the howling nonhumans outside. They went to the glass and, cupping their hands around their eyes, peered through.

Outside, though he had expected it to be dark and stormy, it was clear moonlight—one of the rare nights on Darkover when rain and fog had not blotted out the moons. The air seemed filled with swirling dust, through which he saw the Ya-men.

They were hugely tall, nine feet at least, and looked like tall emaciated men, wearing plumed head-dresses, until he saw their faces. They had huge heads and terrible beaked faces like strange birds of prey, and they moved with a clumsy swiftness that was like the wind-tossed branches of the trees which dipped and surged at the edge of the clearing. There were at least three dozen of them, it seemed, and perhaps more. After a little, as if by common consent, the men turned away from the window and went down the stairs again.

Barron, about to follow them, remained behind. The strangeness was growing in him again. Something turning like a thermostat in his brain told him that the tide of the Ghost Wind had turned. There was no change in the slamming noise of the wind, nor in the howling of the nonhumans, but he *knew*.

They will be gone long before dawn. The wind will die and there will be rain. Only the mad and the desperate travel on Darkover by night, but I—perhaps I am both desperate and mad.

An enormous crash, and cries from downstairs, told him that the slamming attack of the nonhumans had crashed an outbuilding. He did not go down to investigate; it was not his affair. Silently, moving like an automaton, he went in the darkness to the chest of drawers where he kept his clothing. He discarded the thin indoor garments he was wearing, put on leather riding breeches, a thick woven shirt and a heavy tunic. He slipped into Colryn's room and appropriated the man's heavy, fur-lined cloak. He had a long way to ride and a cloak was better than a jacket. He regretted that he must steal a horse, but if he lived, it would be returned or paid for, and if not, he reminded himself of the mountain proverb, "when Eternity comes all will be understood and forgiven."

He cocked a practiced ear; the wind was definitely quieting. In another hour the Ya-men would be gone, the rest-less impulse that had led them there entirely gone; they would waken to terror and strangeness and creep timidly back to their caves and nests in the deepest woods. *The poor devils must feel damn near as strange as I do.*

The slamming of the wind was subsiding and even in the incessant howling there were gaps now, intervals grew wider and finally lessened to nothing. Peering through the glass, he saw that the clearing was empty. Not more than half an hour after that, he heard the other men coming up to the large room where they slept. Someone called, "Bar-ron, are you all right?" He froze, then made himself answer in a sleepy, resentful mutter.

In a few more minutes a silence lay over the fire station, broken only by the snores of exhausted men in the far room, and the rattle of occasional branches in the dying wind. Peering through the glass, he saw that fog was rising. There would be rain and it would lay the last traces of the poison from the Ghost Wind.

All was quiet, but nevertheless he waited another hour, to dispel the chance that one of the men, sleeping lightly after fear and tension, would waken and hear him. Then, moving with infinite caution so that the stairs would not creak beneath him, he stole downstairs. He made up a par-cel of food from the leavings on the table. They had left the doors barricaded, but it was no great trouble to un-fasten the bars and take them down.

He was outside, in the bitter cold and fading moon-light of the mountain night.

He had to find a clawed tool to unfasten the bars they had nailed over the door of the stable, and in order to use it, confused by its unfamiliar weight in his hand, he had to close his eyes and let the inner reflexes take over. He thanked his fate that the stable was at some distance from the house, otherwise the racket he made as he wrestled with the heavy boards would certainly have wakened even such weary sleepers, and they would have come down rais-ing an outcry against thieves. He got them loose and stole inside.

The stable was warm, dark and friendly-familiar with the smell of horses. He shut his eyes to saddle up the horse; it was easier to handle the harness that way. The beast recognized him and neighed softly and he began to talk to it soothingly in an undertone. "Yes, fellow, we have a long ride tonight, but quiet, do you hear? We must get away quietly. Not used to going in the dark, are you? Well, I am, so don't you worry about that."

He dared not mount and ride till at some distance. Taking the bridle, he led the horse carefully down the slope and down the mountain road, then paused to take stock. He was ready; he closed his eyes to orient himself. He must go over the ranges and past the castle he could see from the fire tower, skirt the bends of the River Kadarin and beware of trailmen in the forested slopes on the near side. Then the road toward Carthon lay clear before him.

He was warmly clad. He had a good horse; it was Gwynn's, which was the best, one of the finely bred blacks which the Altons bred for the rangers. He had heard Gwynn boast that Valdir had broken this one with his own hands. It was a crime to deprive the ranger of such a beauty; yet —"Necessity would make a thief even of a Hastur," he reminded himself grimly. Yet another proverb came to mind: "If you're going to steal horses, steal thoroughbreds."

He was well provided with money. Nudged by his subtle prodding, Barron had had Valdir change his Terran credits for Darkovan coins.

He spared a thought for Barron. It was almost a pity to do this to the Earthman, but he had had no choice. One of the greatest of crimes on Darkover, ever since the days of the Compact, was to take over another human mind. It could only be done with another latent telepath, and telepaths on Darkover were aware, and they guarded against such invasion. He had hoped to find an idiot mind, so that he would be robbing no man of his own soul. But instead, as his mind ranged in the desperation of trance, unbound by the limitations of space, he had touched Barron. . . .

Were the Terrans even human? In any case, what did it matter what happened to these invaders on our world. Barron is an intruder, an outsider—fair game.

And what could I do, blind and helpless, but this?

At the foot of the path leading to the fire station, he came to a halt and swung into the saddle. He was on his way.

And for a bare instant Dan Barron, confused, disoriented,

surfaced as if coming up from a long, deep dive. Was this another hallucination—that he was riding along a dark road, faint dying moonlight overhead, icy wind whistling around his shoulders? No, this was real—where was he going? And why? He shuddered in terror, jerking on the horse's reins. . . .

He disappeared again into fathomless darkness.

The man in the saddle urged his horse to top speed; by dawn he wished to be hidden from the station by hills, so that when he emerged again, if they sought him from there he would simply be another man on horseback, moving on his lawful occasions through the countryside. He was very weary, but as if he had taken some euphoric drug, not at all sleepy. For the first time in his sheltered, invalid's life he was not resting inert, waiting for someone else to take action. He was going to do this himself.

He had stopped briefly three times to let his horse rest and breathe before the great red rim of the sun peered over the hills. He found a sheltered clearing and hobbled the horse. He rolled himself in his blanket and slept for an hour, then rose, ate a little cold food from his saddlebag and was on his way again.

All that day he rode through the hills, keeping to little-known roads—if Larry had sent for Valdir the one thing he did not dare was to meet Valdir on the road. Valdir had the old Comyn powers, which made his own look feeble by contrast. Valdir would know at once what he had done. The Storns had no traffic with the Comyn; certainly they would not come to his aid, even in this emergency. He must keep clear of the Comyn.

Toward noon it became cloudy, and Storn, looking up, saw gray caps hanging over the far hills. He thought of Melitta making her way toward Carthon from the far side of the ·Kadarin, and wondered, despairingly, if she could make her way across the passes in time. Snow must be falling on the heights; and in the hills there were bandits, trailmen, and the terrible banshee birds, which hunted anything living and could disembowel man or horse with one stroke of their terrible claws. He could do nothing to help Melitta now; he could help them both best by bringing himself safe to Carthon.

All that day he met no one on the road except an occasional farmer working in his fields, or, in scattered villages, miles apart, women chatting in the streets with rosy children clustered around them. None of them paid attention to him, except in one village where he stopped to ask a woman selling fruit by the road for a drink of water from her well; he bought some fruit, and two small boys sidled up to admire the horse and ask, shyly, if it was of the Alton breed, which gave him a moment's shock.

A Storn of Storn, fugitive and thief!

He slept again in the woods, rolled in his cloak. Toward afternoon of the second day he heard hoofbeats on the road, far off, ahead of him. Riding after, hanging at a distance lest he be seen and the horse, perhaps, recognized by the wrong people, he found that the small road he was travelling spread out into a wide, graveled surface, almost a highway. He must be nearing the Kadarin. Now he could see the riders ahead of him. They were a long line of men wearing cloaks of unfamiliar cut and color—tall men, sandy-haired, fair, and fierce-looking. Only a few of them had horses; the others rode the antlered, heavy-set pack beasts. He recognized them—Dry-towners from Shainsa or Daillon returning home after trading in the mountains. They would not recognize him and they would have no interest in him, but, as was customary in these lands, they would let him travel in their company for a small fee, since everyone added to their band was an extra protection against bandits or nonhuman attackers.

He spurred his horse and rode after them, already rehearsing what he would say. He was Storn of Storn Heights, a man who need fear nothing in foothills or mountains. He could ride with them almost as far as Carthon.

He was safe now. He prayed, with gut-wrenching intensity, that Melitta had had equal luck—that she, too, was safe. He dared not let his mind range backward to Storn Heights, to the castle where his body lay entranced behind the blue fire, guarded by magnetic fields; that might draw him back. He dared not think of Allira, brought to a bandit's bed, or to Edric, wounded and alone in the dungeons of his own castle.

He sent his hail ringing out after the caravan and saw the riders stop.

IX

THEY RODE down into Carthon at midmorning, as the morning mist was beginning to burn away under the quick, hot sun.

For five days they had ridden through diminishing mountains and foothills and now they came between the hills into the wide plain which lay in the bend of the River Kadarin—where Carthon lay bleaching on the plains. It had the look of incredible age; the squat buildings were like mountains leveled by the erosion of millennia. It was the first part of Darkover that he had seen where there were no trees. The Dry-towners had been silent and apprehensive moving through the mountainous forests; but now, with the ancient city lying in their gaze, they cheered visibly. Even their pack animals quickened their steps, and one of the men began to sing a heptatonic melody in a rough and guttural dialect that Storn could not understand.

For Storn—despite his fear of being overtaken, the constant and growing sense that he was pursued, and his endless apprehension for Melitta, struggling somewhere in the snows and passes around High Kimbi—the journey had been magical. For the first time in his life he tasted freedom and even adventure; he was treated as a man among men, not as a handicapped invalid. Deliberately he had suspended his fears for his sister, the thought of Edric and Allira in danger and captivity, and his own sense of guilt for breaking one of the most rigid of Darkovan taboos—the meddling with another human soul. He dared not think about these things; if he let his mind roam back or forward, he risked losing control of the man he had mastered; once, in fact, in the night while Storn dreamed, Barron had wakened in astonishment and terror, looking around at the unfamiliar surroundings and ready to panic and run wild. Only with difficulty had Storn resumed the upper hand. He could feel somewhere, at a level beyond his control—in that ultimate fastness of the human spirit where not even a telepath or Keeper could penetrate—Barron watched and defied him. But Storn kept control. He told himself now that even for Barron's sake he must maintain surface control—among Dry-towners, a Terran would not be permitted to live. Small was the contact between Terran and Darkovan in valley and mountain country; with the Dry towns it was absolutely minimal. Many of them had never seen or heard of the Terran Empire cities, and in the Dry towns any stranger walked with his life in his hands. An off-worlder could not have maintained safety for a single day.

As they reached Carthon, Storn realized that his single-minded enjoyment of the journey was of necessity coming to an end. Carthon had been deserted years ago by the valley lords, who had withdrawn into the mountains when the fertility of the land failed and the river changed its course. It had become a no-man's-land, inhabited by the flotsam and jetsam of a dozen civilizations. At one time, Storn remembered—he had travelled here twice in his boyhood, with his late father, long before assuming the heirship of his house—it had been the haunt of half a dozen bands of mercenaries, recruited from mountain bandits, renegade Dry-towners and the gods alone knew what else. It had been Storn's thought that here he might hire one of these bands to aid in freeing High Windward. It would not be easy—Brynat had had no easy task and a captain of that quality would not be simply dislodged—but Storn knew a trick or two, besides knowing every niche of the castle. With an able band of mercenary soldiers he had no doubt of his ability to recapture his home.

He had urged Melitta to meet him there because he was, or had been at that time, uncertain of the ultimate degree of control he could establish over Barron. He could have sent her alone, keeping only telepathic contact with her; but he was not sure of her continuing ability to maintain rapport over long periods of time and distance. What Storn knew of the old Darkovan *laran* powers was of necessity incomplete and based on trial and error. Only the long, idle childhood and adolescence of a man born blind had given him leisure and impetus to explore them, and he had had no teacher. They had been a way to alleviate his terrible boredom and the feeling of worthlessness felt by a physically handicapped man in a society which put great reliance on strength, physical skill and action. He knew that he had accomplished a great deal for a man with his handicap, even in the fields proper to a man of his family and caste: he could ride; he could climb skillfully in his own mountain cliffs and crags with little help; and he administered his own estates, with his sisters and young brother at his side. In fact, not the least of his pride was in that he had won, and kept, the loyalty of his younger brother in a society where brothers were often bitter rivals and he could easily have been relegated to the background, with Edric taking his place as Lord of Storn. To them—until Brynat had appeared and made war—he had seemed strong and competent. Only when the castle was under siege had he tasted the bitterness of helplessness.

But now the other things he had explored were coming into their own. His body was guarded against Brynat, and he was free to seek help and revenge—if he could get it.

The red sun was high and warm, and he had thrown back his riding cloak when they rode through the gates of Carthon. At first glance he could see that it was unlike any of the mountain villages they had ridden through; it felt, sounded and smelled like no Darkovan city he had ever known. The very air was different; it smelled of spice, incense and dust. It was obvious to Storn that in the intervening years more and more Dry-towners had moved into Carthon, possibly in search of the more abundant water from the Kadarin River, or perhaps—the thought crossed his mind —feeling that the lowlands' and valleys' peaceful peoples would lie there at their mercy. He dismissed the thought for later worry.

Nevertheless he felt apprehensive. He was less confident in his ability to win help in a predominantly Dry-town area. Traditionally they had their own concerns and their own culture; he could offend them fatally by a chance word. From what he had heard and what he had seen travelling with these merchants in the last days, their prime motivation was the scoring of points in an elaborate, never-ending game of prestige. No outsider could hope to win anything in this game, and Storn, travelling in their company, had been ignored, as men intent on a gambling game will ignore the cat by the fireplace.

It was humiliating, but he knew it was safer that way. He had no knowledge and no skill in knife fights, and they lived by an elaborate dueling code under which the man who could not defend himself to the death against enemy or friend was dead.

It was a forlorn hope that he could find Dry-towner mercenaries here. Still, there might be mountain or valley bands here, even though the predominant culture now seemed Dry-town. And even Dry-towners might be tempted by the thought of sacking Brynat's riches. He was prepared to offer them all the loot of Brynat and his men. All he wanted was the freedom of Storn Castle and peace to enjoy it.

They had passed the city gates, giving their names at the outworks to fierce-looking, bearded men; Storn saw with relief that some of them wore familiar mountain garments and heard them speaking a dialect of his own language. Perhaps they were not all Dry-towners here. The city was wide-flung, not like the huddled mountain villages cramped behind protective walls or the *forsts*, the forest forts behind high stockades. The outworks seemed little manned. Everywhere were the tall, fair-haired Dry-town men, and women walked in the open dusty streets—slender Dry-town women, sun-burnt and swift, carrying their heads proudly and moving in the tiny chiming sound of chains, the jewelled fetters that bound their hands, restricted movement and that proclaimed them chattel to some man of power and wealth.

At the main square of the city the caravan turned purposely toward the Eastern quarter, and Storn was reminded that their agreement terminated here. Now he was on his own—alone, in a culture and country strange to him, where any moment might bring some fatal blunder. But before he began to rack his brains as to how he could best explore the possibilities, the leader of the caravan turned back and said bluntly, "Stranger; be reminded that in our towns all strangers must first pay respects at the Great House. The Lord Rannath will be better disposed toward you if you come of your free will in courtesy, than if his men must hail you there to give an account of yourself."

"For this my thanks." Storn gave the formal return and thought that these Dry-town newcomers had indeed moved into Carthon in quantity; nothing like this had obtained when he came there as a boy. The bitter thought crossed his mind that this Lord Rannath, whoever he might be, had no doubt moved into Carthon much as Brynat had moved into Storn Castle, and with as much authority.

It was nothing to him who ruled in Carthon. And in the Great House he might learn what he wanted to know.

In Carthon all roads led to the central plaza of the city. There was no mistaking the Great House, a vast structure of curiously opalescent stone lying at the center of the main plaza. Low, dusty beds of flowers grew in great profusion in the outer courts, and the Dry-town men and women came and went through the halls as if moving in a formal dance. The women, safe and insolent behind the protection of their chains, cast him sidelong smiles and bright-eyed glances, and murmured phrases he could not well understand. Only the repeated murmur of *charrat* was familiar; it was another form of *chaireth*, stranger. *Stranger indeed,* he thought with a flash of unaccustomed self-pity. *Doubly and trebly stranger, and just now without even the time and freedom to answer these bold looks . . .*

He had expected to be stopped somewhere and asked his business, but evidently formal manners either did not exist here or were so alien that he did not recognize them as such. Following the shifting crowds he finally came into the main hall, and realized that it was evidently the hour for audience.

Elegance and a bleak luxury there was, but it was barren and alien here; this room was meant for rich hangings and the luxurious furniture of valley nobility. Stripped to the bare Dry-town manner it seemed as if it had been looted; the windows were bare, letting in harsh light, and there were no furnishings apart from low pallets and a great central thronelike chair on which lay a crown and sword, with hieratic formality in their arrangement on the gold cushion. The throne was empty. A young man, his chin just fuzzed with blond beard too sparse for shaving sat on a pallet beside the throne. He wore a fur shirt cloak and high, exquisitely dyed and embroidered leather boots. As Storn approached him, he looked up and said, "I am the voice of the Lord Rannath; I am called Kerstal. My house is the house of Greystone. Have you feud or sworn blood with me or against me?"

Storn desperately mustered what little he knew of Dry-town customs. He started to answer in the formal and stilted Cahuenga tongue, *lingua franca* of Darkover between mountain and valley, Dry-town and river folk, then suddenly dropped the pretense. He said, drawing a deep breath and stiffening his backbone, "Not to the best of my knowledge, no; to the best of my knowledge I never heard of your house and, therefore, I have never offended against it, contracted debts to it, nor do they owe me anything. I come here as a stranger, strange to your customs; if I offend against them, it is done unwittingly and seeking peace. On my last visit to Carthon the Great House was vacant; I offer such respects as a stranger should—no more and no less. If other courtesy is required, I request that you tell me."

There was a little chiming of chains as the women in the hall turned toward him, and a small breath of surprise ran all round the room. Kerstal seemed very briefly taken aback by the unaccustomed answer. Then he said, with a brief nodding of his head, "Bravely spoken and no offense given or taken. Yet none walk in Carthon without leave of the Lord Rannath and his House. Who is your liege lord and what business brings you here?"

"As for my liege, I am a free man of the mountains, with fealty sworn to none," Storn returned proudly. "I am my own man, and in my own place men give me loyalty at their own will, not from constraint." It flashed over him that pride would serve him better here than any other commodity. Dry-towners seemed to respect arrogance; if he came as a suppliant, they might kick him out without listening. "My house is the house of High Windward, in the Domain of the Aldarans, ancient lords of the Comyn. As for my business here, it is not with you; does your custom require that I must make it known? In my place, a questioner must show that his question is neither idle curiosity nor prying malice; if it is otherwise here, show me reason to respect your customs, and I will do so."

Again the little ripple of surprise ran round the room and Kerstal moved to lay his hand on the hilt of the sword which lay on the vacant throne, then paused. He rose to his feet, and now his voice had courtesy rather than negligence. He said, "In the absence of sworn blood feud between us, then, *charrat* of the house of Storn, be welcome in Carthon. No law requires that you make your affairs known, if they are your own—yet a question locked behind your lips will be forever unanswered. Tell me what you seek in Carthon, and if I can honorably answer, it will be my pleasure to do so." A faint smile touched his face, and Storn relaxed, knowing he had won. Dry-towners valued control above all else; if a Dry-towner relaxed enough to smile, you were probably safe with him.

Storn said, "My ancestral house has been attacked and laid under siege by a bandit known as Brynat Scarface; I seek men and aid to redeem my house's strength, honor and integrity." He used the word *kihar*, that untranslatable idiom for face, personal integrity and honor. "My kinsmen and the women of our people are at their mercy."

Kerstal frowned faintly. "And you are here, alive and unwounded?"

"Dead men have no *kihar*," Storn answered swiftly. "Nor can the dead come to the aid of kinsmen."

Kerstal paused to consider this. Behind them, in the outer hallways, there was a stir and an outcry, and some vague familiar sound in that cry touched every nerve in Storn to immediate response. He could not identify it, but something was happening out there. . . .

But Kerstal paid the noises no heed. He said slowly, "There is some justice in that, stranger of Storn, and—your ways are not ours—no ineradicable loss of honor. Nevertheless, our people will not, I warn you, become entangled in mountain feuds. The House of Rannath does not sell their swords in the mountains; there is enough *kihar* to be found on our own plains."

"Nor have I asked it of you," Storn replied quickly. "When last I visited Carthon there were many who were willing to sell their swords for the chance of reward. I ask only freedom to seek them."

"Freedom of that sort cannot be denied you," Kerstal replied, "and if your tale is true, the House of Rannath will not forbid any free and unsworn man to give you his service. Speak then your name, *charrat* of Storn."

Storn drew himself up to his full height.

"I bear my father's name, with pride," he said, and his voice, although it sounded strange to himself, rang loud and clear—a strong bass voice—through that hall. "I am Loran Rakhal Storn, Lord of Storn, of High Windward."

Kerstal looked at him flatly and unreadably and said, "You lie."

And all around the hall, another sound ran; Storn had never heard it before, but nevertheless, he could not be mistaken. All around the hall, men were drawing their swords. He cast one quick look around.

He stood in a ring of naked blades.

X

MELITTA had stopped struggling now. She walked between her captors, her head down, thinking bitterly, *I've failed. It wasn't enough to fight my way across the passes, hiding from banshee birds at night, getting lost in the snow, the horse freezing to death in the heights. . . . No, I manage to get all the way to Carthon and the first thing that happens is, I'm grabbed up as soon as I walk into the city!*

Think, Melitta, think—there must be a way. What do they want with you, what law have you broken? Storn would never have sent you here if it was impossible for you to find help. But did Storn know?

She drew herself up to her full height, wrenching herself to a stop between the tall, fair-haired men. "I will not go another step before I am told what is my offense," she said. "I am a free woman of the mountains, and I know nothing of your laws."

One of the men said briefly "Masterless wenches"—the word he used was untranslatable into Melitta's own language, but she had heard it used as a particularly filthy insult—"do not walk free here in Carthon among decent people, no matter what your custom may be beyond the Kadarin."

"Have you no courtesy for the customs of strangers?" she demanded.

"For customs in common decency," said one—the dialect so thick and barbarous that she had trouble understanding —"but every woman who comes here must be properly owned and controlled, and her master known. It is for the Lord of Rannath to say what shall be done with you, wench."

Melitta relaxed her taut muscles and let herself be drawn along, among staring men and the soft laughter of the women. She saw their chained hands with something like horror, and was shamed for them and astonished that they could hold up their heads and walk with something that looked like pride. Seeing their robes and their fair hair bound with ribbons and jewels she was more than ever conscious of her travel-worn riding cloak, the patched and faded breeches she wore—even the relatively free manners of mountain girls on Darkover did not accept breeches for riding, and only desperation had driven Melitta to wear them—and her hair, damp with sweat and dirty and straggling with the dust of the road. She flushed dull red. It was no miracle indeed if they thought her the lowest of the low. She wanted to cry.

Lady of Storn, she thought. *Yes, damn it, don't I just look like it!*

They were going through a bare archway now and she saw men and women gathered in a ring around a throne where a standing man, one of the fair-haired Dry-towners but taller and better dressed than most, was questioning a man in mountain clothing. Her captors said, "The Voice of Rannath is not at leisure; wait here, wench." They relaxed their grip.

Melitta's command of Cahuenga was not very fluent, and she stood without listening, trying to recover her own self-possession and glad of the respite. What could she say to convince the lords of this city that she was a free and responsible human being and not a chattel to come under their stupid laws about women? Perhaps she should have sought help in the foothills. The Comyn lords at Armida and at Castle Ardais were no kin to her family but they might have shown her hospitality and then she could have proceeded to Carthon dressed as befitted her rank, and properly escorted. She had heard that the lord Valdir Alton was a wise and enlightened man who had done much to safeguard his own people against the raids of mountain bandits and had led an expedition to root out the *forst* of the notorious Cyrillon des Trailles. Everyone in the Kilghard hills, Storns included, had slept safer in their beds after that. *Certainly he would have been willing to come to our aid against Brynat,* she thought.

She was not trying to follow the conversation between the man her captors had styled the Voice of Rannath and his prisoner, but the prisoner caught her attention. He was unusually tall, with reddish-dark hair and a heavy and sombre face, with something strange about his expression and eyes. She wished she could see him more clearly and understand his words. She could see that he was making some impression on the Voice of Rannath, for the Dry-towner was smiling. Then, before Melitta's electrified ears, the very voice and accent of her brother rang through the hall, drawing her upright in a frenzy of bewilderment.

"I am Loran Rakhal Storn, Lord of Storn, of High Windward!"

Melitta stifled a cry. It had evidently been the wrong thing for him to say; the smile was gone from Kerstal's face. He rapped out something and suddenly every man in the room had drawn his knife and they were closing in on the unlucky stranger at the center of the circle.

Kerstal said, "You lie. You lie, stranger. The son of Storn is not personally known to me; but his father is known to mine, and the men of Storn are known to our house. Shall I tell you how you lie? Storn men are fair-haired; the eyes of Storn men are gray. And it is known to me, as it is known to every man from the Hellers to Thendara, that the Lord of Storn has been blind from birth—blind beyond cure! Now state your true name, liar and braggart, or run the gantlet to save your wretched skin!"

And suddenly, with a gasp of horror, Melitta understood. She understood what Storn had done—and quailed, for a thing that was a crime beyond words—and why he had done it, and what she must do to save them both.

"Let me through," she said, her voice clear and high. "He lies not. No Storn of Storn lies, and when my words are heard let any who belies us call challenge on either or both. I am Melitta of Storn, and if the House of Storn is known to you, father and son, then look in my face and read *my* lineage there."

Shaking off the hands of the startled men who held her, she made her way forward. The closed ring of knife-wielding Dry-towners parted before her and closed after her. She heard a rippling whisper of wonder run round the circle. Someone said, "Is this some Free Amazon of the lowlands, that she walks shameless and unchained? Women of the Comyn Domains are shamefast and modest; how came this maid here?"

"I am no Free Amazon but a woman of the mountains," said Melitta, facing the speaker. "Storn is my name and Storn is my household."

Kerstal turned toward her. He stared at her for some minutes; then his hand fell from his knife hilt, and he bent in the formal bow of the Dry-towners, his hands spread briefly.

"Lady of Storn; your heritage speaks in your face. Your father's daughter is welcome here. But who is this braggart who calls kin with you? Do you claim *him* as kin?"

Melitta walked toward the stranger. Her mind was racing. She said quickly, in the mountain tongue, "Storn, is it you? Loran, why did you do it?"

"I had no choice," he replied. "It was the only way to save you all."

"Tell me quickly the name of the horse I first learned to ride, and I accept you for who you are."

A faint flicker of a smile passed over the stranger's face. "You did not learn to ride on a horse, but on a stag pony," he said softly, "and you called him *Horny-pig*."

Deliberately Melitta went to the stranger's side, laid her hand in his and stood on tiptoe to kiss his cheek. "Kinsman," she said slowly, and turned back to Kerstal.

"Kinsman of mine he is indeed," she said. "Nor did he lie when he named himself Storn of Storn. Our mountain ways are unknown to you. My brother of Storn is, as you say, blind beyond cure and thus unable to hold *laran* right in our house; and thus this cousin of ours, adopted into our household, wears the name and title of Storn, his true name forgotten even by brother and sister, *nedestro* heir to Storn."

For a moment after she spoke the words she held her breath; then, at a signal from Kerstal, the knives dropped. Melitta dared not let her face show relief.

Storn spoke softly: "What redress does the Great House of Rannath give for deadly insult?"

"I am the Voice of Rannath only," Kerstal countered. "Learn our customs another time, stranger."

"It seems to me," Storn said, his voice still gentle, "that

Storns have suffered grave ills at your hands. Deadly insult given to me, and my sister—" His eyes turned on the two men who had haled Melitta into the Hall. "Is this your courtesy to strangers in your city?"

"Amends shall be made," Kerstal said. Beads of sweat stood out on his forehead. "My House has no quarrel with you, Lord of Storn; be then our guests and receive gifts consonant with your quality. Let the exchange of courtesy wipe out memory of offense given or taken."

Stern hesitated, his hand on the hilt of his knife, and Melitta, reading the gesture with astonishment, thought, *He's enjoying this; he half hopes that Kerstal will call challenge!*

But if this was Storn's intention, he remembered his primary intention in time. He said, "Be it so, then. My sister and I gratefully accept your hospitality, kinsman of Rannath," and all round the circle, there were small sighs and stirs of relief or, perhaps, of disappointment.

Kerstal summoned servants and gave orders, then detained Storn a moment with a raised hand. "You claim this woman, then? See you to it that she does not walk abroad free in defiance of our customs!"

Melitta bit her tongue on an angry retort, feeling Storn's hand dig hard into her shoulder. This was no time to start any further arguments.

A few minutes later, they were in a large guest room, bare as all Dry-town rooms, with little more than mats on the floor and a shelf or two. When the servants had withdrawn, Melitta faced the stranger who bore her brother's voice and manner. Left alone with him, she hardly knew what to say.

The stranger said softly, in their own language, "It's really me, you know, Melitta." He smiled. "I must say—you came at exactly the right moment. We couldn't have planned it better!"

"No planning of mine, but good luck," she conceded. She sank down wearily. "Why did you send me here?"

"Because at one time there were mountain-born mercenaries all through this part of the country, gathering at Carthon. Now, with the Dry-towners moving in here, I'm not sure," Storn said. "But we are free; we can act. We could do nothing, now, at High Windward." He threw himself down on one of the pallets. Melitta too, was tired beyond words and she was also ill at ease with a man who still seemed a stranger to her. At last she said, "Who is—the man—"

"His name is Barron; he is a Terran, an off-worlder. His mind lay open to me; I scanned his future and saw that he would be coming into the mountains. And so—" Storn shrugged. Another of those silences fell between brother and sister, a silence which could not be talked about. They both knew that Storn had broken an ancient taboo, forbidden from the earliest years of the Darkovan Compact. Even though the victim was a Terran, the horror remained with Melitta.

They were both relieved when servants of Rannath entered, bearing trays of food, and a pair of chests which, the servants explained, were gifts from the House of Rannath to the Lord and Lady of Storn. When they had gone away again, Melitta rose and approached the pile of gifts, and Storn laughed softly. "Never too tired to be curious—just like a woman! As a matter of fact, Melitta, enjoy these gifts with clear conscience—Rannath's Voice, or whatever that official calls himself, knows that he is purchasing immunity from a blood feud that would run for years and cost him a hell of a lot more than this! If we were Dry-towners, that is. He'll despise us a little because we can be bought off, but I for one don't care a scrap for what a patch of unwashed Dry-towners think about us, do you? I accepted the gifts because, among other things"—he surveyed her—"you looked as if you could use a few gifts! I've never seen you look so hoydenish, little sister!"

Melitta felt ready to cry. "You don't know half of where I've been, or how I've had to travel, and you're making fun of what I'm wearing—" Her voice broke.

"Melitta! Don't cry, don't—" He reached out and took her into his arms, holding her tight, her face on his shoulder. "Little sister, *breda*, *chiya* . . ." He cuddled her, crooning pet names from their childhood. Gradually she quieted, then drew away, vaguely embarrassed. The voice, the manner, were her brother's, but the strange man's body and touch were disconcerting. She lowered her eyes, and Storn laughed, embarrassed.

"Let's see what Kerstal has sent us, and we'll see how high he rates the *kihar* of the House of Storn."

"Not cheaply, at any rate," Melitta said, opening the chests.

There was a sword of fine temper for Storn. He buckled it on, saying, "Remember, these are Dry-towners—it does not mean what it would mean in our mountains. Worse luck, or it would be a pledge to come to our aid." With the sword was an embroidered vest and baldric. For Melitta, as she had hoped, were gowns of linen trimmed with fur, hoods and coifs—and a gilt chain with a tiny padlock. She stared at that, unbelieving.

Storn laughed as he picked it up: "Evidently he thinks I'm going to put you on a leash!" Then, as her eyes flashed again, he added quickly, "Never mind, you don't have to wear it. Come, *breda*, let us eat, and then rest for a little while. We're safe here, at least. Time enough tomorrow to think about what we're going to do, if Rannath decides that no one here can help us."

XI

STORN HAD proved an accurate prophet. However eager the House of Rannath might be to avoid a lengthy blood feud with the Storns, the word had evidently gone out all over Carthon; no one was "at leisure," as he told them regretfully, to pursue a war in the mountains.

Storn, privately, didn't blame them. The Dry-towners were never at ease in the foothills, let alone in the high passes; and the House of Rannath had enough to do to hold Carthon, without scattering such armies as he could command on missions in the far Sierras. For that matter, Dry-town mercenaries, unskilled at mountaineering and ill-guarded against snow and cold, would be more trouble than they were worth. They needed mountain men, and there were none in Carthon.

When the brother and sister insisted on taking their leave, Kerstal besought them to stay and managed not to sound nearly as insincere as they both knew he was. When they pleaded urgent necessity, he found Melitta an excellent riding horse from his private stables and pressed it upon her as a gift.

"And thus," Storn said cynically as they rode away from the Great House, "the Voice of Rannath serves his lord by cutting another tie with the mountains and making it less likely that more mountain folk will come here. That makes it more convenient for the few who remain in Carthon to go elsewhere—I wonder what happened to all the Lanarts? They used to hold land near Carthon," he explained, "and they were a sub-clan of the Altons, along with the Leyniers and the people of Syrtis. I hope the damned Dry-towners haven't killed them off by entangling them in blood feud and picking them off one at a time; they were good people. Domenic Lanart offered his eldest son in marriage to you, once, Melitta."

"And you never told me."

He chuckled. "At the time you were eight years old," Then he sobered again. "I should have married you off, both of you, years gone; then we would have kinfolk at our call. But I was reluctant to part with you. Allira had no great wish to marry. . . ."

They both fell silent. When they spoke again, it was of the past of Carthon and how it had fallen to this deserted state. Not until they were free of the city did Storn again broach the subject of their next move.

"Since Carthon has proved a false hope—"

Melitta broke in: "We are within a few days ride of Armida, and Valdir Alton has banded together all the men of the foothills against bandits—look what he did against Cyrillon Des Trailles! Storn, appeal to him! Surely he will help us!"

"I cannot," Storn said somberly. "I dare not even meet with Valdir's men, Melitta. Valdir is a Comyn telepath, and has Alton powers; he would know at once what I have done. I think he already suspects. And besides"—he flushed darkly, ashamed—"I stole a horse from one of Alton's men."

Melitta said dryly, "I wondered where you got such a beauty."

Storn's own thoughts ran bitter counterpoint. *Valdir's foster son pledged himself with a knife—but it was to the Earthling, Barron. He knows nothing of me and has no friendship for me. And now that road is closed, too. What now?* He said at last "We are far kin to the House of Aldaran. I have heard that they, too, are a rallying-point for the people of the mountains. Perhaps they can help us. If they cannot help us for old kinship's sake, perhaps they will know where we can find mercenaries. We will go to Aldaran."

Melitta, reflecting that meant recrossing the Kadarin and turning back into the mountains, wished they had gone there first; but then she remembered that Storm—Barron—had come all the way from the valley lands far to the other side of the foothills. Carthon had been the best intermediary place they could locate, and furthermore Storm had had every reason to believe they could find help at Carthon. It was the strangest thing; when she did not look at him, it was easy to believe she rode with her brother Storm; the voice, unfamiliar in timbre and tone, had still her brother's familiar mannerisms and speech rhythms, as if it came filtered through distance. But when her eyes alighted on the strange figure which rode so easily on the great black horse —tall, dark, sullenly alien—the unease overtook her again. What would happen if Storm withdrew and she was left alone with this stranger, this off-worlder, this unbelievably alien man? Melitta had thought, after her terrible trek through the mountains, that she had little left to fear. She discovered that there were fears she had never thought of before this, the unknown hazards of an alien man, an alien mind.

She told herself, grimly, *Even if he—gets out—he couldn't be worse than Brynat's gang of toughs. I doubt if he'd want to murder me, or rape me.* Surreptitiously she studied the strange face, masked in her brother's familiar presence, and thought, *I wonder what he's really like? He seems a decent sort of man—no lines of cruelty, or dissipation—sad, if anything, and a little lonely. I wonder if I'll ever know?*

The third evening out of Carthon, they discovered that they were being followed.

Melitta sensed it first, with senses abnormally sharpened by the tension and fear of the journey; as if, she was to say later, "I'd gotten in the habit of riding looking over my shoulder." She also suspected that she was developing, perhaps from contact with Storn or from some other stimulus, from a latent telepath into an actual one. She could not at first tell whether it was by the impact on her mind, or through some subliminal stimulation of her five sharpened senses—sounds too faint to be normally heard, shapes too distant to see—in any case it made little or no difference. When they found shelter in an abandoned herdsman's hut on a hill pasture, she finally told Storn of her suspicions, half afraid he would laugh.

Nothing was further from his mind than laughter. His mouth pinched tight—Melitta knew the gesture if not the mouth—and he said, "I thought so, last night; but I thought I listened only to my own fear."

"But who could be following us? Certainly none of Brynat's men, at such a distance! Men from Carthon?"

"That's not impossible," Storn said. "The House of Rannath might not mind seeing another of the old mountain families disappear—but then, sooner or later he might have to deal with Brynat's raiders himself. Raiding parties have been known to come as far as Carthon, and I dare say he would find us more towardly neighbors than the Scarface— he might not help us, but I doubt if he would hinder. No, what I fear is worse than that."

"Bandits? A raiding nonhuman band?"

Somberly, Storn shook his head. Then, seeing Melitta's fear, he tried to smile. "I'm no doubt imagining things, *breda*, and in any case we are armed."

He did not say what he most feared: that Larry, through sworn friendship and fear for Barron, might have set Valdir on his track. He had not meant any harm—quite the opposite. But Barron had twice—or was it three times—asked questions about Carthon. It would have been simple enough to trail him there. And if no Terran had come there—well, Valdir at least would know what he had done and why Barron the Earthling had vanished. From what little Storn knew of the Comyn, once on the track of such an offense against the ancient laws of Darkover, they would make little of chasing him over half a world.

And when they caught him—what then?

With the uncanny habit she was developing, of reading his thoughts (Had he done well, to waken *laran* in the girl?) Melitta asked, "Storn, just what *are* the Comyn?"

"That's like asking what the mountains are. Originally there were seven Great Houses on Darkover, or Domains, each with a particular telepathic gift. If I ever knew which House had which Gift, I have forgotten, and in any case, generations of inbreeding and intermarriage have blurred them so that nobody knows any more. When men spoke of the Comyn, they usually meant Comyn Council—a hierarchy of gifted telepaths from every House, who were responsible, first, for surveillance over the use of the old powers and gifts of the mind—and later, they gained temporal power, too. You've heard the ballads—originally the seven houses were descended from the sons of Hastur and Cassilda, so they say. It might even be true, for all I know, but that's beside the point. Just now, they're the givers of law—such law as there has been since the Compact—all over this part of Darkover. Their writ doesn't run in the Dry Towns, or in trailman country, and the mountain people are pretty much out of their orbit—you know as well as I do that we mountain people live under our own customs and ways."

"They rule? Doesn't the King rule in the lowlands?"

"Oh, yes, there is a King in Thendara, ruling under the Comyn Council. The kingship used to rest with the Hasturs, but they gave it up, a few generations ago, in favor of another Comyn family, the Elhalyns, who are so intermarried with the Hasturs that it doesn't make much difference. You know all this, damn it, I remember telling you when you were a child, as well as about the Aldarans."

"I'm sorry, it all seemed very far away." They sat on blankets and furs inside the dark hut, crouched close to the fire, although to anyone accustomed to the fierce cold of the mountains it was not really cold. Outside, sleety rain whispered thickly along the slats of the hut. "What about the Aldarans? Surely they're Comyn too?"

"They used to be; they may have some Comyn powers. But they were kicked out of Comyn Council generations ago; the story goes that they did something so horrible nobody knows or remembers what it was. Personally I suspect it was the usual sort of political dogfight, but I can't say. No one alive knows, except maybe the Lords of Comyn Council." He fell silent again. It was not Comyn he feared, but Valdir, specifically, and that too-knowing, all-reading gaze.

Storn did not have to be told how Melitta felt about what he had done. He felt the same way himself. He, too, had been brought up in the reverence of this Darkovan law against interfering with another human mind. Yet he justified himself fiercely, with the desperation of the law-abiding and peaceful man turned renegade. *I don't care what laws I have broken, it was my sister and my young brother in the hands of those men, and the village folk who have served my family for generations. Let me see them free and I don't care if they hang me! What good is an invalid's life, anyhow? I've never been more than half alive, before this!*

He was intensely aware of Melitta, half-kneeling before the low fire, close to him on the blankets. Isolated by the conditions of his life, as he had been till now, there had been few women, and none of his own caste, about whom he could care personally. To a developing telepath that had meant much. Habit and low vitality had made him indifferent to this deprivation; but the strange and newly vigorous body, in which he now felt quite at home, was more than marginally aware of the closeness of the girl.

It crossed his mind that Melitta was extraordinarily beautiful, even in the worn and stained riding clothes she had resumed when they left Carthon. She had loosened her hair and removed the outer cloak and tunic; under it was a loose rough linen shift. Some small ornament gleamed at her throat and her feet were bare. Storn, weary from days of riding, was still conscious of the reflex physical stir of awareness and desire. He let himself play at random with the thought, perhaps because all his other thoughts were too disturbing. Sexual liaisons between even full siblings in the mountains were not prohibited, although children born to such couples were thought unfortunate—the isolated mountain people were too aware of the dangers of inbreeding. With the grimmest humor he had yet felt, Storn thought, *In a stranger's body even that would not be anything to fear!*

Then he felt a sudden revulsion. The stranger's body was that of an alien, an Earthling, a stranger on their world—and he had been thinking of letting such a one share the body of his sister, a Lady of Storn? He set his jaw roughly, reached out and covered the fire.

"It's late," he said. "We have far to travel tomorrow. You'd better go to sleep."

Melitta obeyed without a word, rolling herself in her fur cloak and turning away from him. She was aware of what he was thinking, and intensely sorry for him, but she dared not offer him overt sympathy. Her brother would have rejected it as he had done all her life, and she was still a little afraid of the stranger. It was not the low-keyed throb of his desire, which Melitta could feel almost as a physical presence, which disturbed her, of course. She did not care about that. As with any mountain girl of her caste, she knew that, travelling alone with any man, such a problem would in all probability arise. With Storn's own person she might not have thought of it, but she was much more aware of the stranger than Storn realized. She had been forced to think about this eventuality and to make up her mind about it. She felt no particular attraction to the stranger, although if his presence had been uncomplicated by the eerie uncanniness of knowing that he was also her brother, she might have found him intriguing; certainly he was handsome, and seemed gentle and from the tones of his voice, likable. But if she had even inadvertently roused desire in him, common decency, by the code of women of her caste, demanded that she give it some release; to refuse this would have been, wrong and cruelly whorish. If she had been unalterably opposed to this possibility, she would not have agreed to travel entirely alone with him; no mountain girl would have done so. It would not have been impossible to find a travelling companion in Carthon.

In any case, it seemed that at the moment the matter was not imminent, and Melitta was relieved. It might have been entirely too uncanny; *like lying with a ghost*, she thought, and slept.

It was still dark when Storn's hand on her shoulder roused her, and when they saddled their horses and began to ride down the dark mountain path, they rode through still-heavy sleet which only after an hour or more of riding turned into the light rain which presaged dawn at this latitude and season. Melitta, cold and shivering, and even a little resentful, did not protest; she simply wrapped her cloak over her face as they rode. Storn turned into an inordinately steep and forsaken path, dismounted and led her horse along the slippery path through the trees until it was safe to ride again. She was thinking, *If it is Comyn on our trail, we may not be able to lose them. But if not, perhaps we can shake off our followers.*

"And we may gain two or three days ride on them this way, if they are not accustomed to the mountain roads—they or their horses," Storn said, out of nothing, and Melitta understood.

All that day and the next they rode through steeper and steeper mountain paths, with storms gathering over the heights, and at night they were too exhausted to do more than swallow a few mouthfuls of food and roll, half asleep already, into their blankets. On the morning of the third day after they had first sensed that they were followed, Melitta woke without any uneasy sense of a presence overshadowing their moves, and sensed that they had lost their followers, at least for the moment.

"We should reach Aldaran today," said Storn, as they saddled, "and if what I've heard is true, perhaps even the Comyn don't care to come this far into the hills. They may be sacrosanct in the lowlands, but not here."

As soon as the mist cleared they sighted the castle from a peak, a gray and craggy height enfolded and half invisible in the hills; but it took them the rest of the day to approach the foot of the mountain on which it stood, and as they turned into the road—well-travelled and strongly surfaced—which led upward to the castle, they were intercepted by two cloaked men. They were asked their business with the utmost courtesy but nevertheless entreated to remain until the Lord of Aldaran knew of their coming, with so much insistence that neither Storn nor Melitta wanted to protest.

"Inform the Lord of Aldaran," said Storn, his voice sounding gray with weariness, "that his far kinsmen of Storn, at High Windward, seek shelter, counsel and hospitality. We have ridden far and are weary and call on him in the name of kin to give us rest here."

"Rest in safety is yours at the asking," said the man with exquisite courtesy, and Melitta sighed relief; they were among people of familiar ways. "Will you wait in the gate

108

house, my lord and *damisela?* I will have your horses looked to. I cannot disturb the Lord of Aldaran without his consent, but if you are his kinfolk, I am sure you need not wait long. I am at your service, and there is food for all travellers if you are in need of it."

Waiting in the bare, small gate house, Storn smiled briefly at Melitta; "Aldaran keeps the old ways of courtesy to strangers, whatever else may have befallen his household."

In an almost unbelievably brief time (Storn wondered if some signaling device had been used, for there hardly seemed time for a messenger to come and go to the castle on the heights) the guard returned: "The Lady Desideria bids me conduct you to the main house and make you welcome, Lord and Lady; and when you are rested and refreshed she will receive you."

Storn murmured to Melitta, as they climbed the path and the steps leading upward, "I have no idea who the Lady Desideria is. Old Kermiac would hardly have married; I suspect it is one of his son's wives."

But the young woman who greeted them, was no man's wife. She could hardly have been more than fifteen years old. She was a striking red-haired beauty whose poise and self-confidence made Melitta feel shy, countrified, and ill at ease.

"I am Desideria Leynier," she said. "My foster mother and my guardian are not at home; they will return tomorrow and give you a proper welcome." She came and took Melitta's hands in her own, searching her face with gentle eyes. "Poor child, you look tired almost to death; a night's sleep before you face your hosts will do you good; and you too, Master, you must rest and not stand on ceremony. The Storns are unknown to me but not to my household. I give you welcome."

Storn returned thanks, but Melitta was not listening to the formal words. In the presence of this queerly self-possessed child, she sensed something more than poise; an awareness, an inner strength, and the touch of an uncannily developed sensitivity, so far beyond her own as to make her feel like a child. She made a deep reverence. "*Vai leronis*," she whispered, using the ancient word for a sorceress wise in the old skills.

Desideria smiled merrily. "Why, no," she said. "Only one, perhaps, who has a little knowledge of the old crafts— and if I read rightly, child, you are no stranger to them! But we can talk of that another time, I wished only to give you welcome in my foster parents' name." She summoned a servant to conduct them, and herself went before them along the long halls. It was evidently a busy hour before the evening meal; people went back and forth in the halls, including some tall thin men whose presence and careless regard made Storn draw breath and clamp his fingers hard on Melitta's arm.

"There are Terrans here—this deep in the mountains," he whispered, "what in the name of Zandru's hells is going on here at Aldaran? Have we walked from the trap to the cook pot? I would not believe that any Terran alive had ever come into these mountains. And the girl is a telepath —Melitta, keep your wits about you!"

Desideria turned Storn over to a servant and conducted Melitta into a small room at the top of a tower, one of four tiny pie-shaped rooms on that level. "I am sorry the accommodations are not more luxurious," she apologized, "but there are a great many of us here. I will send you wash water, and a maid to dress you, and although you would be more than welcome in the hall, child, I think you would be better to have dinner here in your room, and go to bed at once; without rest you will be ill."

Melitta agreed gratefully, glad that she need not face so many strangers tonight. Desideria said, "He is a strange man—your brother," but the words held no hint of a prying question. She pressed Melitta's hands and kissed her cheek. "Now rest well," she said in that oddly adult way, "and don't be afraid of anything. My sisters and I are near you in the rooms across the hallway." She went away. Left alone, Melitta took off her dirty and cold riding clothes and gratefully accepted the services of the quiet, incurious maid who came to wait on her. After bathing and eating the light, delicious food brought to her, she lay down in the soft bed and for the first time since the alarm bell had pealed Brynat's presence at the walls of Storn, she felt she could sleep in peace. They were safe.

Where is Storn? Is he, too, enjoying this luxury of safety

*and rest? Surely he must be mistaken about Terrans here.
And it's surely strange—to find a* vai leronis *deep in the
mountains.*

XII

STORN WOKE in the early light, and for a few minutes had
no notion of where he might be. Around him were unfamiliar airs and voices, and he lay with his eyes closed,
trying to orient himself, hearing footsteps ringing on stone,
the sound of animals calling out for food, and strange voices
rising and falling. They were peaceful morning sounds, not
the sounds of a home in the hands of conquerors, and then
memory flooded back and he knew he was in Castle Aldaran.
He opened his eyes.

A curious apprehension lay on him, he did not know why.
He began to wonder how long he could keep the upper
hand over Barron—if it would be long enough to carry
through his aims before he lost hold and found himself back
in his own body, lying helpless in trance, guarded against
personal attack, but still unable to do anything for his family
and his people. If that happened, he had no illusions about
what would happen, sooner or later. Barron would go his
own way, confused by a period of amnesia or perhaps false
memories—Storn really did not know what happened to a
man in Barron's position—and Melitta would be left alone
without anyone. He would never know what happened to
her in that case, he supposed.

And he did not want to return to his own body, blinded
and helplessly imprisoned. If he did, what would happen
to Barron, an Earthman alone in these strange mountains?
For the very sake of his victim, he must maintain hold at
all costs.

If there *were* Terrans at Castle Aldaran, what could it
mean? Sick with unanswered and unanswerable questions,
he flung back the covers and went to the window. Whatever
happened in the end, he would enjoy these few days of
sight out of a lifetime in darkness. Even if these days were
his last.

From the window he looked down at the commotion in the courtyard. Men were going to and fro with an indefinable sense of purposiveness; there were Terrans among them, a few even in the leather dress of the spaceports— *how do I know that when I see it, never having been there?* —and after he had watched a while there was a stir among the men. One man and two uniformed attendants rode through the gate.

The man was tall, dark-bearded, well past middle age, and had an air of authority which reminded Storn vaguely of Valdir, although this man was clearly one of the mountain people. Storn realized from the hubbub surrounding him that he must be looking down at the arrival of the Lord of Aldaran. In a few hours he must face this man and ask for his help. Deep depression lay on Storn, for no discernible reason. Could even a whole army, if Aldaran were willing to put it at his disposal (and why should he?) dislodge Brynat? Storn Castle had been besieged before and it had never even been necessary to defend it. *Now that Brynat holds it, could anyone retake it? Army? We would need a god.*

The scene below melted away and Storn seemed to see within himself the great chained shape of Sharra, flame-crowned, golden-chained, beautiful and awesome. It was the vision he had seen when he lay helpless and blind behind the magnetic force-field at Storn Castle, his body tranced, his mind free and ranging time and space in search of help from *somewhere.*

Sharra again! What does the vision mean?

Melitta came for him late in the forenoon with Desideria, who told them that her guardian was ready to receive them. As he followed the girls down the long corridors, stairs and hallways, Storn was quietly evaluating the poise, the strength and the obvious telepathic awareness of this very young girl, and coming up with a disquieting answer. She must be a Keeper—one of the young girls trained from infancy to work with the old matrix crystals and screens which would have made the few things at Storn Castle look like children's toys. But, overhearing snatches of conversation between them —Desideria seemed to have taken a fancy to Melitta, and talked to her freely—he gathered that there were four of them. In the old days a matrix circle, isolated from the world and giving all their time to it, had barely managed to train one Keeper in about ten years. If Aldaran had managed to train four in the few years since Storn had been here last, what was going on in this place?

But when he asked her a random question, using the polite form of address, *leronis,* Desideria gave him a merry smile and shook her head. "No, my friend, I am not a *leronis;* my guardian does not like the word and its connotations of sorcery. I have been trained in a skill which anyone can learn who is a good telepath, just as anyone who is strong and fit enough can learn hawking or riding. Our world has accepted foolish ideas like sorcery for all too many years. Call me, if you like, a matrix technician. My sisters and I have learned this skill, far better than most; but there is no need to look at me with reverence because I have learned well!"

She went on looking at him with a girlish, ingenuous smile, then suddenly shivered, flushed and dropped her eyes. When she spoke again it was to Melitta, almost pointedly ignoring Storn.

He thought with a certain grimness, *Training or not, she is still conventional in the old ways—and I owe my life to that. If she were old enough to look at it that way—a trained telepath of her caliber need only look at me to know what I have done. Only the convention that girls of her age may not initiate any contact with men other than their blood kin, has saved me so far.*

The thought was strangely poignant—that this young girl of his own mountain people, of his own kind and caste, and trained in all those things which had been the major solace of his life, was so guarded against him—and that he dared not reach out to her, mind or body. He felt as if he could have wept. He set his lips hard and followed the girls. He did not speak again.

Aldaran received them, not in a formal audience chamber but in a small, friendly room low in the castle. He embraced Storn, calling him cousin, kissed Melitta on the forehead with a kinsman's privilege, offered them wine and sweets, and made them sit beside him; then he asked what had brought them there.

"It is far too long since any of your kinsmen have visited us at Aldaran; you live as isolated at High Windward as eagles in their aerie. It has come to mind in the last year or so that I have neglected kinship's dues and that I should ride to Storn, there is much astir in the mountains these days, and no one of our people should hold himself aloof too far; our world's future depends on it. But more of that later, if you are interested. Tell me what brings you to Aldaran, kinsman? How can I help you?"

He listened to their story gravely, with a gradually darkening and distressful face. When they had finished, he spoke with deep regret.

"I am ashamed," he said, "that I offered you no help before this, to prevent such a thing. For now it has happened, I am powerless to help you. I have kept no fighting men here for more than thirty years, Storn; I have kept peace here and tried to prevent feuds and raids rather than repelling them. We mountain people have been torn by feuds and little wars far too long; we have let ourselves go back to barbarian days."

"I, too, had no fighting men and wanted peace," Storn said bitterly, "and all I gained from it was Brynat's men at my outworks."

"I have Terran guards here and they are armed with off-world weapons," Aldaran said. "Would-be invaders knew enough, after a time or two, to let us alone."

"With—weapons? Force weapons? But what of the Compact?" Melitta gasped in genuine horror. The law which banned, on this world, any weapon beyond the arm's reach of the wielder, was even more reverenced than the taboo against meddling with the mind. Aldaran said quietly, "That law has delivered us to petty wars, feuds, murders and assassins. We need new laws, not stupid reverence for old ones. I have broken the Darkovan code and as a result, the Hasturs and the Comyn hold my family in horror; but we are at peace here and we have no hooligans at our doors, waiting for an old man to weaken so that he can be challenged and set down as if the stronger swordsman were the better man. The law of brute force means only the rule of the brute."

"And other worlds, I believe," Melitta said, "have found that unrestricted changes in weapons leads to an endless race for better and better weapons in a chase to disaster which can destroy not only men, but worlds."

"That may even be true," Aldaran said, "and yet look what has happened to Darkover, in the hands of the Terrans? What have we done? We refused their technology, their weapons, we insisted on refusing real contact with them. Since the Years of Chaos, when we lost all of our own technologies except for the few in the hands of the Comyn, we've slipped back further and further into barbarism. In the lowlands, the Seven Domains keep their old rule as if no ships had ever put forth into space. And here in the mountains we allow ourselves to be harassed by bandits because we are afraid to fight them. Someone must step beyond this deadlock, and I have tried to do so. I have made a compact with the Terrans; they will teach us their ways and defenses and I will teach them ours. And as a result of a generation of peace and freedom from casual bandits and learning to think as the Terrans think—that everything which happens can and must be explained and measured—I have even rediscovered many of our old Darkovan ways; you need not think we are totally committed to becoming part of Terra. For instance, I have learned how to train telepaths for matrix work without the old superstitious rituals; none of the Comyn will even try that. And as a result—but enough of that. I can see that you are not in any state to think about abstract ideas of progress, science and culture as yet."

"But what all this fine-sounding talks means," said Storn bitterly, "is that my sister and brother, and all my people, must lie at the mercy of bandits because you prefer not to be entangled in feuds."

"My dear boy!" Aldaran looked aghast. "The gods help me; if I had the means to do so, I would forget my ethics and come to your aid—blood kin is not mountain-berry wine! But I have no fighting men at all, and few weapons, and such as I have could not be moved over the mountains."

Storn was enough of a telepath to know that his distress was very real. Aldaran said, "We live in bad times, Storn; no culture ever changed without people getting hurt, and it is your ill-fortune that you are one of those who are getting hurt in the change. But take heart; you are alive and unhurt, and your sister is here, and believe me, you shall be made welcome here as kin; this is your home, from this very day forth. The gods seize me, if I am not as a father to you both from this moment."

"And my sister? My brother? My people?"

"Perhaps some day we will find a way to help them; some day all these mountain bandits must be wiped out, but we have neither the means nor any way."

He dismissed them, tenderly. "Think it over. Let me do what I can for you; you certainly must not return to throw your lives after theirs. Do you think that your people really want you to share their fate now that you have escaped?"

Storn's thoughts ran bitter counterpoint as they left Aldaran. Perhaps what Aldaran said made sense in the long run, in the history of Darkover, in the annals of a world. But he was interested in the short run, in his own people and the annals of his own time. Taking the long view inevitably meant being callous to how many people were hurt. If he had had no hope of outside help, he would gladly have sent Melitta to safety, if nothing more could be salvaged, and been glad there was a home for her here. But now that hope had been raised for more, this seemed like utter failure.

He heard, as from a distance, Desideria saying to Melitta, "Something draws me to your brother—I don't know; he is not a man whose looks I admire, it is something beyond that—I wish I could help you. I can do much, and in the old days, the powers of the trained telepaths of Darkover could be used against intruders and invaders. But not alone."

Melitta said, "Don't think we are ungrateful for your guardian's good will, Desideria. But we must return to Storn even if all we can do is to share the fate of those there. But we will not do that unless all hope is gone, even if we must rouse the peasants with their pitchforks and the forge folk of the hills!"

Desideria stopped dead in the hallway. She said "The forge folk of the caverns in the Hellers? Do you mean the old folk who worshipped the goddess, Sharra?"

"Indeed they did. But those altars are long cold and profaned."

"Then I can help you!" Desideria's eyes glowed. "Do you think an altar matters? Listen, Melitta, you know, a little, what my training has been? Well, one of the—the powers we have learned to raise here is that associated with Sharra.

In the old days, Sharra was a power in this world; the Comyn sealed the gates against raising that power, because of various dangers, but we have found the way, a little—but Melitta, if you can find me even fifty men who once believed in Sharra, I could—I could level the gates of Storn Castle, I could burn Brynat's men alive about him."

"I don't understand," said Storn, caught in spite of himself. "Why do you need worshippers?"

"And you a telepath yourself, I dare say, Storn! Look—the linked minds of the worshippers, in a shared belief, create a tangible force, a strength, to give power to that—that force, the power which comes through the gates of the other dimension into this world. It is the Form of Fire. I can call it up alone, but it has no power without someone to give it strength. I have the matrixes to open that gate. But with those who had once worshipped—"

Storn thought he knew what she meant. He had discovered forces which could be raised, which he could not handle alone, and with Brynat at his gates. He had thought, *If I had help, someone trained in these ways—*

He said, "Will Aldaran allow this?"

Desideria looked adult and self-sufficient. She said, "When anyone has my training and my strength, she does not ask for leave to do what she feels right. I have said I will help you; my guardian would not gainsay me—and I would not give him the right to do so."

"And I thought you a child," Storn said.

"No one can endure the training I have had and remain a child," Desideria said. She looked into his eyes and colored, but she did not flinch from his gaze. "Some day I will read the strangeness in you, Loran of Storn. That will be for another time; now your mind is elsewhere." Briefly she touched his hand, then colored again and turned away. "Don't think me bold."

Touched, Storn had no answer. Fear and uncertainty caught him again. If these people felt no horror of breaking the Darkovan League's most solemn law, the Compact against weapons, would they have any compunctions about what he had done? He did not know whether he felt relieved or vaguely shocked at the thought that they might accept it as part of a necessity, without worrying about the dubious ethics involved.

He forced such thoughts from his mind. For the moment it was enough that Desideria thought there was a way to help. It was a desperate chance, but he was desperate enough for any gamble, whatever that might be—even Sharra.

"Come with me to the room where my sisters and I work," she said. "We must find the proper instruments and —you may as well call them talismans, if you like. And if you, Storn, have experimented with these things, then the sight of a matrix laboratory may interest you. Come. And then we can leave within the hour, if you wish."

She led the way along a flight of stairs and past glowing blue beacons in the hallways which Storn, although he had never seen them before, recognized. They were the force beacons, the warning signs. He had some of them in his own castle and had experimented until he had learned many of their secrets. They had given him the impregnable field which protected his body and had turned Brynat's weapon, and the magnetic currents which guided the mechanical birds that allowed him to experience the sensation of flight. There were other things with less practical application, and he wanted to ask Desideria question after question. But he was haunted by apprehension, a sense of time running out; Melitta must have sensed it too, for she dropped back a step or two from Desideria and took his hand, glancing up at him with unease.

He tried to smile. "Nothing. It's a little overwhelming to learn that these—these toys with which I spent my childhood can be a science of this magnitude."

Time is running out. . . .

Desideria swung back a curtain, and stepped through a blue magnetic shimmer. Melitta followed. Storn, seized by indefinable reluctance, hesitated, then stepped forward.

A stinging shock ran through him, and—for an instant Dan Barron, bewildered, half-maddened, and fighting for sanity, stared around him at the weird trappings of the matrix laboratory, as if waking from a long, long nightmare.

"Storn—?" Desideria's hand touched his. He forced himself to awareness and smiled. "Sorry. I'm not used to fields quite as strong."

"I should have warned you. But if you could not come

118

through the field you would not have enough knowledge to help us, in any case. Here, let me find what I need."

She flicked a small button and motioned them to seats. "Wait for me."

Slowly, Storn became aware of the strange disorganizing humming. Melitta was staring at him in astonishment and dismay but it took all his strength not to dissolve beneath the strange invisible sound, not to vanish. . . .

A telepathic damper. Barron had been aware of one, at Armida, with his developing powers, he had just been disturbed at it, but now . . . now . . .

Now there was not even time to cry out, it was vibrating through his brain—through temporal lobes and nerves, creating disruption of the nets that held him in domination, freeing—Barron! He felt himself spinning through indefinable, blue-tinged, timeless space—falling, disappearing, dying—blind, deafened, entranced. . . . He spun down into unconsciousness, his last thought was not of Melitta left alone, nor of his victim Barron. It was Desideria's gray eyes and the indefinable touch of her compassion and knowledge, that went down with him into the night of an unconsciousness so complete that it was like death. . . .

Barron came to consciousness as if surfacing from a long, deep dive.

"*What the bloody hell is going on here?*" For a moment he had no idea whether or not he had spoken the words aloud. His head hurt and he recognized the invisible humming vibration that Valdir Alton had called a telepathic damper—that was all his world for a moment.

Slowly he found his feet and his balance. It was as if for days he had walked through a nightmare, conscious, but unable to do anything but what he did—as if some other person walked in his body and directed his actions while he watched in astonishment from somewhere, powerless to intervene. He suddenly woke with the controlling power gone, yet the nightmare went on. The girl he had seen in the dream was there, staring up at him in mild concern—his sister? *Damn it, no, that was the other guy.* He could remember everything he had done and said, almost everything he had *thought*, while Storn commanded him. He had not shifted position but somehow the focus had changed. He was himself again, Dan Barron, not Storn.

He opened his mouth to raise hell, to demand explanations and give a few, to make everything very clear, when he saw Melitta looking up at him in concern and faint fright. Melitta! He hadn't asked to get involved with her, but here she was and from what he could realize, he was her only protector. *She's been so brave; she's come so far for help, and here it is within her reach; and what will happen if I make myself known?*

He was no expert on Darkovan law and custom, but the one thing he did know from walking with Storn for seven or eight days was that, by Darkovan standards, what Storn had done was a crime. *Fine—I could murder him for it, and God willing, some day I will. That's one hell of a thing to do to a man's mind and body!* But none of it was Melitta's fault. *No. I'll have to play the game for a while.*

The silence had lasted too long. Melitta said, with growing fear in her voice, "Storn?"

He made himself smile at her and then found it didn't take an effort. He said, trying to remember how Storn had spoken, "It's all right, that—telepathic damper upset me a little." *And boy, was that a masterpiece of understatement!*

Desideria came back to them before Melitta could answer, carrying various things wrapped in a length of silk. She said, "I must go and make arrangements for transportation and escort to take you into the hills near High Windward, to the caves where the forge folk have gone. You cannot help in this, why not go and rest? You have a long journey behind and ahead, and difficult things—" She glanced up at Barron and quickly away, and he vaguely wondered why. *What's the matter with the red-headed kid?* He suddenly felt faint and swayed, and Desideria said quickly, "Go with your brother, Melitta; I have many plans to make. I will come for you at sunset."

Too disoriented and confused to do anything else, Barron let Melitta lead him through the suddenly strange corridors to a room where he knew he had slept the night before but which he had never consciously seen before. She stood looking down at him, distressed.

"Storn, what's happened? Are you ill? You look at me so strangely—Storn! Loran!" Her voice rose in sudden panic, and Barron put out a hand to quiet her.

"Take it easy, kid—" He realized he was speaking his own language and shifted back, with some effort into the tongue Storn and his sister spoke together. "Melitta, I'm sorry," he said with an effort, but her eyes were fixed on him in growing horror and understanding.

"The telepathic damper," she whispered. "Now I understand. *Who are you?*"

His admiration and respect for the girl suddenly grew. This must have been just about the most terrifying and disconcerting thing that had ever happened to her. After she'd been so far, and been through so much, and with help so near, to find that her brother was gone and she was alone with a stranger—a stranger who might be raving mad, or a homicidal maniac, and in any case was probably mad —and she didn't run or scream or yell for help. She stood there white as a sheet, but she stood up to him and asked, "Who are you?"

God, what a girl!

He said, trying to match her calm, "I think your brother told you my name, but in case he didn't, it's Dan Barron. Dan will do, but you'd better go on calling me Storn or some of these people may get wise. You don't want that to happen when you've been through so much, **do** you?"

She said, almost incredulous, "You mean—after what my brother's done to you, you'll still help me? You'll go back with us to Storn?"

"Lady," said Barron, grim and meaning it more than he had ever meant anything in his life, "Storn is the one place on this damn planet that I want to go more than anything else in the world. I've got to help you get those bandits out of your castle so that I can get to your brother— and when I get my hands on him, he's going to wish he only had Brynat Scarface to deal with! But that's nothing against *you*. So relax. I'll help you play your game—and Storn and I can settle our private difficulties later on. Good enough?"

She smiled at him, setting her chin courageously.

"Good enough."

XIII

THERE WAS an airplane.

Barron looked at it in amazement and dismay. He would have sworn that there were few surface craft on Darkover; certainly no fuel was exported from the Zone for them, and he had never known of one being sold on Darkover, except one or two in Trade City. But here it was, and obviously of Empire manufacture. When he climbed into it he realized that all the controls had been ripped out; in place of an instrument panel was one of those blue crystals. Desideria took her place before it, looking like a child, and Barron felt like saying, "Hey, are *you* going to fly this thing?" But he held himself back. The girl seemed to know what she was doing, and after what he had seen on Darkover, he wouldn't put anything past them. A technology which could displace possession by another mind was worth looking into. He began to wonder if any Terran Empire man knew anything about Darkover.

Melitta was afraid to climb into the strange contrivance until Desideria comforted and reassured her; then, looking as if she were taking her life in her hands and didn't care, she climbed in, resolved not to show her fear.

The queer craft took off in an eerie silence. Desideria put on another of the telepathic dampers inside, saying almost in apology, "I am sorry—I must control the crystal with my own strength and I dare not have random thoughts intruding." Barron had all he could do to endure the vibrations. He was beginning to guess what they were. If telepathic power were a vibration, the damper was a scrambler to protect the user of the force from any intruding vibrations.

He found himself wondering what Storn would have thought of covering in a few hours, the terrain which he and Melitta had covered so laboriously, on foot and horseback, in several days. The thought was unwelcome in the extreme. He did not want to think about Storn's feelings. Nevertheless, his beliefs about the backwardness of Darkover had been gravely shaken in the last few hours. Their refusal of weapons other than knife and sword now seemed an ethical point—and yet Aldaran, too, seemed to have a valid ethical point, that this kept them struggling in small wars and feuds which depended for their success on who had the stronger physical strength.

But don't all wars depend ultimately on that? Surely you don't believe that rightness of a cause would mean that the right side would be able to get the biggest weapons? Would the feud between Brynat and Storn be easier settled if both of them had guns?

And if this was an ethical point rather than a lack of knowledge, was it just possible that their lack of transit, manufacturing and the like might come from preference rather than lack of ability?

Damn it, why am I worrying about Darkovan ways when my own problems are so pressing?

He had deserted his work with Valdir Alton's men at the fire station. He—or Storn in his body—had stolen a valuable riding horse. He had probably irredeemably ruined himself with the Terran authorities, who had exerted themselves to give him this job and his career was probably at a permanent standstill. He'd be lucky not to find himself on the first ship off Darkover.

Then it struck him that probably he need not go. The Empire might not believe his story but the Altons, who were telepaths, certainly would. And Larry had given him friendship, while Valdir was interested in the field of his professional competence. Perhaps there would be work for him here. He suddenly faced the awareness that he didn't want to leave Darkover and that he had at last become caught up in the struggles and problems of these people whose lives he had entered against his will.

I could kill Storn for what he did—but damn it, I'm glad it happened.

But this was the briefest flash of insight, and it disappeared again, leaving him lost and bewildered. During the days as Storn he had grown used to Melitta's companionship. Now she seemed strange and aloof and when he tried to reach out and touch her with his mind, it was an almost automatic movement and the low-keyed vibration of the telepathic damper interfered, making him feel dull, sick and miserable. He had expected to feel more at home flying than riding horseback but after a short time all he wished was that the flight would be over. Melitta would not look at him.

That was the worst of it. He longed for the flight to be over so that he could speak to her, touch her. She was the only familiar thing in this world and he ached to be near her.

Inconsistently, he was distressed when the flight ended and Desideria brought the craft expertly down in a small valley as quietly as a hovercraft. She apologized to Melitta for not coming nearer to Storn, but explained that the air currents around the peaks were violent enough to crash any small craft. Barron wondered how a girl her age knew about air currents. *Oh hell, she's evidently something special in the way of telepaths, she probably feels 'em through her skin or her balance centers or something.*

Barron had no idea where they were. Since Storn had never seen the place—being blind—Storn's memories were no good to Barron. But Melitta knew. She took charge, directing them toward a mountain village where Darkovans swarmed out, welcoming Melitta with delight, and showing Desideria a reverential awe which seemed to confuse the young girl—the first time Barron had seen Desideria taken aback—and even make her angry.

"I *hate* this," she told him, and Barron knew she still thought she spoke to Storn. "In the old days there might have been some reason for treating the Keepers like goddesses. But now we know how to train them, there is no *reason* for it—no more than for worshipping an expert blacksmith because of his skill!"

"Speaking of blacksmiths," said Barron, "how are we going to round up these forge people?"

She looked at him sharply and it was like the first time she had seen him. She started to say, "You and Melitta will have to manage that; I have never been among them," and stopped, frowning. She said, almost in a whisper and less to Barron than herself, "You have changed, Storn. Something has happened—" and very abruptly turned away.

He had almost forgotten that to her he was still Storn. Elsewhere the masquerade was over; the village people ignored him. He realized that if these were people who lived near High Windward, they would know all the Storns.

He did not try to follow what Melitta was saying to the villagers. He was definitely excess baggage on this trip and he couldn't even imagine why Melitta had wanted him to come back to Storn with her. After a time she came back to Storn and Desideria, saying, "They will provide horses and guides to the caverns of the forge folk in the hills. But we should start at once; Brynat's men patrol the villages every day or two—especially since I escaped—just to make sure that nothing is happening down here; and if it were known that they had helped me—well, I don't want to bring reprisals on them."

They started within the hour. Barron rode silently close to Melitta, but he didn't try to talk to her. There was some comfort in her mere presence, but he knew that she felt ill at ease with him and he did not force himself on her. It was enough to be near her. He spared a thought for Storn, and this time he pitied him. *Poor devil, to have come so far and been through so much and then be forced offstage for the last act.*

He supposed Storn was lying entranced, high in his old wing of the castle, and if he was conscious at all—which Barron doubted—not knowing what had happened. *Hell, that's a worse punishment than anything I could do to him!*

He had been riding without paying much attention to where he was going, letting the horse choose his own road. Now the air began to be filled with the faintly acrid smell of smoke. Barron, alert from his days at the fire station, raised his head to sniff the wind, but the others rode on without paying attention.

Only Melitta sensed his attention and dropped back to ride at his side. "It's not fire. We are nearing the caverns of the forge people; you smell the fires of their forges."

They rode up along a narrow trail that led into the heart of the mountains. After a while Barron began to see dark caves lining the trail. At their entrances, small, swart faces peeped out fearfully. There were little men dressed in furs and leather, women in fur cloaks who turned shyly away from the strangers, and wrapped in fur, miniature children who looked like little teddy-bears. At last they came to a cavern gaping like a great maw, and here Melitta and Desideria alighted, their guides standing close to them in a mixture of fear and dogged protectiveness.

Three men in leather aprons, bearing long metal staves and with metal hammers thrust into their belts—hammers of such weight that Barron did not think he could have lifted them—strode out of the cavern toward Melitta. Behind them the fearful people came up and gathered, surrounding them. The three men were dark, gnarled, short of stature but with long and powerful arms. They made deep bows to the women. Barron they ignored, as he had expected. The central one, with white patches in his dark hair, began to speak; the language was *Cahuenga,* but the pronunciation so guttural and strange that Barron could follow only one word in three. He gathered, however, that they were making Melitta welcome and paying Desideria almost more reverence than the village people had done.

There followed a long colloquy. Melitta spoke. It was a long speech that sounded eloquent, but Barron did not understand. He was very weary, and very apprehensive without knowing why, and this kept him from the attempt to reach out and understand as he had done with Larry and Valdir. *How the devil have I picked up telepathic gifts anyhow? Contact with Storn?* Then the white-haired forge man spoke. His was a long chanting speech that sounded wild and musical, with many bows, again and again Barron caught the word *Sharra.* Then Desideria spoke, and again Barron heard *Sharra,* repeated again and again, to cries and nods from the little people gathered around them. Finally there was a great outcry and all the little people drew knives, hammers, and swords and flourished them in the air. Barron, remembering the Dry-towners, quailed, but Melitta stood firm and fearless and he realized it was an acclamation, not a threat.

Rain was drizzling down thinly, and the little people gathered around and led them into the cavern.

It was airy and spacious, lighted partly by torches burning in niches in the walls, and partly by beautifully luminescent crystals set to magnify the firelight. Exquisitely worked metal objects were everywhere, but Barron had no leisure to examine them. He drew up beside Melitta as they walked through the lighted carven corridors, and asked in a low voice, "What's all the shouting about?"

"The Old One of the forge folk has agreed to help us," Melitta said. "I promised him, in turn, that the altars of Sharra should be restored throughout the mountains, and that they should be permitted to return, unmolested, to their old places and villages. Are you weary from riding? I am, but somehow—" she spread her hands, helplessly. "It's been so long, and now we are near the end—we will start for Storn, two hours before the dawn, so that when Brynat wakes we will surround the castle—if only we are in time!" She was trembling, and moved as if to lean on him, then straightened her back proudly and stood away. She said, almost to herself, "I cannot expect you to care. What can we do for you, when this is over, to make up for meddling in your life this way?"

Barron started to say, "I do care, I care about you, Melitta," but she had already drawn away from him and hurried after Desideria.

With jewel lights and with music provided by small, caged tree frogs and singing crickets, there was a banquet that evening in the great lower hall. Barron, though he could eat little, sat in wonder at the silver dishes—silver was commoner than glass in the mountains—and the jewelled, prismed lamps which played unendingly on the pale, smoke-stained walls of the cave. The forge people sang deep-throated, wild songs in a four-noted scale with a strangely incessant rhythm, like the pounding of hammers. But Barron could not eat the food, or understand a word of the endless epics, and he was relieved when the company dissolved early—he could understand enough of their dialect to know that they were being dismissed against the ride before dawn—and one of their guides took them to cubicles carved in the rock.

Barron was alone; he had seen Melitta and Desideria being conducted to a cubicle nearby. In the little rock room, hardly more than a closet, he found a comfortable bed of furs laid on a bed frame of silver, woven with leather straps. He lay down and expected to sleep from sheer exhaustion. But sleep would not come.

He felt disoriented and lonely. Perhaps he had grown used to Storn's presence and his thoughts. Melitta, too, had withdrawn from him and he was inexpressibly alone without her presence to reach out to, in that indefinable way. He reflected that he had changed. He had always been alone and had never wanted it any other way. The rare women he had had, had never made an impression on him; they came, were used for the brief emotional release they could provide and were forgotten. He had no close friends, only business associates. He had lived on this world and never known or cared how it differed from Terra or from any other Empire planet.

Soon it would be over, and he did not know where he would go. He wished suddenly that he had been more responsive to Larry's proffered friendship; but then, Storn had spoiled that contact for him, probably for all time. He had never known what it was to have a friend, but then he had never known or realized the depths of his aloneness, either.

The room seemed to be swelling up and receding, the lights wavering. He could sense thoughts floating in the air around him, beating on him, he felt physically sick with their impact. He lay on the bed and clutched it, feeling the room tipping and swaying and wondering if he would slide off. Fear seized him; was Storn reaching out for his mind again? He could *see* Storn, without knowing how it was Storn—fair, soft-handed and soft-faced, lying asleep on a bier of silks—face remote and his human presence simply not there at all. Then he saw a great white bird, swooping from the heights of the castle, circling it with a strange musical, mechanical cry and then sweeping away with a great beating of wings.

The room kept shifting and tipping, and he clung to the bed frame, fighting the sickness and disorientation that threatened to tear him apart. He heard himself cry out, unable to keep back the cry; he squeezed his eyes tight, curled himself into a fetal position and tried hard not to think or feel at all.

He never knew how long he lay curled there in rejection, but after what seemed a long and very dreadful time he came slowly to the awareness that someone was calling his name, very softly.

"Dan! Dan, it's Melitta—it's all right; try to take my hand, touch me—it's all right. I would have come before if I had known—"

He made an effort to close his fingers on hers. Her hand

seemed a single stable point in the unbelievably shifting, flowing, swimming perspective of the room, and he clung to it as a man cast adrift in space clings to a magnetic line.

He whispered, "Sorry—room's going round. . . ."

"I know. I've had it; all telepaths get this at some time during the development of their powers, but it usually comes in adolescence; you're a late developer and it's more serious. We call it threshold sickness. It isn't serious, it won't hurt you, but it's very frightening. I know. Hold on to me; you'll be all right."

Gradually, clinging to her small hard fingers, Barron got the world right-side up again. The dizzy disorientation remained, but Melitta was solid, a firm presence and not wholly a physical one, in the midst of the shifting and flowing space.

."Try, whenever this happens, to fix your mind on something solid and real."

"*You* are real," he whispered. "You're the only real thing I've ever known."

"I know." Her voice was very soft. She bent close to him and touched her lips gently to his. She remained there, and the warmth of her was like a growing point of light and stability in the shifting dark. Barron was coming quickly back. At last he drew a deep breath and forced himself to release her.

"You shouldn't be here. If Desideria discovers you are gone—"

"What would it be to her? She could have done more for you; she is a Keeper, a trained telepath, and I—but I forgot, you don't know the sort of training they have. The Keepers—their whole minds and bodies become caught up into the work they do—must keep aloof and safeguard themselves from emotions—" She laughed, a soft, stifled laugh and said, almost weeping, "Besides, Desideria doesn't know it, but she and Storn—"

She broke off. Barron did not care; he was not interested in Desideria at the moment. She came close to him, the only warm and real thing in his world, the only thing he cared about or ever could . . .

He whispered, shaken to the depths, half sobbing, "And to think I might never have known you—"

She murmured, "We would have found one another.

129

From the ends of the world; from the ends of the universe of stars. We belong together."

And then she took him against her, and he was lost in awareness of her, and his last thought, before all thought was lost, was that he had been a stranger on his own world and that now an alien girl from an alien world had made him feel at home.

XIV

THEY STARTED two hours before dawn in a heavy snowfall; after a short time of riding the forge folk on their thick-set ponies looked like polar bears, their furred garments and the shaggy coats of the ponies being covered with the white flakes. Barron rode close to Melitta, but they did not speak, nor need to. Their new awareness of one another went too deep for words. But he could feel her fear—the growing preoccupation and sense of desperation in what they were about to dare.

Valdir had said that the worship of Sharra was forbidden a long time ago, and Larry had been at some pains to explain that the gods on Darkover were tangible forces. *What was going to happen? The defiance of an old law must be a serious thing—Melitta's no coward, and she's scared almost out of her wits.*

Desideria rode alone at the head of the file. She was an oddly small, straight and somehow pitiable little figure, and Barron could sense without analyzing the isolation of the one who must handle these unbelievable forces.

When they came through the pass and sighted Storn Castle on the height, a great, grim mass which he had never seen before, he realized that he had seen it once through Storn's eyes—the magical vision of Storn, flying in the strange magnetic net which bound his mind to the mechanical bird.

Had I dreamed that?

Melitta reached out and clasped his hand. She said, her voice shaky, "There it is. If we're only in time—Storn, Edric, Allira—I wonder if they're even still alive?"

Barron clasped her hand, without speaking. *Even if you have no one else, you will always have me, beloved.*

She smiled faintly, but did not speak.

The forge folk were dismounting now, moving stealthily, under cover of the darkness and crags, up the path toward the great, closed gates of Storn. Barron, between Desideria and Melitta, moved quietly with them, wondering what was going to happen which could make both Melitta and Desideria turn white with terror. Melitta whispered, "It's a chance, at least," and was silent again, clinging to his hand.

Time was moving strangely again for Barron; he had no idea whether it was ten minutes or two hours that he climbed at Melitta's side, but they stood shrouded by shadows in the lee of the gates. The sky was beginning to turn crimson around the eastern peaks. At last the great, pale-red disc of the sun came over the mountain. Desideria, looking around her at the small, swart men clustered about her, drew a deep breath and said, "We had better begin."

Melitta glanced up uneasily at the heights and said, her voice shaking, "I suppose Brynat has sentries up there. As soon as he finds out we're down here, there will be—arrows and things."

"We had better not give him the chance," Desideria agreed. She motioned the forge folk close around her, and gave low-voiced instructions which Barron found that he could understand, even though she spoke that harsh and barbarian language. "Gather close around me; don't move or speak; keep your eyes on the fire."

She turned her eyes on Barron, looking troubled and a little afraid. She said, "I am sorry, it will have to be you, although you are not a worshipper of Sharra. If I had realized what had happened, I would have brought another trained telepath with me; Melitta is not strong enough. You"—suddenly he noticed that she had neither looked directly at him, nor spoken his name, that day—"must serve at the pole of power."

Barron began to protest that he didn't know anything about this sort of thing, and she cut him off curtly. "Stand here, between me and the men; see yourself as gathering all the force of their feelings and emotion and pouring it out in my direction. Don't tell me you can't do it. I've been trained for eight years to judge these things, and I know you can if you don't lose your nerve. If you do, we're probably all dead, so don't be surprised, whatever you see or whatever happens. Just keep your mind concentrated on me." As if moved on strings, Barron found himself moving to the place she indicated, yet he knew she was not controlling him. Rather, his will was in accord with hers, and he moved as she thought.

With a final, tense look upward at the blank wall of the castle, she motioned to Melitta.

"Melitta, make fire."

From the silk-wrapped bundle she carried, Desideria took a large blue crystal. It was as large as a child's fist, and many-faceted, with strange fires and metallic ribbons of light. It looked molten, despite the crystalline facets, as she held it between her hands, and it seemed to change form, the color and light within it shifting and playing.

Melitta struck fire from her tinderbox; it flared up between her hands. Desideria motioned to her to drop the blazing fragment of tinder at her feet. Barron watched, expecting it to go out. Desideria's serious, white face was bent on the blue crystal with a taut intensity; her mouth was drawn, her nostrils pinched and white. The blue light from the crystal seemed to grow, to play around her, to reflect on her—and now, instead of falling, the fire was rising, blazing up until its lights reflected crimson with the blue on Desideria's features—a strange darting, leaping flame.

Her eyes, gray and immense and somehow inhuman, met Barron's across the fire as if there were a visible line between them. He almost heard her voice within his mind. "*Remember!*"

Then he felt behind him an intense pressure beating up—it was the linked minds of the forge folk, beating on his. Desperately he struggled to control this new assault on his mind. He fought, out of control, his breath coming fast and his face contorted, for what seemed ages—though it was only seconds. The fire sagged and Desideria's face showed rage, fear and despair. Then Barron had it—it was like gathering up a handful of shining threads, swiftly splicing them into a rope and thrusting it toward Desideria. He almost felt her catch it, like a great meshing. The fire blazed up again, exuberantly. It dipped, wavered toward Desideria.

It enveloped her.

Barron gasped almost aloud and for a bare instant the rapport sagged, then he held it fast. He knew, suddenly, that he dared not falter, or this strange magical fire of the mind would flare out of control and become ordinary fire that would consume Desideria. Desperately intense, he felt the indrawn sigh of the men behind him, the quality of their worship, as the fires played around the delicate girl who stood calmly in the bathing flames. Her body, her light dress, her loosely braided hair, seemed to flicker in the fires.

With a scrap of awareness on the edge of his consciousness, Barron heard shouts and cries from the wall above, but he dared not cast an eye upward. He held desperately to the rapport between the girl in the flames and the forge folk.

An arrow flew from nowhere; behind them someone cried out and an almost invisible thread broke and was gone, but Barron was barely conscious of it. He knew without full consciousness that something had roused the castle, that Brynat's men knew they were under strange attack. But his mind was fixed on Desideria.

There was a great surge of the flame, and a great shout from behind them. Desideria cried aloud in surprise and terror and wonder, and then—before Barron's eyes, her frail fire-clad figure seemed to grow immensely upward, to take on height, majesty and power. And then it was no delicate girl who stood there, but a great veiled Shape, towering to the very height of the outworks and castle, a woman in form, hair of dancing flame, tossing wildly on the wind, wrapped in garments of flame and with upraised arms from which dangled golden chains of fire.

A great sighing cry went up from forge folk and village people crowded behind them.

"Sharra! Sharra, flame-haired, flame-crowned, golden-chained—Sharra! Child of Fire!"

The great Shape towered there, laughing, tossing arms and long fiery locks in a wild exultation. Barron could feel the growing flood of power, the linked minds and emotions of the worshippers, pouring through him and into Desideria—into the flame-form, the Form of Fire.

Random thoughts spun dizzily at the edge of his mind. *Chains. Is this why they chain their women in the Dry Towns? The legends run, if Sharra ever broke her chains the world would explode in flame. . . . There is an old saying on Terra that Fire is a good servant but a poor master. On Darkover too; every planet that knows fire has that by-word. Larry! You! Where are you? Nowhere here; I speak to your mind, I will be with you later.*

He dropped back into rapport with Desideria, vaguely knowing he had never left it and that he was moving now outside normal time and space perception. Somehow Storn was there too, but Barron shut out that perception, shut out everything but the lines of force almost visibly streaming from the worshippers—through his body and mind, and into the Form of Fire. With multiplied perception he could see into and through the Form of Fire—see Desideria there looking tense and quiet and frail and somehow exultant—but it was not with his eyes.

Arrows were flying into the crowd now, dropping off men who fell strangely rapt and without crying out. One arrow flew into the Form of Fire, burst into flame and vanished in soundless, white heat. The Form loomed higher and higher. There came a loud outcry from behind the castle walls as the great Form of Sharra stretched out arms with fingers extended—fingers from which ball fires and chain lightning dripped. The men on the walls shrieked insanely as their clothes burst into flame, as their bodies went up in the encompassing fire.

Barron never knew how long that strange and terrible battle raged, for he spent it in a timeless world, beyond fatigue and beyond awareness, feeling it when Brynat, raving, tried to rally his fleeing, burning, dying men; sensing it when the great Form of Fire, with a single blow, broke the outworks as if they had been carved in cheese. Brynat, desperate, brave against even the magic he did not believe in to the very end, charged along the walls, beyond the reach of the flames.

From somewhere a great white bird came flying. It flapped insanely around Brynat's head; he flung up his arms to batter it away, while it flew closer, stabbing with its glittering metallic beak at his eyes. He lost his balance, with a great cry; tottered, shrieked and fell, with a long, wailing scream, into the ravine below the castle.

The fires sank and died. Barron felt the net of force thin and drop away. He realized that he was on his knees, as if physically battered down by the tremendous streams of force that had washed over him. Melitta stood fixed, dumb-founded, staring at the heights.

And Desideria, only a girl again—a small, fragile, red-haired and white-faced girl—was standing in the ring of the dying fire, trembling, her dress and hair unscorched. She gestured with her last strength and the fire flickered and went out. Spasmodically, she thrust the blue stone into the bosom of her dress; then she crumpled unconscious to the ground, and lay there as if dead.

Above them the great wall of the castle breached, with none left to resist them except the dying.

XV

THE forge folk picked up Desideria with reverent awe and carried her, through the break in the walls, inside the castle yard. They would have done the same to Barron, except that he made them put him down, and went to Melitta, who stood weak-kneed and white. The forge folk disposed of the dead simply, by tossing them into a deep chasm; after some time the wheeling of the *kyorebni,* the corbies and lammergeiers of Darkover, over the crags marked their resting place. In their enthusiasm they would have thrown the wounded and dying after them, but Barron prevented them and was astonished at the way in which his word was taken for law. When he, had stopped them he wondered why he had done it; what was going to happen to these bandits now? There weren't any prisons on Dark-over that he knew about, except for the equivalent of a brig, in Trade City, where unprovoked fighters and obstreperous drunks were put to cool off for second thoughts; anyone who committed a worse crime of violence either died in the attempt or killed anyone who might try to prevent him. Perhaps Darkover would have to think again about penalties less than death, and he frankly wished Aldaran the joy of the task.

At Melitta's orders they went down into the dungeon and freed young Edric of Storn, whom Barron found, to

THE WINDS OF DARKOVER

his surprise and consternation, to be a boy of fifteen. The terrible wounds he had sustained in the siege were healing, but Barron realized with dismay that the child would bear the scars, and go lame all his life. He welcomed his rescuers with the courtly phrases of a young king, then broke down and sobbed helplessly in Melitta's arms.

Allira, numbed and incoherent with terror—she had not known whether they were being rescued or attacked by someone eager to replace Brynat—they found hiding in the Royal Suite. Barron, who had formed a strange picture of her from Melitta's thoughts, found her to be a tall, fair-haired, quiet girl—to most eyes more beautiful than Melitta —who came quickly back from terror. With dignity and strength, she came to thank their helpers and place herself at their service, and then to devote herself to reviving and comforting Desideria.

Barron was almost numb with fatigue, but he was too tense to relax even for an instant. He thought, *I'm tired and hungry, I wish they'd bring on the victory feast or something*, but he knew firmly in his mind, *This isn't the end. There's more to come, damn it.*

He realized with disbelief that the sun had risen less than thirty degrees above the horizon; the whole dreadful battle had been over in little more than an hour.

The great white bird, glittering as if formed of jewels that shone through the feathers, swooped low over him; it seemed to be urging him upward. Melitta behind him, clutching at his hand, he climbed the long stairs. He passed through the archway, through the blue tingle of the magnetic field and into the room where the silken bier lay. On it lay the form of a man—sleeping, tranced or dead—like a pale statue, motionless. The bird fluttered above it; suddenly flapped and dropped askew to the floor, lying there in a limp dead tangle of feathers gleaming with jewels, like some broken mechanical toy.

Storn opened blind eyes and sat up, stretching out his hand to them in welcome.

Melitta flew to him, clasping her arms around his neck, laughing and crying at once. She started to tell him, but he smiled bleakly. "I saw it all—through the bird's eyes—the last thing I shall ever see." He said, "Where is Barron?"

Barron said, "I am here, Storn." He had felt that at this

moment he would be ready to kill the man; now he felt all his rage and fury drain out of him. He had been a part of this man for days. He could not hate him or even resent him. What could he do to a blind man, a frail invalid? Storn was saying in a low voice, ridden with something like shame, "I owe it all to you. I owe everything to you. But I have suffered for it—and I will take whatever comes."

Barron did not know what to say. He said roughly, "Time enough to settle that later, and it won't be me you have to settle it with."

Storn rose, leaning heavily on Melitta, and took a few fumbling steps. Barron wondered if he were lame, along with everything else, but Storn sensed the thought and said, "No, only stiff from prolonged trance. Where is Desideria?"

"I am here," she said from behind them, and came forward to take his hand.

He said, almost in a whisper, "I would have liked to see your face once, only once, with my own eyes." He fell silent with a sigh. Barron had no longer any anger against Storn, only pity; and he knew, with that new and expanded awareness that was never to leave him, that his pity was the worst revenge he could have taken on the man who had stolen his work, his body, and his soul.

A horn sounded far below them in the courtyard, and the women rushed to the window. Barron did not have to follow them. He knew what had happened. Valdir Alton, with Larry and his men, had arrived. He had followed them through half the mountains, and when he lost them, had come directly here, knowing that sooner or later, it must end here. Barron no longer wondered how his masquerade had been known for Storn. Larry had been in rapport with him too long for any surprise.

Storn drew himself upright, with a quiet assumption of courage that did much to dilute the pity and redeem him in Barron's eyes. "My punishment is in Comyn hands," he said, almost to himself. "Come, I must go and welcome my guests—and my judges."

"Judge you? Punish you?" Valdir said, hours later, when formalities were over. "How could I punish you worse than the fate you have brought on yourself, Loran of Storn? From freedom you are bound, from sight, you are blind again. Did you really think it was only to protect their victims that we made what you have done our greatest taboo?"

Barron had found it hard to face Valdir; now, before the man's hard justice, he looked directly at him and said, "Among other things, I owe you for a horse."

Valdir said quietly, "Keep it. His identical twin and stable mate was being trained for my guest gift to you when you had finished your work among us; I shall bestow him upon Gwynn instead. I know you were not responsible for leaving us so abruptly, and we have you—or Storn," he smiled faintly, "to thank for saving the entire station, and all the horses, the night of the Ghost Wind."

He turned to Desideria and his eyes were more severe. He said; "Did you know that we had laid Sharra, centuries ago?"

"Yes," she flared at him, "your people in the Comyn would rob us both of Terra's new powers—and Darkover's old ones."

He shook his head. "I am not happy with what the Aldarans are doing. But then, I am not entirely happy with what my own people are doing, either. I do not like the idea that Terra and Darkover shall always be the irresistible force and immovable object. We are brother worlds; we should be joined—and instead—the battle between us is joined. All I can say is—God help you, Desideria—any god you can find! And you know the law. You have involved yourself in a private feud and stirred up telepathic power in two who did not have it; now you, and you alone, are responsible for teaching your—victims—to guard themselves. You will have little leisure for your work as a Keeper, Desideria. Storn, Melitta and Barron are your responsibility now. They must be trained to use the powers you broke open in them."

"It was not I all alone," she said, "Storn discovered these things on his own—and it will be my joy, not my burden, to help him!" She glared at Valdir defiantly, and took Storn's pale hands between her own.

Larry turned to Barron, with a glance at Valdir as if asking permission. He said, "You still have work with us. You need not return to the Terran Zone unless you like—and, forgive me, I think you have no place there now."

Barron said, "I don't think I ever did." Melitta did not

move, but nevertheless he felt as if Melitta had come to stand beside him, as he said, "I've never belonged anywhere but here."

In a queer flash he saw a strange divided future; a Terran working both for and against Terra on this curiously divided world, torn relentlessly and yet knowing where he belonged. Storn had robbed him of his body and in return had given him a heart and a home.

He knew that this would always be his place; that if Storn had taken his place, he would take Storn's, increasingly with the years. He would master the new world, seeing it through doubled eyes. The Darkover they knew would be a different world. But with Melitta beside him, he had no fears about it; it was a good world—it was his own.

The ship's controls had been set for destruction, and agent Selena Ash realized that someone else knew she was not the idle playgirl she seemed. Whoever had sent her into uncharted space against her will must have known of her mission to trace the path of a long-dead Space Scout and find a miraculous tree. But they could not have known that in her attempt to escape she would stumble upon the fabulous planet they sought.

It was a world like Paradise, perfect in its serenity, until the advent of man aroused its sleeping powers, forces which knew nothing of good or evil. Once on the planet, Selena dared not turn back, though she found herself in the company of deadly and hostile plant life, monstrous carnivores, and the strange savage who was to lead her through a dream—and a nightmare—in search of the Tree that is All Things.

Turn this book over for
second complete novel

JOHN RACKHAM
has also written:

THE DOUBLE INVADERS
ALIEN SEA
THE PROXIMA PROJECT
IPOMOEA
TREASURE OF TAU CETI

THE
ANYTHING
TREE

JOHN RACKHAM

AN ACE BOOK

Ace Publishing Corporation
1120 Avenue of the Americas
New York, N.Y. 10036

THE ANYTHING TREE

Copyright ©, 1970, by John Rackham

All Rights Reserved

Cover art by John Schoenherr.

——————————

THE WINDS OF DARKOVER

Copyright ©, 1970, by Marion Zimmer Bradley

Printed in U.S.A.

ONE

SELENA ASH was whistling to herself. It was not a tune, but just the soft sibilance of preoccupation as she carefully stripped herself of artifice and pretense. Away into storage went her shimmer-silk absurdity of a dress, the jewel-studded shoes and the expensive but pointless knicknacks; tissues and pin-prick tweaking cleaned away the hectic bloom of cosmetics and false hair; she used cream to eradicate the last traces, and it was all done without any thought. Her mind was elsewhere. Around her, the versatile little space-coupe pursued its set course. There was no hurry; she had more than four days. The mad rush of butterfly brainless-ness which spelled out fun for the idle rich on the paradise continent Shangri-La of the playground planet of Tau Ceti III dwindled into her past. She buttoned herself into a white papertex coverall, put her feet into sandals, and went back up the ladder to the control room, not because there was anything to control—the auto mechanisms handled that—but simply because it was where she felt organized.

And she might need the services of the computer to help her with a problem or two. She settled into her seat, cast a routine eye over the dials assembled—blinked—and looked again. She felt an icy chill at her stomach. There was some-thing wrong, something so blatantly wrong that, for a mo-ment, she couldn't accept it. The read-out figure for time of arrival stood at a few minutes over four hours, which was monstrous! She spent a second going over her take-off pro-cedure. Lift-off had been automatic and all clear. In that interval she had preprogrammed for her destination and set the relay switch to kick in the warp as soon as she was clear of the planetary field. That had all happened.

Her program had been for Luna Base, well over a week's journey even at this light-bending speed. She had been flying this little space-coupe or one like it for the past five of her twenty-five years, and it was just not possible that she could have made such a mistake. There were other things wrong, too. She drew a deep and steadying breath and did the

first thing one must always do in doubt—stop everything and take stock. She hit the manual dewarp, shivered through the instant of nausea, then eyed the glowing screens which gave her several pictures of vast expanses spotted with stars.

"Now, then," she murmured, and started by pushing down on the interlock. It was already hard down, as it should be. The interlock is the last button one pushes, when everything is set up and smoothly rolling. Then, should anything fail, the interlock throws everything out and screams for attention. It wasn't that. But there is, also, an interlock cancel button, and that, too, was down—which in theory was impossible. She peered closely at it and tugged. It rose sluggishly, leaving a thin layer of some kind of cement.

"Oh, very tricky!" she congratulated someone as yet unknown. Stick a layer of gum on the cancel, press it home, and there you are. No matter what someone else does, no matter what goes wrong, there will be no alarm—neat, simple and deadly. A cold fury began to stir in her mind. Blaming herself was just part of it. She had found it necessary to play the part of an empty-headed social butterfly, and one couldn't do that *and* openly own a ship that was stiff with crafty protective devices and unorthodox equipment. She had set her watchogs in abeyance; she deserved this sabotage, or whatever it was. But who was responsible? Belatedly she remembered that she hadn't eliminated *all* her guards. There was one, a spy-eye. She touched certain switches on the computer, and a side-screen lit up to give her a picture of a young man about her own age, a handsome —perhaps overhandsome—fair young man with a forelock of bright yellow hair, laughing eyes, and very white teeth. She knew him. It was Pierre Lacoste, only son of a wealthy manufacturer of domestic robot equipment. She wondered whether he would know enough to be able to gimmick her ship. Before she could decide, the spy-record stuttered and shifted to another picture, this time of a taller man of the same age. He was lean and satirical, dark-haired, and self-consciously tough, and she knew him also. The man was Robin Delmar, the current hero and star of the jet-boat set, winner of just about every event in the known Galaxy that involved rockets or jets.

"Well, now," she breathed, halting her electronic stool-pigeon. "There's something, by God!" She took her time re-

viewing what she knew of the two people involved. Together they might just possibly possess enough knowledge to monkey with the ship. Both of them owned and flew their own ships, superficially the same as this one. It was possible but unlikely unless she could think of some reason why. Pierre and Robin and she had been a merry-making trio for some time. Both men had made the expected and routine passes at her and missed. It was part of her art that she could fend off such men without offending them; and they were friendly rivals. But it was nothing more than that, she would swear. She would stake her life that neither man believed her to be anything more than the gay daredevil daughter of Conway Ash—a somebody in reflected glory, for Conway Ash, as chief scientific advisor to the United Planets Office of Technological Strategy, was a force in his own right—but in herself just another rich playgirl.

Stake my life, she mused over her own thought. She might have to do just that, if either of them had found out what she really was, and why. She put the thought away, determined to come back to it only if driven. Assume, then, that Pierre and Robin had gimmicked her ship somehow—for what? The immediate and appropriate answer came back—a joke—and it fitted. If that pair had anything at all in common it was a hilarious (they thought) sense of the absurd. She shook her head wryly, her fury abating somewhat. She spent another moment fitting herself into their viewpoint, then touched another control on her computer, which was not the standard model it appeared to be, but had refinements known only to her and the experts who had installed it.

"Definition," she stated. "Tracer. For your purpose a tracer is any contrivance or device which can be lodged in or on a ship or person such that it will generate a signal detectable at a distance and thus enable its location to be pinpointed by some other appropriate device. Understood?"

The blink signal came up instantly, and she shifted to another button. "Inspect this ship now—thoroughly, inside and out—and contents, including me, for signs of a tracer, and then report."

The answer was thirty-five seconds in coming, which surprised her. The answer itself surprised her even more.

"Four extraneous objects," the computer reported, "match

the given definition. All are broadcasting powerful and continuous signals on the uhf waveband. One has been incorporated into the ship radio console, the others are attached to the hull on the outside. Locations—"

"Never mind, we'll get to that later." She cut the report off and shook her head. "Four? My, my, that doesn't sound like Pierre and Robin. The plan is fine: monkey with my course computer, strand me somewhere, then come dashing to the rescue—the fools! But *four* separate tracers?" She gave up that thought and went back to her spy-eye to try again, more from curiosity than anything else. She got another shock—more faces. The first one was gross and barely human—a fleshy gargoyle of a man with a nose and chin to batter down any obstacle, a craggy brow overshadowing two black eyes, and a mouth that had no lips at all. The next was as different as could be imagined. It was a mature and controlled woman with a face like an underworld madonna—sculptured and flawless—and jet-black hair framed by a glossy helmet. That face could charm away a man's senses—like a snake. Selena ran those two again.

"Those I have never seen before," she breathed. "I couldn't possibly forget a pair like that. God knows how they come to be in cahoots with Pierre and Robin, but the four tracers now begin to make a little more sense. Still, they surely weren't so naïf as to believe that they could toss me light-years into the unknown and then find me on the tail of a uhf tracer!" The answer to that one was obvious, once she saw it. One of them had preprogrammed a rendezvous, and then gimmicked the course computer so that her program was void. But there had to be more.

"I get to where they have planned and dewarp; that's all right. But then I take a fast look around, realize something has gone wrong, and—so, they must have fixed something else, to stop me from doing just that. Let's see just what, shall we?"

She swung her chair out of the way, grasped at quick-twist bolt-heads, loosened them, and swung out the entire front casing of the course computer. Her anger was seeping back, not at the joke which had been played on her, but at the posture she would now have to adopt because of it. If she went ahead and used her skills to get out of their childish trap, bang went her false front as Selena Ash, brain-

less butterfly. And it had cost her time and trouble to set up. On the other hand, if she stayed in character and just sat there, helpless and afraid, waiting to be picked up—but what about those two vultures she had seen who were also in on it?

She pulled open a drawer and fished for tools, clicked on a tiny pencil-torch, peered within at the works—and felt another chill. There were the neat rows of second-order relays. Seven of them were tip-tilted to various settings and neatly disconnected from the panel controls so that they couldn't be altered. The pattern was not immediately obvious but she could discover it later. What chilled her right now was a small aluminum capsule that was patch-wired into the warp-out relays. That innocent-looking tube had markings on it, but even without those she would have recognized it for what it was, because she had seen things like it before. The picture burned in her mind. The course computer would run to its completed setting, relays would close, others would open—and that small but deadly destruct module would explode—and that would be the last useful work that computer, or that ship, would ever do. She felt cold sweat break out on her when she realized that if she had not dewarped on the emergency manual control, she would be dead now.

She looked at it for a long while, making herself think. Less and less did this feel like Pierre and Robin. Fools they might be, but this kind of senseless and dangerous destruction was not in their picture. Perhaps it fitted the other pair, though, and that only made the mystery more confusing. At length she backed away and returned to the drawer for more tools. She took long bits and blades and very delicately cut loose the little bomb. With that done, she thought a bit more.

The false front was finished, that much was obvious. Sexy Selena would never have been able to find that bomb or recognize it, much less remove it. But it couldn't be allowed to rest there. Whatever the score was, she had to find out just what was going on. The obvious way to do that was to go wherever it was they had planned her to go, and see what was laid on. That called for a little preparation and thought. First she made a careful note of the relay settings, and, with spider tongs, adjusted the board from

below until she could reconnect and make everything good. Then she closed the console again, put away her tools, checked that everything was in order, hit the warp switch and held her breath.

Apart from the customary instant of nausea as the ship leaped into its interrupted path, nothing happened. She breathed again, buttoned down the interlock, and then applied herself once more to the computer's special circuitry.

"First," she said, "you will check right through the ship, looking for anything—any other extraneous devices or anomalies—anything!"

That drew a highly reassuring blank. "Now," she said more easily, "extrapolate from the course settings and identify destination. Read it out for me."

The shimmering blue figures came up almost at once and didn't mean a thing. She scowled, shaking her head.

"Halfway to nowhere. Celestial reference chart, please!"

The tabulated data dissolved, gave way to a schematic star map with a small blue winker to indicate the spot she was headed for. She eyed it, shook her head again. "Any further data?" The picture stayed steady.

"That's it," she sighed. "And what a waste of time that was. 'Way out in the wilds—uncharted space at least thirty lights away from Tau Ceti, and more than twice that from anywhere known."

She cancelled the display, glanced at the ETA figure, saw just under four hours, and nodded. There was a glint in her gray eyes that would have astonished her recent cronies.

"Time for a meal," she said, "and a nap. And then I set up a few odd things on my own hook. If somebody really is trying to kill me, I want to know who, and why, and maybe to register an objection or two."

TWO

SHE AWOKE with fifteen minutes to spare before her deadline, just long enough to sweep the fog from her thoughts and be ready as the passing seconds counted down. Her instructions were all keyed in and ready. The arrival warning bonged sonorously, there came that instant inside-out feeling, star-fields lit the screens, and in the same second her computer was gobbling a mass of data, processing it, and getting ready to go. She read the situation with grim delight. Luck! There was a small sun and planetary system no more than four-tenths of a light away. And there was one small, solid, metal, power-emitting object much closer than that—as she had expected. She saw this all in one fast survey, then, as fast as her fingers could move, she aimed for that insignificant sun-system and buttoned for a hop. Sliced seconds later there was a raving glow in her forward screens, and it called for hasty but sure adjustments while she spun into orbit about it. That done she sat back.

"All right, whoever you are," she challenged. "Let's see how long it takes you to sort your tracers from this mush. Try and find me, if you can!"

She felt sure they would, but not immediately, and that was as much as she had hoped for. She now had a breathing space in which to dig a better hiding place. She got busy with scanner and analysis; her radio was on to listen to the blanketing wash of static from the unnamed sun. Whoever was in that ship was hardly likely to broadcast his presence yet. Before anything else, he was going to have to think up some reason why she was not just hung there helpless. And that might make him pause a little. Meanwhile she went over the data on this sun's planets in the hope of finding somewhere to stop. She did not fancy being attacked in space. Her ship was special, and versatile far beyond its routine appearance, but it wasn't that good. On the ground she could even the odds quite a bit. And she was lucky again. One of the slow-circling planets, the

second out, looked promising. Indeed, as she went over the data again, it was more than that.

"Very nice!" She approved. "Sub-tropical primitive, slightly smaller than Earth, acceptable atmosphere and temperatures—might have been made to order." She got busy again, but not rashly. Distant figures and analyses give only a part of the picture. A lushly welcoming planet might turn out to be anything but that on closer acquaintance, and this place was completely off the charts. She slid into a thousand-mile orbit and gave the detection complexes another workout. The acceptability still stood up, so she studied the surface and selected her spot with care and an eye to the questions of cover and defense. There were many minor landmasses, and one enormous one lying athwart the equator. At its northern tip was a beaky promontory, a long flat plain backed by rugged mountains, with dense forest on either side of them.

"That," she decided, "will do me very well. Down among the trees, with the plain in front, the mountains at my back, sea on either side, and let them come and get me—if they can!"

She went down, using the ship's extra-powerful grav-fields to check her fall right up to the last minute, and then settled stern-first among the trees with the absolute minimum of scorching and burning to leave marks for others to notice. And then, with a sigh, she was able to sit back once more. She had an hour in which the sensitive sniffing systems would subject every indrawn molecule to severe scrutiny and assess it for danger. That particular analytical plant, too, was not standard on a ship like this, but Selena by now had abandoned all shadow of pretense of being standard. Whoever it was who had initiated this round of fun-and-games would soon find that he had taken on more than he realized. She reviewed her strategy. They had been laying for her, that much was proven. She had no idea why, but that could wait. Her evasion had been fast, but she was not kidding herself that she had escaped without detection. They had seen her arrive. The ship's bulk itself, even without their tracers, would have rung that bell. But she had warped out again, and that might throw them for a while, especially as they had every right to assume that she would be helpless.

She pondered it. They would have to assume that the bomb damage was not as total as they had planned—but that she *was* damaged, partly crippled. Therefore, in logic, she would have to find landfall somewhere close—which she had done. They would come to look; but she had time to listen to the thousand and one small noises of the surrounding forest re-establishing itself after her arrival. There was time to admire the view in her screens. The forward cameras had two pictures: on one there was a waving mass of tree-tops, and beyond those a mountain range, purple with distance and, in one or two instances, white-crested with snow; on the other she saw more treetops, a glimpse of a silvery yellow beach, and the rolling sea. The stern viewers showed her a quiet wilderness of tree trunks and a profusion of tangled bushes and creepers heavy with multicolored blooms.

"This is quite a place," she declared. "If the life systems check out—and that is quite a big *if*, of course—this is quite a find! Might even be worth laying claim to!"

The idea amused her for a while. Because of a number of nasty legal hassles over rights to the first few desirable planets that had been discovered, there were several iron-clad statutes on the books, one of which effectively stopped any whole-planet claims by individuals or minorities. The first person to locate, establish and record the existence of a new planet had an inalienable right to claim one square mile of its surface—any square mile—as his property, to dispose of as he saw fit. But that was all.

That line of speculation filled the time until the life systems yielded up their verdict. She studied the data carefully. Everything was in the green, except for two items which were underlined for her attention. One was an inconclusive harmless measurement of longwave electromagnetic radiation of unknown origin. The other was an activation analysis of certain complex organic molecules common to the local botanical spectrum; it was not harmful either, but unusual and unexplained.

She frowned, went back to the longwave electromagnetic radiation, then clicked her tongue in chagrin. One might as well try to measure the temperature with a foot rule! Of course one wouldn't expect a chemical analysis to recogize radio! But why was it on the longwave band? It had to be local, from the surface. Longwaves could not push

through the ionosphere. Maybe that was the reason—so that no one outside would get them! She turned on her radio, which was still yielding hushed static, and there it was, on the tell-tale—a winking green neon that said something was coming in. She made adjustments and tuned down, and suddenly there was a drawly male voice in the middle of a sentence.

"—liked that. I did, too. Here's another one you're going to like, by a feller named Strauss. It's called Morning Papers, which can't mean a thing to you, because you never saw a morning paper—nor yet an evening one, for that matter—but who cares about that? Here it comes, now," and the slow voice, an outrageous caricature of hillbilly drawl, went away and on came the classic Strauss waltz.

Selena felt the first faint twinge of unreality. She stared at her radio in frank unbelief, and tapped it just to make sure. Rational explanation eluded her completely. That someone else had found this planet ahead of her and had landed wasn't so hard to take. She had considered that very possibility, although in a slightly different context. But that such a predecessor would refrain from making contact in the normal way, by uhf or a visual signal and would then broadcast, like this, as if to an audience—on longwave was incredible. She put her thumb on the transmit switch and hesitated uneasily. So many unlikely things had happened that she wondered if maybe the trouble was in herself.

"Curiouser and curiouser," she quoted wryly, and managed a smile. "I'm sure I was perfectly normal when I took off!" It was something of a shock to count up the hours and realize just how recently that was. Then, bracing herself, she pushed the button and drew breath.

"This is space-coupe K.T. one-oh-four, out of Luna and Shangri-La; Selena Ash, owner-pilot, speaking. Who are you? Identify!"

She repeated it, then released the button and waited. The Strauss lilt went on. There was neither reply nor any sign she had been heard. She shrugged it off, getting a little tired of trying to answer questions without data. Whoever it was, she could try again later. She had other things to attend to, such as the four tracers. The module in her radio was simple, she could deal with that at once and did so. It had been patched in and was a standard broad-channel

whistler which told her nothing at all. She crushed it and tossed the fragments into the disposal. The outside ones would need something a little more elaborate.

She tried her tool drawer again, took a small satchel and loaded it with what she hoped would be enough and slung it over her shoulder. Then she got out a small beamer and grip and buckled it about her hips, smiling her wry smile as she realized just how wide-eyed either Robin or Pierre would be if they could see this—or would they? Her smile became a cold menace as she reflected that she had not yet properly evaluated the possibility that those two apparently innocent young men may have taken her for a very fast ride! She didn't want to add in that value, because it would mean she had lost what was possibly her biggest advantage.

She went out and down the gangway ladder, debating in her mind whether to rig it with a few safety precautions. Then she glanced around at the peaceful greenery and decided against it. She had no intention of going very far away, just far enough to be able to get at those tracers. And she was quite confident of her ability to handle anything obvious that might come up. There was a circle of scorched vegetation around the base of the ship which gave her a clear walkway until she could come to one of the landing feet. She saw the thing she was after where a strut crossed and merged with the hull. A small chunk of dull silver metal clung limpetlike to the nook between strut and hull; it was the sort of thing no one would notice without having it pointed out. There was another on the other side and one right under the stern, by the steering venturi. They were slick, professional jobs, not at all in keeping with Pierre and Robin.

She rummaged in her satchel and brought out a thick tube of plastic nine inches long. Into one end she fitted an alloy chisel bit; the other end carried a knurled band, which she twisted while gripping the shaft of the tube. She twisted hard, and the tube grew lengthwise as it shrank in girth, telescoping out, longer and longer, but still rigid. She aimed it upwards and kept on squeezing until it was long enough to reach the offending object. Now —unless it was welded on, and she didn't think they'd had time for that—she was going to chip it off. Taking careful

aim, she gripped both hands, lowered, and then jabbed upwards strongly. After another solid jab she thought she could see the beginnings of a crack and nodded. It was epoxy-resin, most probably. She shifted her position slightly, took another swing—and the thing flew apart with a flare and explosion which deafened and blinded her for a moment. She felt the quick heat of it on her face, and the jerk as the explosion whipped her tool out of her grasp and out of sight among the bushes.

She stood still, her ears jangling and her vision full of dark spots, then shook her head grimly. Very nasty—someone was playing very rough indeed. This was not *her* playmates, at all. Suppose she had, somehow, climbed up there to remove that thing! As soon as she could see and hear well enough she stooped, ducked under her ship and out the other side; this time she wasted no motions on delicacy. Drawing her beamer, she laid her wrist alongside the hull, took aim, shut her eyes and fired. Once more there was a bright flash and a thunderclap explosion, but this time she was ready for it and untroubled.

"I think," she murmured, "we'll leave him just one. After all, I'd hate to have him miss me, after all the trouble he's gone to."

She crouched and passed under her ship again to where she had started from, and tried to recall which way her long chisel had flown—not far, surely. Reliving the moment and remembering, she worked out a direction, and started off cautiously to look for it, parting the bushes and taking care not to get confused. Three steps got her to more bushes, and then, as she eased through them and stood, she was looking across a small clearing, an open space about six or seven yards across. There by the foot of a tree, was her chisel. But it wasn't just there. It was held firmly by the man who had picked it up.

THREE

HER FIRST impression was of bulk pared down to the precise needs of efficiency. He was over six feet tall, but the relaxed yet alert way he stood and the shift and play of the long

ropy muscles in his forearm as he turned over her rod to inspect it, modified that first impression into a more accurate assessment of power, not just size. He belonged here, in some indefinable yet positive way, as fittingly as the tree against which he stood. She took another breath to study him in detail: the broad sloping shoulders, filled-out chest, lean waist, strong legs, leather-tanned skin, but most of all his neck and the set of his head. A god of the greenwood—the term came unbidden and unwanted. In her instinctive rejection of it she drew her beamer and leveled it at him.

Then she was able to take time for closer study still because he seemed totally unaware of her presence. His blond hair, very pale and washed out by exposure, hung in a rude shock to his shoulders. About his hips, either as a ragged belt or a skimpy loincloth, was a band of curiously woolly stuff, some kind of fiber, which served to support a bright bladed knife and a curious pouch. Her eyes narrowed at the latter. It contained soil. From it sprang a slim green stem with tiny regular leaves; the stem climbed up and over his chest, around his left shoulder and then vanished into the thicket of his hair. Just beyond him, leaning against the tree, was a seven foot spear of yellow-brown wood, the final foot of it shining metal like his knife. Was he a native—a wild man? She couldn't quite believe that, not by the way he was studying her chisel. Not when he gripped it experimentally and began twisting the knurled end, so that it began to contract again.

The moment stretched. What does one say in a case like this? Then she received a shock as her eyes again followed that twisting, climbing stem to where it lost itself in his hair —and saw a big and bright blue eye peering out. An eye? She caught her breath again as she realized that it was no more than a flower head, that only *seemed* to be staring at her. But it was enough to sharpen her mood. She stepped one more pace to be clear of the bushes and waved the beamer for reassurance.

"Hold it!" she advised firmly. "Hold it right there!" He didn't move as much as a single muscle. "I don't know whether you can understand me or not, but don't do anything fast. Just turn, slowly." He turned quite easily and with no sign of surprise whatever. His head came around first, then the rest of him, and she met a calm stare from

17

the brightest and yet most impersonal eyes she had ever seen, uncannily like the one-eyed look of the blue flower. If there was an expression at all on his face it was of guarded curiosity.

"This is a weapon," she warned, waving the beamer again. "Who are you?"

After a moment for seeming thought he said, "Call me Joe. Better put that weapon away out of your hand, ma'am." His voice was a soft drawl, seeming to drop the words half-way between them. The same drawl she had heard on the longwave with the music.

"You're civilized! Why the primitive savage bit?"

"Why not? Who's to notice? Better put away your hardware."

"Why should I? What are you afraid of?"

"Not me. I live here. It's you. All the time you're clutching that thing you're feeling aggressive. That's a reflex. You can't help it. But the plants around these parts are sensitive to that kind of thing. They don't like it a bit. I'm doing all I can to comfort 'em, else they'd have had you long ago. Better put it up. I can't hold 'em still forever."

He was very calm, almost indifferent, nor had he made another move after facing her. His bland superiority irritated her.

"You're out of your mind. You're masterminding plants! Do you really expect me to believe that?"

"Don't expect you to believe nothing," he said, with what could have been a small smile tugging at the corner of his mouth. "Guess you're the kind as has to be shown. Just don't blame it on me, that's all. It's all right, Friendly, you can relax!" He moved his right hand slowly across his chest to reach the inquisitive blue flower on his shoulder, to spread his palm, still slowly, and cover that bright blue eye.

Selena saw his hand curl into a cup—and shrieked as lashing twigs fastened on her ankles, her wrist, curled about her waist, stooped down to tangle in her hair—twigs with thorns, stringy and strong twigs that gripped and tore and contracted with pressure. Needles of pain erupted from her skin where the sharp-toothed thorns bit. Pressure constricted her breast, her waist, slimp ropes dragged at her legs until

18

she began to totter, and the more she struggled the harder the coils tightened, until panic blossomed in her heart.

"Now stop!" His voice suddenly had the edge of authority. "You been shown, now? How much more do you want? Quit struggling!"

His scorn sliced through her panic, biting deeper than plant's venom. Breathlessly she held still, feeling the slow glide and coiling of more ropy twigs. "Better. Just hold still, and pay attention to me, I can't do it all by myself, you have to help. First off, drop that fool weapon, you hear?" She unclenched her hand and heard the beamer thud to the turf. "That's fine! Now, comb the fright out of your mind. You have to feel friendly, real friendly, to the plants and me and everything. Go on, feel friendly. Pretty flowers! Nice, kind plants. You didn't mean them any harm. You *like* plants! Go on, do it!"

She couldn't—not at first. The inescapable awareness of physical helplessness wouldn't allow it. There were tightly constricting bands of living fiber about her body and a thousand small scratches burned painfully on her skin. But she did realize, as she held fearfully still, that the snaky plants were still, too.

"Me and Friendly can stop 'em," he pointed out, still with quiet scorn, "but we can't make 'em back up, not while you're boiling like that!"

I'll get you, she vowed. *Later!* And then, swallowing and making a great effort, she took charge of herself; she willed herself to feel kindly towards the ropy green horrors—no, that wouldn't do—towards the pleasant and pretty plants which were caressing her to show their delight at her presence. *Nice plants, pretty bushes, such beautiful flowers and leaves*—it was almost the hardest thing she had ever done. It was ridiculous, offensive to common sense and destructive to dignity, but she made the silly phrases form in her mind and repeated them. She felt the capturing strands loosen, little by little. Fervently she filled her mind with beneficent thoughts towards all vegetation, and the snaking strands began to uncurl, to withdraw and to leave her free. That sensation was a strange and creepy one, but she buried that thought deep under a flood of sickly praise and flattery until the last leathery bond had shifted away and she was free.

Aloof and superior, he was still standing there watching her. She moved a step, catching her breath at the instant agony from a host of scratches. Another, and she stooped like someone with rheumatism to take up her beamer. In that moment she caught sight of her hips and legs, and the once-neat coverall was a shredded and rapidly dissolving ruin, melting even as she stared at it; it was rotting away under the sticky green ichor of the venomous plants. That, somehow, was more than she could stand—on top of the other humiliations. She seized the weapon, intending to run clear of the horrors behind her, and then she would make him—but she never got so far as deciding just what punishment would be fitting. It was as if a mighty padded fist slammed down on the top of her head, drove her down into the ground and into darkness.

She came back to consciousness flat on her back, with a sour-acid taste in her mouth and the instant intuition that it would be unwise to move. The assurance of pain was very close. The ceiling looked familiar; it was her own. She stirred, became aware that she was stretched out on her own bunk and covered by the thin foil of an insulex blanket; the pain wasn't as bad as she had dreaded. Half sitting, turning her head, she could see through the half-open cabin door into the control room. This was the upper-deck cabin, just big enough to take a cot and necessaries; it was the one she used when on a solo flight, so that she could be near enough to the controls to get there fast, if necessary. The living cabins proper were one deck down. Why had he carried her all the way up here? She sat all the way up, disturbed by the implications of that thought; and there he was, Joe the non-savage, seated at her panel, listening curiously to her radio, so muted that all she could hear was a buzzing murmur. Disquiet grew in her mind as she realized she was quite nude under the crackly foil blanket.

"Don't try anything violent," he advised, without turning his head and without threat. "Those plant scratches carry a venom—not lethal, but it can be a pesty itch for a while. You have a real cute diagnoster unit here. I used it to whip up an injection for you that should take off the worst, but you have to give it time. Just hold still. I have coffee ready. I'll get it." He rose and went silently away on bare feet, posing her a little problem. Where before had she seen a man

move like that? It was not catlike, not at all tigerish, but flowing. Male ballet dancers—that was it. Then he was back with a self-heat carton for her and one for himself. He settled on the far edge of her cot.

"That's doped," he said, handing it to her. "Make you feel better fast. Mine's just to be sociable. How d'you feel?"

"I'm fairly comfortable." She sat up, grasping the thin foil and sipping the welcome warmth. "I suppose I ought to thank you."

"No matter. That venom, like I said, isn't lethal. You get enough of it in your system and it acts like alcohol—puts you down. That's what it's for. So the plants can take their time about tearing you apart and combining the remains with the soil. Don't mean anything; it's just their way of living."

"I see!" She repressed a shudder at the mental images which came. "I owe you my life, then. Are all the local plants like that?"

"More or less—all I know about. They don't do a thing if you keep calm and friendly. Sort of protective device, you could call it. Sensitive to emotional fields, I reckon."

Selena became sensitively aware that she was naked under the thin foil. "I'm grateful, of course, but was it absolutely necessary to take my clothes off?"

"Weren't none to take off," he retorted blandly. "That's one more bit you need to know. The local life is savage with any strange molecules. So far as I know, they bend their teeth on bright metal, like T-alloys, and one or two of the plastics, but they sure destroy anything else they don't like. That's why I wear this stuff. It's a local fiber."

"I see," she said again, feeling inadequate, and once more irritated, because it was not her pattern to feel diminished by anyone else, least of all a man. "You seem to be able to manage quite well."

"I live here," he said, as if that explained everything. "Been looking over your ship, ma'am. It's a dilly. Sure have been some improvements since—" he hesitated there, went off on another tack. "You seem to be in some kind of trouble, ma'am. Don't want to push it, but have you any plans in mind?"

"Trouble? Plans?" She put the carton aside. "You seem to know a lot about it?"

"Used my head a little, that's all. You had radio tracers stuck to your hull. You got rid of two, left one."

"You were watching me?"

"Right! You came down in a hellova hurry and then kept quiet. It all adds up this way. Somebody stuck a tail on you, and you were on the run. You scratched some of the tail, but left some, too. Means you want to be found, you maybe aim to put up some kind of resistance. By your board there, the enemy is right on to it and will be homing in any time."

"How long was I unconscious?"

"About twenty minutes. I figure it will take those birds up there a while yet to work out what they're going to do. Plenty of time for you to take off and blow!"

"I have no intention of taking off! Why do you imagine I came down here in the first place?"

"No idea, ma'am. I just want you to up-ship and get."

"Why? What's it to you?"

"This is my planet. I like it just the way it is."

"Your planet? *Your* planet? Who d'you think you are, anyway?"

It was as if an impenetrable shutter descended before his eyes and face and he went away, not physically but in some mental fashion. "I sort of figured you'd take it like that," he said softly and rose; he turned and was almost gone from sight before she could find voice.

"Wait! Stop! Where d'you think you're going?"

"Away. Out of the way. This is nothing of my affair."

She scrambled from the bunk, clutching at the foil cover, forcing unpleasant words into her mouth. "No, don't go. Look, Joe, I need your help!"

"Nothing I can do."

"But there is. Listen. I don't know who those people are up there or why they are after me. You've seen their style, the way those tracers were boobied with detonite. They play rough. Now, if I take off, I'm wide open. If you know anything about ships at all, you know that. This isn't an armored ship; I wouldn't stand a chance. This way, down on the ground, they have to land and come at me on the level. At least I'll have a chance to see who they are and maybe find out what this is all about."

"You don't need my help to sit here and wait for that."

"But I'm not going to sit here. I'm going out there. I'll

leave the ship sealed so they won't be able to get in—it's designed for that—and hide out somewhere near, and watch. Honestly, I don't know what this is all about, and I need to know, and that's the only way I can think of. And, for that, I need your help. You know this terrain!"

He stood blank-faced a long while, as the curious flower eye peered at her from over his shoulder. Then he stirred, and shook his head.

"All right, I reckon that's the best way to settle this thing. Come on, then!"

FOUR

SHE MADE a step then realized the state she was in. "Oh! What'll I wear?"

"Can't help you there, ma'am. Less you have something made of metal—maybe that foil would make a kind of wrap."

"Hardly. Besides, it would be visible for miles. Oh, I know!" and still clutching the inadequate foil sheet around her she scurried down one deck to her living space and dug into her wardrobe locker to produce a dress she had worn only once and never expected to wear again. It was made entirely of inch-diameter titanium rings cunningly interlinked—some limp-brained designer's notion of a chain-mail shirt, she believed. She had felt an utter fool wearing it the first time, and she didn't feel much happier about it now, but at least it would serve.

She went back up, to find him listening at the radio once more. "Are they sending?" she asked, and he wound up the volume so that she could hear.

". . . if you can. Reply if you can. This is G.R. six-oh-five calling ground. Are you reading me? Reply if you can, please!"

"Sounds friendly," he commented, cutting the sound. "Mean anything?"

"Yes indeed. G.R. six-oh-five—that's Robin Delmar's ship. She's very fast and fancy. He's a jet ace. I thought he was a friend of mine, but now I don't know; I'm not so sure.

Certainly not sure enough to go waltzing up there and be blown apart. No, hold on while I fix a thing or two."

He stood by the down hatch and let her get on with it, apparently much more interested in her tool bag than in what she was doing. She set certain mechanisms into watchfulness, established a code signal, caught up a tiny portable sender and her beamer, and buckled both to the metal belt of her dress. He, apparently, hadn't even noticed it; that piqued her a little. She was ill-accustomed to being ignored.

"This is quite a gadget, this expanding rod," he murmured, turning it over in his lean fingers. "New to me."

"New to almost anyone," she said. "You've seen a pair of lazy tongs? That molecular structure is the same. Lateral pressure creates a linear deformation in the structure. It's handy. Not on the open market yet, though."

"Yeah." He dropped it back in her satchel and lifted his head. "You ready? I'll show you a place to hide."

"Just a minute." She was beginning to catch nuances in his tone and attitude. "I don't mean that you shall show me somewhere—and then decamp!"

"This is none of my affair," he repeated stolidly. "I don't aim to get involved any more than I have to. You fight your own battles!"

"Now see here!" She sharpened her words angrily. "I am Selena Ash. My father is Conway Ash, chief advisor to the U.P. Office of Technological Strategy. You must have heard of him. You know he is a very important man. If anything should happen to me, he will want to know why, and who, and heads will roll. On the other hand, if I can tell him that you helped me . . ." She was talking to his back. He went down and away so fast that she had to scramble and run to catch him just at the head of the gangway.

"You're a coward," she snapped, and he halted easily.

"No, ma'am, just a disinterested bystander. Even if you are all you say—and there's no proof—your father can't do anything for me or to me."

"But I can!" She had a sudden and vindictive inspiration. "You had better be interested. If and when I get away from here—or someone gets away from here—there'll be talk, and you won't be able to stop it. This is a nice pleasant planet—highly desirable. The word will get around. People will come here in droves, thousands of them. I promise you that!"

There was no visible change in his stone-wall look, but she could feel the change in tension, and she knew she had him. The blue flower head suddenly ducked back out of sight into his hair.

"You're really twisting my arm, now, ma'am. Reckon I'll have to do what you want." Startlingly, he grinned, and it was like an animal showing its teeth. "What do you have in mind?"

His immediate capitulation took her off balance for a moment. Then she said, "Let's get out of the ship and away first—somewhere safe. I'll have to play it by ear from there. Lead on!"

Minutes later she stood shoulder to shoulder with him among the thick bushes that had so recently tried to destroy her in their mindless fashion, and held her portable sender close to her face. Deliberately she whistled into it the first bars of Beethoven's Fifth and watched as the gangway drew itself up and the exit hatch swung shut.

"So much for that," she said. "It's up to you, now."

"Right!" He spun and went away at what looked like an easy stride, but which made her stretch her long legs to keep up.

"What about your ship and that longwave broadcast?" she panted, and he nodded without pausing.

"That's first. I have things to button up. Won't take a minute. Then we hide out. We have time. I know the spot."

He knew the area, too, she realized as he led her a stiff course in and out between massive boles and through riotous undergrowth. He went up and over the irregular ground, occasionally leaping a small stream and striding as easily as if the way were a broad, smooth boulevard. Within five minutes she had no breath for questions and in another five she was sweating. However ridiculous the chain-mail dress might be, it was light and extremely well-ventilated. She slogged on grimly.

Eventually they reached a small clearing, and he halted on the edge of it and waited for her. She heard the faint lilt of an orchestra playing yet another Strauss waltz.

"You stay right here," he commanded. "I won't be a minute."

"No!" she panted in instant objection. "What are you going to do?"

"Turn off the music, for one thing. Friendly's folks will have to get along without it for a little while. Don't want nosy strangers hearing it and coming to snoop. Hold this."

He thrust the spear at her. "No, wait," she protested. "Can't I come with you?"

His bleak stare went oddly with his gleaming smile. "You don't trust me, I know. Why should you? I don't trust you, neither. Once I shut off that music and do a couple of things —well, you can't see my ship from here, and when I'm through you'll never be able to find it. You, nor anyone else. That's the way I want it, ma'am; that's how it's going to be. You can twist my arm just so far. After that it just breaks off in your hand!"

"But"—she objected uneasily—"you're going to leave me all alone, here, by myself."

"You're among friends. Nothing to be scared of, not that you strike me as the nervous kind. Anyhow, Friendly's folks will let you know should any danger happen by."

The last she saw of him was his broad back disappearing through the further wall of bushes ablaze with scarlet blooms. She would have said, herself, that she was not the nervous type, but her recent experience with predatory vegetation had planted a seed of uneasiness in her. She gripped his spear, but was a lot happier at the thought of the beamer on her hip. Standing still, she had time to cool off a little. Properly, she should have been wearing something under it and the bare metal wasn't very comfortable, but the mere thought of something close and clinging made her sweat all over again. The distant music stopped, leaving a gap in the sound scene.

A phrase of his came back—friendly flowers. The way he said it gave it the status of a pet name, almost of someone called Friendly—and his folks. She became aware that the quiet glade was ringed with wide-eyed blue flowers like the one he wore. They were all turned her way, staring at her; there could be no doubt about it this time. In all that host there should have been a few at least that were turned some other way—but no. And then it burst upon her mind. These were Friendly's folks—relatives! And it seemed that the blue-eyed host nodded gently at her understanding. She felt giddy. *I'm going out of my mind!* she thought, but then she painfully recalled those other plants and their deadly

offensive on her. And what had he said? That they were sensitive to emotional fields? It was that peculiar molecule her life-systems analysis had found! The giddy sense of unreality grew. Any moment now, she realized, she would be talking to them and expecting them to answer back, like Alice in Looking-Glass country. To rescue herself from gibbering insanity she turned her attention to the spear in her hand.

It was six feet of light, rigid wood, with regular rings like some kind of bamboo—and then a twelve-inch tip, which was a strange silver-gray metal that she couldn't identify. It started off round and gradually became flattened and pointed, and edged like a razor. But there was something else. She brought it close, but she couldn't see how the metal was jointed to the wood. It just was. It was wood, and then it was metal. A flicker of movement caught her eye. Joe was coming back again with a battered pair of binoculars on a glossy black strap.

"Knew I had these someplace." He held the glasses to show her, then slung the strap over his shoulder. "Been so long, I couldn't recall just where I had 'em cached. Might come handy. Let's go."

"Where to now?" she demanded, returning his spear.

"You'll see. We're going to cast around in a circle now. There's a big rock stump right near where you came down. From the top of that we can see where your friends light and something of what they do."

He led off again, once more at that distance-eating pace so that she had to scramble, and in places, break into a stumbling trot, to keep up. She gathered breath enough for a question, though.

"Joe, tell me—how long have you been living—like this?"

"Never bothered to count the days. It's been a good while. You happen to know the date, off-hand, I could tell you better."

"It's month four, twenty-forty-four. The fifteenth, I think."

"That so? Then it works out about four years and a bit. Useless information, but you're welcome to it."

Four years—her mind chewed on that while her arms, legs and lungs labored to keep up with him over the exacting terrain. A person could go native, or primitive—or mad—in four months in a place like this. But any man who could

so thoroughly shrug off civilization and learn to adapt this well had to be something special. Suspicions began to ferment in her mind; she itched to know more. It would have to wait for now, but it wouldn't be forgotten.

"Whoa up," he ordered, all at once. "Pretty soon now we'll be leaving the shrub cover and moving out into the open, then on to bare rock. You need to know one thing—pay heed, now. If and when I say 'Down!', you go down flat. Don't argue, don't waste any time, just hug the ground hard as you can 'till I tell you to stop. Got that?"

"Wouldn't it help for me to know why?"

"No time to explain. Hear that thunder? Sounds like your company is getting all fixed to land. Come on."

The rocks were hot, sandy-brown and rough to her feet. He scrambled over them like a goat, his tan blending well with the background, while she felt as conspicuous as a street lamp on a dark night. And his agility was heartbreaking, especially when she considered that he carried a spear in one hand, while she had both hands free and needed them. The overhead muttering was louder now. They came to a crest of sorts, and he halted, allowing her to catch up and stand beside him.

"See 'em?" he asked, and she looked, putting up a hand to shield her eyes from the sun. Barely visible in the burning blue she saw a slim silver needle.

"Yes, I can see the ship."

"Reckon he'll come down somewhere over that way, out in the open not too far from the trees. That's quite a trick, coming down the way you did, and he probably won't chance it—not having any need to take cover." She dropped her gaze to follow where his long arm pointed, out over the plain and the beach. "Taking cover is something we ought to do, though," he went on. "No sense in asking to be shot at. We—hold it!" Urgency shivered in his voice.

"What?"

"Get set to drop. When I say—when I say—now, down!"

She threw herself down, saw him go down by her side, and slicing the air where they had been standing came a vicious whine like the grandfather of all hornets in a temper. It flicked by—not just one, but many—and they were gone as abruptly as they had come.

"What?" she asked, again, without moving.

"I call 'em arrow birds, only they're not birds at all, but a kind of winged lizard, with feet like razors and beaks like swords. Fool things spot something moving, they take a bead, and just dive straight at 'em. They can't change aim in mid-flight, so all you have to do is wait for the moment, and then duck, and they go right on by."

"Will they be back?"

"Sure, if you wiggle about."

"How big are they, average?"

"About a foot long, nine inches of which is beak—and deadly."

"So," she muttered. "They go right on by, do they? We'll see about that!" and she turned over and sat up, drawing her beamer as she did so, and combing the nearby sky for traces of movement.

FIVE

SHE WAS ready for his protest, but nothing came. He just lay there, quite still, and she didn't know which she hated most, him, or the unknown and as yet unseen arrow birds. She saw them only just in time, three vivid green and orange blurs power-diving out of the blue straight for her head. She aimed and fired with desperate speed and tore the last one apart so close that she was showered with scorched debris and assailed by a vile stench.

"That's all there is." He sat up casually, dusted himself off, and turned toward her. "You're pretty good with that thing. Most I've ever tried is batting at them with my spear. For that you need to be flat up against a vertical. They're stupid, but not so they'll run themselves into a rock."

"Have you ever examined one in detail?"

"Couple of times. Takes patience, but you can sometimes lure 'em to dive and get within reach of a bush. That does it. But I just duck out of the way now. It's no trouble. Friendly can feel them half a mile away. We'd better take cover now. Come on."

He moved over a ledge, dropping to where there was enough overhang to provide a shadow for them to crouch

in. The noise was enough to feel on her bare skin now, and she saw the sunlight gleaming from the pencil-slim outline of a space-coupe very like her own as it set down over a raving tail of fire and put it out. Then there was echoing silence. That, she felt sure, was Robin Delmar at the controls. It was his kind of professionalism."

"A neat, clean job," he drawled. "That'd be the jet ace you spoke of, I reckon."

"Yes. I can almost see the markings from here."

"What did you say the registration number was?" he murmured, and she turned to see him hoist his binoculars and peer through them. She saw something more, an oddity that exploded a fire-cracker burst of questions in her mind and to her tongue.

She choked them down and managed to say, "Gut-Ripper, six-oh-five. Can you see it?"

"Try a look yourself." He passed the battered instrument across to her and she put it up as he had done, just to be sure, then fiddled with the focusing adjustment and other things.

"That's it—my friends. I'm pretty sure Pierre will be in there with him, maybe some others."

"You sound sort of mixed up," he said. "Talking about it might help some. It would sure help me, anyway, to know what kind of deal I've been roped into."

"I'm sorry about that," she said, and meant it.

"You have plenty of time to talk. The way he chopped her down, that hull will be too damned hot to get out for close on an hour yet. I'd appreciate whatever you can tell."

"Yes. Well, you'll have heard of Shangri-La, even if you've never been there, yes?"

"I know it. Millionaire's playground. Tau Ceti Three."

"Right. And you'll know the kind of affair, too. Good friends and fun partners, nothing more than that, although both Pierre and Robin would have liked it to go a little deeper, perhaps. Anyway, I got an ethergram that called me back urgently to Luna. I didn't tell anyone, but I suppose there are ways of finding out such things. At any rate, I programmed for Luna, and thought no more about it until I happened to notice—well, that the board didn't tally with my program." She told him the rest of it briefly, and

he made no comment at all until she reached the part dealing with the destruct module. Then he grunted.

"I don't blame you for being mixed up, ma'am. Bollixing a courser is one thing—laying tracers, that fits, too. I could pass that off as some kind of practical joke, although I don't care for them, and they ought to be barred in space-craft. But that destruct, and the boobies on the tracers—that's another smell entirely." He stared again at that silent ship away over there. "Somebody seems to want you dead!"

"I've been considering that, of course, but isn't it a bit extreme? I mean, I was never supposed to tamper with the tracers anyway—if a certain party was assuming that the destruct module would be enough to cripple me, the tracers wouldn't come into it."

"That's pretty thin, and it won't hold up in any case. Unless they have changed the design considerably, your courser complex is sitting right on top of your environmental master-board. Did you know that?"

"I suppose I did." She frowned, and then chilled as the implications came to her. "Oh my God!"

"All of that, ma'am. Maybe whoever did it didn't think any more than you, but I wouldn't care to chance my skin on it. Maybe you'd have been able to suit up fast enough, but I wouldn't care to bet on that, either. In the dark, with no air, no power, no tripping-and-closing supply—everything out and dead? I wouldn't care to try it, myself."

There was a long and thoughtful silence between them. Her thinking was severely handicapped by the growing mass of intriguing evidence about him, all the odd twists and quirks of clues that didn't quite add up, and nagged at her when she should have been giving cold and rational consideration to the plight she was in. He stirred suddenly.

"Reckon your friends will bear watching, ma'am. And that hull ought to be cool enough for them to start moving. Soon's they do, we'll take off and beat them back to your ship. That's where they'll make for."

"Yes, of course."

"Thing is to watch *how* they do it. If they just run out the gangway, and then walk away from it, leaving it open, well, that ought to say that they don't mean all that much harm."

"But we have already assumed otherwise, surely?"

31

"No. We figured *somebody* was playing rough, sure, but let's not be too quick to decide—that's the gangway now!"

She lay still, watching as a tiny and distant sliver of metal came out and down to the ground. Then two gaudily clad figures came into sight and tramped steadily away from the ship, quickly disappearing from sight among the fringing trees. She was about to give vent to her surprise when she heard, up above, the whispering thunder of another ship. He had his head back, too.

"That is more like what I had figured," he murmured. "High-jackers! Third party steps in to scoop the pool. Don't move just yet, ma'am. Let's see what this lot do."

It was an entirely different kind of ship. That was apparent by the stronger note of the jets as it rode down, and was also obvious to the eye. She stared up in astonishment, and then looked at Joe, but he had his head down on his chest and his eyes closed. Some intuition made her keep silent until he raised his head and looked at her bleakly.

"This one is the trouble," he said softly. "That first pair were full of fun—the jokers. But this lot—they aren't playing patty-cake!" He showed his teeth in what she was coming to realize was his anger response. "Feels like two people, not friendly at all!"

The last word was the key that fitted everything into place in her mind, confirmed as she stared at him and saw the bright blue flower head poking out from his hair and aiming at the ship.

"Look here," she demanded, the words refusing to be stopped now. "Just how far can that flower thing reach anyway? And what does it do, whisper in your ear?"

Disconcertingly, she now saw him smile in real amusement, a grin that wiped ten years off his age in as many seconds. "You catch on fast. Took me a long while to find out just what Friendly could do. I wouldn't be hard and fast about range. It depends a lot on the quality and intensity of the emotion, I reckon. And I don't know how, either—not in technical terms. Just educated guessing is all. I told you about the plants being sensitive to emotional fields, didn't I? Well, Friendly, here, goes a step better than that. He acts like a kind of transducer-amplifier. He detects 'em, and I feel 'em through him, like a kind of antenna. There's a bit more to it than that, but that's enough—"

He fell silent. Shock waves began to smash to and fro between the forest and the mountains at their back.

"Sounds like a Navy craft," he said, pitching his voice over the din. "Better watch this, it feels pretty bad!"

She cupped her hands over her ears and watched the squat black bulk of the ship hammer down over its own jet-braking. She could identify the profile now; a medium-range Fleet Scout with the marking erased.

"A pirate!" she shouted in amazement.

"Couldn't be anything else," he snapped back. "That's no service crew aboard there. See what he's doing?"

She saw, and at first she didn't believe it and wanted to think that it was a trick of vision or an accident. It was no accident that kept the spouting fire-tail aimed directly at the slim, helpless ship that stood there. Down and down, under the ruthless hand of a competent pilot, the scout pitched and swayed but never lost aim. The seething cascade of blue-white fire swept down and licked and blotted out Delmar's ship altogether—and held there remorselessly, while Selena let out an anguished breath in a soundless cry of protest. Then, with renewed fury, the black ship lifted up and away, to come down efficiently about fifteen yards clear. Again the echoes rushed in to fill an aching silence, and she stared at the warped and sagging, molten caricature of what had been an elegant space-coupe.

"Like I said"—Joe's matter of fact drawl was jarring in the quiet—"not the friendly type. I wonder where in time they learned *that* stunt?"

"Who . . ." It came out a squeak, and she tried again. "Who would do a thing like that? And why?" Anger hadn't come yet. She was still getting over the stunned shock of seeing a ship destroyed.

"Looks like somebody didn't want your friends to leave."

"If that's all it was. Suppose they had still been in there?"

"They must've been seen to get out. Let's hope so, anyway. Thing is, what do we do now?"

"We must do something." She was urgent about that. "We can't just—"

"Just what? Whoever's in that ex-Navy ship is liable to take a poor view of anything we do in the way of interference."

"You're being a coward again."

"No, ma'am, just careful. We still don't know a great deal about what's going on. We could find out a bit more."

"How?"

"You ever climbed a tree?"

"I have. I might not be as good at it as you are, but I'll manage."

"That's fine. Let's go." He ducked out of their shallow refuge and around the crest of rock until they were out of view from the plain. Then he halted her with a sharp stare from his bright eyes. "Get one thing, though. We're going to snoop—to lie low and listen—maybe learn a thing or two. That's all. Don't go horning in with that weapon of yours. Remember there's at least four of them, maybe more, and there's only two of us."

"You don't have to spell it out."

"Just so long as we know how it is. Come on." He went away down the rugged rock slope like a sleek cat. She plunged after him, and it took her only seconds to realize that he had been holding himself back previously. Now he seemed to be in a hurry, and no matter how she slid and scrambled she was far behind him when he achieved level and plunged into the first of the undergrowth. By the time she reached it he was nowhere to be seen or heard, and she plowed to a standstill, feeling lost and terrified in a way she hadn't known since childhood. Panic fed on itself, and, too late, she felt the touch and clutch of snaking twigs, of eager branches and prickling thorns insinuating themselves in and around her chain-mail dress and pressing hungrily close to her skin. She tried to duck, to dodge, but that was worse than useless, and within gasping seconds she was caught fast. It was all she could do to make herself be still, shivering. And there he was, showing his teeth and sneering at her.

"What are you throwing a panic for? You *want* these plants to eat you?"

"I was lost—I didn't know where you'd gone!"

"Take a breath. Be glad to see me, even if you aren't. Work on that. I thought I told you there was nothing could hurt you here so long as you're friendly? Don't you believe that?"

"I can't help it," she snapped, as the clutching strands re-

fused to let go. "I'm no wood nymph. I was brought up civilized."

"That's nice. You'll die civilized too unless I can do something to stop it. We haven't a lot of time, so you'll have to excuse me. Maybe this'll help you out." He came close, put out his hand and touched her at the joint of neck and shoulder. His fingers were firm and strong, yet cool—and she was hard put to resent his touch, although she wanted to—but then something else came. All at once the entire scene was subtly different. She heard all of it thinking. It was not in words, not in any way she could translate; it was just an awareness of life like the instruments of some muted but mighty orchestra. Sighing trees breathed huge sleepy organ tones; grass rippled a constant piccolo chatter; the clutching bushes scolding and suspicious, yelped, aggressively angry at being disturbed and upset. She gasped at the revelation and denial rose into her mind instantly.

I didn't mean to hurt you, to intrude. Truly! I didn't know. I really am sorry. This is your home, and I'm blundering in. The thoughts modulated as she felt the hostility ebbing away. The binding strands loosened, curled away, withdrew, and the bad-tempered yelping abated to a murmur. Then he took his hand away and it was all gone, like switching off a radio.

"I'd no idea," she breathed. "Not that it was—like that! They're just like people!"

SIX

"DON'T BEAR down too hard on that," he warned. "Friendly is inclined to exaggerate a little. They do have personality, though."

"Is it like that for you all the time?"

For the first time, she saw him discomfited a little. "That's a big question, and we don't have gabbing time, right now. We need a tree."

He led once more and she had a gritty moment of irritation in thinking that she seemed to have done nothing these past hours, except trail at his heels. But that went rapidly

as she struggled to keep up to him in the winding wilderness all about them. Perhaps that momentary contact with the sensitive plant had cracked some unguessed barrier in her mind, for it now seemed that the wild luxuriance of bushes, creepers and great standing trees was a kindly and welcoming place. Perhaps it was imagination, but it no longer seemed as if she had to push through or watch her feet for tripping roots—as if the wildlife was edging aside to let her through. He stopped again.

"This will do us."

She stared indignantly up into the spread of a forest giant, the trunk of which was at least five feet through. "The nearest branch is all of nine feet up," she pointed out. "What do we do, fly?"

"Hold that!" He thrust the spear at her, and proceeded to walk up the knotty trunk on his fingers and toes. It was impossible, but she watched him do it as if he had hooks on his fingertips and toes. She breathed hard. Selena Ash was long accustomed to commanding admiration and awe, to being in front of the competition and to affecting disdain for compliments because she knew she had earned them. It was not so here.

"If you expect me to do that . . ."

"The spear," he called. "Grab the pointed end and hold on; pass the other end up here."

She did that. He stooped, took hold, and she was swept into the air like a feather, until her feet could kick out and find rest on the branch.

"I reckon you can manage the rest." He set the spear aside in a fork and scrambled around and up. She breathed hard again, then followed. "We have a little while," he called down to her from above. "Your friends are getting close. But we have a while."

A thousand questions choked her mind as she climbed. One question in particular bothered her: If he could sense and evaluate people at such great distances, by means of that plant, why was it that she had felt absolutely nothing of him when he had touched her? Did he know what she was thinking and feeling? If so, he didn't seem to care much. But now, with a heave and kick, she was around to where she could see her own ship, and hear thrashing sounds at a distance to tell her that someone was not far away. She

hauled herself on to a branch close to him, blowing hard.

"I wonder you don't just take off and hurl yourself from branch to branch. Wouldn't that be quicker for you?" she muttered.

"Brachiation," he murmured, and the word came oddly in his hillbilly drawl. "That's for fiction. You ever see a competition athlete? Those laddies who do stunts on the rings and bars? Even the best of them couldn't swing far hand to hand. Can't be done. The human frame isn't built for it. And getting mad about things don't change them any. 'Comes your friends, now."

The ship was so close she could have hit it with a thrown stone. She lay along her branch and turned her head in the direction of the coming noise. Voices became intelligible.

"Can you see the ship yet, Robin?"

"I see it. And about time! What the hell was she thinking of, to sit down in this damned jungle?" Robin Delmar staggered into view through the bushes, and Selena caught her breath. He was tall, black-haired and bronzed as an Amerind, with his head high and that sardonic, crooked grin on his lean face; it was the triumph of poise over reality. He was a mess. The dark close-fitting tunic with the up-and-down stripe that he favored because it made him look even more angular and lean than he was was a ruin, hanging in torn and molten shreds from shoulders and waist. His bared skin was streaked with green and scarred with angry red scratches and patches. As he halted, she saw that his belt, boots, and the strap that held his tracking instrument were whole—and that he shook, visibly, either from strain or shock.

In a moment she saw Pierre Lacoste coming after and he was worse. He looked scared out of his mind, his butter-blond hair dangling in his eyes and his jaw slack, no sign remaining of his boyish Gallic charm. He, too, had been clawed by the plants, and both men were gleaming with sweat.

"Go on," Lacoste cried. "What are we waiting for? Let's get aboard and away from here."

"Me, too," Delmar declared. "Only, how? No gangway out."

Lacoste ran unsteadily, to where the exit hatch stood shut, and stared at it. "Selena," he screamed. "Open up. For

God's sake, let us in!" He drew breath for another scream and reeled as Delmar hit him.

"Button it, Pierre. Just button it, see? You want to point the whole world right at us? If she's in there, she knows we're here. No need to scream your stupid head off!"

"They're so scared," Selena murmured aside to Joe, "it's a wonder they got this far through the bushes."

"Scared of whoever might be chasing 'em. I doubt they so much as noticed the plants—so they wouldn't attack all that hard. Just get a little stirred up, is all."

"What do you mean, if she's in there?" Lacoste demanded, from his knees. "Where else would she be? She's got to be in there, if she's alive."

"Cut that talk! Why wouldn't she be alive?"

"Why is she here, anyway? You told me—you *told* me—the ship was fixed to warp out in space—"

"That's right. And I disconnected her courser so she couldn't move anywhere else; and we were waiting for her. We saw her warp out. So?" Delmar sounded as if his patience had worn thin; Lacoste had lost his altogether.

"So?" he shrilled. "If you fixed it so damned clever, why is the ship here, and not there!" Under stress his French origins began to show.

"Because," Delmar growled, "our Selena is just that much smarter than we figured. I *told* you the whole scheme was a damned juvenile notion. All I did was disconnect six or seven relays. She could be just smart enough to unfix those."

"But what is she doing here?"

"Having a big laugh at us, I reckon. She's earned it."

"But our ship? And that other ship?" Lacoste was shaking, pleading. Selena felt ashamed for him. "We could have been all burned up!"

"Cool it." Delmar sneered. "That was a Navy craft. You know who her old man is; you know the kind of strings she could pull—and you know how she can spit when she has a mind."

"I don't believe it. She wouldn't do anything like that!"

"You have a better answer?" Delmar swung away from his companion, raised his gaze to the camera immediately above the exit hatch, and made a parody of a bow to it.

"I hereby pronounce *uncle* for both of us, my dear Selena," he said, "but don't linger too long to gloat, sweetheart.

There could be several unkind characters on our tail right now. We'd like in!"

Selena stirred, and Joe hissed an instant warning.

"Now look," she muttered. "This has gone far enough. Those boys are in bad trouble."

"Trouble is right. Worse than you think, and headed right this way. Coming fast. We're safer on the outside."

She hesitated, and then it was too late.

"Turn around. Make it slow." The grating voice was harshly thick with authority. Both men swung much too fast, but froze as they stared into a magnum-beamer, steady as death in the hand of the man who held it. "Well, well," he growled. "Hot-Shot Delmar and Lover-Boy Lacoste. Where's the dame?"

"Who the hell are you?" Delmar challenged, then staggered back as the turf at his toes poofed into smoke and stink.

"I'm asking the questions, mister. If it matters, I'm Pardoe. Bernard Pardoe. And this"—he jerked his head slightly to his rear—"is Miss Scorpia Martine. You know who you are. Now, where's the dame? I mean, Miss Selena Ash, no less."

"We don't know!" Lacoste found his tongue. "We haven't seen her. We suppose she's still in there."

Pardoe grinned. "You suppose, huh? Maybe we can sharpen that up a bit. Scorpia, take a gentle stroll around and see if she's hid out somewhere close by. Don't take any chances now."

"Who, me?" Miss Martine smiled. Watching them, Selena had wondered how they had come so far through the same undergrowth that had savaged Delmar and Lacoste without being affected at all, now she knew. Miss Martine had a magnum-beamer of her own set now to broad beam and low power. She used it lavishly to scorch a way through any bushes that stood in her path. And she was efficient, too. Selena watched her and felt resentful, for a moment, that any woman should be so flawlessly beautiful, so outrageously shaped.

She shifted her stare to Pardoe, remembering him from the spy record but realizing now that this solid slab of a man was even uglier than his picture. His cold black eyes never once left his two captives until Miss Martine had thoroughly covered the perimeter of the ship.

"All clean, Buck. No sign. Reckon she is inside?"

"She's no fool." Pardoe frowned horribly. "Going to take some hooking out of there."

"Stand-off!" Delmar taunted, and Pardoe glared at him.

"You talk too much, Hot-Shot. Just try remembering that I don't need you all that much."

"All right." Delmar shrugged wearily. "Just what do you need, if not us? What are you doing here anyway, apart from destroying my ship?"

Pardoe hunched over his weapon, then slowly relaxed. "No," he muttered, arguing with himself. "Let's not discard something we might be able to play. You crumbs are friends of hers. If she *is* in there, getting an eyeful and listening, maybe she'll think again if she sees her friends getting fried, nice and slow. What d'you reckon, Scorpia?"

"I'd like that. Especially him, he's so tough!" Miss Martine showed her teeth and moved back to be out of range of the smell she anticipated. Pardoe smiled.

"I don't know what happened to your drapes, Hot-Shot, but it saves a minute, doesn't it? And this is gonna hurt you more'n it does me—"

Miss Martine stepped back just a bit too far. Selena saw, from a different viewpoint, what she had experienced only a few hours earlier. Two luxuriant head-high bushes leaned together in unison and flung their snaking branches eagerly around Miss Martine's neck, waist, arms, and legs. She screeched once, and went over backwards, struggling wildly; relays of twigs and branches folded over to grab at her. Pardoe froze with his chin on his shoulder.

"What the hell are you doing?"

"Get—me—out—of this!" The confused mass of greenery thrashed wildly; Miss Martine screeched again. "Help! I'm being eaten!"

Pardoe whirled, took half a dozen heavy steps, crouched to stare and then used his beamer on the wrist-thick stem of one bush, slicing it apart in a spurt of green smoke. Then the snakelike coils were still. He plucked and pulled, flinging the leafy things away as he coughed at the stench and fumes. Delmar saw what he thought was a chance and launched himself at Pardoe's back. The big man reacted like lightning, spinning, straightening up and swinging his hand

around with the beamer in it. It struck Delmar's head. Pardoe glared at Lacoste.

"You care to try something like that, Lover-Boy?" Lacoste cringed and Pardoe turned his head. "Scorpia, you all right? What the hell happened?"

"I don't believe it!" She was shrill with indignant astonishment as she struggled to her feet and threw away the last dead coils of bush and twig. "Those damned shrubs went for me. They're alive!"

"Of course they're alive."

"That's not what I mean, dammit! They grabbed me! I tell you, they were dragging me down and starting to eat me. Just take a look at my duds!"

Pardoe looked, and made what was probably his idea of a laugh. "I would never have believed plants had them kind of ideas. They got you down to the buff, nearly."

"They got further than that!" she dabbed at herself and winced. "Hey, maybe this stuff is poisonous."

"Forget it. Those two are still breathing, aren't they? At least—take a look at Delmar, will you? Maybe I hit him too hard."

"The hell with him! What about me? You expect me to stroll around this damned jungle in the raw?"

"You'll crawl on your knees if I say so, and like it. Take a look at him and let me think."

SEVEN

UNWILLINGLY, trying to rescue the shreds of her clothing, Miss Martine went to kneel by Delmar and investigate his condition—none too gently. Pardoe turned to the silent ship; he scowled at it.

"I'm going to toast your friends, Miss Ash. It will be interesting to see how much of it you can stand." He turned again and aimed his weapon at Lacoste. Selena stirred.

"I can't take any more of this."

"You hold still," Joe muttered. "He's only bluffing. He can't scare that feller any more than he's scared right now, and he knows it."

The beamer held steady. Lacoste shut his eyes in terror. Pardoe snarled and lowered the weapon.

"Bitch!" he growled. Miss Martine glanced at him from her crouch.

"She's no fool, Buck. Why would she come out? What's to gain?"

"Yes. How's the tough guy?"

"He'll live." She got to her feet again, and with an angry vehemence, dragged at the last shreds of her clothes and flung them away. She began patting and rubbing herself in a vain attempt to get ease. "Look, think of something, will you? And fast—I'm going crazy with this itch!"

Pardoe turned once more to stare at the ship. Frustration was obvious in every line of his bulky body.

"I play you one more game," he growled, and strode to where one landing foot had settled into the turf. It was a pointless sign of his need to get close, to get violent. He glared up.

"I know you're in there!" he roared. "Smart, huh? Well, you just listen to me. You better come out, and soon!" He swung his free hand into a fist and slammed it against the metal. Selena winced, knowing what was coming next. The high-frequency twister field that lurked invisibly in the metal wrenched Pardoe's arm away, spun him completely around and sent him careening away in knotted convulsions. The beamer fell from his twitching hand. Before he could regain control he had plunged headlong into a thicket nearby. Once again the eager bushes closed in, smothering, binding, gouging, constricting and biting. This time it was Miss Martine's turn to stand and stare open-mouthed, and then to hoist her beamer and run.

Then she halted, frantically trying to weigh the situation. This time it wasn't so easy to spot the main stems. She adjusted to needle-beam and sliced away at one side, right down to the soil. Coughing as the acrid fumes rolled out, she swung and sliced at the other side. Selena could hardly see her for the smoke; but her voice was audible.

"Hold still, Buck. I can't get at the roots at all. I'm setting for wide on low and I'll toast them off you. Hold still, now!"

Out of the roiling smoke came muted sizzlings, then yells from Pardoe as the temperature rose. In a moment, Miss

Martine came backing out to whip round and flourish the weapon at Lacoste. There was no threat, and she relaxed, backing away to let Pardoe come staggering out of the smoke. He slapped at singed twigs and cursed fervently. Bits of his tailored black tunic came away. He was more gross uncovered, and his body was coming up in red weals. Miss Martine did not stare at him, nor did she make any comment about his condition.

"Let's get out of here, Buck, huh? What say we just fry this pair and blow? I've had just about all I can take of these damned educated plants!"

"Hah!" He shivered, then stared at her strangely. "What did you call them?"

"You ought to know by now. They grabbed you, didn't they? And didn't they play possum until you were close enough to grab? What else would you call them?"

"Yes. That's what I was thinking, too. Come over here a minute."

The pair moved away to be out of earshot of their captives, and, unwittingly, directly under the tree where Selena and Joe were hidden.

"What's on your mind, Buck?"

"This place. Add it up, Scorpia—an uncharted system, right off the charts and—your words—educated plants. What else could it be?"

"If you're thinking what I think you're thinking—nuts! Look, we listened in on those crumbs, didn't we? Delmar deliberately picked his spot to be far away, but random. And neither of those dims knew a thing about this place before they landed here, that's sticking out a mile."

"So all right, they drew it out of a hat. I'm not saying different. I'm saying that this is it."

"You mean, by accident?"

"Why not? Look, Columbus went looking for China, and see where he ended up. Stranger things have happened. Unless there are two planets like this, which I don't believe."

"All right." She shrugged, scratching herself. "What's the play?"

"It wants figuring to do it right."

"Why don't we just fade, let them get together and blow and then take possession?"

"Use your head. If we let them get away, they'll be

back with half the damned fleet, busting to take us apart. Remember who the Ash dame is, will you? Besides, those three aren't all that dumb—especially her. Give them a chance to think it through and they'll get it, just like you did. And everybody has heard of Jensen's Planet, even if they don't believe it."

"All right," she repeated impatiently. "So what do we do?"

"I think I know. Somehow, we have to keep 'em all here until I have checked out and made sure this is the place I think it is. After that, we'll see. But first I have to fix this Ash dame. I think I'm wise to her."

The pair turned and marched back to where Lacoste was kneeling and Delmar had raised himself on an elbow, blood staining the side of his face.

"Beauty and the Beast," he said, and Pardoe grunted.

"You don't learn, do you, comic? Pay attention, both of you. When you two comedians worked out your little scheme to play a trick on Miss Ash, you picked your coordinates at random, right? Want to qualify that, now?"

"You seem to know all about it already," Delmar retorted.

"Most of it. That's my business, and I'm good at it. Me and Scorpia, here, we study folk like you for pickings. Either one of you would be worth about half a million stellars to your friends. But then there was Miss Ash too, and she's worth a bit more than that, quite a bit. So, when you handed us the chance to knock off all three of you at once, naturally we were delighted to play along. You picked this area at random?"

"I had nothing to do with that." Lacoste spoke quaveringly. "The idea, it was mine, but Robin worked out the details."

"Not at random," Delmar said. "You think I'm a fool? I picked a spot that was far away from everything—off the charts and main trade routes. So what? I'd like to know how you got on to it. You never bugged us on that detail."

"Tricks in all trades—and we all have questions. I would love to know how this ship got from there to here. When we followed you aboard and checked over what you had fixed—and made a note of the courser settings—I wired in a destruct module, all set to blow the guts out of her as

soon as she warped out. You could've thought of that, Hot-Shot!"

"A destruct in the courser?" Delmar sat up, got all the way to his feet and stood, swaying. "You fat slab of filth!"

"Watch the big words, crumb, or I'll straighten out your head. You will kindly notice that it didn't happen. She not only located your monkeyshines and fixed them, she also fixed my little blessing. And, I can tell you, I had three tracers stuck on her hull, just in case yours folded. She had scratched yours and two of mine. And mine were boobied with detonite. You chew on that a while, Delmar, and see what it adds up to. You were trying to get a rise out of her? Man, she's been playing you and just about everybody else."

He turned to face the ship again. "You better pay attention, Miss Ash. You're all through with the popsy playgirl bit, so forget it. And you are, like it or not, right up to here in something bigger than you may realize. You will have heard I'm sure, of a man called Jory Jensen?"

"Jory Jensen?" Delmar echoed, and even Lacoste showed interest.

"What is this all about now, Robin?"

"Search me. Pardoe, you're talking about that crazy scout who went and lost himself in space about four years ago. A nut—what has he got to do with anything? Don't tell me *you* believe all those fantastic yarns?"

"I'm through telling you anything." Pardoe did not turn. "You better listen, Miss Ash, and think. I'll draw you a diagram. Me and Scorpia are going back to my ship. We're taking your playmates with us. You should have knocked off that third tracer, but you didn't. I have an ear on it. If it stops I'll be back here, with muscles, and you'll be sorry. If you try to lift off with it still there, I'll catch you before you can warp out, and you'll be even sorrier. Mine is an ex-Navy ship, and it can do nasty things to you. So take a hint. Just stay right here and do nothing. You try anything —anything at all—and this bright pair will fry, immediate— and I'll send the cooked remains to your old man, with full details."

He waited, but there was no sign. He shrugged, turned to his visible audience. "All right, you two, get moving. That way."

"Look, be your age," Delmar shouted. "How the devil can

we walk anywhere? We wouldn't get ten steps through those bushes."

"It's a point, Buck," Miss Martine declared. "One of us better go on in front and clear a path. You?"

"Why me?"

"Because I'm modest," she snapped. "Why should I do these two any favors? You go ahead; I'll follow."

The last Selena saw of the strange parade was Miss Martine's shapely rear disappearing through the screening undergrowth. She stirred, feeling stiff and old, then turned to meet Joe's bright stare.

"Can you tell if they are really going away, that it's not just a trick?"

"Up to a point, sure. They're going away so far. What have you in mind to do?"

"I want to get into my ship and do a thing or two."

"Like lifting off?"

"Don't be stupid! Pardoe meant what he said and you should know that with that ship of his he could blast me into scrap without trying. No, I just want to fix something. It won't take long."

"Still going away. You have time enough, I reckon." He squirmed and went down the tree as easily as a squirrel. He was standing under the tree long before she had reached the lowest branch. She slid down to her stomach, then painfully to arm's length and dangled.

"You'll have to help me, please."

He turned, touched her ankle and caught her as she let go. In that moment she had, again, that awesome sense of being surrounded by murmuring life, but it vanished as he put her down and stood away.

"Still going away," he said. "You'll have time."

"I don't want you to run off."

"You don't need me now. Nothing either of us can do anyway. Pardoe holds all the cards."

"I have no intention of sitting stupidly in my ship awaiting Mr. Pardoe's pleasure. A sitting duck?" He shrugged fractionally. "I'd rather hide out, and for that I need your help again."

"I have things to do for my own self, ma'am."

"Oh well, at least wait there until I come out again, and

we can talk about it a little. Will you? I'll be no more than ten minutes. You can keep watch."

He shrugged again. "All right, ma'am. Can't hurt."

EIGHT

THE MOST important thing she had to do didn't take her more than one tenth of her bargained-for time, which left her an interval in which to do a few other things. One was to study herself in a mirror much more critically than she had done in a long time. Then realizing that she was wasting time, she got out a long-range beamer rifle and a three-pack of spare charges, and her portable code sender, and went out.

He stood close to a tree, turning his head as she stepped clear of the gangway and whistled the notes that sealed her ship again. She searched around and found a hiding place for the small set—by the foot of the tree where he stood.

"That's it," she announced. "I'm in your hands now. How's the enemy, by the way?"

"Still going. That Pardoe's a bad man to play with," Joe said.

"I don't intend to play. I intend to let others do it for me. Joe, I've deceived you, just a little. I'm sorry. You didn't ask what it was I had to do, just now, in my ship. I'll tell you. Do you know what a Dirac-sender is?"

If she had kicked him in the stomach he couldn't have wilted more visibly. His face was gray under his tan as he muttered, "You can't mount a Dirac in a little hopper like that."

"Oh yes. It's a rather special ship."

"You don't have enough power!"

"I do—only just. It is set to repeat just one message, at fifteen minute intervals, and that, as you seem to know, eats up every erg the drive can store up. So, you see, I couldn't take off even if I wanted to, and I don't. You are surprisingly well-informed, Joe."

"For what good that is, now. You know what you've done?"

47

"I think so." She felt compunction at his obvious misery. "Joe—it was also right, what Pardoe said, about this planet, wasn't it?"

"You know it all, don't you? A damned Dirac! I told you" —he grew suddenly savage—"that I had things of my own to do. You have any idea what? You heard what Pardoe said. Do you have any notion what he's going to be doing, as soon as ever he can?" She felt his fury like a blast of heat, noting with an inconsequential part of her attention that he had forsaken his pose. "He'll break out a skimmer—a jet-copter—and he'll go looking for something. His proof, as he called it."

"Yes," she agreed. "I can understand that. He will go looking for a particular tree—Jory Jensen's miracle tree, on the planet of educated plants."

"The Tree," he groaned, his tone putting it into capitals.

"That's right, the Tree. But isn't that quite a task, finding one tree among millions? Or are there a lot of them?"

"Only the one that I know of. And he'll find it. Not right off, maybe, but he'll find it. I was meaning to get there first."

"To do what? Tangle with Pardoe? After warning me not to?"

"There's a difference. I live here; I know this place and the Tree; I know what it can *do*."

"And you know what Buck Pardoe can do, too. Joe, let me help."

"Help? What's the point, now you've alerted—whoever you're sending the Dirac for?"

"Let me worry about that when the time comes. Joe, don't be so damned stubborn. You can't go up against Pardoe on your own, with just a spear. And what about those two boys? All right, they got themselves into the mess, but they're friends of mine. They need help; and so do you. Go on, damn you, admit it! You've been independent so long you can't think any other way, that's your trouble."

He was racked with indecision, and she kept after him. "I have a beam rifle and I know how to use it. You know where the Tree is, and he doesn't. It's going to take him time to find it, which gives us an edge—and the chance to figure out some kind of strategy. Two heads are better than one. I was the unwitting cause of all this mess; let me help you."

He sighed and hunched his shoulders. "All right, ma'am, you sold me. Don't seem to have any choice, not now."

"Do me just one small favor, will you? Stop calling me ma'am. I am not ancient, academic or married. My name is Selena."

"Whatever you say. Can we go now?"

"I think so—hey, what about food? I've just realized I'm as empty as a drum."

"If you can hang on for maybe half an hour, that can be fixed. Let's go."

Here we go again, she mused, *him leading the way and me tagging along after.* As they plunged into the trackless riot of undergrowth, it seemed that the tangled bushes and creepers did tend to get out of the way—or was it just accumulating skill and experience? Either he was holding himself back on her account or she was getting good at moving through jungle, having little trouble keeping up with him. So many questions bubbled in her mind as they strode along that she ventured to put some of them into words.

"Of course they get out of our way," he said, with just a tint of surprise in his voice at her question. "Plants don't like being knocked and bruised and trampled on, any more than you do."

She demurred, "It's not as obvious as you make it sound. It wants a bit of getting used to, meeting plants that think and have emotions."

"They don't think," he corrected. "Not what we would call thinking. But they do have senses. Why shouldn't they? What's so surprising about that? Anything that lives has senses of some kind?"

"Senses?"

A faint but genuine smile plucked at the corner of his mouth. They moved on a while in silence. Then he veered aside and brought her to a small clearing by a tree and halted.

"Senses," he murmured. "You ever wondered why bushes don't grow under and around a tree?"

"Because they need sunshine, I suppose. That's not intelligent—just chemistry, isn't it?"

"It might be, only some bushes, and creepers do grow around the bases of trees—the parasitic kind. Chemistry? And what about grass, doesn't it need sunshine?" He had

no need to point to the thick carpet of grass they stood on. She frowned. "Did you ever wonder why most trees have spaces around them, between them?"

"Look—I don't know. I'm no botanist. I imagine it's purely mechanical. Seeds, nuts, or whatever fall and try to take root, and can't unless there is room enough for them to grow properly. You tell me."

"It's better if you find out for yourself. Take a good look at any tree. Do you ever see the branches bumping into each other? Look at the leaves—all carefully separated. Or just look, really look, at a patch of grass—this grass. Come on." He squatted down and invited her to do the same. "A host of leaves, millions of them, all separate from each other —because this is something a plant has: a sense of space, it's own space. All plants have the ability to work out enough space for their needs. It's territorial awareness—just like birds or bees—or most animals. Or people, for that matter; only, with people it's so weak that they don't use it. They just feel neurotic and go mad when they are overcrowded."

She knelt, put one hand on his shoulder to steady herself, and moved instantly into that strange and fascinating dimension of awareness of the seething sentience all around. Little voices and shrill, big sighs and deep, restless gossiping, an ocean of minds—and she felt him start to lean away.

"Oh, please, no. Don't spoil it. Who'd ever believe that even the blades of grass talk to each other? It's so wonderful!"

"It's not talk," he corrected mildly. "Remember what I said about birds? And I suppose it is stretching a point to call it emotion. They have a way of knowing when they have enough room and when something is getting too close, which causes distress of some kind. I suppose maybe it is emotion, at that. We humans tend to make a lot out of very little, when you think of it. There are only two basic feelings about anything. Either it's favorable—for you—or it isn't. You like it, or you don't. Shade it whichever way you like, but it works out the same. Positive or negative. Every living thing has it. You know yourself, surely, that feeling of being close to something that disturbs you?"

"Yes. Yes, I do." She veered away from that quickly. "But what about the mobility?"

"That's something I don't know. Mobile plants aren't new.

Even on Earth you can find them: mimosa, fly-catchers. And all plants move, anyway, only very slowly. Maybe there's something in the soil or air here. But the sense of space is old. And that's what Friendly is good at, and what you're getting, through him."

"And much more," she declared. "Much more than just space—feelings, too. But why does it sound like music, almost?"

"I don't know that. Why does some music make you feel good, or happy, or like dancing, or sad? I suppose plants just feel good when they have all the room they need, and upset when anything threatens that. And so they can respond to anything else that happens to feel something, like an echo. But that's just a guess." He stood up slowly, and she arose with him, keeping her hand on his shoulder; she was reluctant to lose contact.

"I hate to part with all this," she confessed, "but I can't very well keep my hand on your shoulder all the time. Couldn't I hold your hand?"

That invisible curtain slid down over his face. "That might not be such a bright idea," he declared. "Not right away."

"Whatever do you mean? Are you afraid that I would be intruding on your space, or something?" She snatched away her hand, and the unseen orchestra winked out of her mind. "If you object to me touching you, just say so."

"That's one of the reasons," he said, baring his teeth in that biting smile. "You tend to get spitty real easy— the least little thing—and I can feel it bad enough at a distance, without getting it full blast firsthand."

"Oh!" She snatched a hand to her face, felt the hot blood of chagrin burning there and then all over her body as mingled shame, and rage and humiliation shook her. "Did you have to be so brutally frank about it?"

"And that's another thing. Plants don't have a lot of crazy mixed up feelings. They don't try to hide anything or fake anything. You know exactly what the score is, with them."

"I see. And you're not capable of dealing with anything more complex than a vegetable, is that it?"

"Now you're real scratchy. And all knotted up, too. Your words say one thing, your voice says something else and Friendly tells me something altogether different from either. I let you hold my hand, you're going to get *me* all tangled

up, too, and I just don't have time for that. We have quite a way to go yet."

Suddenly it struck her that he was speaking nothing but the plain truth, that she was mixed up, inside—and that he must have been getting the full blast of that, raw and undiluted, every time he touched her. That idea ran to its logical conclusion and she flamed hotter than before. He must have sensed her feelings, *all* her feelings. She turned away helplessly, wishing herself a million miles away.

"No need to feel so bad about it, ma'am," he mumbled. "Can we get on now? Be time to eat in a while. It's not far."

"You go on ahead," she said, drilling herself to be calm. "I'll try not to offend you too much."

He hunched his shoulders in resignation and led off.

NINE

As THE best way to banish her shameful display from mind, Selena started paying extra attentoin to the surroundings, trying to get some idea of the variation in species and appearance of the various plants. She wondered about wildlife that ran. Surely, too, there had to be insects where there were flowers? Otherwise, what about pollination? It seemed a safe topic to be curious about, and she asked him as they moved along.

"Never seen any insects," he admitted, "big or small. Never thought much about it. I suppose they wouldn't have much chance with flowers like we have here—probably never got started. As for pollination, that's not always necessary. What is important, more, is the ability to disperse seeds and these bushes have all sorts of ways of doing that."

He showed her a few, indicating them as they came up on their way. She saw one gorgeous bush that threw parachutes into the air, another that exerted pressure on its berries until they popped out and one, with a particularly red bloom, that he warned her against.

"Not now—it's in flower. But around seed time, that's a good one to keep away from. The seeds form in a long row

along a flexible spine, all sticking out like the teeth on a comb. And as they mature, the spine gets bent more and more, until it rips loose at the thin end, and flips the seeds off like needles—in a shower. The least thing will set them off, and they travel anything up to thirty feet."

Now their way was uphill and the luxuriance began to thin a little. The undergrowth dwindled, and the trees were slighter and not so tall. Long open vistas between the trunks were more and more common, affording her occasional glimpses of the mountains ahead. They came to a larger stream, almost a torrent, and he halted, waiting for her.

"This next bit is going to be unpleasant," he warned, "and you might wonder why, so I'll tell you now. Saves argument. This water leads where we want to go, and you'd think we would travel along the bank, but we're going to wade *in* it, because there's a peculiar kind of amphibian to be found hereabouts, that lurks mostly close by the water. They're about three inches long, but with teeth like a crocodile. I call 'em crock-beetles, and they're the one thing Friendly can't pick up—can't, or won't. So we take no chances. You'll hear 'em; they click. But they move like slick lightning, too, and by the time you hear 'em they're going away again, with a piece of your toe. So—it will be chilly, but it's the best way. Right?"

"Whatever you say."

"All right, but remember, it's cold. And no point in stopping, once we start. Be about twenty minutes, at most. Here we go."

She watched him plunge in almost to his knees, and turn to go upstream, and she followed—and was hard put not to squeal at the icy bite of the water. She plunged on, gritting her teeth against the pain—and saw first one, then another and then scurrying swarms of the things they were avoiding. They did click, and when she saw what with, she was almost resigned to the bitter cold of the water. They were hideous things with eight scaly legs. They glittered in shades of blue and green like animated jewels—but she saw the jaws and set her teeth.

They fought their way around a slow arc and came to a shelving stretch of silver sand. He went ahead and out. She staggered after him on lifeless stumps, and caught her

breath as the circulation started trickling back like liquid needles.

"It's rough," he said, sympathizing with her unspoken ache, "but you feel fine in a while. All right to drink, too, if you're dry?"

"My stomach will feel insulted, it's so vacant."

"That's all right." He waved an arm ahead. "Food and drink just in sight. Go ahead and drink, if you want to. Get a real appetite!"

"All right." She knelt carefully in the sand and laved her face with the chilly water, managed to swallow a mouthful or two of it, and it made her teeth ache. But it also made her feel ravenous and she followed eagerly to where he had settled under a broad-spreading tree.

"Call this my bed-and-breakfast tree," he told her, plucking away at what seemed to be a mass of gray wool. Looking up, she saw that the tree was laden with similar bundles, each about the size of a cushion. Kneeling beside him she saw that he was uncovering a solid kernel. It was a dark green thing with a skin like a watermelon and about the same size. Balancing it on his left palm, he chopped at one end with his knife and uptilted it quickly.

"Here, that's yours. I'll get another. Drink first, and I'll split it afterwards."

It was more than half full of a pinkish liquid the texture of thin cream, but which tasted acid-sweet.

"It's certainly taken the edge off my appetite," she said, and he grinned up from carving one for himself.

"Filling, that stuff. I reckon you'd get fat as a pig if you lived here very long."

He got to work with his knife again, splitting the husk into three for her.

She munched heartily, enjoying the flavor and watched him with all her bottled-up curiosity returning. Yet she was reluctant to ask him personal questions in case he said anything to shatter this easy companionship that was so pleasant. He was neat in his movements and totally without self-consciousness; he was as natural as a wild animal and yet he was a man, and a cultured man, too, when he could be persuaded to stop acting innocent.

"I just don't understand you," she admitted at last, putting aside the last gnawed section of husk. "You seem to

belong here so completely, and yet just four years ago you were an ordinary civilized human, like anyone else. Not that I'm blowing any trumpet for civilization," she added hastily as he got a bad-taste look on his face. "Right now I would have a hard job choosing between civilized luxury, and this. But that's an argument for some other time. What I mean," and she stretched and settled herself in comfort, using the discarded woolly fiber of the fruit as a kind of pillow, "is the way you have learned so much, so well. I count myself pretty resourceful; I've been trained to be. But I wouldn't care to take on this planet from scratch. I'd have been in a mess had it not been for you. And you had no one to help."

"I had the Tree," he said quietly.

"Is this it?" she queried, frowning up at the green spread and the gray-white hangings.

"No, not at all. You don't know so very much about the Tree, after all, or you wouldn't ask. But this one is pretty important, in its way. I'll show you, in a minute. First I have to tend to Friendly. He needs a drink, and he likes this stuff, too."

He went down to the river's edge and was back in a very short while, stuffing shredded bits of the fruit-meat into the pouch where the little plant had its roots.

"I said I had help from the Tree—the famous tree. But I also had a lot of help from Friendly, here. As I said before, it's more than just a sense of space and a sensitivity to emotions. I'm pretty sure he's learned something from me, and I sure have learned a lot from him. Like for instance." He reached out and took up the fleecy mass of stuff he had picked away from his own meal. "Watch this," he said, beginning to tug at the mass with careful fingers. In a moment she saw that he was unwinding it in a broad strip about nine inches almost like sheer linen. A silly question came to her mind.

"It just struck me—doesn't the tree mind when you pick its fruit?"

"No, why should it? The fruit, the seed, the spore, even the embryo within the mammalian body—is a separate entity. As soon as it's ready for a life of its own, it's discarded by the parent, isn't it? So why should the tree mind? Now this"—he had what looked like yards of the stuff by now—"is worth studying. It's light and fluffy so that it will catch

any small breeze and be carried away. Or, if it falls into the water, and this kind of tree prefers to be near water, it will float and be carried away. And it's sensitive to temperature. Call that a chemical effect, if you like, but if I let go of it, it will roll itself up into a ball until it reaches a certain heat, on the inside. Then it will maintain it."

"That's something like incubation."

"That's right. Keeps the fruit at the right temperature for full growth, until it is ready to burst. But it's more than that, if you think a moment."

"You tell me," she prompted, feeling full and lazy. "I can't think around the corners the way you do."

"Well, it's close on sundown, and I need to sleep, so I guess you do, too. This is as good a place as any, right here. And this is your blanket. You just wrap it around yourself loosely, and it will do the rest. And there is more to it than that, even. We'll move as soon as it's light enough to see. And we will be heading up into the mountains. Not right to the top; I know a pass. But it will be pretty chilly up there."

"I see! But won't it be awkward, just wrapped around? Won't it keep coming undone all the time?"

"A few thorn hooks will fix that, and then you'll be fixed for the cold. Better than shivering in the thin stuff you're wearing now."

"Yes, of course. Thank you."

"Better get some sleep, now."

"Just like that? Both of us at once?"

"No danger, not here. In any case Friendly will warn me if anything does come up. Good night, ma'am."

As abruptly as that he stretched out, rolled over once or twice in the spread out fleece, wriggled and was still. She shook her head in quiet astonishment, spread and patted her own bundle until it was right, wriggled it around herself, and settled down. But there was far too much bubbling in her mind to let sleep come easily. The light faded rapidly, smudging everything into a purple blur; and then there was murmuring darkness. How pleasant it was! If only one could live like this, with no cares or worries, no duties or responsibilities—and no thought of the danger that was so close, postponed only for a brief while.

She let her mind drift back to the life that had been hers

only a short while ago, and the very memory of it was a bad taste. The remark of a colleague came back to her—a remark made in the shaking aftermath of a nearly fatal brush with certain citizens who objected to the law: "Just who are we busting a gut for—people? Are people really any better off now than they were in Cro-Magnon times? The good life! When you come right down to it, all the good life does for most people is make them fat, lazy and discontented."

That was an extreme, of course, but there was a lot of truth in it. She had never bothered to work out whether she was happy or not. She had been busy chasing the next thrill, the next sensation. Lying in the dark and thinking it over, she knew she had never been happy—not ever as blissfully contented as she was at the moment.

Then that thought went away. Pierre and Robin weren't having it as good as this, that was certain. She did have a job, duties, obligations. She hadn't dreamed it was going to be like this when she was assigned to find a planet. Memory played back to her a recording of her briefing interview.

"It's a bad one, Miss Ash." Admiral Longstaffe had been curt, possibly a bit upset by the peculiar turn of events that had put his employer's daughter in the chair opposite him. Longstaffe, thick-necked, red-faced and hard to please, was the presiding brain of Conway Ash Security, and he had every right to be hard to please. With disasters of the past still recent enough to chill the memory and not yet defeated, no new technological effort could be passed until it had been scrutinized down to the last atom, and that called for security of an order that permitted nothing less than one hundred percent. It also empowered Longstaffe to call in the help of a quasi-mythical organization known simply as the Philosophy Corps, when he found himself chewing on something big but outside his immediate competence. It must have shaken him considerably to have the fast reply from P.C. headquarters that his employer's daughter was the nearest and handiest agent they could supply. "You've had time to study the dossier?"

"Fully, what there is of it. Jory Jensen, space scout. Eccentric—what scout isn't? A man would have to be bent upstairs in some way, to take on the job in the first place. Brilliant, or he wouldn't qualify. So, a mad genius lost him-

self in space, somewhere in the general area of Epsilon Aurigae about five years ago. The details about him are trimmings, but give no hint why you want him found. Why?"

"We don't. You won't find him. He's dead."

TEN

SHE JABBED at the dossier with a finger, then sat back. "Dead, eh? Why isn't it mentioned there? And what's the point in my reading it?"

"Last first. You need all the information you can get, because we have so little. And his file is not closed simply because—well, there's a lot more that could come."

"You are sure he's dead? You want his remains traced and located, brought back, is that it?"

"Nothing like that. He lost himself on purpose because he knew he was dying. A damned foolish thing to do, but if a man can't choose what he wants to do with his last moments it's a poor world." Longstaffe coughed gruffly to cover his sentimental lapse, and looked like going on.

"Just a minute. Dying?"

"Definitely. He went through the regulation physical and mental check as soon as he reported from his last mission. The signs indicated that he had at some time suffered a bad exposure to mu-radiation. An accident with his warp generator. He wasn't told that, mark you—just handed a blue card and told to come back for a second check. That is routine; it means hang on a bit, the machines have found something wrong and we're checking. And that is true, too. You don't jump to conclusions on a matter like that. But he did; he knew. He left the reception complex and went straight back to his ship and took off. That is the last anyone has seen of him—or ever will, in all probability. Prognosis four months, give or take a few days—and that's over four years ago."

"Seems conclusive. But where do I come in?"

"Forget Jensen; let him lie, wherever he is. What we're after is something he found and did not report. On the way back from wherever, he stopped off for a bender on

Tau Ceti III—place they call Shangri-La. I imagine you
know about it? Right, well, it's an old story. He fell in with
a gang of sharpies. They got him stoned out of his mind,
rolled him clean and left him to wake up with a hangover
and regrets. So far as is known he came straight home from
there—and the rest happened the way I've told you. He
made no report at all, either there or at base, about the crooks.
You can't figure a man like that."

"How do you know about it?"

"The same bunch got hooked by the Shangri-La law, a
couple of days later, trying to clip and clean a tourist who
happened to be a somebody and screamed. They were
rounded up, and when the pressure went on them, they
cracked. The point is that among the loot found in their
possession was stuff identifiable as the property of Jory
Jensen. A part of it was some sort of seeds. They claimed
that Jensen had said those seeds were worth anything you
cared to ask—a fortune. Shangri-La shipped the whole bundle to us, story and all—his chrono, pocketbook, lucky charm,
solidos of half a dozen girl friends—the usual stuff—and
the seeds. Of course, Jensen himself was gone by the time
the package landed."

Longstaffe paused. "Miss Ash—we planted some of those
seeds—the research department, that is. The results are
pushing our best botanical research people—and others—
into a slow mumble. They are so far from finding explanations that they are having trouble just believing their own
results. Miss Ash, we have to know where that tree is."

"What were their findings?"

Longstaffe coughed again and looked portentous. "This is
top security, remember—but what would you say to a plant
or tree, that grows whatever you want? They selected ten
of those seeds and each lab grew one. They were separate.
One says, 'This looks very like a kind of citrus plant to me.'
That specimen produced oranges—and lemons. Says another, 'I've seen something like this. I will bet it is related
to cinchona.' He got what he was looking for. Then they
started comparing notes—and with others. Flowers, creepers,
other fruits, smells—you name it, or just imagine it—and
the seeds deliver. The last reports I had was that the bota-
nists were recruiting from chemists and physicists for complicated and tricky molecules to dream up, and getting

them. They did not dare to bring their separate experiments together—for just one thing, if those damned plants can read a human mind, they can certainly read each others'—and you think about it for a while and you'll go light-headed, too. We need that tree!"

She took a careful breath and objected. "But if Jensen is dead, as you say, and made no report on whatever the planet was where he got those seeds—four years ago—how can it be found?"

"I know; it's hopeless. We have every unit we can spare out looking as diligently as possible without stirring up curiosity among others. A needle in the biggest damned haystack anyone ever thought of. But Jensen talked once, that much we know; he may have talked to other people. Somebody might have seen something, heard something, probably without realizing it was anything important. You'll start from Shangri-La. You can pass yourself off as—yourself. And keep your ears and eyes open. If you get anything, anything at all—report. We, the forces of order and sanity, have to find that Anything Tree first!"

Selena could have given him a number of arguments about the forces of order and sanity, but she had to find the mysterious plant.

The forlorn impression that the search would be for nothing had grown swiftly as she listened to the fanciful rumors that were like an aura around the name of Jensen's Planet. Either Jory Jensen himself had talked very freely in his cups, or Longstaffe's laboratory personnel were not nearly as security minded as he was. Each tale she heard was taller than the last; each started from the concept of a magic tree and went from there—with only one saving grace, that no one really believed a word of it, not even those who told the best tales. She had chased the story all over Shangri-La's diverse panderings to wealthy pleasure, and it was, again, like the fabulous Indian Rope-Trick. It was always someone else who had had it at first hand, never the speaker. With the passage of time, the accumulation of repetitions and variations—and her own inner distaste for the frivolous role she had to assume—she had come to disbelieve the whole thing, despite Longstaffe's seriousness, and her trip back to Luna had been meant as her moment to declare it nonsense. Only *then* did she find it.

She had a drowsy image of Admrial Longstaffe's weathered face as she broke it to him that there was a man on the planet who had been living with the tree and its lesser relations for years. She tried to imagine his dismay and anger and it didn't work. Somehow the old man's face turned green, and scarlet flowers blossomed from his ears. He leaned across his desk and nipped her with lobsterlike claws, snarling. . . .

"Don't just lie there smirking. Wake up and do something. Wake up."

Joe's quiet voice splintered her dream, and she stirred drowsily as he called, "Time to start out again, ma'am. You want a bite and fresh up?"

"Oh! Mmmm!" She stretched and sat up. There was just enough light to see. "This is the life," she sighed incautiously. "I haven't slept like that since I was a little girl."

"Make the most of it then; it isn't going to last much longer."

"You really don't like people, do you, Joe?" She stirred and went as far as the river-bank to splash her face with the stingingly cold water. He had a kernel all ready to share with her by the time she was done.

"Got nothing against individuals," he corrected, "it's only when they group up into a thing called society that the devil is born."

"The devil? Personified evil?"

"That's what I mean, all right. It always surprises me that the same people who will agree that society is an entity, a thing other than the people who comprise it—those same people boggle at the idea that good and bad can be similarly regarded as entities."

"It's a thought," she mused through a mouthful. "Society is something sociologists have accepted for a long time—measured its dynamic and formulated rules about it. But I must confess I had never thought of gods and devils in the same style. What particular devil had you in mind?"

"We can go into that some other time," he said. "You have things to learn right now. In about an hour we'll break free of timber and then the green belt altogether. And we will be in danger, as well as being cold."

"Something Friendly can't handle?"

"Right. The cold slows him down a bit. That's why I

61

want to be into the pass and going through by noon, to get the best of the daylight and sun for him, keep him awake."

"That makes sense. Just what will we be up against?"

He rose, gripping his spear, and they set out through a gray light rapidly turning golden-green. "There's the arrow birds. You know about them. And there are browsers and mountain cats. Those are just my names for 'em. The browsers are huge—anything up to thirty feet long—and eat green stuff, grass, bushes and such—and they know exactly how far into the green belt they can wander before they bite off something too big to chew up."

Selena felt an uneasy tingle along her spine at the idea of massive herbivores accustomed to doing battle with sentient plants. "It must be fun for them," she suggested, "going to nibble at a succulent bunch of leaves and have it try to nibble back."

"Not a lot of fun for us if we run into a bunch of them. They're strong, and all armor-plated around the head and muzzle, and the front feet are clawed like scythes; and they're always hungry—will eat anything they can get hold of—including each other's carcasses."

"What's the strategy for them?" she asked, and he nodded approvingly.

"Depends. Basic precaution is to pick a way that leads in between boulders and rocks, someplace narrow—when you can, that is. And that way they can't come close enough to harm, anyway. Failing that, all you can do is keep a keen ear open all the time and be ready to run like hell for cover. They're slow starters, but they can work up a clip." He let it rest as he negotiated a small gully and an ice-cold stream. He took up the account when they had gained the far side.

"Mountain cats are something else again. There aren't many, which is all the good news. The rest is completely bad. They come about the size of a tiger, maybe smaller, and are always and ever killing mad. Like the browsers, they are always hungry, and that's the one weakness they have. They kill and eat—and nothing will turn them from eating until it's all gone. They have all the teeth and claws any animal ever had and then some. And they almost always lurk high, so they can drop down on their prey. On the ground they wouldn't get much fun out of tangling with a browser, they'd just get tromped."

"And what's the strategy with them?"

"It's tricky," he admitted. "The best bet is to stay right away from overhangs of any kind—but you can't always do that if you're picking narrow trails to baffle the browsers."

"Difficult?" she queried. "It sounds insane to me. Joe, you've made this trip a time or two, obviously, on your own—with just a spear and a knife?"

"The spear," he said, "is just a symbol, I guess. Only thing I ever use it for is to pick fruit sometimes—or to lean on. I've never killed anything with it. Never tried to. All I aim for is to keep out of the way." He leaned into a steep rise, at the top of which the bushes were scantier; there were no trees ahead. "The way I see it," he said, "I'm the interloper here. This is their planet, what right have I to kill them?"

"That may suit you," she retorted, "but—I hope you won't mind—any arrow bird, browser, or mountain cat that shows any sign of being a threat to me had better be able to move faster than I can push the stud on my rifle."

"That's your privilege," he admitted evenly. "We better look out for some thorn hooks now, and I'll give you a hint or two on how to drape this stuff so it will maintain your temperature. That breeze has a bite in it."

It was more than a bite. Sharpened by the rapid change from close jungle heat, it felt to her like knives scraping past; she was eager to learn how to use the hooking thorns to arrange the fleecy material to its best advantage. It was best, he explained, to wrap it around in many layers, but to leave arms, shoulders and legs free for movement. A dangling length between the shoulder blades would come in later for a hood.

"And make it loose," he emphasized. "Might feel insecure and breezy, but it will cuddle up by itself if you get real cold."

"Colder than this?"

"This is just cool, on the skin. Once we move that will pass off. You ready?"

She was, and they went on, soon into bleak rocky terrain where all there was to see of life was the stubborn greenish moss on the rocks. He went ahead now, holding out his spear butt first like a guide rod, tapping ahead.

"Forgot to mention the snakes," he explained. "They move

out of the way if they have the chance, but they object to being stood on."

She pretended to accept the explanation, but it didn't fool her at all, and she marched at his back with her beamer ready, just in case.

ELEVEN

THEY MADE THE peak of the pass as near to noon as she could estimate by the sun, precisely on schedule and without coming too close to any hazards. The peaks on either side, far from providing any kind of shelter, seemed to funnel what had been a constant breeze into a gale. Her extremities complained, but the rest of her was cozily warm inside the creeping fiber. There, she mused, was an idea that, properly exploited, would get someone a considerable fortune. She tried tactfully suggesting it to him.

"When other people start coming here, Joe," she said, "as they will, what will you do? Establish claim, or move out?"

"Hadn't thought much about it. I won't leave, that's for sure. I'll get by."

The edge on his tone warned her to leave that topic. She tried another one on him.

"How did you happen to find this place?"

"I'd rather not talk about it."

"All right. What were you before you came here?"

"Nobody much. Just one more in the rat race, I guess. Wondering what it was all about, what it's all for?"

"Did you find any answers?"

"Not until I came here and had time to think things out. This place is real; it makes sense. Plants don't spend their time trying to be something else. They just live and grow and mind their business."

She took the hint and saved her breath for the climb, and to pump blood against the increasing chill. They had seen a herd of browsers, but fortunately from a safe distance. They were graceless creatures, lumbering mountains of gray-green scales and matted fur—and even while she

was imagining what that combination would do to the biologists who maintained that no animal could have fur and scales at the same time—she saw the herd attacked by a stray covey of arrow birds. She was surprised. Big and lumpish they might be, but they could wheel fast enough in their tracks when threatened.

"It's the fool birds that don't learn," he pointed out, as they hid and watched. "Even if they don't smash up on those scales, they don't pack enough punch to kill one of those wallopers."

She saw one diving lizard hit and penetrate right up to its head in a browser's matted fur. And before anything else could happen the mighty fang-filled maw came around and snapped, and there was just the stump of the beak there, still buried in meat.

"But surely," she suggested, ordering her stomach to behave, "enough wounds like that and the biggest beast must go down?"

"Right. And his buddies will eat him, and any arrow birds that try to carve something for themselves. The only time the birds win is if there's a swarm of them, or they happen on a youngster on his own."

It had been an arduous trip. According to him they were over the worst and it was all down hill. She could have admired the view, the sweeping panorama of forest, mountainside and distant sea, had it not been far too cold for hanging about. Besides which she was hungry and said so.

"Me, too," he admitted. "There's plenty of food down there, so let's get on; the sooner we get back among the trees the better I'll like it—and Friendly. He don't care for altitude at all."

She hadn't seen the little blue flower head in some hours. Cowering away from the abnormal chill and the thin air, it had long since retreated from his hair and was safely snuggled somewhere inside his woolly garment. She had a pretty good idea just how dependent he was on the flower's senses, and how uneasy he must be with them partially blunted, yet he showed no sign of hesitation as they began the steep descent.

They were scrambling down a gorge that showed every sign of becoming a young valley. The river in its cleft leaped and chattered as if in a hurry to meet it's fate among the

green that was tantalizingly close below. Selena came up to his shoulder, in a moment when he was casting about for the next drop, and declared, "I tend not to like people who abandon things—a chase, a race, a duty, things like that. I'd much rather someone rocked the boat than jumped out."

"It's a point of view," he admitted as he crouched and scrambled down another ledge. "Lots of people have claimed that it's the malcontents and misfits in society who make all the changes—and they claim that's a good thing—keeps progress progressing."

"And there's something wrong with that?"

"I didn't say so. All I know is that if you keep right on butting your head against a brick wall, you'll end up with a concussion. The wall won't change any. Mark Twain said, once 'If at first you don't succeed, try, try again, and then quit. No point in being foolish!' If I don't fit into society, why should *it* change to make room for *me?*"

"Why shouldn't it?" she retorted. "The ideal society should be such that people do fit into it."

"When I hear about one of those maybe I'll go."

"You're a difficult man to like," she complained, bracing herself and leaping down after him. The gorge was getting quite deep now. "You have all sorts of admirable qualities, but you're so prickly."

"You should quit feeling sorry for me."

"You can feel that? I'm sorry, I don't—look, Joe"—she dredged up one of her favorite gambits—"just think about a little grain of sand that gets into an oyster shell and sets up an irritation—and then what happens? A pearl."

"Great—now tell me what the oyster thinks about it."

"You're impossible! You could have been successful at all sorts of things if you had put your mind to it; you know that."

"It's my life," he snorted, and plunged on ahead of her, around a bend in the gorge. Exasperated, she tramped after him, around the corner and into the most foul stench she had ever met. He got it at the same time and froze.

"Cat," he muttered. "Close, too."

She heard him, but her attention was held by the more immediate danger ahead. Up the gorge in lumbering flight came three of the browsers, two large ones and a baby about

nine or ten feet long. Now he heard and felt them, and flattened against the rock-wall.

"They're running away from a cat!" she cried, seeing the slinking yellow-furred shape where it bounded hungrily in chase of meat.

"Right into another one. He's waiting here. Can you see him?"

She glanced up and about rapidly and was just in time to see a snarling fury launch itself from a ledge directly above, clawed feet wide and ready to slash and rend. She swung her beamer and fired at the beast. She heard the echoes of its scream and saw it crash into the rock wall where he was standing with his spear braced. Man and mortally wounded animal went down in a thrashing tangle.

"Lie still!" she yelled, and aimed again, seeing the cat's body burn. Then the lumbering monsters were too close to ignore; they couldn't stop even if that idea could have penetrated their thick wits in time. She dropped to a knee and leveled the rifle, drilling a hole through the little one in front. She saw it lurch and skid into a heap. The others ran into the body, whoofed with the impact, and immediately forgot their panic and began to eat it. Sickened by the sight of them, she shot both—but they did not die immediately.

The yellow pursuer caught up and sprang onto one of the big browsers. She lowered her beamer and moved cautiously to where Joe lay dreadfully still with the dead mountain cat sprawled on top of him.

"Joe?" she whispered. "Are you conscious?"

There was no reply, and she crept still closer, not taking her eyes off the grisly feast for one moment. The noise from the struggle between cat and browser was painful; the steep gorge caught and amplified the screech of the cat and the rumble of the browser. She shook her head, took careful aim, and blasted the cat first, crisping it into silence. Then she shot the two browsers, steeling herself to hold down the lever until there was no possible doubt.

Her stomach lurching, she grasped the dead cat's fur and heaved at it until she had Joe uncovered enough to be able to investigate. There was blood on him, and scratches, none of which looked serious—and he was unconscious, but, as far as she could tell, that was only the effect of a blow on

the head. She struggled to free him from the cat altogether; and then she took a good breath and tried to remember everything she had been told about how to lift and handle an unconscious body. He stirred.

"Huh? . . . What? . . . Holy jumping jets, my head!"

"You must have struck it against the rock when the cat fell on you. Don't move yet, I haven't had time to examine properly—can you feel if there's anything else?"

"There's a stink." He kept his eyes closed and made a tentative movement or two. "I guess I'm all right. Bruised, nothing more than that. What happened, anyway?" She told him, briefly, and he shook his head as if to deny something. "I owe you my life, I guess. I'm grateful, but I'm sorry you had to kill them all."

"What else could I have done?" She watched him sit up and touch himself where the bloodstains were. "We were right in the track of the things."

"I suppose you're right." He reached around and gathered his spear, yanking to free it from the carcass of the dead cat. There was distaste on his face. "First time this thing has ever had blood on it," he said. And she gave way to irritation.

"Excuse me for living!" she snapped. "You may not value your life all that much, but I do mine, and I was looking after it. Do you mind?"

He got to his feet, stretching gingerly, then made his way down to where the stream lashed at the bend in the track, plunging in and squatting down in it to clean himself. She shivered in sympathy, but he made no sign of feeling the chill. After a while he stood again, shook himself like a dog, and rejoined her.

"We'd better get on," he said, and they went on and down, after scrambling past the odorous carcasses. She felt ruffled and knowing that he was tuned in on her feelings didn't help any. She made a point of changing the power pack on her beamer and keeping the spent one for future recharging.

"Now look," she said at last, unable to repress her indignation any longer. "It's all very fine and good to be averse to killing things. I would go along with that myself most of the time. But when it comes to self-defense—"

"To a choice between you and them, you mean?"

"If you want to put it that way, yes."

"I've been here a long time—four years, according to you. I have never had to kill anything yet."

"How many times have you made this trip to the Tree?"

"Twenty, maybe. I haven't counted."

"Well, all I can say is you've been lucky."

"Maybe. I prefer to keep out of the way of trouble."

"They kill each other anyway!"

"I know. But this is their world. We're interlopers. You know, if you take the long view, mankind is an interloper anyway. Wherever we go we interfere and change and mess things up, playing about with powers and forces we don't understand—upsetting nature—fouling it."

"Oh, well," she sneered. "That's about as far as you can go, isn't it? Now you want to opt out of the whole human race."

"Wish I could. I reckon I'd be better off as a plant."

"Do you, indeed! Then, for Heaven's sake why don't you settle down where we're going, along with your precious Tree, and live right there—instead of on the other side of the mountain?"

"You'll know why soon enough. Getting warmer. We'll be there in about three hours or so."

TWELVE

IN LESS THAN an hour they were into scrubby grass and bushes. The sun was warm, the breeze only a gentle breath. The little blue flower came out of hiding and settled itself around his neck and over an ear as if peering ahead. The relief of tension was as tangible as putting down a heavy load. Selena wasn't sure whether it was her own relief—for the mix-up with the stampeding browsers and the murderous cats had shaken her more than she cared to admit—or whether it came from the strange pair she was traveling with. Joe showed nothing on his face, of course, but there was an easier spring in his step. And as for the small flower, she had quite accepted it as an independent entity, more so because it never turned its one-eyed blue stare on her now, but kept its attention ahead.

THE ANYTHING TREE

Analyzing her own feelings was getting to be her way of passing the time, as all attempts to strike a conversation with Joe seemed to lead straight into differences of opinion. This positive awareness of reduced tension, now; could it be that something of the peculiar sensory ability of the plant life was rubbing off on her? She took an internal look at it and had to admit that she had a definite feeling of welcome from the tangled greenery they were now passing through. And she felt affectionate towards the plants, too. There had been little of nature, the wide open spaces, wind-on-the-heath kind of thing in her life. Earth was rapidly running out of that kind of luxury in any case, and most of her adult life had been spent in arduous conditions where the opportunities for contemplating the harmonies of nature were strictly confined to staring at stars and more or less forbidding environments.

"Joe," she called him, all at once. "Hold on just a minute. I've not seen one like this before. Look."

He came back a step or two to contemplate a thick bush that was laden with bulbous and juicy-looking berries, each about the size of a big Earth grape, but golden yellow in color.

"They look delicious," she confessed. "Are they edible, do you know?"

"You can eat 'em," he admitted, "but go easy with them. They pack a punch like neat alcohol. In fact, most of the saps and juices I've run into have that effect. I don't know the chemistry of it, only the effect."

"Hangovers you've had?" she suggested, and he shook his head, not rising to her mild wit.

"They don't do that. But they will make you falling-down stinko if you eat too many. Watch it."

"I will," she promised, and approached the bush with caution and a mental request. Would it mind if she took some? It didn't seem to, and she collected several laden sprays, tasting one as she stepped out to overtake him. The grape-appearance was deceptive. It was more like a tomato inside; the flavor was delightful—and powerful, reminding her of a liqueur. Something like Cointreau? She tried another and a warm glow grew in her stomach, warning her that he had not spoken idly. She thought she could handle just one more, and she did. *What a quiet and pleasant place*

this is! If only one could live here, starting from scratch. Forget the past. Pretend it had never existed—she stopped and shook her head in mild irritation as her wraparound slithered into dangling folds for the fourth time.

It was loose and floppy, no matter how she tried to pin it into place with the thorn hooks. She was trying to keep it as a two piece, one band about her bosom and shoulders, the other like a skirt, but the stuff kept snaking away, curling back and coming undone.

"I'm too hot for it," she muttered, "that's the trouble," and she had a sudden mental image of this freak material made into a dress and worn by some unsuspecting female who happened to walk into somewhere hot. *My God!* she thought, *it would just fall off, all by itself!*—and the thought pushed a giggle up into her mouth and it spilled over into a shake of laughter—until she caught herself in sudden apprehension. She shook her head violently.

This won't do. I'm close to being stoned! And he did warn me! I'm a fool! She breathed hard, ordered her whimsical faculties to behave, and took the traitorous silky fiber in both hands, hooks and all.

"I don't need you. I can always get more, if I have to. Goodbye; thank you for keeping me warm when I needed it."

She dropped the bundle by the side of the track—what she hoped was the track—and set out to catch up with him. She couldn't see or hear him, but she knew where he was, and she hurried. The giggles came again, but she swallowed them down and came up about three paces clear of his broad back, and marched demurely along as if nothing was in any way unusual. A few minutes farther on she saw another bush, this time ablaze with scarlet flowers, and she couldn't resist the urge to catch one big one and twist it into her hair over her ear. Just to show him she was quite unconcerned, that was all. Ten paces more, and he stopped.

"You're wearing a flower," he accused. "Why?"

"Why not?" she retorted. "Does it bother you? Is it dangerous?"

"No, to both those. Bothers Friendly a bit, though."

"Oh!" She thought that over, and malice came into her mind. "Maybe he doesn't care for this particular shade of blue?"

"Colors don't have anything to do with it, ma'am. You want to look like a flower, that's your privilege." He didn't shrug, but it was there in his tone. He turned and led on, leaving her to follow, as usual. In a little while her small jest seemed sour, and she withdrew the flower from her hair and let it fall discreetly. *Those damned grape things, and on an empty stomach, too!* That thought stimulated the sensation and she really was hungry.

They were well into the forest by the time he called another halt; there was no need to explain this time. Not only could she see the bed-and-breakfast tree ahead, she had been sensing it for some six or seven minutes earlier. That realization made her thoughtful as they gathered a meal and squatted to enjoy it properly. She blessed the fact that he was the sort of person with whom one could be silent without provoking a lot of questions. It gave her time to think through her sensations and arrange them. Then she brought out the problem for him to comment on.

"I knew this tree was here before we got to it," she told him. "And I think I am beginning to sense you—your reactions, at least. Do you suppose something of the peculiar magic of this place is infecting me, or is it mental extension —practice, I mean."

"I don't know about the tree," he muttered, taking her question quite literally and seriously, as she had known he would. "That could be just wishful thinking, because you had an appetite. As for reading me, that could be just cues and learning—tone of voice, expression, attitudes and posture. You can do a lot with that, sometimes without knowing it."

"Now you're being evasive. Do you know anything at all about basic psychology?"

"Some. I've read up on it. A man has plenty of time to—" He let that rest and changed the subject a little. "You could be barking up a tree that isn't there, if you'll excuse the allusion, ma'am. I told you, these plants are not intelligent —not as we define it. If you want to be clinical about it, no plant has a brain, or anything anyway resembling a brain."

"That," she retorted, "is no argument at all. We know quite a bit about the brain, these days, enough to realize that the old notion about the brain being the seat of consciousness is hard to maintain."

"Don't see how you can avoid it," he came back, showing interest. "When you put out the brain, everything else is out."

"But the whole body is you. The whole body is intelligent and alive. The brain is just a part, a special part no doubt, but only a part. You aren't *you* with just a brain—it's a relay center, but it doesn't make experiences, or thoughts either, really. If you have any skills at all you must know that your body has them. A plant doesn't need our kind of brain because it has no need to maintain mobility, to be constantly dealing with changing environment. But the whole-body intelligence can be there, just as it is in us. And it can be just as intelligent as us—only it doesn't talk about it."

"And we can understand and deal with abstractions. A plant can't ever do that if, as you say, it is material-intelligent—just a recorded memory of its own sensations."

"I didn't say it like that, but you have a point. Yes, I suppose we are all the result of what has happened to us."

"Plus what we have learned from everyone else, and what they've all learned, and it goes on." He discarded a section of husk, and added, "A plant can only know its own small world and nothing else at all, whereas a person knows a whole history of the human race merely by learning how to talk."

"Yes," she admitted, and scowled.

He took up the last bit of his fruit meal and began to gnaw it. Her thoughts went along a new tack now, a surprising one for her. In her hectic twenty-five years of life Selena had come to know that she was every bit as good as anyone else and far superior to most. She had come to accept that as a matter of course. Now, in a few short hours, she had been defeated and made to look amateurish at almost everything by this strange man. She discovered that she didn't really mind—because he didn't lean on it or take advantage of it. Her curiosity, never very far from the surface, blazed into renewed heat and suggested a strategy.

"Joe," she said gently. "As we're just sitting here for a bit, may I touch your hand again? Please? I just want to know whether the plant life here sings the same song, speaks the same language as the others did, back there."

He looked at her, his curiously bright eyes very keen.

Then, without a word, he extended his left hand so she could reach and clasp his fingers. In that simple contact the magic came once more, only stronger and more vividly. Instinctively she closed her eyes, and held her breath at the wonder of it. It was so like mighty music, yet utterly soundless, not in her ear at all. She felt great booming organ notes from the trees; a rushing running obbligato of violin-whispering and gossiping from the bushes and climbing creepers, trails of silver sound; bell-like chimes that were flowers; and the scurrying piccolo busy-body shrillness of the grass. And then, faint and far away, something caught her mental ear and held it: a silver horn-note, an invitation, both a plea and promise in one. That call stirred her all the way down inside to depths she never knew she had. She opened her eyes and stared at him.

"What's that?" she breathed. "Something a long way off, calling to me?"

"You asked me, some time back, whether Pardoe would be able to find the Tree—one tree, out of all these millions. I said he would. Now you know."

"That's the Tree, that call?"

"That's it. Couple of hours away yet. Call it fifteen miles. And that's just its normal curiosity, not stirred up. It doesn't know you're here, not yet. When it finds out—" He let the sentence die unfinished and she released his fingers hurriedly.

THIRTEEN

"It will find out about you, discover that you are here. And when it does, it will call you. If Pardoe runs true to form, he will do his looking with a chopper, from above, and it will find out about him a lot faster than it will about you. Can't miss—and it will call him, too."

"Call?"

"Oh yes, it can put the pressure on. Not the way you heard it; that was idle—dreaming, you might say. Once it gets stirred, though—"

Selena felt a chill tickle the back of her neck and her

spine. He must have sensed it, for he put on his teeth-baring smile.

"I don't know whether you're right to be scared, or not. I could say not—that you're in no danger. I could say the Tree won't harm you. It's just curious about anything new and different, that's all. I could say that, and it would be the truth as I know it. But I might be wrong, too. What I can say is that the Tree never did me any harm at all— just the reverse. But I can't expect you to believe that. In the final analysis, I suppose it comes down to what kind of a person you are."

"And what sort of person you are, too," she said. "That's something I don't know, Joe. I've seen you, heard you, watched you—but how do I really know what you are, inside?"

"That's the oldest and still unsolved problem in the world."

"Oh now," she denied. "You have an assist. You can detect me; you've admitted it, and demonstrated it, too. You know what I'm feeling. You have even allowed me to know what the plants and trees are thinking and feeling, through your helper. But, every time, I have never been aware of you in that. You've kept yourself out, somehow. Now why would you do that?"

"Just a habit of mine. Don't like being pushy. Don't talk about myself much, either."

"That may be, but without something like that, how do I know what to believe? You may be leading me into a trap of some kind. You could even be a slave of that—that thing, whatever it is!"

She saw the shutters come down over his face again. "You don't have to go any further, ma'am. You can stop right here, or go back. Suit yourself."

"Don't let's start that again. I want to help, and I *can* help, but I have to know what I'm getting into, who I can trust."

"All right. If that's the way you want it, if it will help at all, just this once can't hurt." He held out his hand to her again. She looked at it, at him, and had to drive herself to reach and take his fingers this time. At first there was nothing at all, not even the orchestral vegetation. His face was a guarded mask, his eyes blank—then he started to fade away, to become shadowy and unreal, even as she stared.

Shaken by that impossibility she shut her eyes tight. Now, with a sense of being suspended in mid-air without support, she began to receive him—or something that she felt was him. An in-depth color-sound-emotion blend: a steady flame without heat, the straightness of a sword blade, steel, transparency that was serenity, curiosity without intrusion, fellowship, kinship, and warmth that infused and soothed, that was total self-confidence. Words and inadequate images tumbled over themselves in her mind and she abandoned them impatiently and let the mystery that was him flood in and become known to her.

Then he took his hand away, and he went away like a quick-fading image in sand. She opened her eyes.

"Never did anything like that before—only once," he muttered. "I hope it helped you, ma'am."

It seemed that she hadn't breathed in a long while. She caught up on it, trying to clutch at a fading impression of something wonderful, but it erased itself, leaving only an afterglow.

"I don't know about help, Joe. I don't know how much of that to believe, but I'm going to accept it just as it came and trust it—and you. You say the Tree won't harm me. All right, I'll accept that. We can go on just as soon as you say."

Without another word he rose and started. She followed, drifting in a half-dream through the luxuriant green, bathed in the scents and senses of murmuring life all around, and utterly bemused. Part of her mind could isolate and cling to one hard fact, that she had been permitted to know one other person in a way she had never believed possible. For her it meant a complete redefining of the term to know, as applied to anyone else. She thought back to the Jory Jensen dossier she had studied. What had it told her? He was born at a certain date in a certain place. He had this, that and the other certificates, degrees and skills. He was so high, of such a color skin and eyes, and weight—and all the rest of it. But it had not told her what sort of a person he was because there was no one to know that, nor words to express it. But she knew, now, exactly what sort of a person Joe was.

She knew him, and it was a wonderful, a humbling thing. It was even more humbling, in the midst of the warmth

that was remembering him, to realize that he must know her just as completely. Did she come out of the experience as handsomely? She went deep down into self-examination and doubted it and felt herself a mass of submerged frustrations and petty bitternesses, conceits and contradictions. Then she thought of the blue flower; that flower was the key.

She imagined how it might be if someone could gather seeds of the flower and propagate them far and wide, making them available to the scattered and seething millions of suffering humanity. *The barriers would come down in ruins. People would really be able to know each other. Away would go all the inadequacy of signs and symbols and clumsy words, the deceptions and half-truths. Personalities revealed*—and then her inborn common sense called a shuddering halt.

Would that be so good? She wondered. Would it be wonderful to encounter a mind and personality like—Buck Pardoe or Scorpia Martine?—or, indeed, any one of hundreds of undesirable characters she could call to mind out of a lively past? Shrinking from that, she modified the thought a little. *Why select the known bad ones? Wouldn't it be just as shocking to unveil ordinary people? Nice people? Wouldn't it be something like entering unannounced a bedroom or bathroom? Invasion of privacy!* She grew so immersed in this line of speculation that the matter-of-fact world went by her unheeded. It was with a sense of shock that she suddenly realized that she was standing quite still.

Real-time awareness came to her in discreet bits.

Now that she was paying attention, a presence knocked gently but insistently at the door of her mind. It came in as soon as she was aware of it. It was strong yet gentle, warm, embracing, promising, inviting, and almost saying, "Come to me, let me know you, let me know all about you. Come!"

She retained just enough selfhood to flash an urgent appeal to Joe, who stood waiting for her. He shrugged helplessly.

"You can turn around and walk away if you want to. But you don't want to, knowing you. I don't think it will harm you—but I have to say just this. Back there a bit we were talking about devils and gods, the personifications of

abstractions. I can define one devil for you that bites hard into all civilized people. Call it willing self-deception, the ability to think of rational excuses for all the stupid and wrong things we do and believe in."

With an effort she detached her mind from that insidious call, and shook her head at him. "Is that relevant now?"

"I think so. Deception's a nice devil. He helps you believe yourself, helps you kid yourself that you're not really bad at all, that all the evil and wicked things you think and feel and do are not really bad at all—just force of circumstances, or misunderstanding by other people. A comforting devil to have. But the Tree doesn't know about such things. Without knowing, it casts out devils."

"That can't be bad," she said, and smiled, and then surrendered herself to the insistent and urgent call in her mind. She went into the cool stream, across it and up the bank beyond, passing Joe with another smile. Over the ridge were scattered bushes of all kinds in profusion, so that she had to pursue a winding path, weaving in and out but always following that Lorelei call. It grew stronger and more confident, throwing her inner emotions back into childhood, creating for her the image of father-mother benevolence and vast affection. There was an almost tangible embrace and welcome. Then there were no more bushes, just a clear space and a hanging green veil. She paused, mildy curious until she saw what it was. The Tree was inside somewhere, like the central pole of some immense tent, and this veil was the drooping fronds of its outermost branches.

She put out her hand to part the curtain, but it drew aside for her, opening a lane in the green and inviting her in. Beyond the curtain itself there was a cool turf-floored expanse that gave her the impression of a church, of being imbued with reverence. It was immensely high, seeming to fade away into a sunlit green haze. The trunk itself was large—by any standards an old and enormous forest giant. Selena was not awed by the size alone. She had walked in sequoia groves, among trees that would dwarf this one, but none of those had ever impressed her with such majesty. The vast trunk, some twenty feet through, was dark green, almost black; and it was glossy, without a single branch to in-

terrupt its soaring rise until the eye had followed it at least a hundred feet into the green haze.

Her irrational fears had vanished. There was no hazard here, only a vast and curious benevolence, patiently serene. She stood for a while just bathing in the presence, feeling it like a caress on her skin. Then she remembered the beamer and charges that she carried, and felt wrong about them. Apologies came to her mind as she peeled off the straps and laid her weapons on the turf. Then the call came so plainly that there could be no error, and she advanced, put out her hands and laid her palms flat on the trunk of the Tree.

As when Joe had revealed himself to her, the outlines of sight began to blur, fade and dissolve, and she closed her eyes. Time hung still; existence became unreal, unimportant. There was a tingle in her fingers and arms as if the Tree itself rippled and moved. A phrase came to her mind out of the long ago, *"Goodness went out of me!"* Who had said it? It was as if everything she was and ever had been flowed out of her through her palms and into the Tree. At first, it was good, a tingle of pleasure and greeting. Then it was lassitude and misgiving—and fear. Shaking waves of dark fear swelled up in her and became terror that drowned her into panic. Aghast, clinging to that cool trunk, shaking and weak, she felt wave upon wave of stupefying dread, helplessness and emptiness, as if all her substance were melting away to become nothing.

She clung desperately to the tree as the only real thing in the nightmare; there came pain in rushes and spurts, and the strong soundless music again, shaking and vibrating, tearing her to pieces, ripping small agonies from her body like plucking hairs—and yet there was no hurt, no injury. The pain swept over and through her like a flood, but it was a fire that burned without consuming, that left strength and clarity. Purification—dimly but happily she knew that the flow was not all one way, that something surged back into her from the Tree—something that was good, strong, and bold. The last vestiges of cowardice and dread washed out in that comforting flow. She knew, as plainly as if it had been shouted in her ear, that she was now whole, healthy and clean. And this the Tree had done for her, and to her,

and she was thankful in a way that made an everlasting bond between it and her.

With a silent but sincere gratitude she lowered her hands and turned, to see Joe standing a few feet away, watching her. She felt gratitude to him, too, and a sense of sharing something wonderful with him. She put out her hand in greeting, started to go to him, and her legs folded under her, the glade and everything in it fell away into darkness and silence.

FOURTEEN

WHEN SHE CAME back to consciousness she was stretched out flat on turf and able to stare up into the vast vault of the Tree. She was quite at ease, knew where she was, had no fear, and just lay there in peace, savoring the rare pleasure of being completely comfortable and happy. The completeness of it was in itself remarkable, and she was just beginning on that thought when she grew aware of a low muttering, quite close. She sat up and turned to look; there was Joe. He squatted before the Tree with his hands out to touch it, and he was talking to it. She wrinkled her brow at that, for a moment, but then let it go. Surely speech, she thought, was neither necessary nor of any use, but maybe it helped him with mental imagery. She lay back on an elbow and returned to contemplation of her own well-being. She looked up as he came padding across the grass to her and sank into a squat by her side.

"How do you feel?" he asked. She smiled.

"You know I can't describe it. I've read quite a lot by people who have had striking spiritual experiences, and it always comes to the same thing—it can't be described."

"That's in the Tao," he said unexpectedly. "If you can describe it, that's not it. I think that is what the Bible passage means—the peace of mind that passes all understanding. Something like that."

"I am through being surprised at anything you say, Joe. After that experience, nothing will surprise me. I feel as if I had been taken apart, molecule by molecule, and put back

together again properly, the way I should have been all along. Isn't it crazy?"

"Say it like that and it is, but it's true. That's what I meant about casting out devils. We humans carry about with us all sorts of lies and illusions to preserve us against the sometimes unpleasant realities. That's why so very few people are really fit and healthy, and well. They don't know the right way to live, which is determined by the design of the body itself."

"I think it's more than that. I know something you don't, perhaps. Scientists have investigated the seeds of that Tree, and I know this about their results: those seeds grow and produce plants that have the power to take a construct from a human mind and create it in solid reality. It can deliver what you want."

"So?"

"So I suppose everyone has some kind of meaningful image of what he or she would like to be, a kind of super-ego picture of what we could be. And I think the Tree uses that as a working base."

"Maybe." He sounded doubtful. "It has limitations. It's only a tree, after all."

"You mean, this euphoria could be some kind of illusion in itself? That's a possibility I hadn't considered—hypnosis and suggestion."

"How do you tell the difference?"

"Well." She pondered. "If it really is repair and restructure—I have a scar or two. Mementoes of a lively past. Excuse me." She searched for a scar—and there was no scar.

"It's real, all right. Instant healing!"

"Not instant," he corrected. "It took an hour for you, maybe more. And maybe not healing, either. I told you, it's mental pictures it gets. If that's true then it fixes you up the way you want to be, as far as possible. And that's not always good, is it?"

"I suppose not," she agreed, and fled hastily from any possible revelation of her vanity. "But what do you mean by limitations?"

"Never mind. Look, we'd better get out of here to where we can keep an ear out for Pardoe and the others. This place is close to being soundproof, and Friendly isn't any

help either. He's a relative of the Tree, you see, and completely paralyzed all the time he's here."

"Sort of 'Keep quite while Grandad is talking,' you mean?"

"That's about the size of it." He rose and she went up with him as if new springs had been fitted into all her sinews. The delight of it was like wine and she had to fight to remain calm.

"I confess I'd forgotten all about Pardoe," she admitted as they left the glade, through the curtain of leaves and into the reddish glow of late afternoon. They headed for the stream. "Do you think he will harm the Tree?"

"I think so. I'm not sure. The only thing I have in mind is to stop him from getting at it, somehow. You're pretty good with that beamer."

"Yes, but if you think I'm going to shoot him down out of the sky, think again."

"I know. He'll have your friends aboard. He's no fool. He will figure that you value their lives."

"And I do, at least as much as my own, or yours."

"As much as the whole of the rest of humanity?" he challenged. She started to be angry with him. Then she was struck rigid as he threw her anger right back at her, as positively and unarguably as if it had been a ball.

"Good Heavens!"

"Right," he said grimly. "That's just one of the tricks I've learned from that Tree. You had some before, remember? When you tried to go for me, out by your ship? You probably thought that I hit you with something, and, in a way, I did, but all it was—I threw your own mental attack right back at you."

"Why wait until now to demonstrate—this ability?"

"Because, to do it, I have to touch you mentally to sense what you're doing, so I can reverse it. And—before—I didn't care to do that."

"Very delicately put. In other words, I was repulsive?"

"Put it like that, if you want. The point is, it can be learned. All I did was ask for it. I needed it, or so I thought, to protect myself in a place like this. I don't use it now, and you can see why."

"Yes, but I've lost your point somewhere. What has this to do with Pardoe and my friends?"

"And humanity, remember? Your trouble is, you're stuck

on yourself. You're Selena Ash; your old man's a big wheel; maybe you've all the right in the world to think you're it."

"You won't make me angry again."

"Not trying to. I'm trying to tell you something. You've had a fumble or two, a knock or two, since you got here. But it didn't teach you a thing. That was just alien plants and such. You didn't feel you needed any help. You're still way up there."

"I take it you do have a point."

"Coming to it. Even when you met the Tree, you just swapped curiosity with it and got yourself a swift check-over and repair, that's all. No—you hold still and listen." Now he had somehow placed an invisible clamp on her, and her back hair began to lift at this further evidence of power.

"When I first came to the Tree I needed help in the worst way. That's how I found out what it could do. I thought I needed protection from the plants, and it gave me powers—you've seen some. Now I know a better way, by being friendly, but that's by the side. I thought I needed a weapon, and I had to explain to the thing just what that was, because it's only a tree, remember? And it grew me a spear. You've seen it. I carry it about to remind myself what a damn fool I was. This knife, though, was sensible. It grew that, too—for me."

He paused, and she began to understand what he was trying to explain. He went on, still calmly grim. "Let's run through it again. The Tree will do for you whatever you want, as far as it possibly can, as much as it can understand. It doesn't know good from bad or right from wrong. You want the strength of ten men? You want to be fifteen feet tall? You want power? You have only to ask, to want in the right way—the way it can understand—and you've got it. So—I ask you—what do you think Buck Pardoe will do with that? Do you have any idea what desires are squirming in his mind?"

He released the power that held her, but she didn't move. She felt sick as he went on stonily. "What do you think all the crooks, the dregs, the scum of humanity will do with it, when they get it? You've just said that certain scientists have investigated its fruit. That means there can be, and there will be, other Trees—hundreds of them. God alone knows all the tricks this one can get up to. I only know some, but

that is enough to convince me that wiping out Buck Pardoe and that woman is a small price to pay, and the lives of your friends, and your life, and mine, aren't much more, against the whole of humanity."

"And I've sent a Dirac," she said emptily. "It's too late to call that back."

"That's the least of our worries," he retorted swiftly. "If I know anything about Space Service, there'll be—hold it!" He halted, grew still and tense like a pointer, turned his head to listen, and the little blue-eyed flower turned with him. "Here they come now," he muttered. "You hear it?"

She strained, and then nodded. Very faintly came the puttering sound of a jetcopter. He breathed hard.

"Right!" he grunted, and went away like a blur. There was no hint or request for her to follow. She picked up her feet and went after him as fast as she could, exulting in her new-found vitality, but soon realizing that he had a turn of speed she had not seen until now. And he seemed to have an unerring instinct for the way through, or around, and she was streaming with sweat as she came up to him at the base of a tree.

"You want in on this?"

"Of course," she panted. "I said I'd help."

"Give me the beamer. I can climb the tree faster with it than you can without."

"Oh, can you, indeed?" Her momentary indignation was wasted as he vanished upwards like a squirrel. She shook her head ruefully and set herself to follow. She managed quite well, but he was out of sight long before she had gained the first few branches. She caught him right at the top, where the tree's limbs were perilously slender and yielding, and squirmed on her stomach along a thin branch to be close to him.

"Over there," he told her unnecessarily, as she had already seen the distant blot of the buzzing craft. "He's quartering. He can't miss. As soon as the Tree gets that noise it will perk up and call him."

She accepted the beamer from his hand, stretched out on the uneasy perch and took tentative aim. It was about twenty-five miles, which was too far for accurate marksmanship.

"I can't do it, Joe. You know that, don't you?"

"I know." He sounded resigned. "Never thought you would. You and me, we're not the kind that can kill in cold blood. Can't help being what we are, I suppose."

"True enough, but let's not abandon all hope yet. I know a trick or two once he gets close enough."

"What kind of trick?"

"How well do you know the terrain about here? Is there somewhere he can land that thing close by? I mean, once he gets the feel of the Tree he will look for somewhere to come down, won't he? Where?"

"Two or three spots. Nearest is a clearing about two miles off, over to the right. Not very big, but enough for what he wants."

"Just one more detail. That's a hybrid craft, isn't it? Part copter, with jet assist?"

"Right."

"Well, if he's close enough, and is about to land, I can clip his wings for him, so that he may be able to get down safely, but he won't get back up again."

"That's a trick, all right. Where'd you learn it?"

"Not in school. I need a firmer branch than this." She backed and let herself down to a stouter limb, settled on it and kept her eyes on the dark machine. On a thought, she called up to him, "Can you let me know when he decides to go down?"

"I'll try. There—he's got the message! Watch him go!" She saw the jetcopter heel over and come swooping towards them, growing bigger rapidly. She could imagine the jubilation in Pardoe's mind at the first solid intimations that the Tree was real. The forward flight halted and the cab oscillated under its winged canopy. She set the rifle for needle focus and full power, set the stock against her cheek, and waited for the right moment.

FIFTEEN

"JUST MAKING up his mind to land," Joe advised in an urgent whisper, and she spent an idle thought wishing she could pick up emotions at a distance like that. Then the swaying

machine within her sights began to drop, its note changing. She drew a bead on the very edge of the blur that was the rotating blades, pressed the lever, and a fine thread of electric blue sprang out to lose itself in the evening sunlight. At once the flying machine shivered and swayed violently. The stuttering beat became a clamor, and she heard the sudden frantic whine of jets as whoever was at the controls threw in the lifters to prevent a total crash. The black shape bucked crazily and then went down fast. She peered over the sights of her weapon anxiously, but there was no crash.

"Neat," Joe muttered, coming to stand behind her. "He's down all in one piece, and they're all in good shape, but he can't get back up. And it will be dark soon."

"What will he do, sit tight until dawn? I would."

"Never can tell. Depends on how strong the Tree calls him. I reckon our best bet is to get along there and keep an eye on him."

In the dark? The query came to her lips, but she halted it as an idea struck her. He put out his hand for the weapon, and she passed it back to him, wriggling around to see him go down, dropping almost as fast as if he were falling. *I'm just beginning to catch on to all this,* she thought as she followed at a slightly less frantic pace. *If you want to learn how to climb up and down trees, who better to go to than the great white chief of all the trees—and ask?* It was so obvious. It was difficult to adjust to the notion that one could have whatever one wanted, merely by asking. She scrambled and dropped, and then stood by his side. He aimed an arm and moved, but she called him back.

"Can we spare a few minutes to call on the Tree, first?"

"It's out of our way a bit."

"Only a little. And I need help, the kind of help the Tree can give me."

"Thin end of the wedge," he said cryptically. "All right, this way." He went off at a smart pace. She followed, trying to deduce what he had meant. It came to her after a while. One could get hooked on a thing like this. If you can have whatever you want, simply by asking for it, what happens to discipline, and effort, and moral fiber?—and pride of accomplishment, and all the other things humanity had held in high esteem for so long?

"What is it that you want from the Tree? Don't tell me, but think about it."

"Why shouldn't I tell you?"

"Can if you want, but thinking about it is the hard part. Not in words—that's no good. You have to feel it, believe it, present it in the form of an accomplishment—call it faith."

She pondered that as she ducked through the undergrowth at his heels. Longstaffe's words came back. The botanical researchers had believed the seeds were this, or that—and so they were. One must make an image, but how does one make an image of being able to see in the dark? She remembered how the Tree had plucked from her mind her own fond image of being a gorgeous gray-eyed brunet with a flawless complexion and a knock-your-eye-out figure. That was hardly a belief, more an ideal to be hoped for, and a delight now that she had it. Her mental waters grew deep and confused, and she was far from having them cleared by the time they reached the dim serenity of the tree-temple again.

"I need your help," she said, outside the leaf-curtain, "to get this thing right. Look, all I'm after is some way of being able to move at ease in the dark. Perhaps the ability to detect living forms over a long distance the way you do."

"That's out," he rejected instantly. "I don't do that. Friendly does it for me. There are plenty of his brothers around here, but it takes time and practice and you have to develop the relationship."

"Can't I have that power on my own?"

"I doubt it. You're human, like me. We don't have that kind of equipment, so far as I know. What d'you expect, instant miracles? I keep telling you, it's only a tree!"

"You keep confusing me," she retorted. "What if I want my night vision improved, then? That's fully consonant with being human."

"All of that," he agreed acidly. "Only you're forgetting again. No tree, or plant ever *had* eyes or vision or anything like it. I've told you about their sense of space; that they do have. But how can you expect a tree to understand vision?"

"Like red to a blind man," she murmured, and inwardly scolded herself for being so blind. "Never mind, it can't hurt to try. Here goes." She walked through the curtain of

leaves and up to the tree, composing her mind as she went, convincing herself that she could see the trunk, the lofty vault above, the branches, all of it plainly and in detail, despite the fact that it was almost totally dark in there. Halting, she revised it just one more time by telling herself that it *was* like that, and then put her hands affectionately on the trunk. Just for a breath there was, again, that sense of something going out of her—and then a warm counter-flow that became a rush, a flood, a bursting feeling—tiny galaxies of sparks erupted and died rapidly in her mind, a barrage of tickling thrills bathed her body and she was giddy. She would have fallen had she not clung tightly to the trunk. She leaned on it, closing her eyes. The all-over tingling subsided slowly.

And she could see the trunk quite plainly. She could see all around it, the grass under her feet and the graceful spreading branches overhead. And she could see Joe, quite definitely, standing there close behind her. *Behind?* She pushed away from the Tree and turned to him, smiling—and then realized her eyes were still shut tight. Opening them, she almost fell at the vertigo inspired by the two different but simultaneous images. By sight he was a hulking object in the gloom, but by this other sense he was there as a person, felt and identified in some delightful and inde-scribable way.

"Give me a minute," she said breathlessly. "This wants some getting used to. And don't ask me to describe it, I can't."

"You got something? You mean it actually did something for your vision?"

"No," she said, very softly because she knew the reason for his urgency. "Not sight. You were probably right about that. But I have something better. Let's go."

It *was* better. With this new perception she could slip through bushes and tangles just as easily as he did, *and* know what was beyond, and all around her too. The dark-ness made no difference at all. She tried it with her eyes shut and it was as if she moved through a living world of bright images, all different and distinct, known and identi-fied exactly as if, in some marvelous way, she could touch them with long and delicate fingers. It was an effort to bring her mind back to more commonplace affairs.

"Do you have any kind of plan in mind?" she asked him.

"Nothing hard, no. Let's find that copter first—see what they are up to. Play it by ear from there. First thing I have in mind is to make sure that machine won't fly, ever again. After that we'll figure out some way of stopping Pardoe from getting to the Tree."

"I can't improve on that. What I don't quite get is why you're so bothered about the Tree itself. You know a lot more about it than I do, of course—" She chopped it off as she sensed the stationary bulk of the machine and four human shapes ahead. Shock waves came from one of them. They went forward together cautiously, making full use of the cover, for there was still enough light to make the risk considerable. Crouched behind a friendly bush, they saw Pardoe grasping a blade and staring at it furiously.

"All four!" he snarled, shoving it violently away. "That's all I need. That was no accident. Somebody took a shot at us."

" 'Way out here?" Miss Martine doubted it.

"What else would fuse the blade tips into globs of metal?" he roared back at her. "Whoever it is"—his voice swelled to a bellow—"you better believe me, one more trick and I burn these two down right away!"

"There's nobody to hear you, Buck."

"Who asked you? You just stay there and keep your burner on the playboys, while I rescue some equipment."

Pardoe scrambled back into the machine, and Joe sighed. "Can't do a thing until he moves out. You say I'm bothered about the Tree itself and that's right. Look, it's a mistake to credit it with too much, as it now is. Sensitive to mental fields. Possessed of certain mimetic powers. That's about it. But alien. I mean, it can't hear. It can detect sounds, sure, but a blown balloon can do that. It can sense light and shade, but not to see. The point is, all the development of those senses is human, and we use our senses because we've been taught how. The Tree hasn't been taught anything. It knows only what it has met and experienced."

"Yes. I can see that."

"And we are the only two humans it has ever met, the only ones it knows. It's had a considerable effect on me, and on you—but we have also had an effect on it. You understand that?"

"Yes, I do." She recalled the sensation of goodness going out, and caught her breath. "Good God! I see what you mean. You're saying the Tree is innocent, naïve."

"That's right. Just like an overgrown child. Now you try and imagine what effect it is going to have when it gets a taste of Buck Pardoe and Scorpia Martine!"

Selena started to ponder the prospect, but before she could get beyond a chill despair Pardoe came boiling out of the craft again.

"You must be out of your mind," Miss Martine expostulated. "Why thrash about in the dark, damn it."

"Because I say so I told you six or eight times already, we have no time to give away. All the time Miss High-and-Mighty Ash is missing there will be somebody—a whole lot of somebodies—looking for her. Maybe it will take them years to find this planet, and then again, maybe it won't. Half the Space Navy is looking for this place right now, and has been looking for a long while; you know what I mean. And maybe somebody has already found it, too, to go by those blades. We don't have any time to sit around and get fat."

"Get fat!" she screeched furiously. "Eaten alive by crazy plants, all my best duds rotted and ruined, two damned invalids to feed and nurse, and now your damned flying egg-box folds up on us—you call that getting fat? And now you expect to march out and find a tree, one tree, in the dark?— with God only knows what skulking in the bushes. You must be out of your mind; you've seen what the crazy things can do!"

"I've seen. You don't have to tell me. It will be just too bad for any plant that tries to get gay with me from here on." Pardoe sounded mean enough to spit acid right back at the surrounding undergrowth. She perceived how the unlikely caravan began to move and felt the first hurt of the plants as Pardoe blasted them to ashes in his path and marched forward.

"That hurts," Selena gasped, and Joe grunted in sympathy.

"Just one more reason for stopping him. Those plants are all my friends. Makes me ashamed to be human. They're almost clear of the craft now. Can you get a bead on it?"

"Just leave it to me." Selena aimed and poured a steady disruptive beam into the machine until it crackled and collapsed.

"That takes care of that," she declared with considerable satisfaction. "Have they noticed anything?"

"Not them. Pardoe is making too much clatter for anybody to notice anything. The way they're headed they should pass close by us. We might as well keep still."

She directed her attention to the oncoming travelers, wincing as Pardoe kept letting go with a heavy-duty blaster to clear a way for himself. *Much more of that,* she thought, *and it won't be so difficult to shoot you down, cold blood or not.*

"Follow my track!" Pardoe commanded, "and if those two drag on their feet just toast 'em up a bit."

"How the hell can you tell which way you're going?"

"You mean to tell me you can't feel it? I always said you were so stuck on yourself you don't know anybody else is alive. Just keep on going, that's all you have to do. I'll take you to it."

SIXTEEN

"WE LIE low, let 'em go by, then I clobber her from the back and we maybe can grab your friends, right? Think you can shoot that beamer out of her hand?" Joe whispered.

"I think so. I'll try to time it for your strike. Careful!"

"I will. You stay right here."

He went away with no more noise than a shadow, but she was able to follow his progress easily.

Behind Pardoe came the captives Delmar and Lacoste, shambling and reeling in acute distress. Each man had his wrists lashed together at his back, and a stout black plastic cable linked them, from the slip-noose about one neck to its counterpart about the other, so that neither man dared stumble and fall for fear of strangulation. There was no sign of any care of nursing, as Miss Martine had claimed, and Selena itched in sympathy as she saw their scars and scratches. Following, looking thoroughly bored and disgusted, came Miss Martine herself, visibly out of humor with the whole situation, but maintaining an alert grip on her beamer.

Joe was behind Miss Martine and ready to strike. Selena

took careful aim and held her breath. Some instinct seemed to warn Miss Martine, perhaps some tiny sound or smell. She stiffened. The spear came down in the same second that she ducked and whirled, and caught her on the arm. She yelled in fright. Selena wriggled frantically, trying to get a clean shot. Miss Martine hoisted her beamer, and down came Joe's spear again, cracking solidly against the weapon. It went spinning away, and in the next second Joe and the woman were grappled and thrashing about in the undergrowth in a confusion of arms and legs.

Up ahead, Pardoe roared in anger, spun around, came galloping heavily back, elbowing the helpless captives out of the way. Miss Martine let out a shrill scream from the tangle and her partner homed in on it. Selena saw his unoccupied hand reach for a fragmentation pistol.

"Get clear!" he roared. "Damn it, Scorpia, get out of the way, let me get a shot at it!"

Selena acted without pause to consider implications. She sent a needle-beam slicing through the cable that linked the captives, then swung and aimed delicately at the heavy-charge beamer which jutted from Pardoe's right hand, now in perfect profile. The lethal metal erupted in a spray of incandescent sparks, and he flung it away from himself frantically, then spun heavily around, snarling, to peer into the gloom. Up came the frag-pistol in his hand, and the night flew apart in thunder as it spat one—two—three—and stopped. His aim was good. Selena heard the slugs rip through the night air where she had been crouched. Then, as they struck, the echoing silence gave way again, this time to a chorus of banshee wails as the lethal fragments sprayed the surrounding darkness.

Face down and still, Selena was able to follow the action quite well. There was another animal screech from Miss Martine, a solid thumping blow, silence—and Joe melting shadowlike into the gloom, leaving her prone. Pardoe came close, kicked her to see if she was conscious, but kept his eyes continually scanning the surrounding gloom.

"Scorpia, you all right?"

She groaned, sat up and rubbed her head.

"Come on, come on," he urged. "What happened? Where'd he go?"

"I don't know, and I don't care, just so long as he stays

gone. He? That was no he, Buck. It was an ape! Wild man of the woods. Something like that. Hey! Leggo my foot, damn it!" She scrambled up rapidly, rescuing her ankle from the grip of a green tendril. "Give that damned shrub a blast, will you? Before it comes after me."

"Some hope," he snarled. "Your so-called ape-man just shot my beamer out of my hand with one of his own. Him, or his friends. Some ape! Use your own."

"If I can find it in the damned dark." Miss Martine stooped complainingly to search, while Pardoe glared a-round into the gloom.

"Damn it!" he growled. "Where'd he go?" and then, giving vent to fury, he loosed off three more thunder-clap shots, and the shrill wails of shattered steel came back. But there were no screams of agony or indications of a hit. "Yah," he snorted. "Got away. Oh, come on, you, and quit that moaning! You and your judo and karate and all that, and you let yourself get jumped—hey!" Surprise choked him for a moment, then the leafy darkness shook to the fury of his cursing as he realized that his captives were gone.

Back by the little knoll from which all the havoc had been done, Selena staggered to a halt and lowered Pierre Lacoste to the ground, gave a thankful sigh of relief.

"Hush now," she warned. "Not a sound. He's too handy with that splinter gun to take chances. Thanks, Joe, for tak-ing Robin. I think he would have been a bit too heavy for me. Let's have that knife—"

A few seconds later the two baffled and battered men were free of their bonds. Lacoste was too far gone to do anything but stare, but Delmar still retained enough spark to peer into the gloom and gasp, "Selena? It is you, isn't it? But who's this character?"

"Call him Joe. He's a friend, on our side. No time to ex-plain just now. Hush. That Pardoe has long ears and a brain. Keep still."

Excitement erupted again below. Miss Martine had found her beamer and something else.

"A spear?" Pardoe demanded incredulously. "Don't tell me we have native tribes on our necks, too."

"That's it, Buck—got to be! We've been jumped by some local tribe, and they've carried off our prisoners." Her agita-tion was plain. "Look, Buck, why don't we go back to the

jetcopter and button up until it's light, huh? This stumbling about in the dark, it's crazy. The next thing you know they'll get us, too."

"Anybody who tries to jump me," Pardoe vowed, "will get a gutfull of splintered steel. I don't like this, Scorpia."

"You don't *like* it?"

"That's not what I mean. Use your skull, damn it. Native tribes don't come complete with beamers."

"You sure it was a beamer?"

"What the hell do you think did this?" He waggled the ruined and partly fused weapon under her nose, and she wailed.

"That only makes it worse! Buck, I'm scared. Can't we go back? Get under cover?"

"We're going back as far as the copter, but only because I have another heavy beamer stashed there. And then we're coming right back and we're going to locate that Tree—if I have to blast every damned plant between here and Tau Ceti."

The unhappy pair went stumbling away, and Selena sighed.

"I don't know what we're going to do, now. They won't be pleased at the state of their craft, but I can't see that stopping Pardoe now."

"The Tree's got him," Joe agreed grimly. "He'll be back."

It took just fifteen minutes to prove him right.

"Looks like we're stuck," Joe declared softly. "The only way to stop Pardoe now would be to kill him, and neither of us can do that."

"What is everything all about, please?" Pierre Lacoste broke his sleep-walking stupor to ask it in a voice that betrayed his Gallic origin. "I keep trying to believe it is all a nightmare, no? But it hurts like real."

"It's real." Selena shook her head in the gloom. "Don't either of you feel anything, a kind of uneasiness or anything like that?"

"I do," Robin volunteered. "Sounds crazy, but its like somebody singing, a Lorelei kind of thing, a long way off. And a sort of itch to go and see what it's all about. That what you mean?"

"Not singing," Pierre contradicted. "It is more like a beautiful woman who is saying 'Come to me, and I will make

you happy.' It is like that, but I do not know how. It is insane. Is it?"

"It's a tree," Selena told them. "Believe it or not. Look, you've both heard stories, most of them fabulous, about Jensen's Planet and the miraculous Tree, haven't you? Well, this is it, and that's it, and it's all true—nearly all, anyway. This is no time to argue, or to explain. Just accept it. Buck Pardoe has, and he's on his way to the Tree right now, following the feeling that you have."

"You make that sound like the end of the world, Selena."

"It could be, Robin. We were hoping and trying to stop him, but short of shooting him down in cold blood from ambush, I don't see how we can, now. It would be absolute insanity to try to tackle him openly, the mood he's in and with the armory he has."

"I could kill him in cold blood, or hot blood, or any other kind," Pierre muttered. "But I am too much of a coward to try it."

"Don't run yourself into the ground," Delmar advised. "We never claimed to be professional heroes, did we? I still can't take it in—that noise in my mind is a tree? And that stuff about Jensen's Planet, is real? Even if so, what's so desperate about it?"

"This is no time to explain, Robin, even if I could without getting it all wrong. But you could try, for size, the idea of putting the ultimate weapon into the hands of a psychopath like Pardoe."

"Maybe you'll think better on a full stomach," Joe said, out of a long silence. "How long since you two ate?"

Selena felt instant contrition, deepened when both men revealed they had been given nothing at all; they had neither eaten nor had anything to drink since leaving their own ship.

"That's almost forty-eight hours. You must be starving! Joe, can we do anything about that?"

"No trouble at all. You ready?"

"Yes, but—what about Pardoe and the girl?"

"We can't do anything to them or about them, not now. The Tree wouldn't let us, now that it's curious about them. Come on."

Twenty minutes of traveling brought them to food and a cool stream where they could all refresh themselves and

regain some measure of ease. But, with that out of the way, the main problem remained.

"They must surely have reached the Tree by now, Joe. Can you tell, from here?"

"By inference," he said. "I was following them, and then they just blended into the background. About five minutes ago. That means they are inside the main area of influence."

"So there isn't anything we can do at all, now?"

"We can follow, if you like, and see what happens. You want to try that? Bring your friends; I'll lead. Better keep a touch on me, Selena, just in case something goes wrong."

"I will," she promised, ridiculously pleased at his first use of her name. "You will be careful, Joe, won't you?"

He went away as silently and smoothly as ever, and even with her new senses, it was difficult to keep up, so she didn't try. It was all right as long as she could keep a mental touch on him. Despite her helpful guidance, her two companions made heavy weather of the dark jungle.

"You must have eyes like a cat," Robin complained, picking himself up from his third fall over sprawling roots.

"That is one thing. What else I do not understand is the plants," Pierre muttered. "Before, they were pulling and clutching with hooks and stings, as if they were alive. But not now."

She was ready to explain when the words died in her throat. Suddenly there was a sense of something missing, an emptiness. Robin and Pierre felt it, too. The Tree—it had stopped calling.

SEVENTEEN

THE ABSENCE of that pervading intelligence was almost a pain to her, like the death of a friend. Pierre put it in almost the same words.

"She has died—the so-beautiful woman who called me!"

"Something just switched off, that's for certain," Robin said. "What the hell, Selena?"

"I don't know." Confused notions came and went in her mind. Her intended explanation that the plants were sentient,

that all one had to do was feel friendly—seemed vapid and unnecessary now. So, too, was her own tentative discovery, that the Tree presented itself in different ways to different people, or, possibly, that each individual interpreted the call in his own way. Whichever it was, it didn't matter. The Tree was dead—or was it? She led the way towards where Joe was waiting, a silent shadow just a few feet clear of the veil of leaves.

"What's happened?" she demanded anxiously, and he shrugged.

"No idea. This is new to me. I've never known the Tree to shut right off like this."

"Do you suppose Pardoe burned it, with his weapon?"

"I doubt it would keep still for anything like that. It can detect a threat just as fast as any of the other plants. Faster."

They stood awhile in silence; their common concern made it a companionable silence. She tried to think aloud.

"Pardoe got this far—got through. Got right up to the Tree and touched it. We can assume that."

"And the Martine female," he added grimly. "It sucked them both dry, because that's how it works. But then what?"

"We have to go in there and find out, Joe. I can't detect a thing beyond that curtain. Can you?"

"Not a smell. Friendly is all curled up in a ball. He doesn't like it one bit."

She shivered, put out her hand to take his, and felt his fingers grip on hers in sudden need.

"No way of telling what will happen if we go in there, Selena."

"Yes, I know. But we have to find out. And we have to believe that it won't hurt us."

"I'd like to believe that, too. All right, let me go ahead."

"No, not this time. You're handier than I am, Joe, just in case you have to take Pierre and Robin back—to my ship—where the Navy will be landing—in case—you know?" She let his hand go and went forward to the curtain. It was strangely still; not a leaf quivered. She reached out and pushed the fronds aside; they were stiff, almost waxy and stayed parted where she had pushed them, leaving a gap. She went into darkness in which she could perceive nothing at all. Could it be that the Tree had snatched back its gift in a moment of anger? That didn't seem likely, or even pos-

sible. She probed and got the feeling that it wasn't her ability that was at fault, but that something like a fog pervaded the whole grove. She had the creepy sense of trying to move into an occluded mind. There was a dull pain, a headache of immense proportions. She aimed her mind at the Tree itself.

"You're hurt," she told it. "You're upset in some way. I can tell that much, but I don't know any more than that. I want to help. Please let me help you. Tell me what I can do. Let me help!"

There was neither pretense nor effort in her call. She really did want to help. Something came to her from the Tree, for the murk around her seemed to swirl and eddy in quick agitation, ghostly fingers of breeze caressing her skin. Then, gradually, the darkness dwindled and vanished and the churchlike dimensions of the grove came into her ken. There was the massive, looming trunk of the Tree, and it ached to her touch. There were blotches on it. She looked around more by habit than from need, for she had already sensed the presence of the two others there. She turned and called.

"Joe! I think it's all right. I don't know what's happened, not yet, but I think it's all right."

He was beside her in a moment, his hand out to take hers in a way that struck warmth into her heart over the sorrow that filled the air.

"It's had a hell of a knock," he whispered. "Do you reckon we can do anything sensible to help?"

"Let's see what happened to those two first. I can't get anything from them. They're just lumps."

Together they paced across the turf to where the intruders were, and halted as a distinct shock tingled them both.

"What?" he grunted, whirling swiftly, and then he relaxed, and she eased also, as she saw. Pierre and Robin had followed, through the gap in the curtain, but only a few steps. Now they stood quite still, frozen like wax models in a store window.

"Poor thing," she murmured in instant understanding. "It can't stand any more strangers."

"I'm not surprised. But they won't come to any harm for a while. Let's look at Pardoe."

It was what she had come to do, but she regretted the necessity as soon as she was able to see just what was left

of the crook. He was sprawled on the turf in a shapeless heap that could hardly be described as squatting, or crouching, or anything else. He was just a shapeless mass of flesh and bone, slumped and helpless, his head sagging down between his knees. Joe reached down, took a handful of hair and hoisted up that heavy head so that they could see his face.

"Nothing there," he muttered, and she had to compress her lips to keep her stomach down where it belonged, for Joe was literally correct. It was a slack and idiot-empty face, devoid of anything like wit or sanity. There was nothing at all. Just a helpless, brainless vegetable.

"Scraped him right out, and there was nothing to put back."

"Joe—that's horrible! And it's probably true, which makes it worse."

"No worse than a whole lot of people I've known." Joe was grimly calm.

Scorpia Martine was very beautiful but just as empty. "She's withdrawn—gone completely."

"They got what they wanted, in a way," he said, taking her in his arms. "I guess the Tree knows a lot more about humans now than it did before."

"But it's all wrong! It's got us all wrong. Somehow it has to learn that those two—"

"Strikes me it doesn't want to know any more about any of us, the way it cooled off your friends. Can you blame it, Selena? I mean, take a look at the trunk there, where those two touched it."

She turned her head to stare. There were angry splotches like scars on the dark smoothness. She eased herself free of his arms and went towards the trunk urgently.

"Don't do it," he called. "Don't—you don't know—"

"I have to. Someone has to show it—" She reached out for the massive trunk, took a breath, and there was Joe at her side.

"Takes two," he muttered. They reached out and touched as one. She felt instant twisting pains in her arms and shoulders, then all over—and caught her breath—but the twinges went as fast as they had come and replacing them came a vast curiosity, a wondering. She spoke aloud because it was the simplest way of arranging her thoughts to make sense.

"I'm sorry you've been hurt and upset. It couldn't be

helped. There *are* people like that. We don't like them any more than you do."

"That's right," Joe endorsed. "We don't like them. The only way anyone can tell what they are like is by finding out, by getting to know them; there's no other way. After a while you'll get to know them by—"

He stopped, and she knew why. Something had gone, dissolved, was no longer there. She looked at him in surmise, but he shrugged and dropped his hands.

"I don't know, Selena. I'm no psychologist, and I doubt if even a proper headshrinking expert would get very far with this. Fugue?"

"I was just about to say the same thing. Flight from reality —all three of them, in different degrees. Pardoe has lost his identity altogether. Miss Martine is inturned, catatonic. And now the Tree has withdrawn itself. Some time ago you said 'Ashamed of being human.' I think I would agree with that, now." She turned away from the lifeless trunk miserably, and distant movement caught her attention. Robin and Pierre came groping in what was, for them, dense gloom broken only by fitful starlight through interstices in the high vault of leaves.

"So this is the famous Tree?" Delmar put his head back to assess the size of it. "It's big, certainly."

"Impressive," Pierre agreed. "So far as one can see. But it is only a tree, after all."

Selena exhanged rueful glances with Joe. He looked sad, and she felt it, as if he had lost an old and valued friend. And yet, she had to be philosophical about it, the Tree had learned something valuable—how to shut itself off from harm and interference.

"Ah well," she sighed. "Perhaps we should be thankful that's all it is. The next problem is, somehow, to get these two back to my ship by the time the Navy gets here."

That took three of the roughest and most arduous days Selena had ever known. Pardoe—the empty shell of him— had to be fed, led, constantly prodded, urged, and watched. Miss Martine was easier, but still a worry, because she would just stop like a mechanical doll as soon as she was left alone. Robin and Pierre were willing but ignorant of the area. Selena came to marvel at Joe's infinite patience and resource, and discovered resources in herself that she

had not dreamed she possessed. At the end of those three dreadful days her erstwhile playboy friends had acquired poise, alertness, and muscles. She had grown to feel as close to Joe as the fingers on one hand. It was a comradeship that owed little to words. Somehow she felt little need, or urge, to talk everything out as she had been so accustomed to do. Now it was a silent understanding, shared emotions, knowing what he was going to do next, finding him always ready and anticipating *her* next move; it was a warm thing.

She missed him within moments of sighting the bright spike of her ship. There was relief at their safe arrival, the blessed feeling of being able to relax, the outspoken pleasure of Robin and Pierre at the sight of something familiar and re-assuring—and then, in the middle of it all, he had vanished. She couldn't believe it at first. Then, when she tried pushing out her new senses as far as it was possible to stretch them, and finding no trace, she knew it was so, and that he had once again dropped out and gone into hiding. That was the evening of the third day. That night she slept once again in her own narrow bunk, bathed and clean, between silky sheets and with metal walls and watchdog circuits between her and the hazards of the wild outside—and she felt suf-focated and shut in.

The Navy arrived the following day, just before noon, with urgent messages crackling in her radio, and busy black dots high up in the blue, jockeying for orbit. It was an im-pressive force. Two medium-heavy cruisers, two shuttle ships, and one enormous research monitor, a space-borne laboratory complex crammed with specialists, their equipment, all hand-picked for just this moment. The range of disciplines cov-ered the whole spectrum of anything that could possibly apply to botanical biology, plus a more than fair complement of psychologists and psychiatrists, all unanimous in being firmly confident that there could be no such thing as sen-tient vegetation, but all equally determined to be there, just in case.

Admiral Longstaffe was in the first shuttle to touch ground. He had been briefed by radio about the immediate essentials—beware of the bushes—think friendly thoughts—and he was sensible enough to heed the advice. Selena greeted him warmly, very fit and honey-tanned, efficiently conventional in a fresh set of disposable coveralls, and was

secretly amused to see the way his eyes widened at sight of her.

"No need to ask if you are well, my dear. One look is enough. And this is M. Lacoste, and Mr. Delmar? Congratulations, gentlemen. I'm told you were to a large degree instrumental in locating this planet. I'll want a word with both of you on that, later."

"And we need help with these two." Selena showed him the unfortunate victims of the Tree, and watched as trained personnel took charge.

"And now," Longstaffe declared, "what about the Tree?"

EIGHTEEN

"YES," she said soberly. "We found it. I can give you the coordinates. You have a walkabout there?" She meant the radio that linked Longstaffe with at least one other of his men at all times. As he nodded she resumed, "Better have all your department heads listen in, and make a recording, otherwise you'll all be asking the same questions several times over. And there's too much of it for that. In the first place, when I tell you just where the Tree is, and you mount an expedition, pick good men and women for it. I do not mean technically capable people. I mean good as in honest, sincere, clean-minded—with integrity. You'll see why when I explain the whole thing."

Longstaffe gave her a hard look, but respected her enough to do no more than issue instructions for all senior research personnel to listen. Then she told them precisely what they needed to know, and all she knew, about the Tree itself and the rest of the plant life, so far as she understood it. Impersonal and objective reportage was no new exercise for her, and she did it competently, omitting several items of a purely personal nature. Nevertheless, there was a lot to tell, and by the time she was finished the first impatient wave of scientists were standing looking at the Tree while listening to her. Their guarded comments came back to her via the etherwaves.

"A sense of serenity," one reported, "but no positive activity. You would say it resembles fugue?"

"That's my guess. You'll work out your own diagnosis. All I'm saying is that for centuries, possibly, it knew nothing but what it had learned from other trees, plants and growing things. Then it met honest humans, if I may so describe Scout Jensen—and myself. One can presume a whole new and exciting world being opened up to it. On the basis of your own results with its seeds, you will admit that to be a reasonable assumption. Then, as I have explained, it was so unfortunate as to encounter two rather bad humans, two people who were repulsive even to normal people. Ask Lacoste and Delmar how they were treated, what they have to say about those two. The result? You people are the experts, the psychologists. You'll have your own names for what happens to a mind that believes everything is sweetness and light and then has everything go bad all at once. What will you call it, insanity, overwhelming doubt, flight?"

"This is one for the books," one of the behaviorists snorted. "A neurotic tree."

"That's your problem," she declared. "But I have a suggestion, for what it's worth. If we assume this Tree is merely a reserve of potential, and talent, without what we would call personality—and that the effect, the impact of fully developed human personalities on it has been disastrous, it seems that the wisest thing to do is to study it as a specimen —that is, study its growth pattern, soil conditions, habitat and all that. And then forget *it*, but use that knowledge to develop the seeds properly. And then train *them*. Grow them into the ways you want them to be, as you would grow and educate an intelligent animal—or a baby."

She had had time to think that one through, and it was just as well, because they had many questions. What helped to still the remaining skepticism was the undeniable mobility of the plants. Before that day was over all the researchers were busy, slipping readily into teams, to search for and identify the peculiar molecules which might be responsible, to dissect and examine sections of the plants, to do air, soil and water analyses, cosmic-ray studies, crustal radioactivity tests—and a group of them hovered around the Tree itself, checking it in every way they could devise.

Longstaffe went back to his command cruiser with the

third shuttle, taking Robin Delmar and Pierre Lacoste with him. They were to be sent home just as soon as his men had put them through a total interrogation and had impressed on them the importance of saying nothing whatever about the things they had seen and heard in the past four days. When that shuttle came back down, disgorging more scientists and technicians, it also yielded a tall, gaunt, gray-haired man, with a perpetual dry smile and Selena's gray eyes. She was quietly delighted to see him.

"I hope I didn't give you a scare, Dad. I know you don't like me being in this kind of work, and I worry because you might be worried."

"Don't." He gripped her hand once, then got out the pipe that he was seldom seen without. "I never bothered to tell you, child, but it was my gentle hint that opened the way for you to be considered by the Corps in the first place."

"I suspected something of the kind. I mean, when they sorted me out and offered me the chance to take their tests, I knew someone had been singing my praises."

"And why not?" Conway Ash fired up and wreathed himself in aromatic smoke for a moment. "I know people; I can pick 'em. That's all there is to my job—not expertise, just knowing how to pick the right people for the right job."

"That I can understand." She relaxed in the sunshine by his side, and watched the busy men and gadgetry. She had always been comfortably close to her father in this way, able to relax and talk to him as man to man. "What I don't quite get is how you happened to know about the Philosophy Corps anyway. From the inside, I know that they are—deliberately vague, dispersed, hard to get in touch with, and almost legendary. That is really their strength, that they have no official propaganda, no known chief, or headquarters, and very nearly no rules, either. Very few people even believe there is such a corps, in fact. Something like this planet, until we found it."

"Let you in on a secret." He smiled. "I was one of the founding members of the Corps. Had to pull out because I had talents that were more useful elsewhere. But I keep in touch; I can pull strings occasionally."

"I might have known! Tell me, what's going to happen to this planet, and the Tree?"

"Well now." He emitted a blue plume and studied it.

She knew that he was in fact watching her like a hawk. "I was going to ask you one—why are you hanging on here? Nothing more you can do. Your friends have gone. You're not technical enough to contribute anything further. What's the attraction?"

"It's a lovely place," she said promptly and demurely, and he snorted gently. "I'd like to live here," she added, and he snorted again.

"Bad luck. I've been through the preliminary assessments. We are going to invoke Secregs on this one, make it Q-max."

"Quarantine?" She frowned over that for a moment, then nodded. "Yes, I suppose that's sensible. It's hardly ideal for open colonization as it stands, and it wouldn't be wise to leave it unguarded for more enterprising people like Pardoe and company. But total quarantine? Wouldn't you want to leave someone here, in charge? A look-out?"

"Look out for what? There'll be a network of watch-dog satellites and alarms. And eventually, maybe, we will put down a base team, but not for a long while yet—some years. The scientists will gather and take away enough material to keep them busy that long. You see, if we can't grow the plants and make them do tricks in our laboratories, or in some spot of our own choosing, there's not a lot of point, is there? So who needs a ground base? And, in any case," he added, so negligently that she fell right into it, "who would want to stay here in this wilderness?"

"I would," she said grinning as he stirred just a little. "You like sneaking up on people, don't you? All right, now you know. I want to stay here."

"You look well on it. That glow isn't just health; Selly, I know you that well. There's only one thing could make you offensively radiant like that and willing to pull out of the Corps at the same time. Want to tell me about him?"

She was relieved to be able to talk, and Conway Ash was a good listener. "It wasn't," she admitted, "until I was slanging him for being a drop-out—tucking himself away in the Scout Service, and then here—that I realized I was talking about myself, too. I don't belong anywhere. All my life I've been pretending to be this, that and the other. The only reason I liked being in the Corps was because it set me

apart from the herd. And above them, too—and that's not good. I don't belong out there. But I am at home here."

"All right. It's your life. He sounds quite a character. The way you've drawn him, I don't blame him for hiding out. But, supposing you do find him, and he doesn't think the way you do, then what happens?"

"It's a big planet. I really do like it here, Dad. Leave me a caller, and I'll be official guide and advisor to the base team, when you do send one. But not for a year, please?"

"All right again. May I offer just one piece of advice? That research monitor up there is stuffed with psychologists of all kinds. You have a chat with some of them, learn up a bit. It can't hurt, and in my opinion that boy of yours needs help. You do that, eh?"

"You're ahead of me, as always. I was intending to do just that."

She had her chances. It took the researchers almost four weeks of concentrated effort to get all the material they needed, and for the Navy to establish a four-unit network of guardian satellites, small and far out, almost invisible, but triggered to give warning should anyone try to orbit and land on the planet. Eventually, though, the shuttles went off into the blue for the last time. Temporary base cabins were dismantled and shipped out; people went away in groups— one small crew took care of her own ship and lifted it to swing with the rest—and the planet was still and silent once more.

She was prepared for a long wait. She had managed to find Joe's old ship; it had not been easy because he had allowed the landing feet to settle deep into the soft earth and had encouraged creepers and flowering shrubs of all kinds to drape themselves around it until it was like a part of the living forest, but she found it. Without her special sense of space she might never have succeeded. Having located it, she took no liberties, but made herself at home in a discreet manner with the minimum of disturbance, like a guest. He had made sure it would never fly again, but it was otherwise quite functional and comfortable. There were book tapes and musicassettes enough to make sure she would not be bored, even if she had not had ploys of her own to occupy the time.

Part of her task was to get to know the friendly flowers

all about his home and to revive his custom of playing them tunefull and rhythmic music. They really did prefer waltzes, and it was great fun for her to sit and be aware of their pleasure in the music. Another thing she did was to discard all the artificial trappings of civilization. *"Consider the lilies of the field . . ."* She had quoted the lines from Matthew often, but never until now had she realized the point of them. Quite happily, she went naked and was at one with the peaceful and unspoiled world about her. Warmed in the sun by day, securely dreamless and untroubled by night, she settled into a serene and quiet bliss she had never before believed possible, a state of mind that took her back to the carefree, semi-mystical days of her childhood. And, like a child, she had mischief in mind.

It was in the early afternoon of the ninth day that he came back. She was aware of his approach long before he came into sight, and she assumed that he was likewise aware of her presence. She had counted on it and prepared against it as part of her mischief. She sat, quite still and at ease, on the warm turf by the ship's gangway foot, and waited, sensing his slow movement, guessing at his suspicions and waiting for him to appear through a break in the bushes across the glade from where she was. The slanting sun was on his face as he stood there, gripping his spear and swinging his head from side to side in bewilderment.

"Selena?" he said very softly and in doubt. She kept silent, stealing this precious moment to study him and refresh her memory. He looked lost and baffled searching for her, although she was in plain view.

"It's a trick," he said. "You're playing a trick on me. Where are you?"

"I'm here, Joe. It's all right." She rose and went to him, took his arm and led him back to where she had been sitting. "Yes, I played a trick on you. Several tricks, in fact, but none of them malicious—"

"I watched the ships go. I thought everyone had gone. I thought they would quarantine the planet."

"They did. It's a Q-Max. There'll be no one coming back here for at least a year, and then only a research team. You're quite safe now."

"But you're here. You stayed."

"Do you mind that very much?"

"I don't understand." He looked lost and troubled. "Why are there so many of you—like echoes?"

"I made friends with your friendly plants, Joe, and I trained some of them, four of them, to play a trick on you—on your Friendly. He is picking me up all over the place, isn't he? And, all the time, I am here, right by your side." She touched his hand again, and he shook his head.

"You know?"

"I've known for a long time, Joe, that you're blind."

NINETEEN

HE SAT, just where he was, and she settled down beside him, to reach and take his hand again. It was quite still in hers.

"How long have you known?"

"Almost from the beginning, Joe. You have a very direct stare, and I learned long ago that only abnormal people stare steadily like that. Either they do it on purpose—or the person isn't really looking at all. And then, those binoculars. You hadn't used them in so long, you not only forgot where you'd put them, you also forgot to slip back the lens covers. Yet you pretended to look through them, for my benefit. And you never did mention the color of anything, even the red blossom I put in my hair; you let me call it blue. So I knew, but it wasn't until the Tree gave me the power to sense masses and shapes—like Friendly—that I realized how wonderfully you could manage. So I don't feel sorry for you. If you're all ready to recoil from pity, don't be."

"Why did you stay behind?"

"To any other man the reason would be obvious. If it was any other woman but me, that would be the right reason, too. It might well be"—she hesitated at it—"one of the reasons. There are others. One is that I like this place; I really do. There's another, not so simple. To explain it, I want you to sit still and listen while I tell you a story, a story about a man called Jory Jensen, a Navy Scout."

"He's dead."

"Yes, yes, he's dead. In a way, he is. I know a lot about Jory Jensen. Before I ever came to this planet I had studied his dossier, the full record in the Navy files, so I know all that. But I know a lot more than that, too. I know how and where he died. He was a strange man, an eccentric one, but a good man. To be a scout a man needs to be a bit of an oddball, but Jensen was a near-genius. He could have been away up at the top in anything he tried—but he couldn't stand people—stupid, non-rational, whimsical, emotional, immature people. He was *too* good. It is nothing unusual, that. Such people go strange trying to fit in, or they opt out. Jensen opted out, as a scout. And he was a good one.

"And then one day he happened on a planet of a system that was different. He went through all the routine steps, but he kept running into the awareness that this place was different: pleasant, clean, good, and welcoming. He felt at home. So he omitted to include it in his flight log. And he kept on coming back to this place between commissions. He would have staked a personal claim, but a scout is not allowed to do that, so he had to go on hoping that no one else would ever land on it. And it preyed on his mind. He worried. He had found a wise old tree on this planet and made friends with it. On one trip he had a small accident, nothing serious, and the Tree cured him—just like that. That's when he began to realize what he had found. And then—the law of averages caught up with him. He had a bad accident with his drive, and got an overdose of mu-radiation. He didn't know for sure, but he suspected. He patched up the job and came on home—"

"How do you know all that?" he queried, and she squeezed his hand.

"Part of the job. The mechanics went over his ship for a fast preliminary, spotted the repair, made it good, and reported it while they made an estimate as to the rest of the overhaul. Meanwhile, Jensen went in for his routine checkup, and they gave him a blue card. That was enough to confirm what he suspected. He ran, got back to his ship before anyone thought to slap a distraint on it, and blew. According to the official book he headed out into the big dark and died."

"That's mu-radiation," Joe muttered. "There's no cure."

"Just so. That's fact. The rest is guesswork, but with some

supporting grounds. Jory Jensen came to this planet. He knew what the Tree could do, he hoped it could cope with mu-radiation. He tried—and it did. It was a big job, and in the process Jory got changed quite a bit. A complete overhaul, you might say. You might also say that he was not the same man he had been. So, you might say, Jory Jensen is dead. But you're alive, Joe."

"And blind!"

"Yes. I've been thinking about that. You say the Tree can't understand sight, because it's just a tree. And that's true enough. But there's another side to that, Joe. Those ships that came, and went away again, were stuffed to the rivets with psychologists of all kinds. That's obvious, isn't it? I mean—intelligent plants? So, I've always been interested in psychology and its application to sociology, too. I talked with them. About you. Not by name," she added quickly, as his fingers twitched. "More in the nature of a hypothetical question. And the answers were illuminating. To start with, the effect of mu-radiaion is to induce a slow but irreversible decay in the nervous system. It goes, bit by bit. The senses are the first to shut down. No need to go into all of it, but let's get this straight. You're cured completely. You wouldn't be here otherwise. Is that understood?"

"Not by me, it isn't. I'm still blind!"

"And feeling a bit sorry for yourself?"

He lifted up and away from her all in one sinuous movement, and his face was bleak, like weathered timber. "I'm happy here. I have Friendly. I get by. This is my home."

"I touched a nerve, didn't I, Joe?—admit it. Come back here and face it—and listen." She waited, steeling her heart to be hard and as ruthless as was necessary. He came and sat, defiantly. She reached for his hand again. "Here's a question for you, Joe. Suppose you could see again? Just suppose it could be fixed? Would it make any difference?"

"None at all. I like it here. I'm all through and washed up with people. I decided that when I knew I was losing my sight. What good is a blind scout? I dropped out, as you say. But then, I learned to live with it, with Friendly to help. And this is my home, now, sight or not." He hesitated at that, and she could feel his mind working along with his uneasy fingers. After a while he added, "I don't mind you being here. I thought you had gone along with the rest, and

I was a bit sorry about that. I had begun to think that you could fit in here."

"Thank you. I'm glad; I like it here. I was thinking that I fitted in, too, but I was quite ready to move away to some other spot. I don't want to be in your way."

"That's all right; you belong. But let's not have any more of that about me feeling sorry for myself."

"Why not? Wouldn't you like to be able to see again?"

"I can see all I want to, with Friendly."

"Just so. And that tells me quite a bit. Here's part of it. You say a tree can't see, knows nothing of sight. That's true. Sight is more than just a functional optical system, though. Eyes don't see, Joe. *You* see, with and through your eyes; and your eyes are perfectly all right, Joe. There's nothing wrong with them."

This time he didn't jerk up and away. He sat quite still, but his fingers were tense in hers. "That's not a very good joke," he said quietly. "It's not funny. Do you think I'm just pretending to be blind?"

"No, not quite that. I want you to do something for me, please. It won't take long. And I promise, afterwards, I will go away and leave you alone, if that's what you want. Please?"

"More tricks?"

"In a way, but I'm trying to help not to hurt. You *do* know me better than that, surely?"

"All right, what do I do?"

"Stand up. Stand up just there. Right—now take off your friendly plant, right off and away." As he hesitated she added, "It's quite all right, I'll take care of him, and you shall have him back. I promise."

Highly unwillingly he peeled out of his fiber harness, carefully easing away the coils of the plant-stem from his chest and shoulder.

"I'm all in the dark now," he muttered. She took the small warm bundle and laid it aside, and smiled at him.

"All in the dark and helpless—I know. You fear that, and quite naturally. But not just now. You're with friends, Joe, including me. Just think about that for a moment."

"All right," he muttered. "There's no danger. So?"

"So," she said, mocking him gently, "now shut your eyes. Go on, it can't make any difference, can it?" He shrugged,

closed his eyes, and she stood back a few paces from him, facing him, put an edge on her voice.

"Think, Joe, think hard. Think, Jory Jensen that was, and tell me true. What is it that you don't want to see? What is it you're afraid to face? What are you hiding from? Is it guilt? Do you feel guilty because you've dropped out—dodged your responsibilities? Abandoned your career, your duty, your Service oath? What? What is it that you are refusing to see?" She threw the words at him like darts, leaning on them, putting them in deep as she had been taught, striking right down to his hidden values, stirring up the submerged fears.

She saw him shake and dwindle like a stricken tree. He choked on words that were difficult to get out. Then, in a burst, they came.

"Humanity! You can keep it, have it, forget it—lying, cheating, grubbing, stinking—the whole filthy mess—you can have it all. I want no part of it!"

"You're so right," she agreed. "That's the way humanity is, part of the time. And you are part of it; you're a human being, too."

"No! The hell with it. I want no part of it. I'm out."

"It's no good, Joe. Shutting your eyes to it won't make it go away. It's still here. You think you've gone away from it, but you can't get away from yourself. You can't! Face it, Joe; look at it. Look at me, Joe. I'm human, too. Look at me —you can. You *know* you can. You're not afraid of me, surely? Look at me, Joe. Come on now, look!"

Then she caught her breath, just watching him sweat and struggle, and then open his eyes. And her heart turned over—because he *could* see. It was obvious. The expression on his face was enough to prove it. She stood quite still, blinking at ridiculous tears and trying to smile—and then she held out her arms to him. But he shook his head as if dazed, and the light in his eyes was something to behold.

"No magic," she whispered, suddenly embarrassed. "Don't think that—just applied psychology. Psychic blindness is nothing new nor strange. It's common enough. Joe, don't—"

"Selena!" he said, and there was that in his voice that made heat in her cheeks and giddiness in her heart. "You're beautiful. So beautiful! Friendly told me you were lovely,

but I never dreamed—I can see you—and you're much more beautiful than I ever dreamed."

"It was a chance I had to take," she mumbled, suddenly and dizzily aware that she was completely nude. "I'm so glad it worked—and that you think I'm—nice to look at!"

"I would have known you by your voice. But you—you're so beautiful, I could go on looking at you—I can see!" A shadow darkened his delight. "I can see; you cured me. Now I'll have to go back."

"Oh no you won't," she said, suddenly in charge again, and very positive. "No one knows anything about you except me—and Dad. I had to tell him, you see, because I've dropped out, too. I'm official resident here, at least for a year. And, if I like it at the end of that time, it will be permanent. I think I am going to like it here, but that's really up to you, isn't it? Now that you can see, you may not think that I belong—"

"You belong more than ever, Selena. I'd sooner be blind again than lose you now. I can ask you honestly now, please stay."

"I was hoping you'd ask. You see, my dear, my motives for wanting you to be able to see were not quite impersonal. They were rather selfish, really. Tell me again, am I really so beautiful?"

AFTERWORD

SAFELY BACK in his office on Luna, Admiral Longstaffe took out and re-read the personal memo that Selena had handed him just before he left the planet.

TO Longstaffe, Adml., SEC/CHEF U.P. Off. TECH/STRAT.
FROM Selena Ash, P.C.
RE Jensen's Planet.

Please have the enclosed standard one-square-mile territorial claim processed for me soonest. I haven't yet chosen my spot, but I promise it will be nowhere near the Tree.

When you report to P.C. H.Q. on my behalf, please inform them I hope to be able to recruit a new boy, if I can open his eyes for him.

Finally, when you mark off the date on your calendar one year from now, please include in the party one multi-denominational padre. One way or another, I mean to get this one. Wish me luck.

"Luck?" Longstaffe sighed as he filed the papers carefully and made the necessary calendar notation. "That's like taking an ore crusher to crack an egg. By God, if I was thirty years younger you wouldn't have to twist *my* arm!" And he sighed again. *Some folk,* he thought, *have all the luck.*

ACE BOOKS

SCIENCE-FANTASY ANTHOLOGIES

The best authors and their best stories are sure to be in these top-rated collections of science fiction and fantasy.

WORLD'S BEST SCIENCE FICTION: 1969   91352 — 95¢
Edited by Donald A. Wollheim & Terry Carr

WORLD'S BEST SCIENCE FICTION: 1968   91351 — 75¢
Edited by Donald A. Wollheim & Terry Carr

THE "IF" READER OF SCIENCE FICTION   36330 — 60¢
Edited by Frederik Pohl

NEW WORLDS OF FANTASY   57270 — 75¢
Edited by Terry Carr

**THE BEST FROM FANTASY AND SCIENCE
   FICTION: THIRTEENTH SERIES   05452 — 60¢**
Edited by Avram Davidson

**THE BEST FROM FANTASY AND SCIENCE
   FICTION: FOURTEENTH SERIES   05453 — 75¢**
Edited by Avram Davidson

**THE BEST FROM FANTASY AND SCIENCE
   FICTION: FIFTEENTH SERIES   05454 — 75¢**
Edited by Edward L. Ferman

Available from Ace Books (Dept. MM), 1120 Avenue of the Americas, New York, N.Y. 10036. Send price indicated, plus 10¢ handling fee.

ACE RECOMMENDS . . .

LORDS OF THE STARSHIP
    by Mark S. Geston   49250 — 50¢

PSI HIGH AND OTHERS
    by Alan E. Nourse   68750 — 50¢

THE BROKEN LANDS
    by Fred Saberhagen   08130 — 50¢

THE MOON OF GOMRATH
    by Alan Garner   53850 — 50¢

MOONDUST
    by Thomas Burnett Swann   54200 — 50¢

THE SILKIE
    by A. E. Van Vogt   76500 — 60¢

THE PLANET WIZARD
    by John Jakes   67060 — 60¢

OUT OF THE MOUTH OF THE DRAGON
    by Mark S. Geston   64460 — 60¢

DUNE
    by Frank Herbert   17260 — 95¢

TEENOCRACY
    by Robert Shirley   80200 — 75¢

THE PANDORA EFFECT
    by Jack Williamson   65125 — 60¢

THE WARLOCK IN SPITE OF HIMSELF
    by Christopher Stasheff   87300 — 75¢

DARK PIPER
    by Andre Norton   13795 — 60¢

Available from Ace Books (Dept. MM), 1120 Avenue of the Americas, New York, N.Y. 10036. Send price of book, plus 10¢ handling fee.

ACE DOUBLE BOOKS ... more for your money

72400 — 60¢
THE RIM GODS by A. Bertram Chandler
THE HIGH HEX by L. Janifer & S. J. Treibich

30300 — 60¢
THE GREEN MILLENNIUM by Fritz Leiber
NIGHT MONSTERS by Fritz Leiber

37250 — 60¢
IPOMOEA by John Rackham
THE BRASS DRAGON by Marion Zimmer Bradley

23140 — 60¢
FEAR THAT MAN by Dean R. Koontz
TOYMAN by E. C. Tubb

77710 — 75¢
THE SPACE BARBARIANS by Mack Reynolds
THE EYES OF BOLSK by Robert Lory

81680 — 75¢
TONIGHT WE STEAL THE STARS by John Jakes
THE WAGERED WORLD by L. Janifer & S. J. Treibich

12140 — 75¢
CRADLE OF THE SUN by Brian Stableford
THE WIZARDS OF SENCHURIA by Kenneth Bulmer

42800 — 75¢
KALIN by E. C. Tubb
THE BANE OF KANTHOS by Alex Dain

23775 — 75¢
TREASURE OF TAU CETI by John Rackham
FINAL WAR by K. M. O'Donnell

Available from Ace Books (Dept. MM), 1120 Avenue of
the Americas, New York, N.Y. 10036. Send price of book,
plus 10¢ handling fee.